Modern Magick

Volume 1

The Road to Farringale

Toil and Trouble

The Striding Spire

Charlotte E. English

Contents

The Road to Farringale

Modern Magick, 1

CHARLOTTE E. ENGLISH

1

The troll was not especially large, as trolls go: six feet and a bit, maybe seven at most. He had a run-down look about him, like he hadn't washed in a while and had no plans to do so anytime soon. He wore a ratty zip-up jumper with the air of a charity-shop purchase about it; had it been only second-hand when he'd bought it, or already third? Its faded navy colour did nothing for his sallow complexion, and the tracksuit bottoms and trainers he wore with it were no better. His bulbous eyes rested a moment upon me, took in my coiffed hair and silk dress, then shifted to my colleague, Jay, who stood nervously unsmiling beside me.

I expected an enquiry of some kind. A greeting, maybe, or even a challenge. But he said nothing; only stared at us with dull, incurious expectation.

I tried to look past him into the Enclave, but he'd opened the stone slab of the door only just wide enough to talk to us. Obstructive. Not a good sign. 'Morning,' I said brightly, and it *was* a bright morning: mid-April and balmy, sun high in the sky and rosily smiling. A perfect day for a drive into the hills. 'We're from the Society for Magickal Heritage,' I told him, using my official voice. 'We have received word of a pair of unregistered alikats in these parts. Would you know anything about that?'

The troll's answer was to slam the door on us, setting up a fine, booming echo that reverberated along the grassy hillside.

'He knows nothing,' Jay translated.

'They never do.' I stepped back from the door, or what had once been the door, and surveyed it speculatively. Now it appeared to be nothing but a slab of bare stone in a rocky cliff face, patches of heathery grass scattered above and before it. We were deep in the Yorkshire Moors, not far from the town of Helmsley (or so Jay informed me). I wondered if the powers back Home knew how far the South Moors Troll Enclave had deteriorated. Considering the state of their Doorkeeper, the signs were unpromising.

'Ves,' said Jay, eyeing me. 'What are you doing?'

'I am wondering if there is another way in.'

'There won't be another *legal* way in. You know the rules.'

I rolled my eyes. Jay was only a few years younger than me, I judged, so he was no wide-eyed intern. But he *was* fresh from the Hidden University. The tutors there spend a lot of time drilling the students in The Rules, of which there are many. For example, one does not chatter about magickal stuff to those without the Vision to see it for themselves. And, one does not visit the private spaces of Hidden Communities without their express invitation, which means one is only allowed to use their front door. *With* one of the residents on the other side of it, politely holding it open.

'All very true,' I said. 'But that's the official policy. In our line of work, it is sometimes necessary to bend the rules a bit.'

'Aren't there complaints?'

I smiled mirthlessly. 'They try that, once in a while. It rarely ends well. In this instance, I'm pretty sure these fine folk are illegally holding at least two alikats, and if it's a breeding pair that's even worse. How are they going to report us for misdemeanours without revealing their own transgressions?'

Jay narrowed his deep brown eyes at me. 'That does not make it all right to freely break all the Rules.'

'No? How else would you like to get those kats out of there, then? I make it about half an hour before the first one gets eaten.'

'I'm sure we can come up with... wait. Eaten?'

I couldn't help sighing. These fresh graduates, so... naive. 'Why do you think Trolls are generally discouraged from keeping alis?'

'Because... because alikats are considered endangered.'

Jay obviously hadn't thought that one through. 'Exactly.'

'Ah.' Jay stopped arguing and joined me in searching for a way in. We proceeded to spend half an hour or so inspecting the hillside for something conveniently resembling a back door, and came up with nothing. We ended up back in front of that stone portal, which was still firmly closed.

'Oh well,' said I. 'We'll have to do it the fun way.'

'The fun way?'

'I, um. I meant the questionable way.'

Jay folded his arms and stared me down. 'After you, then.' I do not know why he insists on wearing leather jackets but I do wish he would not; they suit him far too well.

I rang the bell again. It wasn't a bell at all, in the usual way of those things, but the expression's apt enough. I laid my right hand, palm-flat, against the stone and politely requested entrance.

As per the Magickal Accords, the inhabitants of the South Moors Troll Enclave — if they weren't known to be in Recluse — were pretty much honour bound to answer the door. They were required to co-operate with Jay and I as well, of course, but that hadn't held much weight with them, so who knew? Jay and I waited in hope, and our patience was rewarded. Eventually. About four long minutes later, a thread of dull topaz light raced around the cliff face, tracing the outline of a door, and that door creaked open.

They had changed their Doorkeeper. Mr. Tracksuit and Trainers was nowhere in evidence; replacing him was a larger, lumpier, and rather more belligerent fellow — no, *lady* — who wasted no time whatsoever in demonstrating how matters stood between us. She bared her yellow teeth and I waited for the spectacular roar of displeasure, most likely preparatory to tearing off our heads, which would undoubtedly follow.

Trolls have a certain reputation, do they not? Not only among those with the Vision to see them. Even the Magicless tell stories like The Three Billy Goats Gruff, in which trolls are hideous beasts who'll eat practically anything.

Usually, they are wrong. I've encountered trolls whose manners, tastes and general refinement would put the finest of the British aristocracy to shame. Trolls whose delight in beauty, culture and the arts go virtually unrivalled across the world; trolls whose academic aptitude and scholastic achievements far exceed my own.

Then again, I have periodically encountered the other sort, too. The ones the Norwegians were talking about when they began telling that story about the Gruffs. *Those* trolls really will eat almost anything, provided it's fresh, and in a pinch that would certainly include yours truly.

So I had to forgive Jay for his obvious unease, faced as he was with a displeased

Doorkeeper who possibly hadn't eaten for an hour or two. He backed away, leaving me to face the good lady alone.

In his defence, it did look like an involuntary step back. Those survival instincts, they'll put paid to your manly courage any day of the week.

Fortunately, nothing put paid to mine. I smiled my nicest smile at the Doorkeeper — who had not, after all, chosen to treat us to a vocal display of displeasure — and said, in my friendliest tone, 'We'd really like to come in. Just a quick visit, nothing to—'

I stopped because the Doorkeeper was opening her mouth. She was probably preparing to shout at us, or roar at us, or something of the kind, though her movements were peculiarly slow. It seemed to cost her a lot of effort merely to part her lips, which was odd indeed, but convenient because it presented me with a wide open mouth to throw my neighbourly offering into. My gift was a tiny pearl of a thing, all pale, lustrous beauty and lethal potential.

Well, not really lethal. It was a sleep draught, the kind of thing that was once served oddly-coloured and bubbling in peculiar glass jars. The technicians at Home have started compressing them into these bead forms instead. It's the same potency, only smaller, and easier to deliver. Every bit as fast-acting, though; the jelly-type shell that holds everything together dissolves in the mouth in seconds.

It took only slightly longer than that for the Doorkeeper to evince a promising swaying upon her boot-clad feet.

'Back a bit more,' I warned Jay, who'd begun to show signs of plucking up his courage for an advance. I wandered back a bit myself, and waited.

The troll pitched forward, and landed upon her face. All ten feet of her hit the ground with a *thud*, which resonated so powerfully I was even moved to hurry a little.

'In we go,' I said, and grabbed Jay by the arm. 'You can study her later, if you like, but just now we need to get on with the job.'

'I don't want to study her,' Jay retorted, pulling his arm out of my grip. 'I was just interested. I've never seen a troll like her before.'

'You can admire her later, too. Maybe she'll take your phone number.'

'I didn't mean—'

'Alikats,' I reminded him. 'Quickly.'

He muttered something inaudible, then added snidely: 'I just find it hard to take you seriously with that hair.'

I tossed the hair in question, undaunted. Just because it was cerulean-blue, and arranged in impossibly perfect ringlets; did that give him any excuse to question my authority, or my expertise? 'I know you are jealous, and I can't blame you, but this is only our first assignment together and I'd like to survive it intact. If you help me retrieve these kats without anybody losing a limb, I'll get you a Curiosity all of your own. A wardrobe that spawns a new, jazzy leather jacket every morning, say. Or a mirror that shows only your best features.'

All Jay's features are his best features, in fairness. He flicked his pretty, pretty eyes at me in annoyance — they're the colour of dark chocolate, those eyes, and they have that velvety quality, too. It's all decidedly unfair, and I can't decide yet whether or not he knows it. 'Lead on,' he said, choosing (perhaps wisely) to ignore my facetiousness.

I led.

The Enclave proved to be much as I expected: a jumbled mess. The town was built in circles — they do like curves, trolls — and formed of tall, imposing block stone houses built in sinuous lines. Those houses were probably handsome, once, but they'd been allowed to deteriorate. Some of them had lost their original carved oaken doors, and had others tacked on in place; the new ones looked as though they'd been ripped off some shoebox of a concrete dwelling, probably from a local housing estate. Nothing had been painted in at least ten years. Rubbish lay stacked in piles in every corner, and discarded refuse lined the cobbled stone pathways.

The aroma of the place might best be termed Unpleasant. Let's leave it at that.

There weren't too many residents about, which was fortunate for us, though I wondered where everybody was. I saw a few listless-looking souls trudging purposelessly hither and thither, their heads covered with cheap knitted hats. They wore the same fashion of frayed, mismatched clothes as the Doorkeepers.

Nobody stopped us. I'd half expected the noise of the Doorkeeper's fall to attract some kind of attention, but either they had not heard (was that possible? The woman fell like a *tree!*) or they did not care. Nor did they question the sudden appearance of a pair of humans, one all improbably-coloured hair and spectacular fashion sense, the other all cinnamon skin, chocolate eyes and tousled cuteness (should I stop making Jay sound edible...? Okay then). I suppose they had no particular reason to interfere with us. If they were unaware of what we'd done to their Doorkeeper, they'd assume we had been given clearance to enter.

It did not take us long to find out what had become of the alikats. The Enclave was eerily quiet; the sound of a distressed yowl carried nicely. Jay and I veered as one, and made for the alikats at a run.

There proved to be a little square in the centre of the town (or shall I call it a round? For it, like everything else in the place, was pleasingly curvaceous). A cluster of trolls had gathered in an eager knot around a fire pit — or what passed for eager around here; they were at least visibly breathing, which gave them the edge over the rest of the townspeople. The leader of this little group was unquestionably the hunch-backed one in the middle, whose broad shoulders and massive hands looked more than capable of ripping me to pieces. He held a cleaver. To his left stood a troll in a candy-striped jumper that looked like it was knitted by somebody's grandmother. For his convenience, she was obligingly holding out one of our missing alikats. The poor creature's indigo-shaded fur bristled with fright, and it fought mightily to free itself, but to no avail; nothing could dislodge the fierce grip in which it was held.

I noticed that its captor had painted her fingernails a charming cerise, which was a nice effort, even if the lacquer was rather chipped.

'See the other one?' I asked of Jay as we approached.

'Nope. You do this, I'll do that.' He veered off, went around the knot of trolls and disappeared.

I didn't argue, even though his desertion left me to deal with six or eight trolls unaided. Two alikats were missing, only one was in evidence; I felt a stab of fear, for those kats are more than merely *endangered*. Like many magickal creatures, they feed off magickal energies (in a manner of speaking), and there are blessed few of those bouncing around nowadays. Things were different back in, say, the middle ages. In those days, practically everybody was Magickal and alikats, and all their ilk, were a dime a dozen — or comparatively, anyway. Here in the early twenty-first century... well. I can't even guess at the approximate value of a breeding pair of alis, they are *that* rare. The Powers would have my head if Jay and I returned with only one.

And these idiots were trying to *eat* them.

'Stop!' I barked. The trolls' absolute obliviousness to my presence — and Jay's — was curious, and I had to repeat the word twice more at increasing volume before one of them finally looked up at me. This alert, lively specimen fixed his muddy grey eyes upon me with a dull spark of awareness, and nudged the hunchback.

But too late, because that cleaver was already swinging down, aimed unerringly for the yowling alikat's neck.

2

D *amnit.*

I threw caution and dignity to the winds and made a leap for the alikat. We fell in a blur of flying hair and fur and deeply unhappy beast, and I'm pretty sure that cleaver missed my shoulders by a mere two inches but it was *worth it,* because I came up with an armful of kat. The creature was hissing and writhing like a mad thing but she was, blessedly, still alive.

'Right,' I snapped, eyeing the hunchback with all the justifiable anger of a woman who has only narrowly escaped death by cleaver. He stared back at me with the same dull lack of interest as the rest of his kin, which took the proverbial wind out of my sails just a little. 'Society,' I said firmly, and my identifying symbol (a purple unicorn against the Society's backdrop of three crossed wands) flashed briefly in the air before me. I fear the dignity of the moment was somewhat impaired by the antics of my rescuee, which continued to thrash and claw at me as though *I* was its tormentor. Honestly, did the absurd creature not realise I had saved its skin? I tightened my grip upon it, trying to ignore the way its black claws sank deeper into my poor flesh, and lifted my chin haughtily. 'The Rules for possession, care and treatment of Magickal Creatures are well known to you, are they not? And upon this point, they are *very* clear. No endangered species may be owned without a valid permit, and they are *never* to be put on the menu!'

I expected some manner of objection to be raised to this, if to nothing else that I had done. But the hunchback only stared at me for several long seconds, mouth slightly agape.

Then, finally, he shrugged, letting his dirty cleaver drop heedlessly onto the cobbled stone square at his feet. The sharp clatter of its fall split the heavily silent air with a *crack,* and I jumped.

The hunchback made no attempt either to defend his conduct, or to reassert his ownership of the alikat. Instead, he turned away and shambled off, his candy-striped companion shuffling after. One by one, the other half-dozen trolls scattered, leaving me alone in the square. I watched them go, stunned.

There was definitely something odd going on. Why were the trolls so apathetic? What had prompted them to try to make a dinner of an alikat? They *did* know the Rules. These policies had been in place for many years.

The quiet at least gave me an opportunity to pacify my poor alikat. I gentled it with a little charm I learned from my mother — handy when I was a child, she once said, which does not speak well of my temperament at that age, but never mind. The kat relaxed in my arms, affording me with the leisure to observe the toll its understandable distress had taken upon me. My arms were striped with stinging wounds that oozed trickles of blood into the shredded sleeves of my lovely silk dress, and I could not hold back a sigh. This line of work is, all too often, fatal to skin and clothes alike.

Jay reappeared. To my vast relief, he was carrying the other alikat. Definitely a male, this one: it was half again the size of the little female that now lay so quiescent in my arms, its fur dappled in deeper shades of indigo and black. To my mingled admiration and disgust, the second alikat embraced Jay as though the two had been best friends since their earliest youth. It lay twined around Jay's neck and half down one of his arms, its whiskers vibrating with the force of its purr. I detected no signs of injury in Jay, though the thick leather of his jacket might have had something to do with that.

He took stock of my bloodied state and the alikat lying in my arms, and gave a tiny, satisfied nod. I tried not to feel offended by his visible lack of concern for the fate of my poor arms. 'Vaporised the lot?' he guessed, glancing around at the empty square.

'Nothing but dust and ash.'

He grinned. 'What did you really do with them?'

'Nothing. They submitted to my withdrawal of the alikat without a murmur, and left.'

Jay's brows went up. 'Odd.'

'Very. Shall we take these poor little soldiers home?'

'Lead on.'

'Uh, no. You lead on.'

Jay gave me a tiny salute. 'You are the boss.'

'Fine.' I cast a quick look around to get my bearings, and set off.

'That's the wrong way,' Jay helpfully observed.

I stopped. 'Remember why they assigned you to me?'

'I just… didn't think you could really be that bad.' Jay picked a direction almost the opposite of the one I had been wandering in, and marched off.

'I'd love to take offence,' I said as I fell in behind him. 'But the truth is, I couldn't find my way out of a bucket.'

'Noted.' Jay sounded perfectly composed. Not a quiver of mirth could I detect.

'Are you laughing at me?'

'Never.'

'You are.'

His shoulders began to shake, which prompted a dissatisfied *mrow* from his alikat. 'Yes. Yes, I am.'

I caught up with Jay, and expressed my disapproval with a disdainful toss of my cerulean curls. 'I have other talents.'

'I am sure you do.'

'Aren't you going to ask what they are?'

'I've been told what they are. Vast knowledge of magickal history. Specialised knowledge of ancient spells, beasts and artefacts. No insignificant skill with charms.'

'Great hair.'

'*Great* hair.'

I smiled, mollified. 'What are your talents?'

'I,' said Jay, 'can find my way out of a bucket.'

'I am speechless with admiration.'

'*And* the South Moors Troll Enclave. There's the door.'

· · · ● · ● · · ·

Burdened as we'd hoped to be by a pair of frightened (and possibly injured) animals, we had judged it best to eschew flight this time and travel by car. At least, this was the official motive. I prefer cars anyway, for two reasons. One: it is unnecessary to manage the thorny problem of finding one's way to somewhere while maintaining an invisibility or deflection glamour, all without falling off one's choice of steed (chairs are popular). And two: call it vanity, but I hate what the high winds do to my hair. Cars, of course, have heating and sat nav and roofs overhead, which is delightful of them. They also have traffic jams, but I consider that a price worth paying for comfort.

Since Jay would be driving, he had insisted we use his car. I'd half expected it to be some kind of zippy, sporty thing with too few seats and overly glossy paintwork, but instead he drove a shabby-looking Ford Something in a respectable shade of dark red. It displayed the kinds of scratches and minor dents suggestive of a car that is well-used but not quite so well-loved. We carefully loaded our (thankfully uninjured) alis into a pair of cat carriers, settled them in the back, and headed for Home.

When I say "Home", I mean headquarters. The Society for Magickal Heritage is officially called The Society for the Preservation and Protection of Magickal Heritage, or SPPMH for short. But while lengthy and convoluted acronyms might work beautifully for, say, the RSPCA, we summarily rejected the garbling and spitting involved and opted for the serene simplicity of merely: The Society. And the Society is housed in a gorgeous country mansion which is, considering its size, surprisingly hard to find.

We like it that way. The house has no official name; that's why we just call it "Home". Like the Hidden University, it isn't marked on any map. It has no website, and no sat nav will direct you to it. This, as you may imagine, has frequently caused me no little difficulty. I was two days late for my first day of work.

The house dates from the mid seventeenth century. It was once owned by one of the more prominent magickal families among the nobility of England and Ireland, so they say, though reports vary as to which family it was. Officially, it was knocked down after the Second World War, like so many of our country houses; this piece of misdirection, combined with a liberal application of deterrent charms, keeps us largely secure from the outside world. It drowses, quietly hidden, somewhere near the border of South Yorkshire and Derbyshire, ringed by peaceful hills, and as wholly unspoilt as a building that's Home to two hundred people can possibly be.

Not being directionally impaired, Jay got us there within a couple of hours. I felt so many things upon approaching that beautiful house, as I always do. Admiration for its rambling stonework, its fanciful little towers, its long windows, parapets and soaring archways. Fondness, for the place I've called home for more than a decade. Pride, for the work we do; we've saved and restored countless books and artefacts; rescued many species of magickal creatures from the disaster of extinction; tracked down and extracted magickal Treasures and Curiosities without number, sometimes from situations of considerable danger. What kind of work could be more important than that?

This array of warm feelings suffered an early check. As we drove slowly up the spacious driveway, I noticed that Zareen had turned the flanking rows of stately, centuries-old oak trees upside down. Again.

'Is it too soon to revoke her Curiosity privileges?' I sighed, wincing at the exposed roots sagging helplessly in the air.

'It appears to be too late,' said Jay.

'It's never too late.'

'You'll have to talk to Milady. She—'

A great, groaning *creaking* sound interrupted whatever Jay was about to add, as the tree nearest to us flipped right-side-up again. Dislodged earth rained down upon the car like a shower of hail, and I was thankful anew that we had not come swooping in upon a pair of inconveniently open-topped chairs.

'*Definitely* talk to Milady,' growled Jay, narrowly avoiding a falling clot of earth of alarming size with a neat swerve of the wheels.

It was good to be Home.

• • ● • ● • ● • • •

Jay was only recruited by the Society a couple of weeks ago, and it shows.

We parked, retrieved our alikats and made for the house. I was aiming for a side door that would take us straight into the Magickal Creatures wing, but as we approached, the little green-painted portal faded into the stonework and disappeared.

I stepped back.

'Uh,' said Jay, blinking and pointing at where the door had been. 'Is... it supposed to do that?'

'No, but all attempts to dissuade it have failed. I think Milady's given up. Take a step back, Jay.'

'What?'

I don't know whether it was the vanishing door that did it or the inverted trees beforehand, but Jay definitely wasn't at his sharpest. I grabbed him and *pulled*, just as an elegant spiral staircase made from solid wrought iron descended from above, slamming into the ground a little too close to where Jay had been standing moments before.

3

J ay stared at the staircase in consternation.

'Thanks,' he said faintly.

I made a flourishing gesture of invitation, indicating the proffered stairs with a sweep of my free arm. 'After you.'

'Uh. Why don't you go first?'

'Don't worry, the House won't hurt you.'

Jay gave me the are-you-crazy stare. 'I've narrowly missed having my car crushed by a ball of earth the size of four of my heads, almost been flattened by a flying set of stairs, and all of this has happened in the last ten minutes of my life.'

'All right. *I'll* go first.' I picked up my discarded creature carrier and set off up the steps. After a few moments' hesitation, I heard Jay's footsteps ringing behind me.

There was no door at the top, but there was a long window set with many small panes of glass. When I reached the top, about fifty of those panes flickered and vanished, creating an entryway just large enough to admit Jay and myself.

'Thank you,' I said. 'How convenient.' For beyond the makeshift doorway I could see one of the larger, oak-panelled drawing-rooms of the first floor, or what had been a drawing-room once. It was now used as a kind of common room, and one of its occupants was Miranda Evans, our vet and specialist in magickal beasts of all kinds.

'Hi,' I said as I wandered through the window, and set the creature carrier down at her feet.

She was lounging in the kind of shabby, velvet-clad wing-back chair in which Home abounds, her red robes partially open to reveal a chunky hand-knitted jumper worn underneath. Her blonde hair was half out of its bindings, as usual; she took one look at me and Jay and the present we'd brought for her, and immediately scraped it back into a more business-like ponytail. 'More work,' she said with her quirk of a smile. 'Lovely.'

'Alikats, breeding pair. Extracted from South Moors.'

Her brows went up at that, and she hastily swallowed the dregs of her cup of tea. 'Injuries?'

'None visible. I think they're unharmed, they just need a check-up and then resettling.'

By the time I had finished this sentence, Miranda was already on her knees, peeking through the bars at my slumbering alikat. 'Gorgeous,' she commented.

I'd lost her attention altogether, but that was all right. Jay and I watched as she gathered up our beleaguered pair; with a nod to us both, she left the common room at a smartish pace.

Jay glanced behind himself. The door we'd used had sealed itself up again, turning back into a window. 'Is it a coincidence that we found Miranda right here?'

'No,' I said, making a beeline for the kettle and the tea cupboard. 'That was the House helping us out. It does that.'

'When it isn't trying to kill us.'

'It wasn't trying to kill us.'

'Yeah, right.'

'It was trying to kill *you. I* was fine.'

This was a joke, of course, but I regretted it when Jay developed an expression of mingled anxiety and affront. I put a cup of tea into his hands to pacify him, or at least to distract him, neither of which worked. 'Haven't you seen the House do that before?'

'Nope.'

'It's because you're new,' I decided. 'It hasn't figured you out yet. It will soon.'

'Then it will stop trying to kill me?' Jay looked profoundly sceptical.

'No. Then you'll stop being careless enough to get in the way of House's helpful gestures. Or Zareen's pranks, for that matter.'

Jay took a long gulp of tea, like a man chugging something strong and alcoholic. 'Survive a few more weeks for optimum results. Got it.'

I chugged mine, too, for we did not have time to linger. Somewhat to my regret, for the first-floor common room is one of my favourite places at Home. It's something to do with the quality of the light, I think; those long windows somehow admit the perfect degree of it, in the perfect quantity, keeping the room bathed in a peaceful glow that perfectly brings out the mellow tones of the wooden walls and flooring. Those chairs are remarkable, too. We might not have had time, but I sank into one of them anyway, the crimson one. Its proportions immediately adjusted around me, creating of itself a seat of perfect size and dimensions to accommodate my frame. The cushions softened, too, since I prefer a pillowy structure, and the back shortened a little to suit my height — its previous occupant was apparently rather taller than me, which isn't unusual.

'Lovely,' I said, wearing my smile of serene contentment.

'Out you get,' said Jay unsympathetically. 'We've a report to make.'

I sighed, deeply, but he was right. Something was very much amiss at South Moors, and the Powers needed to know about it right away. 'Fine, fine,' I said with decided ill grace. I threw a cushion at him as I rose; unlike the loose earth from Zareen's inverted trees, *this* he dodged with easy grace, and raised a single brow at me.

'Have you *no* mischievous side?' I asked him in exasperation.

'None whatsoever.' He said it with such a straight face, I had to believe him.

'You and Zareen should get on like—'

'Cats and dogs,' he interrupted. 'We do.'

I tossed the tangles from my hair, adjusted my poor ruined dress, and made for the door. 'They should have given you someone *much* more serious to work with.'

'But you're the one who needed me.' Jay somehow beat me to the door, opened it, and held it for me with an ironical little bow.

Considering the most prominent of the reasons why I needed him, that reflection was mildly embarrassing, so I responded only with a haughty look of disdain and strode forth.

Jay was kind enough to fall in behind me without further comment, and I was able to pretend that I didn't hear the low chuckle that was *almost* masked by the sound of the door closing behind us.

· · · • · • · · ·

The process for seeking an audience with Milady is rather particular.

First, one is expected to present oneself in her preferred location, that being at the very top of the very tallest tower of the House. And why not? There is something agreeably fairy tale about it, even if the physical exertion required is not always well received by her supplicants.

Jay managed the ascent of three narrow, winding stone staircases in increasingly strained silence. They are the kind with uneven steps (charmingly worn by time, and the passage of a million footsteps); spiralling construction (tightly wound, so as to make of them the greatest possible obstacle); and occasional landings, randomly dispersed (the kind with dark, shadowy corners, wherein one half expects to find all manner of disagreeable creatures residing). And of course, none of them has fewer than thirty or so steps. All things considered, I was impressed that he made it halfway up the fourth staircase before the complaints began.

'Isn't there a lift?' He sounded faintly breathless but not excessively so, which wasn't bad. Jay obviously kept himself decently fit.

'Of course not,' I said, in the ringing tones of a supremely fit woman (a boast, but what can I say? I've been climbing these staircases every day for more than a decade. That alone will give a woman lungs of steel, and the hind quarters of a racehorse).

'What do you mean, *of course not*? Lifts are wonderful.'

I cast him a withering look over my shoulder. 'This is a seventeenth-century mansion. Where do you suggest we put an elevator? Which priceless and irreplaceable features shall we rip out in order to make room for it?'

'Fair point. What about the house itself, then? If it can present you with a staircase straight up to the common room, it can whisk us up to the top tower in a jiffy.'

'Are you in a wheelchair, Jay?'

'Uh... no.'

'Valerie Greene — have you met her yet? Library? — is wheelchair-bound. Dear House takes the very best care of *her*. Any door she approaches opens upon just the place she wants to go.'

'That's good of it.'

'Isn't it? And quite ingenious.'

'So we're left to haul ourselves up all these stairs because...?'

'Because we are able-bodied, fit young people, Jay, and I don't think House approves of laziness.'

I fancy it was the word *laziness* that silenced him, or perhaps he simply ran out of breath. Either way, he had not another word to advance until we arrived at the top of the sixth set of stairs and stood, briefly winded (or he was, at any rate; I deny all such charges), and taking great gulps of air. We were in a cramped, rounded tower; before us was one of those narrow, arrow-slit type windows filled in with glass, through which we were afforded a fine view of the green, sun-dappled hills beyond the gates.

'Lovely,' I commented.

Jay said nothing, so I turned to the one other feature of that stark little tower: a heavy oak door, closed and barred.

I knocked.

'What now?' whispered Jay, when nothing happened.

'House is consulting with Milady as to whether she wants to admit us.'

'Does she ever decline?'

'Me, no. You, however... who knows.'

Jay allowed that to pass in silence. 'Does she really live up *here*?' he said after a while — just as the door unbarred itself with a *clang* and swung slowly inwards.

'In a manner of speaking.' Jay made no move, so I entered the room first.

Milady's room is only about six metres across, its walls curved most of the way around. Those walls were fitted with panelling at some point in history, though not with the smooth, warm-hued oak that's prevalent across most of the House. The tower's walls are sheathed in iridescent crystal. There's one window, but it doesn't look over the countryside like the one in the antechamber. Through it one can see only swirling white mist.

I stepped into the centre of the room, and positioned myself in the middle of the thick, royal-blue rug that covers the floor.

'Afternoon, Milady,' I said cordially, and curtseyed.

'Uh.' Jay came up next to me and turned a full circle on the spot, neck craning, as though Milady might be hidden somewhere in a room with no furniture and no corners. 'Where is she?' he whispered to me.

I elbowed him. 'Say hello,' I hissed.

'Hello, Milady.'

That was it. I elbowed him again, a bit harder this time, and by way of judicious application of pressure to his upper back I contrived to force him into a semblance of a polite bow.

The air sparkled. 'Cordelia Vesper,' said a low, cultured female voice. 'Jay Patel. What have you to tell me today?'

4

Nothing ever worries Milady. I could tell her an army of hostile magicians was advancing upon the House with a legion of direbeasts in tow, and she would merely say, 'Unfortunate. Very well,' dispense a simple, efficient plan for containing the problem which would work perfectly, and then invite us all for tea afterwards.

She heard our account of the South Moors Troll Enclave in thoughtful silence, a silence she maintained for some ten or fifteen seconds after I had finished speaking. That, it seems, was as much time as she required to consider our information, place it in context, and devise her response.

'You did well to retrieve the alikats,' she said. 'There are but twelve breeding pairs left in England, at least that are known. We could not easily bear to lose one of them. They are in Miranda's care?'

'Yes, Milady.'

'Then they will be well tended to. Regarding the trolls, their behaviour is cause for concern. I will arrange for a consultant to meet with you. He will be here this afternoon.'

This was vague, but I knew by then that Milady's plans always became clear soon enough, so I curtseyed again and murmured something agreeing. Jay gave me the side-eye, and said nothing.

'Return to me once you have met with my consultant, for I shall have a new assignment for you this evening. Jay Patel.'

The name was spoken in a tone so indistinguishable from the rest, it took Jay a moment to realise he was being addressed. 'Yes?' he said hesitantly.

'This was your first assignment with Vesper. Are you contented with her?'

Privately I thought that Milady might have done better to ask this question of Jay when I was not standing right next to him, but he took it in stride. 'We work well enough together, Milady,' he replied.

'Very well. Vesper?'

I thought of the hesitancy he had shown when faced with even the apathetic trolls of South Moors. I had wondered a little about his courage, but that was probably unfair of me. He was new. If he had met any trolls at the Hidden University, it might well have been limited to old Maj, professor of anthropology, and she was ancient, wizened, soft-spoken and totally unintimidating. He had faltered, but he'd held. He would get used to it. 'I am happy to continue our partnership,' I said. 'We made it through the mission without getting even a little bit lost, and I can't remember the last time that has happened to me.'

'He is more than your chauffeur, Vesper.'

'I know that,' said I hastily. Did I though? It occurred to me that I knew little about Jay's specific abilities, and the only reason Milady had given for assigning him to accompany me was my deplorable tendency to lose my way — besides his obvious need for basic induction to the Society, of course, which anybody might have provided him with. It did not much surprise me to learn that there was more to Milady's thinking than that, but as to what it *was,* I was in the dark.

No matter. This, too, would become clear in time.

'You will find chocolate in the pot,' said Milady, which befuddled Jay but I knew it for one of her characteristic, mild dismissals. I made a final curtsey, motioned Jay into a parting bow, and hustled both of us out of the tower room.

Jay was silent all the way down four staircases. Then he said: '*What?*'

'To what are you referring?'

'All of it.'

'More specifically?'

'Let's begin with: who exactly is Milady?'

'No idea,' I said brightly.

Jay stopped, and stared at me.

'Nobody does,' I said with a shrug. 'Some say she's the latest scion of the aristocratic family who built this House, which makes sense. Some say she is the *same* woman who built this House, which is less likely, as she'd have to be centuries old. But who knows? She could be either of those things, or neither. We know her as the founder and benefactor of the Society, She Who Pulls Our Strings, the Bosslady, and that's enough for most of us.'

'Why is she a disembodied voice?'

'I don't know.'

'Why did you keep curtseying to a disembodied voice?'

'Oh, I'm sure she can see us. That window, I think, though I'm not sure how.'

'You don't think that curtseying is a little old-fashioned?'

'So's Milady.'

Jay sighed, and ran a hand through his hair. 'You know, when I got this job offer, they told me. At the University. They *told* me it was strange up here.'

'They weren't wrong.' We'd made it back to the first floor by then; I steered Jay back to the common room, where, as promised, we found a welcome addition to its equipment. An oversized, eighteenth-century silver chocolate-pot stood upon one of the tables, wisps of steam curling invitingly from its spout. A pair of chocolate-drinking cups had been set beside; these, of course, were the delicate, porcelain kind, with gilding around the rims.

'You are kidding me,' said Jay in blank disbelief.

I took a seat and poured out chocolate for both of us. It was sweet and spiced, dark and rich, pure luxury: exactly the way we don't drink it anymore. 'Have a bit,' I encouraged Jay. 'One tends to feel better afterwards.' And I did, already, even after only a few sips. I was less tired, less hungry, and the scratches striping my arms were already stinging less.

Jay did not believe me, clearly — not until he had drunk half of his share of the chocolate.

'Strange but good?' I invited him to allow.

He drained his cup and poured out another. 'Strange,' he said with emphasis.

I raised a brow, and waited. Sure enough, a reluctant smile crossed his face and he sank back into his chair with a sigh, visibly more relaxed than he had been half an hour earlier. 'Strange but good,' he conceded.

· · · · ● · ● · · · ·

We were at leisure to amuse ourselves for the next two or three hours. I spent the time changing my ruined blue dress for a printed cotton one in spring-like rose, worn with a light shawl. It clashed with my cerulean hair, so I employed my wonderful Curiosity — a ring, this one, with a charm embedded — and adjusted the latter to a more complementary blue-lavender hue.

I don't know what Jay did. We separated after we had finished with Milady's chocolate, and did not reconvene until we were called to meet the consultant. I made my way back down to the soaring, marble-floored entrance hall to find Jay already waiting, jacket discarded. He wore jeans, and a simple pale blue cotton shirt which contrived to look simultaneously neat and lightweight and casual. I approved.

My admiration was not mutual, for Jay looked me over and said: 'You look like a bouquet of flowers.' The words sounded complimentary enough, but he spoke them so tonelessly, his face so expressionless, that I could not help concluding that some unspoken criticism lay behind them.

So I ignored this.

'Where—' I began, for the hall was empty other than the two of us; no sign of our promised consultant could I discern. But as I spoke, Nell — Nell Delaney, of media and tech and suchlike — stuck her exquisitely greying head around one of the doors and said: 'Ves? Convention Chamber. He's waiting.'

That made me raise my brows, for that particular room is arguably the finest at Home. It's usually used for large gatherings of the significant kind. We only put individuals in there if they're important, and we want to impress them. Not, of course, if they're the important kind of people we're hoping will agree to fund us. Such a show of magnificence would be quite misplaced there. So who had Milady found to meet us?

I adjusted my hair, checked that my attire was immaculate, and adopted my most confident stride. It wouldn't do to appear unsure.

'I don't suppose...?' said Jay, trailing after me.

'Nope,' I said, without waiting for the rest of his sentence. It didn't matter what he intended to ask about this afternoon's adventure; I had no more idea than he did.

The grand double doors of the Convention Chamber had been invitingly flung open, and we were able to walk straight in — stopped only briefly by Robert Foster, who had obviously been given Brawn Duty outside the doors. He's a big man, Robert, and commensurately impressive at all the arts one might wish to employ if any conceivable variety of threat might chance to be mounted in one's vicinity. Or in other words, he's Scary Rob.

'Ves,' he said to me with a nod. He doesn't exactly cultivate the air of a man of force. He favours the neat, plain attire one might adopt to work as, say, a school teacher, or a general practitioner (the latter of which is not misplaced, since he... is). His tightly-curled black hair is always in need of a trim, and I've never seen him with less than three or four days' worth of stubble. But I suppose he has no need to dress the part. You can *feel* the danger in Robert; not by any overt signs of menace, for he is a careful and essentially gentle man. But he is so chock-full of magickal energy — the *strong* kind — that it's hard to miss.

He cast a vaguely suspicious eye over Jay, who stared back.

Silence.

They could be sizing each other up for half the afternoon, and we had no time for that. 'Jay Patel,' I said quickly. 'My new sidekick. He's with me.'

'Wha — I'm not *with* — sidekick?!'

I ignored these incoherent protestations, took Jay's arm, and at Rob's nod — faintly amused, judging from the involuntary curve of his lips — steered Jay into the Convention Chamber.

The room takes my breath away every time I see it, which is not often. If the entrance hall is impressive, the Chamber is staggering. It has the kind of high ceiling which seems to soar on for half of forever, held up by buttresses of the flying type. Everything is marble and exotic wood and crystal and gilding. It doesn't fit with the rest of the House too well, so it's my belief that it is a later addition. As to when, how or why it came into being, however... who knows. I have been trying to get my hands on a history of the House for years, but if such a book exists, it's very hard to find.

Our contact sat at one of the graceful crystalline side tables, one of Milady's chocolate pots set before him. He had been served with the best our kitchens could offer, which made me mildly envious, for those pastries are to die for. I wondered vaguely if he might be disposed to share.

I could see little of the man himself, for he sat partially concealed behind an enormous folio. So absorbed in his book was he, he seemed unaware of our entrance. I had time to note that he was a man of some height and, apparently, strength; the mere weak and feeble amongst us (like me) would have spread that heavy book open upon the table, but he held it up before him with no sign of strain whatsoever.

Good, then. Milady had found us a representative of the troll communities. An important one.

I cleared my throat. 'Good afternoon, sir.'

The book was instantly closed, and set aside. I received an unimpeded view of by far the most gorgeous troll I have ever beheld, and I mean *gorgeous* in the sense of spectacularly well-presented as well as... well, rather handsome. All height and muscle and perfect posture was he, his bulky shoulders encased in a dark blue velvet coat over a silk shirt. He wore a kind of cravat, and an actual top hat lay on the table beside him. A *top hat*. No wonder he and Milady were acquainted. His skin was a pleasing jadeish hue, his features perfect. All this splendour and privilege might lead one to suppose he'd have an attitude problem, but his vivid green eyes twinkled with good humour as he looked the two of us over. His gaze lingered upon the vibrant mass of my hair.

'The famous Vesper,' he said in a low, rich voice. 'I hear much of you.'

5

I think it was the word *famous* which rattled Jay, for he transferred his attention from the gorgeously arrayed consultant and blinked incredulously at me. '*Are* you?'

'No,' I said crisply, and then amended that to, 'Not really. Baron Alban flatters me.'

'Only a little,' said the baron, and that twinkle deepened. He fingered his cravat and added, 'How did you guess my name?'

'Your reputation precedes you.' Oh, I'd heard about the baron all right. The Troll Court's ambassador to the Hidden Ministry (the magickal government of England), and a prime favourite everywhere he goes. His reputation for flamboyance far exceeds my own — or shall we say, his notoriety? He is also known for his wit, his cleverness and his knowledge of magickal creatures, history and communities, but people don't talk about any of that so much as they talk of his hats, his coats and (by rumour at least) his ladies. I'd wanted to meet him for years.

I was still surprised, though, to find him at the House. When Milady had spoken of a "consultant", I had at least half expected a troll, but I had pictured... what? A scholar like myself, perhaps; someone who was several years into an exhaustive study of troll customs, habits and history, to be published in about fifteen years' time. An anthropologist, a psychologist, a folklorist... *anybody* but Baron Alban.

Since he had made no move to get up and did not appear to wish to stand on ceremony, I took a chair and a cup of chocolate. 'What can we do for you?' I said.

Jay followed my example, but he was wary. I could see that in the rigidity of his posture as he sat across from me, looking ready to run at a moment's notice.

This amused the baron all the more, and he grinned. 'I understand there is a problem at South Moors.'

'Milady spoke of a *consultant.*' I laid a slight emphasis on the last word, hoping my tone would convey a polite question rather than incredulity.

'So I am. I was not born into a barony, you know, and I certainly was not appointed to the post of ambassador at birth. I spent many years of my youth as a rootless vagabond with a tendency to get myself thrown out of every town I lived in, which had its drawbacks. But since I developed an unusually broad knowledge of troll life across most of its strata, it has, on occasion, made me a useful person to consult.'

He spoke with the smoothness, the confidence and the vocabulary of a highly educated man, so I guessed that these rootless, drifting years had been followed by several more of focused study. I wondered what Alban had done to net himself a barony — other than smile gorgeously, which he was doing in my general direction at that very moment.

All right, then.

'What would be your summary of the problem?' Alban asked.

Jay did not seem inclined to lead the way at communicating, which suited me just fine. 'If I had met any of the inhabitants of South Moors individually, I would have said they were... depressed,' I said. 'There is an air of apathy, a greyness, a blankness — though even to call it depression is to state the case too mildly, for they scarcely seemed to hear me when I spoke, and no one vouchsafed any reply. What could possibly afflict a whole village with such symptoms is beyond me to imagine, and I have never heard or read of such a case occurring in history.'

'And the alikats,' Jay put in. 'It is not usual for them to make a meal of such beasts, is it?'

'Not now,' said Alban. 'Some of us will eat just about anything, of course,' — he gave a feral grin as he said this — 'but the Accords have been in place for long enough to deter even a backwater like South Moors from snacking on endangered species.' He winced. 'How many alis were lost?'

'We rescued two,' I said. 'We saw no sign of any others, but who knows what they were eating before word reached us.'

Baron Alban raised his cup to his lips and delicately sipped, silent in thought. The cup ought to have looked tiny and fragile in his huge hands, but it, like the baron's chair, had fitted itself to his proportions. 'Milady was right to summon me,' he finally decided. 'The matter requires the immediate attention of the Court.'

That took the problem neatly out of my hands and Jay's, which was well enough. But I was a little sorry that our meeting with Baron Alban would soon be over, and we would probably never cross paths with him again. I studied him closely, committing points of detail to memory: the exquisite cut of his coat, the sharp points of his superb lapels, that expertly knotted cravat. His sculpted jaw, prominent cheekbones and wickedly twinkling eyes...

He caught me at this scrutiny and gave me a wink, which, for the sake of my dignity, I pretended not to have observed. Setting down his empty cup, he said: 'I'd like to hear the whole story, please. Everything that happened, and everything that you saw.'

This we gave, in as much detail as Jay and I could remember between us. We did a fair job, I think. We are both graduates of the University; we've been taught to observe, and to question. Baron Alban heard us out without interruption, save once or twice to clarify a point of detail. His troubled look deepened as we spoke, and when we were finished he gave a great sigh and rose from his chair. My *goodness*, but he was tall. 'Her Majesty will need to know at once,' he said, gazing down at me with a smile that looked — was it wishful thinking? — a little regretful.

He bowed to us, already taking out his phone, and was gone before I had time to realise that he had given us no insight, no advice, no information at all. But then, he was not there to consult for our benefit; he was there to consult for Milady's.

Jay helped himself to more chocolate — he was swiftly growing to like it, that's for sure — and sat back with a sigh. He had that wide-eyed, flabbergasted look again. 'Strangest day of my life,' he said. 'No contest.'

Poor boy. Little did he know. 'It gets worse.'

'How... how much worse?'

'Or better,' I amended. 'Depends how you look at it.'

Maybe I needed to work on my strategy, for Jay did not look encouraged.

· · · · ● · ● · · · ·

We were back in Milady's tower by nine o'clock upon the following morning. Jay kept his dissatisfaction with the climb to himself this time, which I appreciated, for the morning dawned bright, sunny and beautiful and I wanted to enjoy it. 'Glorious *sun,*' I observed unnecessarily as we toiled up the stairs.

Jay treated this offering with all the interest it deserved, and said nothing.

This time, when we presented ourselves before Milady, Jay bowed without my encouragement. He really *did* like that chocolate.

'Vesper. Jay. Good morning,' said Milady's voice, the air twinkling brightly with every syllable she uttered. 'I hope you are in the mood to travel.'

I perked up at that, for when I am not in the mood to explore? 'Always!' I declared.

Jay's enthusiasm did not quite equal my own. 'Probably,' he allowed.

'You will be familiar with the Farringale Enclave, of course?'

Of *course* I was. Farringale was legend. The site of the Troll Court back in the middle ages, it was renowned for everything — art, scholarship, philosophy, ideas. It was a magickal hub, overflowing with magickal energy; some of the most powerful and most visionary feats of magick ever heard of were developed there, performed there.

Its decline is a sad tale, though not an uncommon one. Time passed, and gradually left Farringale behind. Other schools of magick and ideas supplanted it; other libraries and universities came to be pre-eminent. The Troll Court moved southwards in the early eighteenth century, and Farringale became increasingly isolated from the rest of the world — so much so that there is now considerable debate as to where it is actually situated. Far in the north of England; that is about as much as we can all agree upon. 'Are we going *there?*' I blurted. What a dream! A place steeped in such history, such mystery, such intrigue... what if its legendary libraries were still intact?

'No,' said Milady, and my hopes died. 'You may not be aware that there is suspected to be some key to its decline that is not widely known about, though its precise nature has never been confirmed.'

'Some catastrophe, you mean?'

'Perhaps. Scholars at the Court have traced its deterioration to a mere handful of years, beginning around 1657. In March of that year, the Enclave was thriving. By December, it had shrunk to half its former size. Whether its inhabitants fled or died we do not know, but that there was something gravely amiss is not in doubt.'

'Does Alban suspect a connection with that and the fate of South Moors?' It seemed far-fetched to me, but apparently the baron had access to information I lacked. I felt the familiar envy grow in my breast: a kind of lust for knowledge denied.

Someday I would need to cultivate a connection at the Troll Court, no doubt about that. What other secrets were they hiding in those libraries of theirs?

'It is not an isolated occurrence,' said Milady. 'In 1928, the Garragore Enclave went fully Reclusive. It closed its doors to all outsiders, which is not in itself unusual; but nothing has ever been heard from it again, which is rather more so. It is thought that the settlement faded altogether, and is now barren. But its doors remain sealed, even to the Court. No explanation for its demise has ever been uncovered.'

I'd heard of Garragore as well, though it was nowhere near in the same league as Farringale. Its name appeared in documents from the nineteenth and early twentieth centuries from time to time — mentions in private journals, newspapers, advertisements, that kind of thing. It had not occurred to me to notice that its name had stopped showing up after 1928. I'd had no reason to pay attention to it.

'Are there more such stories?' I asked, feeling slightly sick. Here was a most unpromising pattern.

'There are. Baron Alban is greatly concerned that South Moors may go the way of Farringale and Garragore and the others, if help is not given. But *how* to help is a question no one can yet answer. The baron has requested our assistance.'

'Why?' said Jay. 'Cannot the Troll Court muster the manpower to do it themselves?'

'They are employing their own resources as they see fit. When it comes to the kind of investigation he has in mind, however: we can do it faster.'

'Can we?' I asked. 'How?'

'Because we have Jay.'

That took me aback. Jay? What about him? Alas, my thoughts must have shown on my face, for Jay rolled his eyes at me, his lips twisting in irritation. 'I *am* more than a chauffeur,' he said.

'Oh? What are you?'

Jay's face set into a disgusted expression and he said nothing, so it fell to Milady to explain. 'I recruited Jay the moment he was free to join us, for one particular reason. He is a Waymaster.'

Oh.

6

'Nobody thought to mention this before?' I asked, unable to suppress a trace of bitterness.

'It was not considered wise to make this ability widely known.'

Waymasters are rare. That is an understatement. One who knows the Ways can make use of all the ancient portals that are spread all over Britain — and indeed, the world. Around here they take the form of henges, for the most part. The big, shiny, popular ones like Stonehenge are never used anymore; too many tourists in the way. But the country is littered with the more humble kind, henges of rock and wood and earth. If you can walk the Ways, you can step from one to another in the blink of an eye. It is an ability that used to be common, but like so much else of magick it has been fading away for generations. Nobody knows why.

I understand that some would find all kinds of interesting, nefarious ways to exploit such an ability as Jay's. But *I* wouldn't. Did they not trust me?

'Jay was assigned to you because you were the best person to train him,' said Milady. 'I wanted you to treat him as an ordinary recruit. I wanted *him* to learn how we manage day by day, with or without a Waymaster to hand, for he will not always have the ability freely at his disposal. It was not intended that you should be kept in the dark about it forever.'

I did not feel much mollified, but I kept my dissatisfaction to myself. It is unprofessional to put one's irritations on display. 'Very well.'

'What would you like us to do?' asked Jay.

'Baron Alban is well-travelled, and frequently visits the more populous and central Enclaves. He is not concerned about the well-being of any of those. There are a few far-flung or mildly reclusive settlements, however, whose fate is more in question. I need you to discover whether they are showing any signs of decay, like South Moors, or any unusual behaviour.'

A mission that proposed to take me all over the country in a trice, and gave me the opportunity to explore several places I had never before visited, could only be welcome to me. 'Yes ma'am!' I said with enthusiasm.

'Thrice the usual budget, Ves,' added Milady, 'and take whatever you need from Stores. You have one week.'

Resources: Great. Time: Less so. I swallowed a mixture of mild panic and exhilaration and made my usual obeisance. 'We'd better get started at once, then.'

'That would be lovely.'

· · · • · • · • · · ·

It is possible that when Milady said *take what you need from Stores,* she did not mean *rob the place of everything that might conceivably come in handy, under any circumstances whatsoever.* But if that wasn't what she meant she ought to have particularised, for Jay and I had a daunting job to do and no time at all to do it.

'See, when Milady says "a week",' I said to Jay as I palmed a handy sustenance charm, 'she really means about three days.' I found an unlocking charm — enchanted, unimaginatively, upon a huge bronze key — and pocketed that, too. The Stores at Home are wonderful: half a dozen rooms of varying size, the walls all lined with shelves and cabinets laden with all manner of artefacts, trinkets and Curiosities — and even a few genuine Treasures. Some of them are aged and delicate; you need a special permit to take any of those out. I didn't touch them. I was more than contented with enchantments more recently Wrought, for they offered everything we could need, and one did not have to live in fear of breaking or losing one of them along the way.

'Three days,' murmured Jay. 'Let's see that list again?'

I handed over the slip of paper I'd received from Nell: a computer print-out of all known Troll Enclaves still extant in Britain. The list consisted of twenty-six names, more than half of which she had subsequently crossed out in red pen. Baron Alban's territories,

I presumed; we did not need to investigate those. South Moors and Farringale were also crossed off, which left us with nine places to visit.

Nine towns in three days.

Feasible, I hoped, since one of us was a Waymaster. But *damn*. It was going to be intense.

I could see when Jay had finished counting up the names, for his face registered the same dismay as I felt. I quickly took back the list. 'One at a time. That's all we have to think about.'

'Right.' He returned to watching me strip Stores of everything remotely useful, though I felt that his gaze rested more on me than on the surrounding treasures. How did that make sense? New recruits tended to salivate when we brought them in here, and I'd taken Jay straight to the largest of the storerooms. A fabulous late nineteenth-century statue of a mermaid rested on a shelf about three inches from his face, a lovely thing Wrought from jade and something nacreous which visibly rippled with power. A protection charm of some kind was probably embedded therein; it was the kind of thing the wealthy used to like to keep on display in their fabulous houses, to keep thieves and such away.

Jay didn't even glance at it.

'*What*?' I said after a while.

Jay chewed his lip. 'I, uh. Think we may have got off on the wrong foot, just a little.'

Well, he was right. I turned away again to hide my blush, for I *had* messed up. 'I fear I have been patronising, and I apologise. But *really*. If they'd just *told* me that you were—'

'Relevant?' Jay offered.

'Yes. Exactly.' I took down a sweet little teacup painted with viper's bugloss, but regretfully put it back again. I wanted it, but the chances of either of us coming down with a fever in the next three days were not high.

'Apology accepted. But I was speaking more of myself.'

'Oh?'

'I think it was the unicorn symbol, and your...' He trailed off. When I looked back, his gaze was travelling thoughtfully from my wildly-coloured hair, past my madly-coloured dress and all the way down to my whimsically-coloured shoes. He wisely chose not to finish that sentence. 'Ves,' he said instead. 'That's all anybody ever calls you. But you turn out to be *Cordelia Vesper*.'

'Does that name mean something to you?'

He grimaced. 'I read your thesis. "Modern Magick and—"'

'—Magickal Heritage: The Changing Times. I remember.'

'Right.'

I waited, but that seemed to be it. 'Did you...' I paused to reflect, discarding my instinctive question, because *did you like it?* sounded appallingly needy. 'Did you find it... useful?' I hazarded.

'It was interesting.'

Interesting. Right.

I took down one last Curiosity — a floral charm bracelet which, if I knew my charms, purported to change the colour of any bloom I chose to so deface — and stuffed it into my pocket. There was no possible way we could find a use for it, but what did that matter? Life is complicated, and happiness is made up of the little things. I'd bring it back when we got home.

'Shall we go?' I proposed.

'At once, and immediately. Faster than the speed of light. We'll arrive yesterday.'

I blinked. 'Really?'

'Wha— no. No! It was a joke.'

'Oh.' Anything Jay did could only seem sadly mundane after hype like that, but perhaps that was well enough. Who knew what could be going on behind that impassive visage? Maybe Jay suffered from performance anxiety.

· · • · • · • · · ·

And lo, it was my turn to be ignorant.

Jay led us down into the cellar. This is not a part of the House I have ever had much cause to visit, before. It is mostly used for storage — the boring kind, not relics and artefacts and such — and one or two minor departments I never go to. Our destination therein proved to be a small chamber tucked into one corner, which we reached by way of a lengthy staircase and three winding corridors.

The heavy oak door creaked horribly as Jay coaxed it open.

'Here we are,' said Jay, ushering me inside and closing the door behind me. 'The Waypoint at Home.'

I looked around, unimpressed. The room was barely furnished; naught but a single couch rested against one wall, looking inviting enough with its plump upholstery and overstuffed appearance, but it was not at all elegant. The walls could have used a new coat of paint, or perhaps just a thorough scrubbing; what had probably once been white had dulled to a drab cream. The floor was well enough, but its bare oak boards had not been swept in about a decade either, if I was any judge.

There was nothing else in there, save only for one thing: a ring of nubs of wood, set into the floor. The remains, I judged, of an ancient henge, over the top of which the House had been built.

Clever.

Jay puttered about doing nothing that I could make any sense of, and I waited. I was already beginning to regret my excess of enthusiasm in Stores; the shoulder bag I carried seemed to be growing heavier by the moment. I occupied myself in transferring some of the smaller of its contents into the pockets of my long purple coat, pleased to find that the redistribution helped. A little.

Curse my magpie tendencies.

'So,' I said after a while, when Jay still did not appear to be doing anything productive. 'What happens now?'

'Seriously?'

'Uh... yes?

'How can you have no idea how a Waymaster works?' Jay was incredulous, which was unfair of him.

'Jay. Nobody knows how a Waymaster works. Our last one left eight and a half years ago to take up a tempting employment offer in Jaipur, and that was the last I saw of her. And she never took me travelling with her anyway.'

'Really?' Jay was silent for a moment. 'What kind of employment opportunity?'

'Jay. Focus.'

'Just how tempting was it?'

'Jay!'

He rolled his eyes, and... a lot happened all at once. He was standing in the middle of the room, and when he raised his arms the air swooped and whirled and gathered itself into a vortex of stars. That is the nicer way I can think of to describe it. If I said it also resembled a twinkly tornado, however, perhaps that better conveys its more alarming qualities.

'Why do people call you Vesper?' he yelled. I still couldn't figure out what he was doing, but it involved some effort, for sweat was forming on his brow. 'Why not Cordelia?'

'I hate my name!'

'It's... it's pretty.'

'Cordelia? Yes! It's a doll name, for pretty, well-behaved girls who take a lot of ballet classes and wear their hair in buns.'

I thought he actually laughed, though that might have been a trick of the light — which was turning awfully peculiar. 'Why not shorten it?'

'To what? Cord? That's a type of string. Dell? That's a magickal reservoir. Or a computer.'

'Ves is unique.'

'Exactly. It—'

I did not make it to the end of this sentence, for with a roar and a *swoop* and a nauseating sensation of the world tilting upside down, we were gone from the Waypoint in the cellar and deposited in an untidy, aching heap somewhere altogether else.

7

J ay looked like he was strongly disposed to vomit.

'Are you all right?' I said. Quite uselessly, for he clearly was not.

'Fine,' he replied through gritted teeth.

'Your legs are shaking.'

'My everything is shaking. But I'm fine.' He got to his feet and stood, visibly trembling. But since he was also wearing the clenched-jaw look of a man who *will not* be helped, I left him to it and devoted myself to a largely futile attempt to figure out where we had ended up.

We were in the middle of a henge, of course, though it was not the flashy kind that hordes of tourists come to see. Little remained of it but a ring of decaying wooden posts half-sunk in wet earth, and surrounding that (and us) were... trees. Straggly ones, thick enough to obscure whatever lay beyond but otherwise rather sad-looking.

'Place requires some tending,' I said.

'Most of Britain requires some tending.' Jay took a deep breath, stretched, cast a quick glance around himself and set his face resolutely in what appeared to me to be a completely random direction. 'Ready to go?'

'Where? I have no idea where we are.'

'Somewhere in the vicinity of Glenfinnan. We're a few miles away from Finnan Enclave.' He checked my shoes and, oddly, smiled. 'Boots. Good.'

'Why do you seem surprised?'

'I thought you might have shown up in heels or something.'

'I am not that much of an airhead, Mr. Patel.' I haughtily shouldered my bag. 'Lead on.'

Jay's comment did not much surprise me. I am not expected to be much of a walker; you wouldn't anticipate that about a woman with a fondness for delicate, impractical clothes and improbable hair, would you? But actually, I love to walk. I enjoyed our hike, for the environs of Glenfinnan proved to be green hill country, dotted with patches of woodland, and here and there glimpses of an expanse of clear, serene water. The air was bright and crisp and I breathed deeply, somewhat regretful that our errand was of such urgency as to prevent of our exploring.

Jay clearly had no soul for scenery, for he marched on without ever pausing to admire. Nor did he ever waver as to direction. He certainly had focus. He seemed so little inconvenienced by his obvious shakiness before, I didn't want to admit that my knees were shaking, too, and it took half an hour for the waves of nausea to stop assaulting my stomach. I pretended I was fine and so did Jay, and we accomplished our forced-march in rather less than an hour.

Finnan Enclave's front door proved to be at the base of one of those gorgeous, craggy hills, a bit like at South Moors. We stood in the twin shadow of two swelling peaks, one rising on either side of us. Drifty clouds had raced over the sun, and we stood bathed in a mild, unpromising gloom as we studied the green, heathery slopes before us.

'Are you sure this is it?' I said after a while, when Jay seemed undecided.

'Yes.'

All right, then. I waited while Jay rambled about a bit, looking this way and that in a decisive fashion, and occasionally touching protruding rocks.

'Do you know where the door is?' I said at last.

'Of course I do.'

I waited a little longer, watching in idle delight as a tiny pink skreerat poked its head out from in between a tuft of grasses, eyed Jay beadily, and vanished again.

Jay finally gave up his futile search. 'It's one of these,' he said, gesturing broadly at a tumble of fallen boulders.

'How do you know that?'

'I looked them up on Nell's system before we left.'

Clever of him, though it was not currently availing us much. I rummaged in my satchel, ignoring Jay's disbelief as I extracted rather more objects from within than could reasonably fit inside. 'Aha,' I murmured, drawing forth my oversized key and a pendulum, the kind that had probably once belonged inside a grandfather clock. 'This,' I said to Jay, 'is a basic burglar's toolkit, magicker style.' It was the work of a moment to coax the pendulum into activity and it began to swing gently in my hand, back and forth, back and forth. 'It is a little clumsy, the pendulum,' I observed as the charm did its work. 'I would have enchanted a pathfinder's charm onto something a bit more elegant, myself. A filigree compass, for example, with quartz fittings and a handsome chain. But—' I paused as the pendulum's sway slowed and eventually stopped, leaving the device pointing unerringly at a large, craggy black boulder about six feet away from where Jay had stopped. 'It works, proving that elegance is not at all necessary in life.' I smiled, packed the pendulum away again, and advanced upon the boulder.

We had to go through the usual process of requesting entrance, of course. I laid my palm against the boulder and announced us. When that didn't work, Jay tried.

We were not surprised to find that the silent hills remained silent. There was no promising creak of an opening door, no gust of air to welcome us into a yawning portal.

'Breaking and entering it is, then,' I said, with a sense of satisfaction I could not disguise. I can't help it: I love doing things the sneaky way.

Jay was not so thrilled. He did not object, for Milady had essentially *ordered* us to get into these Enclaves one way or another. But he was visibly uncomfortable as I employed my unlocking charm upon the boulder and...

...and nothing. It did not work. Oh, the *key* worked all right; it glimmered with that promising aura of power, and the boulder glittered in response. There was communication between the two charms, as there should have been, but the boulder declined to be affected by it. The rock remained untouched, stubbornly inert and immoveable.

'Some burglar you are,' said Jay.

I put the key away. 'On to Plan C.' That skreerat had to have come from somewhere. Magickal beasts don't typically wander the wilds as freely as, say, wood mice or stoats or whatever. They mostly stick to the Dells, which are pockets of Hidden landscapes folded between the Ways. Finnan Enclave had firmly closed its outer doors upon the non-magickal world, as they all did, but its regular entrance would undoubtedly be situated on the edge of one of these Dells. If we could not walk straight into the Enclave, we'd have to get into Finnan Dell first and *then* break into the Troll settlement. Their back door, so to speak, was unlikely to be so well protected as their front door.

I went back to the spot where I'd seen the skreerat, and kept walking that way. It wasn't too long before I saw it again: a glimpse of pinkish-grey fur whisking into the concealing cover of a cluster of frondy grasses.

I delved into my satchel again, removed an object which markedly resembled an ordinary torch (because, in essentials, it was), and switched it on. Its beam blazed forth, illuminating the grassy path the skreerat had followed in a haze of misty light.

'Is there anything you aren't carrying in that bag?' said Jay.

'Nope.' I waved the torch around a bit, but the quality of the light did not change.

Hm.

'The wonderful thing about the Society is its forward-thinking attitude,' I told Jay as I clomped around in circles, throwing hazy light everywhere. 'Somewhere in the attic is Orlando's lab. Nobody is allowed in there, not ever, but the most wondrous things come out. Including this torch. It's a hybrid, see? It is electronic in its basic function, but Orlando blends these things with charms in some unfathomable way and comes out with totally unique effects.' There: a flicker of bright energy in the near distance, lancing through the brumous glow like a lightning strike. 'This particular one illuminates traces of magickal energy, making them visible to the eye in ways they usually aren't. See that?'

Jay saw it. He was off before I could say another word, striding ahead of me at such speed I found it hard to keep up.

About twenty seconds later he disappeared.

I found the spot where I had last seen him, and shone my torch about one more time. There was a long, vertical split in the air: a thin, wavering line about twelve feet high, traced in white light.

I turned sideways, and fell through the tear in the atmosphere.

There are those who manage this procedure with rather more grace than I. I can only achieve a chaotic tumble, so of course I ended in an undignified heap upon the floor of the Dell beyond. I chose not to worry about what Jay might think of this display of clumsiness and quickly picked myself up, dusted bits of grass off my coat with studied nonchalance, and took a look around.

Jay, thankfully, was about ten feet off, and not looking my way. No wonder, either, for when one is surrounded by such spectacular beauty, why waste your glances upon me? Finnan Dell was like Glenfinnan, only more colourful. We stood at the top of a low, sloping hill; ranged around us was a lusciously rolling landscape composed of several more peaks and dales, all dusted with heathery grasses ranging in hue from serene jade to vivid emerald. Clumps of bushes painted in shades of blue were dotted here and there, sprouting spring blossoms in glorious profusion. The air was balmy, and held that slightly hushed, hazy quality the outer world only displays at the height of summer, and early in the morning. A lake lay spread at the bottom of the valley before us, adding the clean scent of fresh water to the bouquet of floral nectar I was luxuriating in.

'The Enclave is this way,' said Jay in a no-nonsense tone, proving once again that he has no heart for beauty.

I fell in behind him anyway. We *did* have a job to do.

And there we were, faced with another dreaming hillside, though this one was at-tractively sun-drenched. Finnan Enclave's Dellside door was another huge, black boulder embedded into the hill's face. No one answered this one, either, but my excellent key worked like a charm (...so to speak). The boulder groaned mightily and heaved itself aside, and in we went.

My first impression of Finnan Enclave was that it was, unbelievably, messier than South Moors. The winding, curved stone streets were familiar enough, though their houses were of a different architectural style: stone and wood-built with little arches, and some intriguing polychromatic brickwork. Grand, handsome and sweet in equal measure, and most attractive. I'd live in such a house.

But those streets were thick with debris. A heavy, not unpleasant scent of compost hung in the air, the source of which proved to be the piles of long-rotted *something* heaped up in every sweeping corner. A thick, oppressive silence hung over everything, and though we walked down street after street, we saw nobody about. No one at all.

Jay and I exchanged twin looks of concern. 'I think it is time for a little more breaking and entering,' I suggested.

I expected a refusal from Jay, and he did hesitate, but finally he nodded. 'I don't think we'll even need your key, here. Look.' He indicated the nearest house, whose grand elmwood door hung slightly ajar.

Not a good sign.

'None of this mess is litter,' I said, upon a sudden realisation.

Jay, already halfway up the path to the house, stopped. 'What?'

'There's no litter. This is all leaves, twigs, branches, dead flowers... swept in off the hillsides, probably. There is nothing here that looks like it was dropped by somebody living.'

Jay frowned, and made for the house again at a half-run. I followed.

The house was gorgeous inside, all wood panelling and sweeping archways. There was an entrance hall hung with tapestries, a dining room, two parlours, a handsome stone kitchen... whoever lived here lacked for neither money nor taste, clearly.

Only, it was empty. Not only were there no signs of life, there were no signs there had ever *been* any life. Everything was dust and desolation, like some kind of show home that had fallen out of use.

'This is weird,' said Jay, and I agreed, for it was *weird*.

It wasn't just that house, either, for a quick survey of the next few along the street told the same story. They were all empty, dust-laden, abandoned.

'This entire town is dead,' said Jay wonderingly, when we regained the street.

'As a dodo,' I agreed.

Jay took out his phone. 'We've got a big problem here.'

$$\mathcal{8}$$

That changed things. After Finnan, there was no more wandering through the
spring sunshine admiring the scenery. We had several more distant Enclaves to visit,
and every reason to expect trouble at most of them.

Jay called Nell, and gave her a terse, hurried report. She went away to consult with
Milady, and called back barely ten minutes later. Jay listened in taut silence.

'There's a team on the way to investigate Finnan,' he said when the call was done, shoving his phone back into his pocket. 'And South Moors. We're to go on to Darrowdale.'

'All right.'

'That's in Gloucestershire,' he added helpfully.

'I knew that.'

'Really?'

'No.'

There might have been a roll of the eye in answer, but I couldn't be sure, because Jay
turned his back on me and marched off.

The disappointing part about the Ways is that you cannot drift away to one of them
from literally Anywhere. In that, I suppose it isn't much different from driving. You can
go more or less anywhere you like by car, but if you get out and wander away from your
vehicle, you'll have to go find it again before you can drive on.

At least Jay and I did not have to contend with the misery that is traffic. It was, however,
necessary for us to trawl our way back to the henge, at a pace which left both of us sweating

and winded. From there, Jay whisked us off before either of us had chance to catch our breath.

The process was less disordering the second time, at least for me. I was no longer alarmed by the whirling winds, or the disorienting sensation of far-too-rapid movement. My insides objected a little less, too.

Jay, though, looked every bit as distressed as the first time. He spent a half-minute or so doubled over, elbows on his knees, shaking and gulping in air like a drowning man.

I began to feel concerned for him. We had several more Enclaves yet to visit, and must contrive to travel to at least three a day. Would the impact upon him grow more bearable, or less so? Would he cope?

I knew better than to express any of these thoughts, though. We were strangers to one another, near enough; would he hear concern in my words, or doubts as to his competency? I could not guess, and therefore did not take the risk.

'We're looking for the Giant's Stone,' said Jay once he had dragged himself upright. 'I think that's what they call it, around here.' The henge he had brought us to was even more underwhelming than the last: just a circle of earthworks, no standing monuments of any kind. Had there never been any, or had the remnants faded with the passage of time? The henge was situated in the kind of copse that could exist pretty much anywhere in Britain: a raggety cluster of birch and oak trees randomly spread about, the floor carpeted in ivy and ferns. I could only take Jay's word for it that we were in Gloucestershire — or, in fact, that there was a henge there at all, for the ground was so overgrown with ivy, I saw little but an indeterminate array of dips and slopes.

The Giant's Stone, though, was much more distinct: twin slabs of ancient stone, prettily grown over with moss. I suppose they did look rather like sleeping giants; was that why they had been given the name? Or had somebody once seen an unglamoured troll hereabouts, and misinterpreted the vision? Happily for us, the Stone was not too far from the henge we'd used, perhaps only a mile. Still, it felt far enough away under the circumstances. I am by no means unfit, but I'm not a jogger.

I made a mental note to take up running when I got home. Apparently Jay and I were to be working together for a while, and with him... for all his dissatisfaction with the stairs, I was starting to think I might need to up my game.

Following my earlier lead, Jay set his palm to the nearest stone and entreated entrance. And...

...entrance was granted. Instantly. One of the stones ponderously rolled aside, revealing a grand subterranean entryway. Or in other words, a dirt tunnel heading deep underground.

'That's refreshing,' I said. 'How lovely and hospitable.'

But Jay was frowning. 'I don't think so. It's more like the door was open anyway. I just gave it a little shove.'

Nobody leaves their front door open like that, not intentionally. My heart flickered with alarm. Jay disappeared into the downward-sloping tunnel and I followed; we all but ran the quarter-mile or so until the tall, earth-walled tunnel opened out into Darrowdale Enclave.

There is a large, populous Troll Enclave somewhere else in Gloucestershire: the Enclave of the Forest of Dean. It, too, is subterranean, spread across a network of natural caverns beneath the forest. Apparently Gloucestershire trolls tend to be underground dwellers, for the smaller, lesser-known Darrowdale is much the same. We stepped out into a large cavern, its ceiling so far above our heads I couldn't begin to imagine how far up it was. The rock walls were of mottled colours, scattered with chunks of raw iron ore and daubed with reddish purple ochre. The houses here were built into the rock walls, sloping structures made from irregular stone blocks fitted into place like some kind of Tetris puzzle. They had made significant use of the ochre, I judged, for red, purple and yellowish colours predominated in the paints and stones they had used.

Darrowdale was not abandoned. The trolls there strongly resembled the inhabitants of South Moors, only they were... worse. Jay and I walked the length of a wide main street unchallenged; its residents watched us pass with dull, uninterested eyes and made no move to stop us, to welcome us or to talk to us at all. I saw one old lady stretched across a low bench positioned in a pretty square at the end of the street; she lay covered with crocheted blankets, and looked as though she had not moved in a long time. In fact, she looked as though she may no longer be capable of movement at all. Only the faintest rising and falling of the blanket told me she lived at all: she was still breathing.

Everywhere we looked, the trolls of Darrowdale drifted in some kind of stupor. Many sat slumped upon benches or chairs or even upon the earthy, rock-inset floors, unmoving and uninterested in moving. Those who were still on their feet slouched and shuffled their way around, as though the effort of putting one foot in front of the other was almost insurmountably difficult. If nobody was speaking to us, they were not speaking to each other either, for the Enclave was eerily quiet.

'No one's doing *anything*,' whispered Jay, appalled.

It *was* an appalling sight. So much life, there, in that populous little town, and yet no life at all.

'That's not quite true,' I replied, struck by a sudden realisation. 'They are eating. Look.' The square we were standing in was ringed with houses; a suit-clad troll sat before one of them upon a stone bench, a chunk of raw meat in one hand. He ate with no apparent pleasure whatsoever, no relish, no attention for whatever he was eating. His jaws moved slowly, chewing his food with a methodical, mechanical determination to imbibe.

The image was faintly obscene, perhaps because it was so incongruous. His suit, though in dire need of laundering, was neat and smart and looked quite new; his house, too, had obviously seen a lot of care over the years. But he clutched his hunk of meat in a clawed grip, heedless of the blood that ran over his fingers and down his wrist to stain the cuffs of his white shirt. He was so expressionless I might have taken him for a statue, were he not moving. His teeth were stained, and flecked with torn-off flesh and blood.

Jay eyed him with poorly concealed disgust. 'Trolls aren't normally given to eating their meat raw, are they?'

'Well, you've met Baron Alban. Do you think he'd go for that?'

'He *did* say that trolls will eat pretty much anything.'

'So they will. Lightly fried in butter, delicately sauteed, oven-roasted, a la sous vide, you name it. There is a reason why the Society employs a couple of troll chefs.'

'Then why are they eating raw meat?'

The suited troll wasn't the only one. Now that I thought to look for it, it was every-where: most of the people we could see had a chunk of something raw and bleeding in one hand, even if they had yet to muster the energy to actually consume it. I took a closer look at the old lady on her bench, and saw that she had a morsel of something red and glistening clenched between her teeth. 'Good question.'

'And why are they all eating, all the time? Especially when they aren't doing anything else.'

'Also a good question.' I approached the troll in his suit, moving slowly and carefully. I didn't want to startle him; that would be neither to his benefit, nor mine.

I needn't have taken such care. He did not even look at me as I drew near, only continued his grim war of attrition against the meat he held.

'Excuse me,' I said. 'Good afternoon. We come from the Society for Magickal Heritage, in Yorkshire. May we ask you a couple of questions?'

I was not particularly expecting a response, nor did I get one. But he tried. His gaze flicked to me, and he spent some ten or fifteen seconds merely looking at my face. Then his mouth moved. At first I thought he was chewing again, but no. He made several attempts to form words, his lips struggling to shape syllables which did not emerge.

At length, he abandoned this effort and went back to his meat.

I frowned, noticing something else. The fabric of that natty suit hung oddly. The fit was wrong. That alone is no surprise; few people buy bespoke tailored suits anymore, they are largely purchased off-the-peg. When you do that, who knows what you are getting yourself into? But a perfectly-fitted ensemble isn't likely to be it.

This was different. This troll had lost weight since he'd bought that suit. A lot of weight. The folds of fabric hung off him.

'Why are you eating that?' said Jay, coming up behind me. 'Why is everybody eating all the time?'

He did not receive an answer either. The troll did not even look at Jay, but went on chewing, oblivious.

I turned away from the uncommunicative troll and stared around in dismay. 'You know, Jay, while that's a relevant question and all... I'm also inclined to ask *what* they are eating. Where did they get all this meat?' I was thinking, of course, of the two alikats at South Moors, who had been seconds away from being turned into dinner when we had intercepted them.

'Oh,' said Jay, and then added: 'Shit.'

9

I do not know how Miranda got down to Gloucester so quickly.

It wasn't *that* fast, I suppose; not compared to the (relative) ease with which Jay darts about the country. But she arrived a full hour sooner than I'd expected, and she brought approximately half of the Society with her. Soon, those eerily quiet caverns were awash with frantic Society agents racing to save, protect and preserve as much as they could.

The worst discovery was the crude pit that had been dug at the rear of the Enclave. Its aroma first announced its presence; we lifted our noses to the putrid scent of something rotting, and followed the stench.

It proved to consist of *lots* of somethings rotting. The pit lurked behind a pair of ramshackle, abandoned buildings both leaning dangerously to the left. A narrow track wound in between, and at the rear was the crater: perhaps ten feet deep and eight wide, roughly covered over in tarpaulin in a crude, futile attempt to conceal the horror of its contents. It was a bone pit, and filled nearly to the rim with the half-rotted corpses of dead animals. Most of them had had their flesh roughly stripped from their bones before they were discarded, though by no means expertly. Looking at the mess of bloodied flesh, the pale glint of bone here and there, the thick carpet of maggots crawling with grotesque enthusiasm over the whole, I could imagine the clumsy haste with which each beast had been dispatched to its fate.

They were not all magickal beasts, but too many were. Severed heads and tails and paws, dislocated beaks and feathered crests, claws and teeth, patches of decaying fur — each sad little remnant announced that here lay far too many of the precious creatures we fought so desperately to save.

I wished, too late, that Miranda had been far away when we found that pit. It broke her heart. She stood on the edge of it, shuddering uncontrollably, and looking so near to collapse that I had to steady her.

'How could they?' she gasped. 'How could they do such a thing?'

'Miranda.' I gripped her arm hard, holding her up by sheer force of will if I had to. 'They are sick. Can you understand that? This is not cruelty, it is desperation. They've been eating this much and they are still wasting away. They are *starving*.'

I don't know if she heard me, or registered the import of my words, for she made no reply. She took a deep, deep breath, mopped her damp cheeks on the sleeve of her jumper, and left me. 'Right,' I heard her calling as she walked away. 'There must be some creatures still alive down here, let's find them! Quickly, please!'

Well and good. Miranda's job was to take care of the animals. I needed to find someone who could help the trolls.

They were already being helped, I soon saw as I trotted gratefully away from that terrible pit. But ineptly. The Society had not yet realised how futile it was to try to communicate with the trolls of Darrowdale; we were too late for that. They needed more direct help, though of what nature, who knew?

A young man in a blue jacket raced past on his way to somewhere; I caught hold of him. 'Did they send any of the medical staff down here? I need to talk to them.' I'd asked for a doctor, but requests and instructions sometimes got a little garbled along the way.

'Uh,' said the boy. 'Foster's here somewhere.' He did not stay to argue the point any longer, but dashed off again.

That was all right. They'd sent Rob, and that was all I needed to know. Robert Foster, with all his might, was also a doctor, a fact I sometimes forgot. I went in search of him, but ran into Jay first.

'I was looking for you,' said Jay. 'We're finished at Darrowdale, they can handle it from here. We need to move on.'

'Yes, but first I have to talk to Robert.'

Jay's brow snapped down. 'Can't it wait?'

'No. Help me.'

'Right.' We resumed the search together — a frustrating process, for there were so many people down there, so much furious activity taking place, that it was hard to know where to begin. I saw Miranda once, striding past us with a thunderous look, and Zareen looking unusually grim, but no Robert.

It was Jay who spotted him at last. We had found our way back to that odd little square, where we had met the troll in the suit. Where it had been serene before, it was now swarming with people. 'There,' said Jay, pointing.

Rob was bending over the old lady under her blanket, tending to her with all the gentle care so characteristic of him. He was not trying to speak with her, but examined her face with a look of intense focus.

'Rob,' I said. 'I think there's some kind of a sickness here. They've all got it. Have you been to South Moors?'

Robert straightened up at my words, and directed a frowning look at me. He shook his head. 'Should I?'

'Yes. South Moors is going to end up like this, I know it. They're displaying the same kinds of symptoms, only I think they are at an earlier stage. It's like... some kind of wasting disease, and they're all eating and eating but it's not helping them.'

He nodded thoughtfully, casting an eye over the old lady, who still had not stirred. 'That would make sense with what I am seeing. I'll look into it.'

'There's another thing. The things they are eating — they're mostly going for magickal beasts. Not exclusively, for I saw a fox and a lot of rats in that pit. But either by knowledge or instinct they're targeting the magickals, and that has to be relevant.'

'Thanks, Ves.' He nodded to me and to Jay and turned back to his patient.

'Can we go now?' said Jay.

'Immediately, and at once.'

If I could, I would be delighted to forget the urgent bustle of the next two days. Jay took us across England, into Wales and Ireland and back again; three great, gigantic, exhausting leaps every day. By the end of it, I was ready to collapse. Jay looked like he wished he had died three weeks ago.

From Darrowdale we proceeded to Parrow Hollow, Warwickshire, which to our relief was hale and well — merely Reclusive. Five of the other names on our list proved much the same, but the final one... that one was as bad as South Moors and Darrowdale put together. Baile Monaidh Enclave was a decimated wreck, well on its way to becoming a ghost town like Glenfinnan. Its handful of surviving citizens were skeletal, withered almost to the point of desiccation, and sunk in such deep stupor they were barely breathing. We summoned all the help we could, but we both knew it was bordering upon too late for them.

By the time we finally made it Home, my trembling legs threatened to dump me face-first into the cold, unforgiving stones of the cellar Waypoint, and I came close to decorating them with a liberal helping of my stomach contents besides. How Jay held himself together I do not know, but somehow he did. As the swirling winds of our passage slowly died away, he stood with his arms tightly folded, jaw clenched, sweat pouring off him.

I eyed him with a view to offering assistance, but he would not meet my gaze.

'I want a bath,' I announced. 'A bath, two meals, three desserts, six cups of tea and sixteen hours in bed.'

Jay made a faint sound that might have been a chuckle, or perhaps it was a choked gasp of pure longing. 'Three meals for me, and make that twenty-four hours asleep.'

'You've earned it.' I hesitated, reluctant to give voice to my next thought. But it couldn't be helped. 'Right after we talk to Milady.'

Jay backed up a step, his eyes widening in horror. 'No! I am not doing that climb!'

'Well...' I forced my jellied legs to walk me to the door, and took hold of the handle. 'This might be one of those times when...' I opened the door and took a peek beyond. 'When House loves us. Look.'

Instead of the narrow, dark passage and staircases of the cellar, the room beyond the door was clearly Milady's tower. 'Just six or seven steps and we're there.'

'Three, if you don't have short legs.' Jay demonstrated one of his long strides, which dwarfed mine. But he never made it to a second. He wobbled and stopped, swaying like a sapling in a strong wind.

'Right, come on.' I took his arm, propped him up against my shoulder, and hauled us both through the door.

Jay promptly collapsed all over Milady's floor. I winced, for he hit the ground with a *thud* and that had to hurt. The carpet might be handsome, but it wasn't especially thick.

The air sparkled.

'Jay Patel,' said Milady. 'Are you well?'

'Fine,' croaked Jay. Probably. It was hard to understand him with his face buried in the rug like that.

Milady let the matter drop. 'Welcome Jay, Ves. You have news for me, I collect.'

'Tons of it.' I gave myself permission to sit, too, if Jay was going to, though I managed the business with a touch more elegance than he. With the help of an occasional, muffled interpolation from Jay, I told Milady everything that had happened since she had sent us off to Glenfinnan.

She heard us out in her customary courteous silence, and then said: 'Very good. There's chocolate in the pot.'

I blinked, taken aback, for I had expected some form of comment upon our labours. A question or two, perhaps; confirmation of a point of detail somewhere; even a titbit of information we might yet be unaware of.

Ah, well. If chocolate was all I could have, chocolate I would most certainly take.

'Do take them back down, House?' said Milady, which surprised me again, for I had never yet heard of anybody directly addressing House and actually receiving a response. But Milady spoke with the confidence of being not only heard but attended to, and so she was, for when we opened the door again we found ourselves stepping over the threshold directly into the first floor common room.

'I like you,' said Jay.

'Thank you.'

'I was talking to the House.'

'I know.'

He gave me a tiny smile, barely more than a twitch of his lips, and sank heavily into the nearest arm chair. The chocolate pot, apparently taking its cues from Milady in the same fashion as House, obligingly poured itself out for both of us, and we disappeared into all the sweet, spicy pleasures of hot chocolate for a blissful two or three minutes.

'Is that it?' said Jay, when he had finished slurping up every last trace of chocolate from his dainty cup.

'Doubtful. Now we wait.'

'For?'

I shrugged. 'Milady does not yet know how to proceed, I would guess. She is most likely awaiting the return of our colleagues from Darrowdale and Baile Monaidh.'

'Why do we have to wait for Milady? Isn't there something we can do in the meantime?'

'Besides sleeping?'

'After the sleeping.'

'Maybe, yes, and I do have an idea. But I want to sleep first. Don't you?'

'Desperately.'

So we did that.

• • • ••••• • •

My idea involved a day or two spent searching the libraries; always an appealing prospect, whatever the occasion. But before I had chance to get started, someone swept in upon me and knocked all my plans awry. I was reclining in the common room at the time, stretched across two wing-back chairs and half asleep. It *was* first thing of the following morning, in my defence, and though I had slept a great deal it did not yet feel like enough.

'Vesper?' said a low, beautiful voice, and I jerked upright, for I knew those delectable tones.

Baron Alban was back.

10

And there he was, in all his gorgeous glory. He had chosen a red leather duster coat that day, worn with dark combat trousers, boots to match, and an ivory shirt. No hat; instead, his golden-bronze locks had been brushed into an attractively wind-swept arrangement, and a jewelled pin winked at his throat.

I was suddenly wide awake.

'Hello, the Baron,' I said lightly, wishing I had taken a minute or two longer over my hair before I'd come downstairs. It probably resembled a hedge more nearly than I would like.

The Baron, though, did not seem displeased, for he looked me over with a twinkle and a smile, and made me a bow. 'It is early. I apologise.'

'The pot would like to offer you some tea,' I observed, for the delicate glass teapot I favoured was bobbing lightly up and down, its spout emitting enthusiastic puffs of steam.

'Thank you, pot. I shall be delighted.' He took a seat, and his cup shortly after, and sat looking thoughtfully at me. 'How are you getting along with the matter of the Enclaves?' he said.

I sat up a little more. 'Well, I have a theory, though it has some holes in it. But maybe you can help fill them in.'

He smiled faintly. 'Perhaps I might.'

'I think there is some kind of wasting sickness. They eat and eat and still starve; clearly they are ill. But there has to be more to it than that, because there are too many questions.

It *seems* to be affecting only trolls, but why only a few of the Enclaves? And there is no discernible link between those communities that are sick. They are situated far apart from one another, so how is the disease spreading? And they aren't just starving, they are... it's almost like their minds are starving, too. They have no energy for anything but eating, and barely that. They don't speak; it's as if they have forgotten how to form words, or simply lack the energy or the will to make the effort.'

'All good points.'

'And they are eating magickal creatures, almost exclusively. Why? That suggests it is about something more than mere physical sustenance. Any kind of food would suffice there, but they are going for meat, and the meat of magickal beasts in particular. What's that about?'

Alban's green, green eyes twinkled with amusement. 'So many questions. You have some theories to advance, too?'

'Of course I do. But I did not share them with Milady, yet, for I have no evidence.'

'Let's hear them.'

'Right.' I set down my empty tea cup. 'The disease spreads, but if it were contagious in any conventional way, surely we would be seeing either a wider problem — or a more confined one. Some of the affected Enclaves have been at least partially Reclusive for years, with little or no traffic going in or out of their towns. How did they catch it? And since they did, why hasn't it spread farther? I don't think it is a contagion.

'Meanwhile, their desperate need to eat, eat and eat is telling, but the fact that they are starving anyway tells me that whatever they are feeding, it isn't themselves. I think there is some kind of infecting body — a parasite, if you will. And it is taking so much from each host that it's killing them. But it does not need meat to survive.

'We know that many magickal beings feed as much off magickal energies as from more conventional foods. Trolls are an example. You need meat, grain, vegetables to survive, but you need a replenishing diet of magickal energies in order to flourish. This is why Troll Enclaves tend to be located inside Dells; those structures as a whole are built around sources of strong magickal energy. It's perfect. At a place like Glenfinnan, you eat, sleep and breathe magick, literally.

'These parasites, then. I think they feed off magickal energy. If we go back to Glenfinnan, say, track down what is, or more probably *was*, their source of magick, I imagine we will find it drained. And that is what happened to its citizens, too. Whatever parasite they were carrying sucked them dry.'

Alban just watched me, his face unreadable, and I began to feel a flicker of doubt. The idea made sense to me, but he did not seem to be impressed. 'Is all of this based purely upon logic and deduction?' he asked.

'Is that not good enough?'

To my relief, he grinned. 'I suspect your theory of such a high level of accuracy, I wondered if you had access to some secret source of information after all.'

'Some secret source of information I ought not to be going anywhere near?' I tried to look coy, as though I might have just such a source.

'Exactly.' The grin faded and a frown appeared, the unsettling kind.

So much for making of myself a woman of mystery. 'Alas, no,' I sighed. '*You* do, of course, but the likes of a Vesper can only dream.'

The grin flashed again, wry this time. 'You are occasionally talked of in my circles, you know. Your track record is impressive — so much so, I think there are those who suspect you of harbouring secret resources. But I begin to think it is merely an astuteness of mind that's hard to hide from.'

'So you *do* have a secret library!'

He laughed. 'Point ably proven.'

'May I see it?'

'Of course not.'

Curses. 'So why are you visiting me this morning?'

'Take a guess.'

'There is something you want me to do.'

'You and your partner, yes. Jay, was it?'

'It is.'

Baron Alban paused, and looked around. The common room was mostly empty at that hour of the morning, but not quite: Miranda sat wearily nursing a coffee on the other side of the room, and another chair was occupied by somebody from the Restoration department whose name I can never remember. 'Is there somewhere more private we can talk?'

'It's never promising, when they say that in films.'

His lips twitched. 'I have nothing nefarious in mind, I assure you.'

'I don't object to a *little* villainy, mind. I only draw the line at a *lot*.'

This he acknowledged with a gracious salute, and stood up. 'The matter is somewhat urgent.'

'Ohh.' How interesting. I led him out of the common room at once, down to the ground floor and around to the south side. One of my favourite retreats is the expansive conservatory that occupies about half of the south wall. It belongs to the Botany department, and they do a fine job of keeping it filled with all the most interesting magickal herbs and plants, many of which bloom gloriously and smell delicious. I cannot understand why it isn't constantly swarming with people, but I seem to be one of very few who visit if they don't have to.

As I'd hoped, we arrived to find damp stone floors and the scent of wet earth in the air: the watering had already been done for the morning, and we could expect to have a quiet corner of the greenhouse to ourselves for a few minutes. I chose a sunny nook beneath an arching trellis heavy with something blue-blossoming and fragrant, and adopted a posture of intent interest.

The baron was uncharacteristically hesitant. He looked at the flowers, and at me, and at the clear glass ceiling, and appeared to be struggling to discover what to say.

'I need your help,' he finally ventured.

'So you said.'

'On an errand of a… slightly questionable nature.'

'I was getting that feeling, too.'

His eyes smiled at me. 'There is somewhere I urgently need to get into. It relates to the Enclaves, you see, so it is an emergency. But the place in question is locked. *Extremely* locked. And there are one or two other obstacles…' He trailed off.

'If Jay told you I have a taste for breaking and entering, he is quite wrong, and I deny all charges,' I said serenely.

Alban lifted a brow in my general direction. 'He's said nothing of the kind, in fact. *Do* you indeed?'

'As I said, all charges denied.'

'That might not be a bad thing, at all.'

'I grow ever more intrigued.'

Alban sighed. 'Right, the fact is… there are three keys to the place in question. I have secured two of them, at some risk and cost to myself, but they are useless if I can't get all three.'

Uh huh. 'Where is the third one?'

He smiled at me, hope and mischief and sheepishness mixed up into one rather adorable, hard-to-resist package. 'It's, um. It's here.'

'Let me guess: you absolutely are *not* supposed to have it.'

'Let's just say Milady refused.'

It was my turn to raise a questioning brow.

'She threatened to throw me off the tower top,' he admitted.

'Just how locked *is* this place?'

'Extremely, thoroughly, completely and forever locked.'

'I might guess that it is dangerous.'

'Probably. Maybe. Who knows, anymore?'

I folded my arms. 'So. Milady held the prospect of your swift and inescapable death over your head if you pursue this venture and you still want to find the key?'

'No.' His smile broadened, turned achingly hopeful. 'I want *you* to find the key.'

'That is spectacularly unflattering.'

'Depends how you look at it.' He leaned closer to me, so close that I could smell the fresh, cologne scent of him. 'Do I consider you expendable? In no way whatsoever. Do I think you are a match for Milady? Why, yes. I absolutely do.'

My eyes narrowed. 'You cannot flirt me into it, Lord Baron.'

That smile turned wickedly mischievous, and the twinkle reappeared in his eyes. 'Can't I?'

Damn him, he was far too good.

Though, he did not know me perfectly if he thought he *needed* to flirt me into it. I would have done it just for the sake of curiosity alone. A super-locked, mysterious somewhere, filled to the brim with who-knew-*what* manner of juicy secrets? Yes *please*. You can sign me up for that, zero questions asked.

'What is it that you needed Jay for? I possibly don't need to tell you that he will be firmly opposed to this proposition.'

'Quite,' agreed the baron. 'We do not need to tell him about this particular part of it, perhaps, if you think he will disapprove. I will need his Waymastery skills later on, once we have secured the final key.'

'One last question, then.'

He made a show of bracing himself. 'Let's hear it.'

'What, or where, are you trying to get into?'

'I can't tell you that.'

'No good! Try again.'

'Vesper. I can't tell you that.'

'Right. And you were planning to waltz off there with Jay and leave me languishing at Home alone, I suppose?'

He did not answer that in words, but his face told me everything I needed to know.

'You'll tell me, and you'll take me with you.'

'I can't.'

'No deal.'

'Ves... you don't understand.'

'And I never will, if you keep me in the dark.'

He sighed, ran a hand over his hair — unwise, for those wavy locks were *so* perfectly ordered before, and what a shame — and eyed me with strong disfavour. 'I could find someone else to get hold of the key.'

'If there is a better choice, why are you talking to me?'

'Fine.' He made a don't-blame-me-when-you're-dead gesture and said, with strong reluctance: 'Where we are going, if you really want to know—'

'I do.'

'—Is... is Farringale.'

$$11$$

'Farringale,' I repeated.

'Yes,' said Baron Alban.

'Mythical, mysteriously abandoned, long-lost seat of the Troll Court for hundreds of years Farringale?'

'That's the one.'

'The unfindable version, or is there some other Farringale that's still marked on a map somewhere?'

'Why don't you let me worry about how to find it, while you worry about how to get in?'

'All right. Be right back.' I slid past him and made for the door.

'Uh, Ves?' he called. 'Where are you going?'

'I'm going to ask Milady.'

'What? Why! She will only say no.'

'You don't know that for sure.'

'No,' said Milady.

I'd given it my best shot, honest. I had begun with a polite enquiry after her health, paired with my usual curtsey, and opened the discussion with: 'It emerges that our excellent Baron Ambassador suspects a close connection between the afflicted Enclaves and Farr—'

'No,' said Milady.

'—Farringale, and seeks an opportunity to investigate the precise causes of its demise in a more direct fashion—'

'No.'

'—in hopes of uncovering some new, hitherto unsuspected information which might enable us to save Baile Monaidh and Darrowdale and—'

'No.'

'—any others that might come under similar afflictions in the future, or even to—'

'No!'

'—to learn enough to avert such calamities from ever occurring again at all. '

'Vesper! I do not know how many times you require me to repeat the same word before you find yourself able to comprehend it.'

'But why! The Baron's theory is sound and his cause is more than just—'

'The reasons he saw fit to present to you, and to me, are just, but I suspect the Baron of harbouring a few other ideas.'

'If he draws some other benefit out of the venture while also resolving an *emergency* which threatens the life of many of his people, I see no cause for complaint.'

'His theory might be sound, or it might be hogwash. There are reasons aplenty to avoid Farringale. Why do you think it was closed in the first place?'

'If it *is* sound, much may be accomplished. If it is not, we will have learned something.'

'And the risks?'

'Baron Alban is prepared to face them, and he has already secured two keys—'

'The keepers of those keys cannot have been any more delighted with this plan than I am, so I am moved to question just by what means his lordship secured them.'

'That is his own affair. I did not ask.'

Milady sighed, its manifestation a soft *puff* of glittering light. 'Vesper. I understand your point of view, truly, and I applaud your passion. But consider. The risks involved in opening Farringale are not necessarily limited to those holding the keys. We do not know *what* may come forth, were those doors opened, and therefore we cannot consider ourselves prepared to deal with the consequences.'

'The only way to learn something is to ask! To explore, to find out! No secret ever did anybody any good for long.'

'Vesper.' Milady's tone turned less strident, more... resigned. Wearily so. 'I cannot permit this.'

'I can only continue to fervently disagree with that decision.'

'You are one of my very best, and you know it. But I hope you understand that your job will be in some considerable danger, should you choose to disobey me in this.'

'I understand.'

'Very good. Please accept my regrets, Ves.'

· • • • ● • ● • • ·

I did, of course, with the utmost politeness. But while I understood Milady's position well enough, I do not think she understood that keeping my job was not my primary priority. Oh, I would be devastated if she carried through her threat, and ejected me from the Society. It has been my home and my world for so long, I cannot imagine my life without it. But it is a job with a *purpose.* The work that I do *matters.* I am here because I want to save our beautiful magickal beasts, our wondrous books and charms and artefacts and Curiosities and plants and Dells and all the rest. And yes, if I get the chance, that absolutely includes the Troll Enclaves, whether they fall strictly under my purview or not.

If I lost my job, I could get another. But if we lost half our Enclaves? How could that ever be justified?

So I set forth to disobey Milady, heavy of heart but firm of purpose. And if, lurking behind all those noble ideals, there was another reason — namely, that I simply cannot resist an ancient mystery — well, nobody needed to know about that but me.

· • • ● • ● • • • ·

'The problem,' I said, having rejoined Baron Alban and borne his inevitable I-told-you-so, 'is that I have not the first idea where to look for the key. I do hope you have furnished yourself with something along the lines of a clue.'

'None whatsoever,' he said. 'But I can assure you that it will be virtually unreachable, and secreted somewhere with fiendishly excellent security.'

'How very encouraging you are.'

He bowed. 'Honesty is my policy. Be careful, Ves. I would not make such a request of you, were it not—'

'Urgent. Yes, yes, I know.'

'I have given you a way to reach me,' he said, and when I took out my phone I found a text from an unknown number saying: 'Tally ho!'

'Do you take anything seriously?' I said.

'I'm taking this problem seriously. Just not all the way seriously, all the time.'

'Where would be the fun in that,' I agreed.

The baron gave me a swift grin, and tipped an imaginary hat. 'Good luck, Ves. Text me when you've got it.'

With which buoying words he was gone, leaving me with a big problem and a dearth of possible solutions.

· · · ● · ● · · · ·

Trying to second-guess Milady is… not the easiest task I have ever been given. I mean, where to begin? If I was a disembodied voice with a penchant for tower-tops and chocolate pots, where would *I* hide the key to a lost Enclave? Absolutely no idea.

I thought about all the obvious places, and dismissed them as too obvious. The tower? On the one hand, at least she could keep an eye on it up there. No one was likely to be pilfering it out from under her very eyes. But it did not strike me as likely, because whenever any of us thinks of Milady, we think of the tower. It is the first place any of us would choose to look for something Milady had hidden, and therefore, I had to cross it off the list. She was too subtle for that.

Stores? That made a lot more sense to me, and I considered it an attractive possibility for a while. Where better to hide something like that than in plain sight, so to speak? Buried under so much other, random paraphernalia that nobody would ever realise its importance? Maybe. But this, too, occurred to me too early and too easily, so I had to discount it. Anything that seemed very likely probably wasn't.

I thought about the Enchanting labs for similar reasons. They spend all day tinkering with various charms and imbuing them into various objects, so those labs are always littered with stuff — keys included. But that struck me as too random. Such a key could get lost in there, or worse yet, its operating charm overwritten with something else entirely. Milady wouldn't be that careless.

And so I went on, eliminating every idea I came up with as too obvious, too unlikely, or too risky, until I had nothing left.

I toyed briefly with the idea of asking Jay. I'm not sure why, only that he was bright-minded and obviously saw the world very differently from me. He would probably see some possibility that would never have occurred to me. But I kept coming back to the unavoidable fact that he would heartily disapprove of the whole venture, so I stayed away from him.

In the end, devoid of further ideas, I went to see Valerie.

• • • • ● • ● • ● • •

Valerie Greene has a job I rather envy. She's Queen of the Library, Head of History, Boss of all Secrets, and it is her official duty to uncover exactly the kinds of ancient mysteries that I cannot resist. I applied to join the Library Division when I arrived at the Society, but Milady said my varied talents rendered me better suited to my current, rather more eclectic role, and I cannot say that she was wrong there.

Nonetheless, when I walk into the grand library at Home and see Valerie at the main desk there, absorbed in some promisingly huge and dusty tome and with her name engraved upon a shiny brass plaque, I always suffer a mild stab of regret. It is one of those libraries that dreams are made of: all soaring ceilings and shelves by the thousand, everything all ancient oak wood and leather-bound tomes. It smells like knowledge and mystery and time, and when I went in that day I paused to take a great lungful of that familiar aroma, as I always do.

Valerie looked up from her book. 'Morning, Ves.' She had a smile for me, as usual. She is one of the few people at Home that I would call a close friend; we've both been here for years, and have spent many hours chattering about books and speculating as to the truth behind some mystery or another. She and I are roughly the same age, she being the elder by only a few years. She has a neatness and a chic style about her that I have never been able to match, her dark hair and skin always perfectly complemented by her ensemble. She favours the swept-up look by way of hairstyle, which is practical; when I read, my hair is always falling all over the pages. You would think I would learn.

'Val.' I sidled up to the desk — a mildly undignified form of movement it may be, but it cannot be helped; sidling is exactly what I did — and sat down across from her. 'I need to ask you something.'

'Is this going to be one of those juicy requests?'

'It is the questionable kind. Is that juicy enough?'

'Plenty.' She closed her book with great care and set it aside, laying it atop a soft, protective cushion. 'What are we digging up today?'

I grinned. Val knows me far too well. 'A key,' I said. 'Actually, before we get to the sticky part, let's begin with Farringale. What do you know of it?'

That word definitely got her attention. 'Farringale? Much the same things everybody knows about it, I imagine. Seat of Their Gracious Majesties, the kings and queens of the Troll Court since time immemorial, up until a few centuries ago. Its last known rulers were Hrruna the Third and Torvaston the Second, whose reign ended somewhere in the mid sixteen hundreds but who knows when exactly, because it—'

'—inexplicably faded out of all knowledge. Exactly. That's the part that I'm interested in.'

Valerie folded her arms and gave me the narrow-eyed look. 'Theories abound as to why, as I am sure you know, because you have read every book we own about Farringale from cover to cover. So why are you asking me?'

'I might be under the impression that you know something that isn't in any of those books.'

'I wish I did, but no. The current Court keeps that place shrouded in the kind of secrecy that can only be termed impenetrable.'

I nodded, more impressed than I cared to show. Valerie is tenacious with this kind of thing, even more so than I am, and she has the stature and credentials to make legitimate requests for that level of information. If even she couldn't get past the Troll Court, they were really serious about keeping it under wraps.

'Somebody at the Court disagrees,' I said, and I told her about Baron Alban and his proposition. Her eyes grew rather wide as I hurried through my tale, and when I had finished she said: 'Ves, I don't know whether you should... are you sure about this?'

'Of course I'm sure,' I replied, all incredulity.

And then came the grin I had expected. 'Of course you are. As if I would make any other decision in your shoes.'

'I wouldn't suspect you of it for an instant.'

12

'So you need this key.' Valerie tapped a pen thoughtfully against her lips, a characteristic gesture. I said nothing, letting her think in peace. I have great confidence in Val. She always comes up with something. 'I wonder why Milady has custody of it,' she said at length.

A good question, one I had not really considered. 'The Society's entire existence is about protecting rare old stuff, isn't it?'

'Might be reason enough.' She thought some more, her eyes straying to the books on the far shelves. 'The House predates Milady by quite a margin, of course. I wonder why Alban is so certain Milady is keeping the key.'

A faint suspicion entered my head. 'Predates? By how far?'

She nodded, following my train of thought perfectly — or perhaps I was following hers. 'The House's precise date of construction is not known for some reason, but a few particular architectural features have led me to conclude that it was built somewhere around the early 1660s. Give or take a few years.'

'And the decline of Farringale took place in 1657! Or so Milady said.'

Val's eyes narrowed. 'That was unusually forthcoming of her.'

'Wasn't it? I have no idea what came over her.'

'It makes sense that those three keys were hidden away sometime fairly soon after the close of the Enclave, which was probably somewhere in the 1660s. Is Milady personally keeping the third key, or was it given to the House?'

'Given... to the House?' I was sceptical, I couldn't help it. 'Come on, Val. I know it's an odd House and rather more aware than most Houses are, but still. It doesn't have a mind, exactly, or a consciousness the way we do—'

'Doesn't it?'

It might have been a coincidence, but something creaked in the library just then. I don't mind admitting that it gave me the chills. 'All right,' I said, prepared to accept the possibility, for what was ever normal about the Society? 'But if House has got it, that's a problem. If I couldn't persuade Milady to let me have it, I... have no idea how to convince a seventeenth-century country mansion.'

Valerie smiled. 'House can be very helpful, if it likes you.'

I cast a slightly trepid glance at the stately shelves nearby, and the graceful ceiling arching far overhead. 'How do I know if it likes me?' I whispered.

'I wouldn't worry, Ves. You are very likeable.'

'That's comforting.'

She sat back, eyeing me speculatively. 'I will tell you a secret about the House. Maybe it will help.'

I blinked. 'Wait. There are secrets about the House that you haven't told me?'

'Yes, but we can wrangle about that later. Is this urgent or not?'

'Sorry.'

Out came the secret. 'House has a favourite room. Few have seen it, for it is so well hidden, you really have to know that it's there in order to find it at all. And I don't think House likes visitors in there too often, so it doesn't exactly help you out if you go looking for it. But it's there, somewhere near the heart of the building. A sitting room, prettily decorated, and as far as I can tell it's unchanged since the sixteen hundreds. I believe it most likely belonged to whoever built this House, and House keeps it just the way it is.'

'Fantastic,' I breathed. 'So you've been inside it?'

'Twice.' She did not elaborate, and I didn't push. 'Anyway, if you go there, I think House might listen to you. And if it does... well, House and Milady are usually in accord with one another, but it wouldn't be the first time they have disagreed.'

'Dear Val, you are a jewel in the Society's crown.'

She smirked. 'I know. Got some paper? The directions are a little convoluted, you'll want them written down.'

She wasn't kidding. I left the library a few minutes later with a sheet of notepaper in my hand, both sides of it mostly covered in Val's flowing handwriting. According to the directions, there were at least three times as many staircases at Home than I had ever seen or imagined, and far more corridors than the place should reasonably have room for. Not that this should have surprised me either. I had more than once suspected that the House was somewhat larger on the inside than its exterior would lead a person to expect.

Val's route started, helpfully, from the library, but I soon began to feel that I was lost. I trotted along several winding corridors, up a few twisting staircases and down several more. At first I knew exactly where I was, but after a while I realised I recognised nothing that I saw around me. When I opened an occasional door to take a peek inside, I saw rooms I had never seen before either.

This frankly flabbergasted me. I had lived for more than a decade in that House, and I'd been comfortable that I knew it inside out. How could so much of it have been hidden from me all that time? And what else was there that I still did not know about?

It grew quieter as I walked, a clear sign that I was travelling farther and farther away from the House's centres of activity. There was a stillness to the air that made me feel very alone, and my footsteps rang out, crisp and sharp, echoing off the aged stonework.

And then the corridor ended. I turned a corner and saw before me nothing but uninterrupted stone walls and a clean stone floor — curiously free of dust and debris, for all its remote atmosphere. There were no windows, no doors, no stairs; no way out at all, except back the way I had come.

I consulted Val's directions again, to no particular avail. Honestly, the sense of giving a woman like me so complex a list of directions and expecting me to traverse them without getting lost! For an instant I suspected Val of playing a trick on me, but dismissed the idea. She would not. Her faith in my ability to find my way through this maze of a castle must be rather higher than my own.

Turn left, said the last of Val's notes, which I had just done. Turn left… and then what? I considered calling her to ask, but dismissed that idea, too. She hates to have ringing phones around when she's reading, and would undoubtedly have switched hers off.

I felt my way along the walls for a while, checking for hidden doors, stones that might obligingly slide aside to reveal secret staircases, that kind of thing. No luck there either.

I chose a corner at the end of the corridor and sat down with my back against the stone wall, surveying the empty passageway before me with some dismay. How could I be *so* inept? The answer was probably obvious, so obvious that it had not occurred to Val that I might need help. Jay would have got it in an instant, and treated my confusion with that faint but distinct disbelief I have sometimes detected in his eyes. I could have called him, but my pride revolted against that idea.

'Well, House,' I said aloud as I hauled myself back to my feet. 'Your secrets are safe from me.' I walked back along that puzzling corridor and turned right, following Valerie's directions backwards.

Memory is a strange thing, is it not? I remember names, dates, faces and all manner of minute details with the greatest of ease, but I am not so well able to recognise places I have already been. So it took me much longer than it should have to realise that the passageway I was walking down was not the same one I had traversed perhaps half an hour before. The great stone blocks that made up the walls were limestone of a slightly different shade, and cut a little on the smaller side. The air smelled faintly of chocolate, which I had not noticed before. When I passed a gilt-framed painting of an eighteenth-century landscape I did not remember seeing before, I was certain I had gone wrong.

My stomach fluttered with nerves at finding myself so much at a loss, for I had clearly strayed from Val's directions and had no idea where I was. If I became hopelessly turned about in House's twisting corridors, would it consent to rescue me? I could be lost for hours. Days.

But then there was a door. It obtruded itself upon my notice so suddenly as to arouse my suspicions. Had it been there a moment before? Was I so oblivious as to have missed it? It looked innocuous enough: an ordinary-sized door painted bright white, with a single, large pewter knob set into the centre.

'All right, then,' I muttered, game to try anything that might get me out of that mess of a maze. I grasped the knob, finding it strangely warm under my hand, and turned it.

And there it was: House's favourite room. It could only be that, for before me lay a perfectly preserved parlour whose fittings and furniture clearly proclaimed its provenance. The wallpaper was prettily figured with scrolling flowers, all rosy and lavender and ivory in hue; three elegantly-curved seventeenth-century chairs had been upholstered to match, in handsome ivory silk; portraits in oval frames hung upon the walls, and an exquisite old grandfather clock occupied one corner. It was still ticking, its pendulum keeping time with a drowsy, soothing sway.

A little white tea table stood in the centre, atop which sat a silver chocolate pot not wholly unlike Milady's. A puff of steam drifted from its spout as I stepped over the threshold, and a cup appeared beside it.

'Is that for me?' I said.

The pot puffed steam again, which seemed a clear enough response. So I settled into the nearest chair — carefully, carefully; one is used to treating antique furniture with great care. But these chairs, while they had obviously been much used and loved, displayed none of the frailty or decay they ought to have accumulated over the better part of four hundred years.

I took a moment to examine the portraits, idly curious as to whether I might recognise any of the faces depicted therein. I did not. They were ladies and gentlemen for the most part, sumptuously garbed in the silk and lace gowns, the elaborately curled wigs, the velvet coats and jewelled extravagance of the sixteen hundreds. There were one or two exceptions, however. I saw a young, dark-skinned man clad in much simpler garb, his expression earnest and intense. On the other side of the room, a little girl in a plain dress played with a doll; next to her portrait hung that of an elderly woman wearing an eighteen-thirties day dress and a wide straw bonnet, smiling in the sunlight of a bright spring day.

'Dear House,' I began, setting down my empty cup. 'Thank you for the chocolate, you are always such a gent. Or a lady, it's... hard to tell. I have come to entreat your help. May we talk?'

It felt odd, sitting alone in that eerie little parlour out of time, literally talking to the walls. But a faint *creak* of assent answered my question to the apparently empty air — or at least, I took it as assenting. Nothing leapt out to cut me off, or to hustle me out of the room again. And so I began.

$$13$$

'Dear House,' I said. Only as I spoke those words did it strike me as odd that the house had no other name. Such grand places always have spectacular names of course — think of Chatsworth, or Castle Howard, or Buckingham Palace. Iconic buildings, memorable names. Why was this one so different? Had it ever been named, at all? If not, why not?

I had never heard of its ever being called anything but "House", or "Home", or something along those lines. It had never felt strange to call it such before. But now I was addressing the building directly, and it felt as strange to call it "House" as it would be to address a friend as "Person", or perhaps "Human".

'Dear House,' I said again, trying to sound less doubtful about it. 'I... need your help.'

I paused — to collect my thoughts, and to give House an opportunity to turf me out, if it wanted to. I mean, if it was going to be totally uninterested in rendering me any assistance at all, better to know that right away and save both of us the time.

But nothing happened, so I went on. 'There is a problem with the trolls, you see. They are sick, dying. We're going to lose a few of their Enclaves altogether if we don't figure out why, and who knows where it will end? Perhaps they will all go. Something has to be done, but nobody knows where to *start.*

'We think it might have something to do with Farringale. Baron Alban and I, that is — do you know him? He is the Troll Court's ambassador to the Hidden Ministry, and he knows things about the Old Court, even if he won't confide in me. We want to go to

Farringale, so we can try to find out what destroyed it. If it's the same thing that's wiping out Glenfinnan and Darrowdale and Baile Monaidh, well, maybe we will be able to do something about it. *Before* any more are lost.'

I took a deep breath, encouraged by the continued lack of dire consequences to my narration. 'You've probably guessed why I'm here by now. Alban has two of the keys, but we cannot go without the third. I... may as well own that Milady forbids the venture entirely. I don't really blame her, either. If Farringale was half as vast and splendid as the legends say, then whatever destroyed it was probably not something we want to poke with a stick. But I think we have to try.

'Val thought you might help me, and... I am hoping she is right. Do you have the third key? Will you lend it to me? I promise to bring it back.' An unpleasant thought entered my head and I felt obliged to add, in a lower tone, 'Assuming I get out of Farringale alive.'

Silence. Seconds passed, then minutes, and I heard no sound but the gentle ticking of the grandfather clock; saw nothing move, save the clock's swaying pendulum.

Was that a refusal? Was the House even listening to me? I didn't know, couldn't tell. All I could do was wait, which I did with increasing impatience and dismay as minute after minute passed and the chocolate went cold in the pot.

Five minutes. Seven. Ten.

Fifteen.

How was I going to explain to Baron Alban that I had failed? He had asked me specifically, with a flattering confidence in my ability to deliver. I did not want to disappoint him. And if we could not get into Farringale, how else were we to save the Enclaves? What else could we do?

Twenty minutes, and no sign of a response. Either House had not heard me at all, or it had chosen to side with Milady. 'Very well, then,' I said. 'Thank you for listening to me. And for letting me see your favourite room.' I took a last look around, for the chances were that I would never see it again.

The clock ticked on.

I hauled myself out of the chair — really, they were surprisingly comfortable, for all their formal magnificence — and shook out my hair.

Something fell from my lap with a *clink*.

Ohgod. Was it my cup? Had I left that dainty and probably priceless antique upon my knee? But no; there had been no shatter, no *crash* of porcelain breaking into pieces.

A key lay upon the floor, not three inches from my left foot. It was a large, handsome, silver-wrought thing, intricately engraved, and it bore a blue jewel that glittered with its own light.

'Oh.' I bent to pick it up, carefully, as though it might be fragile. But it was heavy in my grasp, sturdy, and faintly warm to the touch. That jewel shone when my fingers touched it, mesmerising.

'Thank you,' I whispered. This was no small thing. House was trusting my judgement over Milady's — mine and Alban's. 'We won't fail,' I said, so rashly, for I had no idea what we might find in Farringale; how could I be sure that we would not?

My show of confidence pleased the House, though, for a ripple of warm air shivered over my skin like a balmy summer breeze, and the key glimmered on in my hand.

'Onward, then,' said I, and left the parlour. When I stepped over the threshold of the door, I found myself back in the first floor common room.

And there was Jay, lounging in an arm chair not three feet away and looking at me like I had just grown a second head. 'Where did you spring from?'

I glanced about, confused. 'I came in through a door... oh.' The door was on the other side of the room, and I was nowhere near a window.

'You walked out of a wall,' said Jay.

'Doesn't seem unlikely.' Happily, nobody else was around to witness my involuntary feat of defiance of all known laws of nature, if not Magick; the common room was empty besides him. I wandered over to my favourite chair — the wing-back one with the red upholstery — and flopped down into it with a spectacular lack of grace. I was feeling a bit weak at the knees, which was probably a sign of incipient panic. What did I think I was doing, proposing to waltz into Farringale? A place nobody had set foot inside in centuries, which had collapsed due to reasons unknown but undoubtedly dire? I was mad. Baron Alban was mad.

And the next thing I had to do was convince Jay to get us there, the same Jay who was scowling at me with that fierce frown of his.

'Are you okay?' he said abruptly.

'What?'

'Are you all right? You look a little pale.'

'I am always a little pale.'

He rolled his eyes. 'Paler than usual. You look like a bowl of yoghurt.'

'I'm fine.' The question discomfited me, because it was unexpected. From his face, I'd assumed he was displeased with me for some reason. Instead, he had shown concern.

It did make it harder to proceed to knowingly pissing him off.

Oh well. Delaying unpleasant duties never made them any easier to perform. 'Jay, I need your help with something.'

He sat up a bit, and focused a more alert gaze upon me. 'That is why I am here.'

'It isn't exactly why you— oh, never mind. I need to go somewhere quickly, together with... someone else.'

'Someone who else?'

'Baron Alban.'

He nodded, unconcerned. So far, so good. 'Where are we going?'

'I don't... know, exactly, but Alban does.'

The frown reappeared. 'We are following the intriguing baron into parts wholly unknown? Are we trusting him enough for that? He's a total stranger.'

'It isn't... *entirely* unknown. I know where we are aiming for, I just don't know where it *is*.'

'Enough mystery, Ves. What's going on?'

So much for breaking it to him gently. 'We are going to Farringale.'

'Farri— the Troll Court? The lost one? Seriously?'

'That's the plan.'

He stared at me.

I stared back.

If I had harboured any hopes that he might assume Milady had given the order, those hopes were swiftly dashed. 'Why,' said he with detestable and inconvenient astuteness, 'is it you asking me about this? Why aren't we up in the tower hearing all about it from Milady, together?'

'Because she said no.' Screw trying to be subtle, if he was going to be so bloody clever.

'Then we aren't going.' Jay said this with aggravating serenity, picked up the book he'd been reading when I came in, and to all appearances forgot my existence altogether.

'We are. Look.' I fished the key out of the pocket I'd hastily stuffed it into, and held it up. The blue jewel blazed, which made for quite the impressive effect.

Jay didn't even look up.

'*Jay.* Look at this thing!'

He raised his head, and subjected the glittering key to a dull, uninterested stare. 'What of it?'

'It's the key to Farringale. The third key, of three. House gave it to me.'

'The House gave it to you?'

'Yes.'

'This House?'

'*Yes.*'

And I'd got him, I could see that. He still did not like the idea, but he was listening to me. 'Why would House give you that key if Milady said no?'

'Apparently it isn't up to Milady to decide about the key.'

Jay put away the book. 'All right. Why did Milady say no, if House is in favour?'

'She thinks it's too dangerous to open Farringale.'

'She could well be right.'

'She might be, but so what? How else are we going to help the Enclaves? Do you have a better idea?'

'There are probably hundreds of other ways we could find out what's going on with those Enclaves.'

'Probably. Name one.'

He opened his mouth, hesitated. 'The... the library probably has some relevant materials somewhere, or some other library.'

'That could take forever to dig up.'

'There are teams at Darrowdale and South Moors right now, looking for a source of the trouble—'

'Which they apparently aren't finding in a hurry, as we've heard nothing. And this is urgent, Jay.'

'I am not sure why you expect to walk into Farringale and have the answer handed to you on a plate.'

'I don't, but we *might*. How do you know?'

'You could die. *We* could die.'

'Maybe. Maybe not. Meanwhile, a lot of trolls *are* dying.'

Jay began to look a little desperate. 'Ves... you might be able to openly disobey Milady, but I can't. You've a ten-year history with the Society, a blazing track record. However angry Milady might be with you, the chances of her chucking you out are practically zero.

But me? I've only just got here!'

'You're a Waymaster, the only one we've managed to get hold of in about a decade. She won't discard you lightly.'

'It would be neither wise nor classy to presume upon that.'

'House is in favour!'

'Which is useful to know, but House doesn't pay my salary, and House isn't going to be writing me a reference if I have to go looking for a new job.'

'You're a Waymaster, you don't need a reference. You could walk into a new job this afternoon.'

'It's about professional standards, pride—'

'Jay, the important thing here is to get the job done. And the job is to preserve. The Enclaves are folding around us and nobody knows how to stop it. This is the best way I can think of to find out why — the best, the most direct, hopefully the fastest. Can you think of a better one? Really?'

Jay sighed, long and deeply, and shook his head. 'Nope.'

'Right.'

'Right. So.' He scowled at me and chucked his book at my head. 'Damn you and your rule-breaking ways. You'll make a disgrace of me.'

'Or a hero.'

'Or a hero.' He stood up, stretched, shook himself, as if to shake away his doubts. 'Since this is all kinds of urgent, I imagine you want to get going. Where's Alban?'

'I'll find out.' I took out my phone and called the baron's number. His reply was immediate.

'Ves? Did you get the key?'

'Yes.'

'Is Jay with us?'

'Yes.'

'Then we go. Meet me in the conservatory in five minutes.'

'Ten,' I countered. 'We need to grab a few things first.'

'Ten it is.'

14

The things I had in mind were not supplies, as the baron probably imagined. I still had my stash of toys from the Darrowdale expedition, and I keep a basic travel kit ready at all times because I am often sent off somewhere at a moment's notice.

No, the "things" I planned to grab in passing consisted of just the one, really. A tall, reassuringly bulky, Rob-Foster-shaped thing, to be precise.

I like Rob so much. He is so calm, and so obliging. I found him in the infirmary tending to a forlorn-looking soul with her arm in a cast. Broken bones aren't too uncommon around here, at least among those following certain fields of specialisation (mine included).

'Much as I hate to disturb you,' I said to Rob as I swept in, resembling, most likely, a small, vibrantly-coloured whirlwind, 'I have an urgent matter on hand.'

Rob acknowledged my appearance but did not answer me until he had finished whatever he was doing for the girl — I call her such because she *was* very young, perhaps fifteen or so. She seemed a bit too young for a Society recruit, but perhaps she was here on some kind of internship or work experience thing. We sometimes get them.

Anyway, Rob dismissed her, all calm reassurance and comforting professionalism, and the girl — Indian, at a guess, and very smartly dressed — went away looking less forlorn.

'All right, Ves,' said Rob, taking off his doctor's coat. 'What may I do for you?'

'Jay and I are going to Farringale,' I told him.

'Ah.'

Unflappable, Rob. 'Nobody's been there in centuries,' I added.

'Indeed.'

'Since we have no idea what we might find there, and whether or not it will prove to be friendly, I'd like to take you along with us.'

Rob looked curiously at me. 'What do you need me for?'

'I'd like your help with not dying.'

He smiled faint amusement. 'Playing the damsel? You could probably hold your own against pretty much anything, and Jay's no slouch either.'

He wasn't wrong — about me, at least; I had no real idea what Jay's abilities might be. Anybody taking up my line of work with the Society is obliged to take a rigorous series of courses in what Milady, by way of adorable euphemism, terms "the Direct Arts". And while I am no prodigy by any means, I can be plenty *direct* when I need to be. I'm still breathing, aren't I? And believe me, Milady has thrown me at all manner of risky adventures down the years.

However.

'It's the "probably" part that bothers me,' I answered. 'And I'll have Jay with me. He is something of a protege and I do not want to have to admit to Milady that I got him sliced up and made into mincemeat.' Particularly when the mission was unauthorised in the first place.

'I'm surprised Milady didn't think of sending me along,' said Rob, brows slightly raised in mild enquiry.

People are too sharp around here by half. 'She doesn't know we're going,' I told him. I mean, why bother lying? 'Actually, she outright forbade it. But House disagrees, so we're going anyway.'

Rob absorbed this in stoic silence, his gaze on me thoughtful. 'All right,' he said, to my relief. 'You can explain the rest on the way.'

I gave him my best, absolutely my sunniest smile, and my most exquisite curtsey too. 'You are a gentleman above any other, Mr. Foster.'

'I know.'

· · · ● · ● · · ·

It was only once we arrived at the conservatory that I realised I'd forgotten to mention

Baron Alban to Rob. And I had, of course, neglected to mention Rob to Baron Alban. Oops.

The two gentleman took the surprise well, however, electing only to eye one another up in a manner assessing and wary but in no way hostile.

'Our party's expanding,' noted the baron.

'I like breathing,' I told him. 'And Rob's the best we have at keeping all those kinds of procedures going. In numerous ways.'

Alban accepted this with a nod. Rob asked no questions at all, so I left the problem of explaining the Baron's presence for later.

'The key?' prompted Alban.

I fished it out of my pocket and held it up. Rob stared at it with more interest than he had yet shown in anything, that I could remember, but he made no move either to touch it or to ask me about it.

Baron Alban, however, did both.

'No,' I said, snatching it out of his reach. 'I will hang onto this one.'

Alban's eyes narrowed. 'I have the other two.'

'Which you are welcome to keep. House gave this one into my care, however, and I promised to give it back.'

'And so you shall, once we return.'

I shook my head, and tucked the key away again safely out of sight. 'I live here, and I'd like to continue to do so for a while yet. Would you like to break a promise to a castle, voluntarily or otherwise?'

The twinkle returned to the baron's eyes, and he made no further effort to persuade me. 'Where did you find it?'

'That's a secret.'

He rolled his eyes. 'You people eat, sleep and breathe secrets.'

'Pot, meet kettle.'

'Fair.'

Jay arrived just then, looking a little out of breath. I wondered what he had been doing with himself for the last quarter-hour. 'The Waypoint's ready,' he said. He looked at the baron. 'Where are we heading for?'

'I'll tell you when we get to the Waypoint.'

Jay shrugged and turned away. 'Let's go, then.'

A few minutes later we were back in that cold cellar room. It was even colder than last time, and I shivered. Did I imagine the faint, chill breeze coiling sluggishly over the stone floor?

Jay shepherded the three of us into the centre of the floor, right where the winds of travel had manifested last time. Then he looked questioningly at the baron.

'Winchester,' said Alban. 'Or thereabouts.'

Winchester? As far as I had ever heard, scholars were agreed upon just one point regarding Farringale: it lay somewhere in the far north, either in England or in Scotland.

Winchester is in Hampshire. In fact, it is almost as far south as you can go before you hit saltwater. How could so many fine minds be so spectacularly wrong, and about so basic a fact?

Pot, meet kettle. Indeed. 'Misdirection?' I said to Baron Alban, failing to conceal my sourness.

He grinned at me. 'Best way to keep a secret I know.'

'You all have been mighty determined to keep this one.'

He shrugged. 'Not my call, but I'm sure their Majesties have their reasons.'

'They aren't going to be pleased with you.'

'About as pleased as Milady's going to be with you, I imagine.'

There was time for no more words, for the breeze became a strong wind and then a howling gale, and then *away* we were once again.

Winchester made some sense, I thought, and it was a thought I clung to as I was whirled about, doll-like, in the winds of Jay's magick on the way to Hampshire. After all, while ancient England cannot be said to have had a fixed capital in the modern way, Winchester was its principal city before London supplanted it. It did not surprise me greatly that the Troll Court should choose to anchor itself in the same environs as the monarchs of England, though that did not answer the question of why either party had chosen Winchester in the first place. What was it about the city? It was one of the very oldest settlements in England, true, but the same could be said for many another place.

Such reflections carried me through the worst of the journey, until I was at last set down — surprisingly gently — atop a wide, green hill in some pleasingly sun-dappled countryside. Vibrant meadowland stretched before me, dotted with yellow-flowering bushes and low, dark green shrubs. A brisk wind blew up on the heights there, which would have pleased me more if I had not just been subjected to rather an excess thereof.

I cast a quick glance at Baron Alban, who looked unaffected. Interesting. Did they have a Waymaster at the Troll Court? Most likely. He had the serene air of a man well used to travelling by high winds.

Rob, I knew, was considerably less accustomed to it, but he stood admiring the scenery with his customary stoicism, so I felt no concern for him.

Jay was another matter. I swiftly concluded that it must be much harder to convey four people to the other end of the country than it was to convey two, for he had collapsed into a boneless heap upon the grass and was performing a creditable impression of a dead person.

When a couple of minutes went by and Jay did not get up, Rob knelt beside him and subjected him to a cursory examination. 'You all right, lad?' he said quietly.

'Be fine,' Jay mumbled.

Rob did not argue with this announcement, but took a charm bead out of a pocket somewhere and put it between Jay's lips. They tend to be colour-coded; this one was yellow, and as far as I could remember that meant it was a restorative.

A most effective one, for Jay was soon sitting up and then back on his feet, shaking himself like a dog and breathing great gulps of air. 'Ouch,' he croaked after a while.

Rob clapped him on the shoulder. 'How long have you been using the Ways?'

'About five minutes, as these things go.'

'You did well.'

Jay said nothing in reply, but he accepted the praise with an air of quiet gratitude of which I took careful note. It hadn't occurred to me that he might lack confidence, or that a simple compliment would go such a long way.

'To Winchester, then?' said Jay, looking at Baron Alban.

'Actually, to Alresford.'

That won him a blank look. 'Where?'

'It is a tiny old town a ways north-east of Winchester.'

Jay tapped away at his phone for a minute. 'Ten miles away,' he said lightly. 'Or a bit more. No problem, we'll be there by nightfall.'

'We should have brought some chairs,' said Rob.

Jay had the look of a man just barely resisting the temptation to roll his eyes. I didn't blame him. Four chairs, large enough to fly in without falling overboard, would not be easily portable. He set off down the hill, moving at a brisk march. 'Better get going,' he called back.

'Wait, I have a better idea.' It was me who spoke, and by way of response I received from all three gentlemen an identical quizzical look. 'I have, um, a small secret,' I ventured.

'*Really.*' Jay's voice dripped sarcasm.

Baron Alban merely raised a brow at me that said: *Is that supposed to be a surprise?*

I did not try to explain, which might have been a mistake, since my next move was to stick my hand down the front of my dress and start rooting about in there.

'Um, Ves...?' said Jay.

'Hang on.' Almost... ah, there they were. I withdrew my hand, bringing forth a set of tiny silver pipes.

Jay's confusion only grew. 'Panpipes?'

'Syrinx pipes,' I corrected. The baron knew what they were, for his grin flashed bright and he chuckled.

I blew a trilling melody upon my beautiful pipes and in response, a breeze swirled through my hair. Not a frantic, grabbing breeze like the Winds of the Ways, but a gentle wind, warm and serene and scented with flowers.

I shoved the pipes away again and faced the horizon. 'Any moment now.'

'Should I ask why you keep charmed syrinx pipes in your undergarments?' Jay said, apparently more intrigued by that question than whatever might come of my music.

'They're safe in there,' I murmured, not paying him much attention.

If he made any response, I missed it, for there in the sky was a pinprick of colour, growing rapidly larger and more distinct. Three others formed around it. They flew fast, feathered pinions spread wide to ride the winds, and soon they were swooping in to land upon the hilltop nearby.

'*Unicorns?*' said Jay, incredulous. 'You just whistled a quartet of winged unicorns out of your bra?'

'Never underestimate the benefits of a good bra,' I told him with dignity. 'As many a lingerie company will tell you.'

Jay, for once, had nothing to say.

15

Alban took the stallion, of course, it being the only beast large enough to bear the baron's rather bulky frame. Twenty hands high if he was an inch, the stallion rippled with muscle, his hide almost as gleamingly bronze as the baron's hair. They made a handsome pair.

My own unicorn was white, though her coat and horn glinted silvery in the right light. She and I made friends years ago, and we've been on several adventures together. The second time we met I gave her a name: Adeline. 'Addie,' I greeted her warmly, as she nosed and lipped at my cardigan. I gave her a kiss, and a ball of sugar. She dipped a bit to permit me to spring up onto her back; I took hold of the silver rope she wears which more or less keeps me from falling off, and we were ready to go.

Rob, too, was mounted up, sitting competently astride a night-black unicorn I felt a bit envious of. What a majestic creature she was! Her tapering horn was indigo traced with silver, her mane black glittering with stars. I had never seen her before; a new friend of Addie's, obviously.

Jay, though, was in trouble. There was but one unicorn left for him to choose: a little mare of pale golden hide and rippling white tresses. She seemed friendly enough, but somehow they were not getting along. Jay stood several feet away from her, hands on hips, eyeing her with no friendly spirit, and the mare was dancing nervously from hoof to hoof.

'Up, Jay!' I called. 'No time to waste!'

'It may come as a surprise to you to learn that I have never ridden a unicorn.'

'No problem. It's much like riding a horse, only more... airborne.'

'What makes you think I'm capable of riding a horse?'

That *did* surprise me a little. Who didn't know how to ride a horse? But I suppose the arts of chair-riding, and related charmery, are more likely to appear on the university's curriculums these days. Winged horses and unicorns, like so many other magickal beasts, are becoming scarce.

'What do you think, Addie?' I whispered to her, patting her silky neck. 'Do you think you could carry two of us? We're both skinny and on the short side, nothing too burdensome.' That wasn't an altogether fair way of describing Jay when he was almost six feet tall. Compared to the baron, though, he was a lightweight.

My darling Adeline indicated her approval by trotting over to Jay and halting right beside him. She lowered her graceful form to the ground, and waited patiently for him to notice her.

Which he did, though with almost as much delight as he had greeted the rest. 'What's this?'

I patted Addie's back. 'Join me, and the world will be ours.'

Jay raised his brows.

'I'll keep you from falling off,' I translated. 'Not that Addie would ever drop us.'

Jay was not impressed, but he did not argue. Within a few moments Addie had both of us astride her elegant back, Jay sitting behind me as stiff as a board.

'Try to relax,' I told him. 'You only make it harder for yourself otherwise.'

He tried, with some success, but that was before Adeline rose to her feet again and began to walk. Jay clutched me so hard that it hurt, but I let it pass; he'd had a hard day already, and they don't issue unicorns with seatbelts. No wonder he was uneasy.

'Here we go,' I murmured, as Addie began to trot, then to canter. She launched herself into a tearing gallop, her glittering wings spreading wide and beating with long, powerful strokes. Her hooves left the ground and we were away, spiralling up into the sunlit sky.

Jay wrapped his arms around my waist and buried his face in my shoulder. I suppose he didn't want to see the view, which was a shame, because we flew higher and higher; so high, anybody who saw us from the ground would take us for a distant flock of birds. Old Winchester Hill dwindled to nothing beneath us, lost in the expanse of rolling, vibrant green countryside over which we flew.

'Open your eyes!' I called to Jay. 'You have to see this!'

'Gladly,' said Jay. 'As long as you're okay with my vomiting all over your dress.'

'On second thought, maybe stay as you are.'

'That's what I was thinking.'

I was glad of Jay's warmth as we flew, for however glorious the April sunshine, the winds were cold so far above the ground. The journey was not long, for my unicorns were fast beyond belief; those glorious wings gobbled up the miles, green meadows sailing by below us as we flew. Nonetheless, by the time we spiralled down to the ground I was frozen stiff. I did not so much dismount as fall straight off Addie's back, landing on my feet by happy fortune alone.

Jay walked about, waving feeling back into his arms and shaking himself. I expected him to look nauseated or petrified, but if anything he looked exhilarated.

'Not so bad, eh?' I said, smiling at him. 'Air Unicorn, I mean.'

He grinned at that, taking me by surprise again. 'Eight out of ten, would fly again.'

'Eight?'

'One point deducted for sub-optimal temperatures. One point for the screaming terror.'

'Unfair. There was no screaming.'

'In my head, I was screaming the whole time.'

'I salute your courage,' I told him, matching action to words.

He rolled his eyes and turned away from me, which was rather unfair considering I had been serious. But never mind. I certainly wasn't going to admit that my knees were a bit weak, too; I've flown by unicorn a few times, but the combination of height and speed combined with the lack of safety features always takes a toll.

'This is the right place,' said Alban, striding up with his bronze stallion trailing behind him. 'Near enough.' The wind had done terrible things to *my* hair, I had no doubt, but the baron merely looked handsomely windswept. Some people spend a lot of quality time with a hairdryer trying to achieve that effect, and without much success.

We had come down in a field, just within sight of a pretty village — Alresford, presumably. I was not worried about being spotted; Adeline is used to passing herself off as a swan, or a goose, or some other large bird, under the cursory glance of a non-magickal observer. Nonetheless, I judged it best to dismiss her and her little herd as soon as we were certain of no longer needing them.

'Thank you,' I whispered to Addie, kissing her soft nose, and she whickered at me before trotting off.

The closer we got to Farringale, the more Baron Alban's urgency increased. He led us off towards the old town at a storming pace, and I had little time to admire the neat terraced houses with their bright paintwork, the tiny shops, or the delightful old timber-framed mill with its crown of thatch. Sun dappled the broad streets, the air was fresh and bright, and I wished we had gone there with a picnic or something, ready to enjoy the day. But Alban looked as grim as death, which was helpful in recalling my mind to our real purpose. We passed occasional strollers and shoppers as we tore through Alresford, but the baron attracted no real notice whatsoever; no doubt he was adept at concealing his unusually tall frame, unusual features and distinctive skin colour behind a glamour charm.

We stopped at last not far away from the lovely old mill. A sturdy bridge arched over the clear water of the River Alre, a blocky construct built from stone and brick. Clearly ancient, it must date, I guessed, from somewhere in the medieval period — a rare survival from such far-distant days. The bridge dwarfed the narrow waterway running beneath it; its pointed arch rose high enough for us to walk right underneath. We stopped on a little ledge next to the water, and looked expectantly at Alban.

'Key?' he said, looking at me.

I withdrew my beautiful key from my pocket. To my delight, the sapphire blazed when the light hit it; was it the sun that lit its internal fire, or proximity to the gate it was intended to open?

Baron Alban took two more keys out of his own pockets: one shining gold set with a ruby-red stone, the other glinting bronze and cradling a stone of vivid green, like emerald, or peridot. Both keys radiated coloured light, like mine, and I was moved to gratitude that we were, at least for the moment, alone at the bridge.

I thought Alban would know what to do with the keys, but he did not appear to. He stepped back a few paces and stared at the bridge, brow furrowed, clearly perplexed.

I could see why. There were no signs of anything like a keyhole anywhere upon that aged stonework. Not even one, let alone three. How were we supposed to open the gate?

'May I borrow that?' Alban said to me, indicating my key with a nod of his head.

Reluctantly, I handed it over.

'Thanks.' The baron held all three keys in one of his large hands and stepped into the water, heedless of the damage to his polished boots. He walked all the way under the arch, dipping down as the roof sloped lower. Nothing happened, save that he got rather wet. He turned about and made his way back to us, shaking his head.

'I thought merely holding the keys might be enough, but no.' He went back to searching the stonework for a clue, pacing back and forth impatiently.

'There.' Rob pointed a finger over the baron's head, at the smooth stonework just above the bridge's pointed arch.

I saw nothing. 'What? What are we seeing?'

'Wave those keys around a bit again, Baron,' said Rob.

Alban complied, looking like he felt a bit foolish. But as he stretched up his arm and waved the keys back and forth, a faint, answering glitter of colour rippled over the stones.

'Well spotted,' commented the baron.

He was the only one of the four of us tall enough to do anything about this discovery, of course. This was troll country, all right. Alban laid each key in turn against the stones until something else happened: the gold key flashed red and sank into the stone, fitting into a perfectly-shaped depression we had not been able to see before. There it lay, twinkling jauntily red.

The baron had no trouble fitting the second key alongside it: within moments, the bronze key with its green jewel had taken up a neighbouring spot, and the two shone side-by-side like early Christmas lights.

Only one key, my key, was left, and its home was soon revealed by way of a sheen of blue lighting up the grey stone. But Alban hesitated.

'Are we ready for this?' he asked of us, looking over his shoulder and down at his audience of three.

'Yes,' said Rob. He looked prepared, his posture confident, his manner composed. But so he always did. I have never seen Rob at a loss, or afraid.

'I am,' said Jay, though he looked and sounded less certain than Rob.

'Onward,' I said, and tried to sound staunch and imperturbable. Was I ready? How could you be prepared for something you could not predict?

This was no time for doubts, for the baron nodded his acknowledgement of our enthusiasm and reached up to place the third key.

Rather a lot happened.

First, the light. If the keys had shone brightly before, now they fairly blazed, and a rainbow raced, swift and glittering, over the arch of the bridge.

The bridge shuddered under some force we could neither see nor feel, shedding earth and stone dust into the water. I winced, suddenly anxious, for the bridge was irreplaceable; what if the passage of centuries had weakened it? What if it was no longer capable of bearing the pressure of the Farringale enchantments, and collapsed? Milady would never forgive us. I would never forgive myself.

But it held. The shaking stopped, the rainbow of light faded, and all became still once more.

With one change. A serene white light shone from underneath the bridge, marking the outline of an arched portal. A breeze gusted forth from within, bringing with it the musty scent of lost ages.

The way into Farringale was open.

16

As one, the three gentlemen around me tensed, and stared into that pale light with wary intensity.

I didn't. I did not really believe that anything horrible was going to come barrelling out of Farringale the moment the door was opened, nor did it. Nothing happened at all, actually, save that the breeze died down, leaving the air still and fresh once more.

I settled my bag more comfortably across my shoulders, briefly wishing that I had not filled it quite so enthusiastically. 'Onward, then,' I suggested, and went through the gate, water swishing soothingly about my ankles.

The gentlemen let me go first, and alone, which was not very gentlemanly of them at all. But Rob quickly caught up with me, fine fellow that he is, and we advanced together. For a few moments we were walking near-blindly into that cool light and could see nothing that awaited us, which was a *little* alarming, I will admit. But nothing leapt out at us; no unpromising sounds of rapid, unfriendly approach assailed our ears; all we heard was our own footsteps ringing, curiously melodically, upon a hard floor.

The light gradually ebbed. We passed through it, finding beyond an enveloping musty aroma, air thick with dust which caught in my throat; a noticeable drop in temperature, not at all welcome after the warm spring sunshine we had just left; and the silent remains of a dead street.

It was curiously narrow, that road, considering where we were. I had expected more from Farringale than a thin, crooked street lined on either side by high stone walls. Those walls were *golden* somewhere under the caking dust, which was more promising. But still, as entrances went, it did not seem fitting for so legendary a place.

Then we turned a corner, and *there* was the grandeur. The portal we had used was some kind of side entrance, I guessed, for we turned off it onto a wide, sweeping boulevard all paved in golden stone. Ornate lampposts lined the roadsides, each bearing an orb of crackling white light suspended by no obvious means. That those lights still operated appeared at odds with the deathly silence of the city; their eerie, lonely glow illuminated streets abandoned for hundreds of years. Why did they still burn?

Houses of golden stone or white brick were spaced out along the road, set some way back from the street. Each had a wide square of empty space before it, once host to gardens, perhaps, but now as dead and empty as everything else. Pools of still water had collected in some of them and gone green and stagnant; they gave off an unpleasant smell.

Above the hushed remains of lost Farringale rose sky upon sky upon sky. I have never seen sky like that, before or since. It was the deep, rich blue of twilight, though not because evening approached; the sun was high, the city well-lit. Airy palaces of roiling clouds hung heavy above us, as golden as the stone beneath our feet. It was a display of staggering beauty, which ordinarily would have pleased me greatly, but something about that vast sky made me uneasy. I walked a little nearer to Rob.

The boulevard veered gracefully to the left in a smooth curve, and we followed it. Jay and Alban had caught up with us by then, and we walked four abreast, our eyes everywhere. I began to realise something else strange, which did nothing to enhance my comfort: the city was too clean. The passage of more than three hundred years ought to have taken more of a toll, surely; Farringale should have resembled Glenfinnan in its decay, only being more advanced. But the streets were pristine; not even a single leaf presumed to drift over the smooth paving stones. The houses looked aged, but they were whole and sound, not crumbling as I would have expected. I could have moved into one of them and lived happily there, untroubled by leaking roofs or collapsing walls. There was no mess, no disorder. Only the dust, thick and clinging and smelling of dirt and age.

Was somebody keeping the city tidy? But that did not make any sense. We had seen no sign of life whatsoever, and moreover, the city *felt* empty. There was a depth to the silence, a profound hush, that precluded the possibility that Farringale was home to a company of fastidious street-sweepers. Something kept the city preserved — the same enchantments, perhaps, that kept the lights burning in the street lamps.

What any of that had to do with the strange sky was anybody's guess.

'Has it always been like that?' I asked of Alban, gesturing at the sky.

'I've never heard anything of the kind.' He gazed long upon those vast golden clouds, and I saw that his eyes were very wide.

'Interesting.' I was feeling deeply unsettled, this I will admit. But I smothered the feeling and walked on, for I was as intrigued and excited as I was afraid. *Farringale!* My scholar's heart danced with joy at the prospect of so many mysteries, all laid out here for my perusal.

Jay drew nearer to me. 'I have a question,' he said in an undertone.

'Yes.'

I expected a question about Farringale, naturally, or some related topic. Instead he said: 'Where did you get those pipes?'

'That is a secret.'

'Why?'

'Because it pleases me to remain a woman of mystery.'

That won me an unfriendly stare. 'How does that help you?'

'Because I cannot otherwise get you to take me seriously. Something to do with my colourful dresses and mad hair, wasn't it? How else am I going to hold my own with you?'

'Okay, okay. I'm sorry I suggested anything of the kind. Please tell me about the pipes.'

'Why do you want to know?'

'Are you kidding? You whistled up a quartet of *unicorns*. Of course I want to know.'

Fair point. 'I can't tell you,' I said, and cut off his objections with a wave of my hand. 'I really can't. I am not allowed.'

'According to who?'

'The Powers That Be.'

'Aren't you the rule-breaker extraordinaire?'

'When I have good reason. This isn't one.'

Jay gave a long, sad sigh. 'I have another question.'

'Yes.'

'Why do you keep them in your, uh, undergarments?'

'Imagine you suspect me of harbouring some magickal object of deep and ancient power, and you want to take it from me. Where are you going to look?'

'Bag,' said Jay promptly. 'Pockets, maybe.'

'Bra?'

'Never.'

'Right.'

'Very clever.'

'Thank you. I know that—' I stopped talking, distracted by a flicker of colour glimpsed out of the corner of my eye. I turned to look, but saw nothing that could explain the soft flash of light, the blur of colours I'd thought I had seen. Just the same empty street, and a deserted, white-tiled plaza branching off it. Nothing moved.

'What is it?' asked Jay, who'd stopped a few paces farther up the road.

I shook my head, and caught up with him. 'Nothing.'

We arrived at a wide intersection, and there we stopped, for nobody knew which of the three other streets that opened before us would take us where we needed to go. For that matter, nobody knew what we were aiming for. Our plan had not been a sophisticated one; it consisted of "Find Farringale and search it for clues." So far, so good, but since answers had yet to leap out of the air to oblige us, what did we do next?

I looked long and hard down each street, noting that all three hosted buildings of promising-looking grandeur. 'I wonder if any of those is the library?' I mused aloud.

Alban had a piece of paper in his hand, to which he kept referring after every searching glance at the streets around us. I sidled closer.

It was a map, roughly hand-drawn in biro on basic, white A4 paper. But if I was disposed to dismiss its significance on account of its humble appearance, I was soon moved to reconsider, for Baron Alban's thumb was positioned over the outline of an intersection just like the one we were standing on. One of its four converging streets outlined a smooth curve, from the other end of which branched a tiny side-street. Where this terminated, a blocky doorway was crudely drawn in. All of this looked... decidedly familiar.

'My dear baron,' I said. 'Wherever did you get a map of Farringale?'

The look he shot at me could only be termed shifty. 'The library is here,' he said, and I could *see* him dodging my question but how could I care, when instead of an explanation he offered me a library? He was pointing one elegant finger at a hastily-drawn square on his map, which I was encouraged to note was not far away. Unfortunately, he did not excel at drawing. The library seemed to be positioned about equidistantly between two streets; which one actually hosted the door?

'There are four of us,' I observed. 'Two to take the left fork, two to go straight ahead.'

'Haven't you ever played games?' Jay said. 'Never split the party.'

I looked around at the silent, empty city. 'We don't seem to be in any danger. Where's the harm?'

'Not *yet*,' said Jay. 'But something emptied this place, and if it is the same *something* that destroyed Glenfinnan and is presently decimating Darrowdale, I'd rather take a little care.'

'I have to agree,' murmured Alban.

I looked at Rob. I had invited him to be our Captain of Health and Safety, after all. On this point, his opinion mattered to me the most.

'No need to rush, I think,' he said.

Or in other words, no splitting the party. 'Random pick, then,' I said with a shrug. 'We can double back if we get it wrong.'

We went left. The street narrowed there, and I was intrigued to notice a distinct change in its architectural character. The houses were smaller, and very differently built: most of them were timber-framed, with great, dark beams and white-washed walls. Some few farther along were made from brick, the deep-red, uneven kind: hand-crafted, and crumbling a little with age. They were human-sized and human-built, if I did not miss my guess, and dating from the sixteenth century. I'd seen many such buildings all over Britain.

'They must have had a human population here, once,' I said. 'Look at this house! Tudor, has to be. Handsome, but not too grand: merchants? There was once a lot of trading back-and-forth between the Troll Enclaves and our own towns.'

I don't think my fascination was fully shared by my companions. A medical treatise from the fifteen hundreds might have interested Rob, but a building? He cast it a polite glance, clearly did not see what had got *me* so excited, and found no comment to offer. Alban was focused on his map, and did not even look.

Jay, though... 'It's a shame all of that's gone,' he said, gazing at the merchant's house with an air of faint wistfulness. 'Can you imagine trying to get that kind of free trade and travel going nowadays?'

I could not. Magick used to be commonplace; it was widely used among humankind, and universally accepted even among those with no ability. That is no longer the case. It's dwindling in humans, so much so that it now qualifies as a decided rarity. To those with no magickal talent, it simply does not exist. Our magickal communities have shrunk to mere pockets of activity, carefully hidden from the rest of the world. We survive, and we try to carry as much of that heritage forward as we can. But it isn't easy, and for folk such as the trolls, it's much harder to pass unnoticed.

Rob stopped, so suddenly that I almost collided with him. He stood tense, alert, his head lifted, scanning the sky.

'What is it?' I said.

He made no reply for a while, and finally shook his head. 'Nothing, I think.'

But then I heard it, too: a *swoosh* of air from somewhere overhead, like the slow flapping of vast wings.

'Hear that?' said Rob, in a whisper.

'Yes,' I replied. 'But I see nothing...'

'That cloud,' said Jay. 'It's... is that lightning?'

He was facing the other way, arm lifted to point. I spun around, stared hard at the hazy mass of clouds he indicated. Naught but serenity met my eyes, all golden peacefulness like a lazy summer afternoon...

...and then a ripple of searing golden light, there and gone so quickly I almost doubted the evidence of my eyes.

Wingbeats again, so close I almost felt the brush of feathers against my hair...

Rob backed up. 'We might want to get out of the open air,' he suggested.

'You don't think—' began Jay.

'He's right,' interrupted Alban. He was already making for the nearest building: that same Tudor townhouse I had been admiring only a moment before. He talked on as he walked. 'There's an old myth about Farringale Dell. There was once a mountain somewhere in there, so tall that its peak touched the clouds. And nesting thereupon were the kinds of creatures we do *not* want to tangle with, so, Ves? Jay? This way, and quickly.'

'What kinds of creatures?' said Jay, though he did not argue with the baron: he made for the mansion at a jog.

'Big, winged ones,' muttered Rob, who was retreating backwards, his gaze still locked on the sky.

As was mine, for erupting out of the clouds was a mass of big, winged creatures, all wreathed in crackling golden lightning. *Big* creatures. They were tawny in colour or white, their gigantic wings luxuriously feathered. They had the bodies of lions and long, sinuous tails...

'Griffins,' I breathed, torn between awe and fear. Because if we want to talk about rare magickal beasts, it doesn't get much rarer or more magickal than the griffin. We've thought them extinct for years.

I had time only to register that my frozen-in-wonder awe was sadly misguided, for the nearest of the flock was bearing down upon me with alarming speed, and growing larger by the second... good heavens, *how* big were they?

'*Ves,*' shouted Rob. 'These creatures are *not* friendly!'

He was right, for that marvellous bird's beak opened wide and it shrieked at me, unmistakeably a challenge. An *angry* challenge. Its cloak of lightning crackled and blazed with heat, filling the air with the scent of ozone.

'Shit,' I observed, and threw myself to the ground. Wicked talons missed me by a hair; lightning flashed, searing my eyes, and my dress began to burn.

The griffin banked, turned, shrieked its fury anew. Then, with one powerful beat of its sail-like wings, it renewed its attack.

17

M y ears rang with the raucous shrieking of the griffin as it descended upon me, all screaming fury and intent to kill. How beautiful it was in that moment, I thought, as I rummaged frantically inside the neck of my dress. What sleek lines, what elegance, what gleaming, velvety hide—

Then Rob was there. Of course he was; that's what I'd brought him for. He was so heroic as to cover my body with his own, making of himself a shield between me and the griffin. How lovely was that? Unfortunately, he also had a knife in each hand. They were the charmed kind: fearsomely sharp, wrought from something silvery and glinting with the light of enchantment. He would throw them and they would not miss. They would bury themselves in the eyeballs of those fierce, glorious, terrifying creatures and the griffins would die and it would be all my fault.

'*No!*' I screamed, and rolled away from Rob. I had what I needed: my pipes. I scrambled to my feet, shoved Rob aside as the first griffin went swooping past, and raised my precious syrinx pipes to my lips.

The melody I played was markedly different from the tune that had summoned Adeline and her unicorn friends. This one began as a sharp, penetrating sequence of notes, a blast of charmed music intended to interrupt our assailant, to halt it in its tracks. It worked. The griffin stopped abruptly and hovered there, only ten feet from me. What a pity that I could not hold it for long! For I wanted to go up close to it, to study it, to admire it. I could sketch it, take back a detailed record of its surprising existence for the

Society.

But no charm could hold so powerful a creature for long, even with my pipes to amplify the effect. My melody changed: from my silvery flutes poured a slow, languid stream of notes, a drowsy lullaby, a tune to invoke yearning thoughts of nests and safety and warmth and sleep...

The griffin drifted a while, caught in the grip of a waking dream. Then, slowly, it floated away upon somnolent wings, returning to its nest in those glorious golden clouds. Its brethren followed, and soon the skies were clear of griffins once more.

Rob was not pleased with me.

'What did you mean by stopping me?' he demanded. 'It nearly killed you!'

'I couldn't let you destroy it.'

'It nearly killed *me.*'

'I am most assuredly sorry for that, but it did not kill you.' I went to help him up. He took my hand with poor grace and rose with a groan of effort, or perhaps pain.

'I am getting far too old for this,' he muttered, eyeing me with no friendly feelings whatsoever.

Jay and Alban came cautiously out of the mansion again, searching the sky for griffins. 'Are they gone?' said Jay.

'Yes.'

'Was it the pipes? We heard music.'

'It was.' I stashed them in their usual place, a process from which all three gentlemen politely averted their eyes. 'Shall we move on?'

'I *definitely* need to get me a set of those,' muttered Jay.

Rob was not finished with me. 'Ves,' he said firmly. 'If you bring me along to help keep you from *not dying,* then I need you to let me do my job.'

'I will, I promise, and I really am sorry. But I did not expect griffins. Griffins, Rob! They're supposed to be extinct!'

'And *you were almost dead.*'

'Almost! But not! All is well, and nobody had to die. Not me, not you, and not the magickal beasts of legend which we all thought we'd lost centuries ago.'

Rob sighed and said no more, but he trudged on beside me with a weary air that I did not like. He was not as young as he used to be, I supposed, though I had not considered that fact. When I had first joined the Society, Rob had been about the age I was now:

somewhere between thirty and thirty-five. He had been all power and energy and a grim kind of competence that seemed immune to fatigue, or pain, or anything we lesser beings suffered from.

But rather more than ten years had passed. Rob looked almost the same as he had on my very first day at Home: tall, muscled, his sleek dark skin unlined, his curling black hair as thick as ever. But for all his ageless looks, he must be nearing fifty. I shouldn't be hurling him around with such abandon. Not anymore.

'I am sorry, Rob,' I said, with more sincerity.

He side-eyed me, still unmoved. But then he sighed, and gave me a rueful smile. 'You're always an experience, Ves,' he said, which did not quite strike me as a vote of confidence. 'Nobody does things the way you do.'

'It's why I am good at my job,' I said hopefully.

'True. Nobody else would come out of this adventure with the local population of deadly griffins fully intact.'

I beamed.

'Let's just hope we can come out of it with our local population of Society employees fully intact as well.'

Yes. True. 'And our Troll Court representative,' I added.

'Him, too.'

Alban went back to his map. He walked off with the purposeful air of a man who knows exactly where he is going, calling, 'This way! Quickly.'

We followed, and with all due haste. The griffins might be gone for now, but they could certainly come back. Even I could not have said with any certainty how long my charm would hold.

'Do you suppose those griffins are the reason Farringale was abandoned?' said Jay.

'That would make sense,' Rob replied.

I did not want to agree. If Jay's speculation was correct, what did that do to my theory, and Alban's? There were no griffins at Glenfinnan or Baile Monaidh or South Moors, and Darrowdale was underground. If griffins had driven away the residents of Farringale, then its demise had nothing whatsoever to do with the other Enclaves, and we were wasting our time in coming here at all.

Nonetheless, it was impossible to dismiss the theory. Griffins were known to be touchy, territorial creatures, as we had just seen. If a large colony of them had claimed Farringale

Dell as their home, the trolls who lived there might well have concluded that moving on was simpler (and safer) than trying to stand their ground.

Even to the extent of abandoning their Court, though? Would they really? I frowned, unable to make any sense of it. It was all guesswork, whatever we concluded. We needed the library.

'Aha,' said Alban, stopping at that moment before one of the largest buildings we had yet seen. Wrought from snowy stone in great, square blocks, it towered four tall storeys high, and boasted a crowning roof of magnificent proportions. The walls were lit with long, wide windows fitted with tiny diamond-shaped panes of glass. Massive double doors guarded the entrance, set beneath an ornate lintel.

Alban walked up the three wide steps and rapped upon the door.

'I don't think—' I began. I was going to add "that anyone's home", but the doors moved of their own accord and slowly swung open.

Baron Alban gave me a dazzling smile. 'We trolls are known for our hospitality,' he said as he led the way inside. This did not quite fit with my experience of the Enclaves, but I let the comment pass.

Nothing could have exceeded my eagerness to hasten up those steps and into the library. But I was brought up short again by another flicker of colour: something moved in the hallway beyond. Or some*one*.

But when I mounted the steps and stepped through that handsome doorway, I entered a grand white-stone hallway empty of any other living soul save only for Alban. There was nothing there to explain the glimpse of blue I thought I had seen, the flash of gold; just serene white stone and a pair of pale statues.

'Did you see anything odd in here, when you came in?' I asked Alban.

He quirked a quizzical brow at me. 'Like what?'

'I don't know.'

He shrugged, already turning away from me towards one of the great stone arches that led off the hallway. 'Just an empty hall. What else would I expect to see?'

What, indeed? I could not shake the feeling that these glimpses of colour came from no static objects; there was a sense of movement about them, like somebody had just whisked past me. But how could that be? There was no one around but the four of us. That fact was indisputable.

Furthermore, it did not appear that the rest of my companions were suffering from these hallucinations. Neither Jay nor Rob showed any sign of having noticed anything untoward; they were following Alban into the library, leaving me alone in the hall.

Jay, though, noticed my absence and turned back. 'Ves? Everything all right?'

An intriguing oddity it was, and I wanted to pursue it. But where could I begin? I did not know where to look. So I said, 'Yes,' and followed him into the library.

We entered a large chamber with the kind of soaringly high ceiling that can only result in dizziness if you stare at it for too long. Its walls were lined, floor-to-ceiling, with shelf after shelf of books. Books beyond counting, all leather or cloth-bound and looking far too new considering their advanced age. The library had broad, stout, troll-sized ladders via which one could reach those high-up shelves, and a complement of polished wooden research tables, each with its own cushioned chair.

I was in heaven, and clean forgot about the peculiarity of the colours.

All four of us stood just inside the door, staring at that array of ancient knowledge with, I am sure, identical expressions of breathless awe.

'Well,' said Jay at last. 'Next question: how do we find what we need in all of *this*?'

'There are twelve more chambers like this one,' murmured Alban.

'Twelve.'

'Mhm.'

There followed an appalled silence.

'Best get started, then.' That was Rob, of course, unflappable as always.

'*Where?*' spluttered Jay.

'Alban,' said Rob. 'Your map. Is there any indication as to where history books are shelved?'

The baron slowly shook his head. 'I could not find anything so detailed. I hoped that something would guide us, once we got here—'

'Hanging aisle signs, like at the supermarket,' put in Jay, with what I considered to be pardonable sarcasm under the circumstances.

'Something like that,' Alban said, unruffled.

I heard something, then. Not the calm, deep tones of Rob's voice as he made some reply, nor the sound of Jay's boots thudding across the aged wood floor as he wandered off in search of who-knew-what. It was a sound out of keeping with any probable noise the gentlemen might have made: a whisper, a *rustle,* as of stiff silken curtains being drawn back.

Turning away from that glorious array of books, I followed the sound as it came again, and again. Back through the majestic archway and into the hall, across the echoing stone; veering left and through another arch—

I did not make it that far, for someone caught up with me. Someone I could not see, but whose footsteps I clearly heard: the rhythmic *swish, swish* as of silken slippers brushing lightly over those cool stone floors, but how could that be? I was alone in there, or if not precisely alone, none of my colleagues were wearing *silk*—

My thoughts tumbled apart as the world tipped sideways and revolved, dizzily, around me. When it settled and my watering eyes could once again distinguish details beyond an indistinct blur, I found I was... still in that same hall. Despite the sensation of disorienting movement I had experienced, I had not moved at all.

But my surroundings were not unchanged. For one thing, the hall was darker than it had been before, with an odd, flickering quality to the light that soon began to play merry hell with my eyesight. There came odd shifts in the atmosphere with each wavering of the light; shadows leapt across the room, rays of light darted from one archway to another. It was, to say the least, unsettling.

For another thing, I was... no longer alone.

'Art trespassing,' said the author of my woes. 'What will you with Farringale?'

18

The lady was a troll, no mistaking that. She had features of aristocratic character, finely sculpted like marble, though the fine wrinkles that mapped her face spoke of advanced age. Her hair was all white wisps, a mass of snowy locks artfully curled and beribboned. She wore a gown of crisp blue silk, with lace about the wide-cut neckline and wide, full sleeves. The skirt was very full, and at once I understood the source of those rustling sounds. Not curtains, but a *dress*. She had walked right up to us, and though we had not seen her, we had heard the motion of her skirts.

At least, I had. What did that mean?

I made her a curtsey, for she was evidently a woman of stature — in the sense of rank, at least, if not height, for she was only a little taller than me. 'Madam,' I said, with scrupulous politeness, for her faded blue eyes were fixed upon me with no friendly expression. 'We trespass, I cannot deny, but it is not our intention to disturb your peace. We come upon an urgent errand.'

No response was made me, but nor did the lady interrupt. She waited, impassive, listening.

So I went on.

'Is this...' I began, and paused, blinking away the uncomfortable effects of another flickering surge of shadows and light. 'Am I gone back in time?'

'Nay,' said the lady. ''Tis beyond the power of magick, that.'

'Then what is this? Where have I gone? For I am not where I was *before*, of that I am certain.'

'You have not moved, I vow, save in time.'

'But you said—'

'You are caught between the echoes, and shall here remain until it please me to release you.'

I do not know if I was expected to make any sense out of these impenetrable words, but my comprehension or lack thereof did not seem to trouble my reluctant hostess. For the moment, I abandoned my line of questioning.

'My name is Cordelia Vesper,' I said — judging it best to offer my full name, for to a woman who, I strongly suspected, had survived somehow since the fall of Farringale, the old-fashioned formality of "Cordelia" would sound better than the terse modernity of "Ves". 'I work for the Society for Magickal Heritage. I came here with two colleagues, as well as Baron Alban, a representative of the current Troll Court. May I know whose acquaintance I have had the unexpected pleasure of making?' I ended this speech with a winning smile, the kind that invariably puts people at their ease.

She scrutinised me in silence, not softening towards me one whit. 'You address Baroness Tremayne.'

I curtsied again, a gesture she deigned to acknowledge with a nod of her head. I wondered, briefly, why she had selected me, out of the four of us, for interrogation. Would she not more naturally have chosen Alban? 'We are here to—'

She spoke abruptly, cutting me off. 'Long ages have passed, since last came the footsteps of another in these lost halls. How came you here? What arts carried you past our thrice-locked doors?'

'Keys,' I said promptly, wishing I had been able to retrieve one of them on our way in. Presumably they were still embedded in the side of Alresford Bridge. 'Baron Alban secured two from the Court, I know not by what means. Mine was the third, given into my keeping by…' I hesitated, suddenly much inconvenienced by the House's lack of an obvious title. 'By the House in which my Society is based,' I said, much disliking the awkwardness and imprecision of this designation.

But its effect upon Baroness Tremayne was curiously profound. 'A House?' she repeated, laying just such emphasis upon the word as to suggest that she knew precisely what kind of House I was referring to. 'Say on.'

So I told her about Home, but I had not proceeded much further than to mention its approximate location and date of construction before she stopped me.

'It is well known to me.' She looked at me afresh: less with suspicion, more with respect. 'Your errand? Quickly.'

I did not need to go into great detail about that, either. I had scarcely got into the malaise at South Moors before she began to nod with evident comprehension, her gaze sharpening — and turning alarmed. *She knows,* I thought, with infinite relief. She recognised the problem, knew what it was. She would know how to help.

Baroness Tremayne listened in silent sorrow through my account of deserted Glenfinnan, and the moment I had finished outlining the turmoil at Baile Monaidh and Darrowdale, she came alive — all action and urgency where before she had been all silent stillness. 'Something of a hurry, I find it,' she said, and with a rustle of skirts she turned, and marched away across the hall. I trotted after, followed her into another grand library chamber much like the first, only larger. Jay had already discovered it, I quickly saw, for he was on the other side of the room, intent upon the shelves. He was difficult to see clearly, however, for like the shadows and the light, he flickered strangely in my vision, and moved from place to place in jerky, darting motions most unnatural. He did not appear to see the baroness, or me.

'Your companion?' said Baroness Tremayne.

'Yes.'

The baroness made no move to approach Jay or to talk to him, in spite of her question. She ignored him entirely, and crossed instead to a shelf in a different part of the room. A quick, deft movement; she reached out, selected a single, slim volume, which she put into my hands; then away she went, quick of step and purposeful. 'It would be well to hurry, Cordelia Vesper,' she called over her shoulder to me.

I looked longingly at the book. It was bound in dark leather, quite blank; not a single word was embossed into its aging covers. I hungered to open it then and there, devour its contents immediately, and it cost me every shred of willpower I possessed to tuck it carefully away into my bag, unopened.

Jay had seen something. He was at a far shelf, back turned, reading. Then he was on the other side of the room, near where the baroness had stopped, hand outstretched towards the slim gap in the shelves that had not been there moments before.

Mischief welled up in me, irrepressible, and I succumbed to temptation. As I darted past Jay in the baroness's wake I trailed my fingers over the back of his neck, a feather-light touch which would certainly make him jump.

I did not pause to observe the effects of my misdemeanour, for the baroness was disappearing back into the hall. I hastened to catch up, forgetting Jay in an instant when I realised that her ladyship was walking straight into the far wall.

Not into it — *through* it. This was so powerfully reminiscent of what I myself had recently done at Home, courtesy of House, that I was much struck. Were such arts commonly employed, long ago? I needed no further proof of the deleterious effects of time, the way our magick had faded, dimmed. The baroness was mistress of magicks so long forgotten, most of us did not know they existed.

I followed after, approaching the wall with some trepidation. It had swallowed the baroness without trace, but to me it looked as solid as ever.

So it proved to be, for my face met cold, unyielding stone and there I stayed.

'Baroness?' I called.

Seconds ticked past, and my trepidation grew. Had she simply left, and abandoned me? I no longer felt that she intended to leave me stranded *between the echoes*, as she had earlier threatened to do. But since she had not explained what that meant, perhaps she was doing me the undeserved honour of assuming that I knew; that I could manipulate the echoes as she did, and find my own way out. 'Baroness Tremayne?' I called again.

Her head appeared through the wall, devoid of neck or body; a disconcerting sight. 'Follow, child,' she chided me, and I was too embarrassed by my ignorance to take exception to the term *child*. In her eyes, I probably was, and more or less deservedly.

'I cannot,' I confessed.

Her disembodied head tilted strangely; she was puzzled by me. 'Strange,' she commented. Then her arm appeared, reaching for me. I permitted myself to be grabbed. A swift, sharp *tug,* and the wall melted before me.

I fell through, with a regrettable lack of grace.

On the other side was a spiral staircase winding its way down into some subterranean space. There were no doors or windows set into the walls, just unbroken stone. Baroness Tremayne was already halfway down the stairs.

'Wait,' I gasped, hurrying to catch up. 'Who *are* you? What are these magicks you perform with such ease? They are forgotten now.'

'Not forgotten, while the House remains.'

'But they are not learned, not taught. We know nothing of them, not even at the

University.' Her stride was long for her relatively insignificant height, and I had to work to keep up. The air cooled as we descended, the light dimmed; this place was obviously not intended for use by such folk as I. 'I do not know what you mean by the echoes.'

'Spells, rare and strange,' said the baroness, whisking out of sight around a corner; we had reached the bottom of the stairs. 'Dark arts, to the minds of some. They were afeared. No university has ever taught our ways.'

'Our ways?' I repeated. 'Who do you mean by that? How are you here? *Who are you?*'

It did not matter how insistent I was with my questions; they all went equally unanswered. Baroness Tremayne stood motionless at the foot of the stairs, her gaze intent upon something I could not see until I joined her.

Then, all at once, I understood.

We had travelled into the depths of a network of cellars. Low-ceilinged passageways spread before me, intersections branching off into the darkness. The light was so low I could see little but great, craggy blocks of stone stacked into graceless walls, each set with heavy oaken doors held shut with black iron bars. The only light in those cellars was of a faded, sickly character, and its source was no sconce or torch or globe of wisp-light. The light came, somehow, from the floor, and it glimmered and shifted in a way that suggested ceaseless, writhing movement. I did not immediately understand.

I looked closer, stared harder. The floor surged and wriggled in waves of frantic motion, as though it was alive.

Which, effectively, it *was*.

'They are... worms?' I whispered, appalled. 'Maggots?'

Baroness Tremayne shook her head, her gaze never wavering from the mass of pale, writhing creatures that carpeted the floor and the weird light that clung to their tiny, repulsive forms. '*Ortherex,*' she said, and the word struck me as vaguely familiar. I had heard it before, somewhere — or more probably, I had read it. 'Parasites,' the baroness continued. She bent from the waist, a slow, stately movement, and extracted a single worm from the writhing mass. This she held up for my inspection.

I grabbed a glow-sphere from my bag and activated it with a flick of a finger. A clear, bright white light shone forth, a comfortingly *clean* radiance compared to the sickly glow of the ortherex. Thus illuminated, I could clearly see its plump, segmented, legless body, its toothless mouth, its covering of fine hairs. It had no eyes. 'Parasites,' I echoed, intrigued and disgusted. 'They feed off a living host?'

The baroness nodded. 'They prefer my kind, though it is not known why. Inside our soft bodies they lay their eggs. Their young swell and grow, feeding from our heart's energies and the magicks woven into our blood. Such theft will kill us, and swiftly. Then, forth go the ortherex. Their preferred home thereafter is a deep place, dank and dark. Into the rock they go, to drink up such magicks as they find in our Dells and Enclaves, and to find new hosts.'

I felt sick, for by the baroness's words I realised that the carpet of ortherex I could see was but the surface of the problem. *Into the rock?* How far down did that mass of parasites go?

And this was the cellar of the library alone. One building, out of a whole city.

Just how many billions of ortherex were there?

19

To my renewed horror, the ortherex on the baroness's palm was by no means content to lie passive. It twitched and writhed, bunching its body into a tight coil, its mouth fixed upon her skin in a manner that to my eyes looked highly unpromising. The baroness winced, and quickly dropped it back into the mass of its brethren.

The thing was gamely trying to *eat* her.

I stared at the baroness, and I dare say my eyes were as wide as saucers. In the midst of my horror, a thought occurred to me. 'How is it that you are still here?' I gestured at the ortherex. 'I mean, it is not merely the passage of time — for you have been here since the fall of Farringale, have you not? Hundreds of years?'

She looked gravely at me, and said only: 'I have.'

'Time aside, then, how have you survived proximity to these horrors? The rest of Farringale fell!'

She turned away from the wriggling parasites and began, slowly, to ascend the stairs. 'Some few of my kind are resistant to the ortherex. Our blood will not nourish them. From us they cannot feed, and so they die.' Her lips quirked in a faint smile. 'Still, they try.'

I thought of the way that tiny mouth had fastened upon the baroness's skin, the way she had hastily thrown it off. Apparently, the ortherex could still hurt, even if they could not kill her. 'How many of you are still here?' I asked her.

'Three, by my life. Once, there were more.'

They were dying out, then, these lingering guardians of Farringale. I pictured her centuries-long vigil, the loneliness of her state here, cut off from the wider world; condemned only to wait, and watch as her few fellows died around her. I shivered.

A theory as to the nature of her longevity was forming in my mind, and I hungered to ask questions of her. But I restrained the impulse. There was not time, now, to pursue that topic. The matter of the ortherex was far more pressing. We reached the top of the stairs, and those enclosed walls now made sense to me. Perhaps there was the outline of a lost door, somewhere inside that walled-off corridor; someone had bricked it up, perhaps in hope of containing the tide of ortherex which had taken possession of the cellars. A doomed effort, and futile.

The baroness took us back through the wall, and paused. How grateful was I, to return to that light, airy hallway after the dank misery of the passageways below! I stepped into the patch of sunlight which shone through the main doors, welcoming its soft warmth upon my skin. It was faded and wan in this strange place the baroness had brought me to — *between the echoes* — but comparatively, it was bliss. 'Baroness,' I said. 'Please, tell me you have a way to stop these creatures. Can they be purged? Destroyed? Repelled? Anything.'

A faint smile curved her lips: of satisfaction, perhaps. 'I do,' she said, and my hopes swelled. 'Alas, too late we were for Farringale. But down the long ages we've toiled, and our work is finished. The tome I put into your hands; you have it still?'

Of *course* I did. I took it out to show her, and she nodded approval. 'Therein lies the key. Know that nothing can purge the ortherex once they grow too strong; perhaps Glenfinnan is already lost beyond recall. But it is not too late for Darrowdale. If you love magick, Cordelia Vesper, then save our Enclaves. I entreat you.'

'I will. *We* will, now that you have given us the means.'

She nodded again, though her attention had wandered from me, her thoughts turned within. 'If but *one* is saved, all is justified,' she mused, and I saw a sadness and a weariness in her that all but broke my heart. 'It will be enough.'

I wanted to ask more of her. Perhaps I could get away with an enquiry after all; just one or two probing questions about these *echoes,* and her surviving colleagues, and the people she referred to when she said *our.* But the light slowly brightened around me until I stood blinking in pure, unimpeded sunshine, and I realised I was alone. The baroness had faded away like smoke.

'Thank you,' I called. Too late, too late, but perhaps she heard me, somewhere within the echoes of lost Farringale.

I stood for a moment, a little dazed by what had just happened, what I had seen. Had I really spent the last half-hour in conversation with a woman whose birth predated mine by centuries? One of a mere few survivors of the disasters that had destroyed Farringale, a mere *three*, who—

And my train of thought ground to a halt.

Only three?

'Baron?' I called, feebly at first. But urgency swelled my lungs, and I bellowed as loudly as I could: '*Baron Alban!*'

It might have been uncouth of me, standing in the hallway of Farringale's library shouting at the top of my lungs. But it was faster than going from room to room searching for him, and that was rather more important than good manners at that moment.

To my relief, he came into the hall at a half-run only a few seconds later. 'Ves? What's the matter?'

I looked long at him, standing there in all his trollish glory. I pictured those wriggling creatures fastening their hungry mouths upon his perfect skin, sucking him dry of all the magick he possessed. I pictured them laying their clutches of eggs in his ears, his mouth, his hair; those eggs hatching, growing, killing him from the inside out. I took a deep, steadying breath and said: 'Much as it pains me to abandon this library, it is imperative that we get out of here. Right now.'

Rob and Jay had come running, too; all three of them stared at me. 'You can't be serious,' said Jay at last. 'Not after all the trouble we went to.'

I held up the book. 'We've got what we need. I don't have time to explain, Jay, you are just going to have to trust me. We need to get Alban out of here. Now.'

Rob nodded once. 'Right,' he said, and made for the door. He stood there awhile, carefully checking the horizon, and I knew he was looking for griffins. 'Coast is clear, for now.'

Alban looked strangely at me. I detected a trace of alarm in his eyes, though he kept its effects well under control. 'You'll explain, later,' he said, and it was not a question.

He was as reluctant to flee Farringale as I, but I couldn't help that. He would thank me, once he knew. 'I will,' I promised.

That was enough for Alban, who joined Rob at the door.

Jay, though, whirled about and vanished back into the library.

'Jay!' I called, furious. 'Jay! This is *serious*.'

He reappeared twenty seconds later with an armful of books — books he clutched tightly to his chest, with as much care and desperation as he might cradle his own child. 'I'm here,' he panted. 'Go.'

My heart warmed to him on the spot.

· · · ● · · ● · · · ·

Our retreat from Farringale could at best be termed *disorderly*. I did my best to keep the baron away from anything that looked like rock, which inconvenienced us several times, and confused my companions to no end. I had neither time nor attention to spare for explanations.

To their credit and my relief, they followed my lead anyway.

Or Alban's, in the end, for nobody in their right mind would trust *me* to find our way from the library back to the gate. That map of his proved invaluable again. We wound our way back through those beautiful, heartbreakingly empty streets, and this time I barely glanced at the structures we passed, hardly paused to speculate at the contents of those abandoned houses. If Alban got infected it would be *my fault*, and what then? I hoped that the baroness's journal might include a recipe for a cure, but perhaps it would not. She had made no such promise.

For the first time in my life, I felt deeply, personally responsible for someone else's safety, and under circumstances which made it deplorably difficult to be certain they would make it out okay.

I made a mental note not to keep putting myself, or anybody else, in that position.

The griffins, thank goodness, did not bother us on our return trip. We moved too fast, perhaps, or they were still drowsy from the charm I had spun. I thought I saw unpromising flickers of lightning in those distant clouds as we arrived, breathless, at the gate, but I could not be sure.

We surged through the door en masse, snatched the keys from the worn stonework of the bridge, and watched, panting with exertion and tension, as the door shut behind us. The light of Farringale faded.

Carefully, Baron Alban folded his map and returned it to a pocket in his trousers. It was covered in writing, which it had not been before, and I wondered what the baron had found to make notes about, while I was busy wandering the bowels of the city. He put away the gold and the bronze keys, too, and held out the silver one to me.

I took it.

'I think,' said Baron Alban, 'that it's time for you to explain.'

'*Please*,' said Jay.

So I did.

· · • · • · · · ·

I troubled my Adeline, again, and her trio of friends. They came to us at Alresford, and bore us back to Old Winchester Hill. How comforting it was to feel the warmth of her flanks beneath me, to wind my fingers through her silken mane. It is hard to dwell on darkness, disease and fear when you have a unicorn nearby.

Jay's windstorms swept us off that hilltop and back Home, where we parted ways.

But not without some argument.

'The book, please,' said Alban, and held out his hand to receive it.

'Not yet,' I said, making no move to hand it over.

He stared at me. 'What?'

'I need to give it to Milady. It has to be processed by our library, its contents given over to our technicians. Then it may travel to the Troll Court. Believe me, the Society will fully understand the urgency of the situation. I imagine a copy will be made for our use, after which the book will be sent along to you with all due speed.'

'Nonsense,' he said sternly. 'This is a matter for the Court. We have all the right people to—'

'How many Enclaves are there?' I interrupted.

'I don't know, quite a few—'

'Exactly. Do you want help, or not?'

He stared helplessly at me, and heaved a great, exasperated sigh. 'If that book doesn't find its way to the Court within two days — preferably less — I'll be back.'

His tone fully conveyed what that would mean for me. 'Yessir,' I said.

He smiled at that, albeit crookedly. 'Bid you farewell, then.'

I glanced, briefly, at Jay, whose state was much as I imagined. But Rob was tending to him, so I had a couple of minutes. 'Wait,' I said to Alban.

He paused, one brow raised.

'It is not my place to interfere, but I'm going to anyway.'

That crooked smile flashed again. 'All right, I am duly braced.'

'This problem should have been caught sooner. It's telling that it wasn't. Am I right in thinking that the Court allows full autonomy to each Enclave? That they may live as they choose, according to their own rules and laws?'

'More or less. There are some laws which apply to all our kind, but Their Majesties do take a general policy of non-interference with individual Enclaves.'

'Right. And sometimes Enclaves choose to go Reclusive. They shut their doors, cease to communicate with the Court at all — or anybody else, much — and nothing is heard from them for years.'

'Decades, sometimes. Yes.'

'Yes. So. If someone had made a point of checking up on these people, maybe Glenfinnan wouldn't have been wiped out.'

Alban began to show signs of a great, heavy weariness. His shoulders sagged, and shadows deepened under his eyes. He dragged a hand across his brow. 'Oh, Ves, you are opening a whole can of worms with that one. You have no idea...'

'I don't need to have an idea. I'm just pointing it out. This one's a matter for the Court.'

He nodded and straightened, all business once again. 'I understand.'

With that, he was gone, striding through the door without so much as a farewell. I watched as he turned towards the stairs that would take him out of the cellars at Home, and from thence away. Back to his own world, where I could not follow.

Then I turned back to the others. Rob had Jay on his feet again, though Jay's books had not fared so well. I stooped to pick them all up, stacking them carefully atop one another. They were old and fragile and infinitely precious, and my heart fluttered with excitement. When I took a quick look through the titles, I almost fainted with joy.

'Jay,' I said gravely. 'I love you, just a bit.'

'Help yourself,' he said, with only a faint trace of sarcasm.

'Oh, I *will*. And believe me, Val is going to love you too.'

'Great,' said Jay, and swayed as his knees gave out. 'I could use some love.'

'You and me both. Next stop: Milady. And she is *not* going to be pleased.'

20

Later, Jay and I lay slumped in opposing chairs in the first-floor common room. We had adopted identical postures of exhausted inactivity, flopped like a pair of stringless marionettes.

On the table before us stood an emptied chocolate pot.

We had not spoken for a while. Neither of us had the energy, I think, or perhaps our minds were too busy with their own thoughts. It *had* been an unusual week, after all.

But it occurred to me that Jay wore an expression of particular, and deepening, despair, and I felt moved to enquire.

'My first assignment,' he said, as though that explained everything.

When nothing more was forthcoming, I cautiously prompted: 'And?'

'Going to get fired.'

'For what?'

'Disobeying a direct order.'

I scoffed.

'What?' he said. 'You heard Milady.'

'Yep.'

He nodded, confirmed in his woes. 'How long does it usually take them to give notice?'

Like he was expecting the letter of doom any moment now. 'In your case,' I told him, 'I'd say you'll be losing your job in about fifty years. More, if you eat right and exercise regularly.'

He blinked at me. '*You heard Milady.*'

I had indeed. And it was fair to say that Milady was not at her most delighted with us. She had not been outright angry; that was not her way. But there had been a crispness to her tone, a certain air of cool, brisk efficiency not characteristic of her, which was only apparent when she was displeased. Despite his inexperience with Milady, Jay had certainly picked up on that.

On the other hand...

'See that?' I said, pointing to the shining chocolate pot.

Jay's frown deepened. 'The pot? Yes. I see it.'

'Means we've done well.'

'But—' Jay began.

I cut him off. 'No. It *always* means we've done well. If you've underperformed but given it your best shot, you'll probably get tea. Good tea. Or coffee, if that's your preference. If you've really screwed up and it's genuinely your fault, well... I once heard of somebody getting a bowl of stagnant rainwater.'

Jay grimaced. 'Harsh.'

'Not really, he was a prat. But you see my point.'

Slightly, slowly, Jay shook his head.

I tried again.

'We *did* disobey a direct order. And Milady can in no way endorse our actions because she *is* our boss, and no employer alive wants to encourage a regular display of such outright disobedience. But we had due reason, and she knows that now.'

I recalled the high points of the conversation well.

'How did you get the key, Cordelia?' Milady had said (like a displeased parent, she resorted to my true, full name when she was unhappy with me).

'The House gave it to me,' I'd replied.

Prior to that moment, she had been all cool displeasure. That disclosure was the turning point. The chill in her manner did not noticeably dissipate, but I'd been able to recount the outcome of our journey without interruption.

And the chocolate had been waiting for us, upon our descent.

'I suppose,' said Jay dubiously.

'Due reason,' I repeated. 'And the support of the House, which is by no means inconsequential. On top of which, we came back from Farringale alive, without leaving the place a smoking wreck behind us, and with the means secured to help Darrowdale and South Moors and the rest. The chocolate is Milady's way of acknowledging our blinding heroism, without having to go so far as to own herself mistaken, or to congratulate us upon our disobedience.'

Jay began to look more hopeful. He sat up a bit. 'Maybe you're right.'

'I am,' I said serenely. 'You're not getting fired, because by consequence of being my partner in crime, you're the hero of several Troll Enclaves. And who knows! Maybe Farringale can be restored.'

'Maybe.' Jay was dubious, and I didn't blame him. He hadn't seen what I had seen at the lost Troll Court, but my account of it had been graphic enough.

Nonetheless. Milady had given orders that the book, or at least its contents, were to be put into Orlando's hands without a moment's delay — orders which I had been absolutely delighted to perform. Orlando is a genius, there is no other word to describe him. He and his technicians would blend the contents of Baroness Tremayne's book with the very best that the modern world had to offer, and come up with... well, a miracle. Maybe.

Copies of the book were also slated to go out to some of the other teams — Rob's, for one. There *was* a cure in there. It was not described as being fully effective in all cases, and some of the trolls we had seen would undoubtedly be too far gone for help. But some could be saved. South Moors would survive, and there was hope for Darrowdale and Baile Monaidh. While Jay and I lay, inert and weary, in our matching arm-chairs, many of our colleagues were preparing to depart the House for the days, weeks or months necessary to pull the Enclaves back from the brink of destruction. In this, I had no doubt they would be joined by the Troll Court's best — led, in all likelihood, by Baron Alban.

Silence fell again, for a little while. It was broken by Jay, who said, with the randomness of a man emerging from deep reflection: 'I am glad we did it.'

'Me too,' I fervently agreed. 'Not least because of those books! A hero on two counts, Jay! I told you Valerie would adore you.'

She really had. Assuming at first that the theft — er, *retrieval* — of the books had to be my doing, she had showered me with such delicious praise and affection, I had been reluctant to admit that I'd had nothing to do with it, thereby transferring all her heart-warming admiration onto Jay. But it was deserved. 'You are her new favourite person.'

'Next to you, perhaps.'

'You're my new favourite person, too,' I said, letting this pass.

His head tilted, and he regarded me thoughtfully. 'Am I?'

'Assuredly.'

A faint grin followed, tentatively mischievous. 'I thought that was the baron.'

I thought about that. 'He does have excellent hair,' I had to concede.

'He was asking me questions about you. While you were off in the library's cellars.'

'Oh?' I sat up, too, my interest decidedly piqued. 'Like what?'

'Just, general stuff about you. How well I knew you, what kind of a person you are. I got the impression...' He hesitated.

'Go on.'

'I thought he might be angling for information on whether or not you're involved with anyone.'

Aha. 'What did you tell him?'

'Nothing. I have no actual insights on that point myself.'

That went some way towards explaining the text I'd received from Alban an hour or so earlier. Our brief conversation went like this:

Alban: *Will take time to sort out this mess, but how about coffee after?*

Me: *Make it tea?*

Alban: :)

So, I would be seeing the baron again.

Jay waited, leaving space for me to respond, but I chose not to. After a while, he hauled himself out of his chair with a groan, saying, 'I don't care what time it is, I am going to bed.'

'Good plan.'

He paused on his way past, and looked down at me with a slight frown. 'Ves.'

'Yes.'

'Thanks for being a bad influence.'

He sounded sincere, but with the frown? I couldn't tell, so I decided to take it at face value. 'You're more than welcome.'

Jay nodded, apparently satisfied, and dragged himself to the door. 'No doubt you'll get us into plenty more trouble,' he called back. As he vanished into the corridor beyond, I heard him say, distantly: 'Hopefully the heroic kind.'

I could be relied upon to do the former, most certainly. Whether it would also be the latter, who knew?

· · · ● · ● · · · ·

It later proved, however, that Jay is more than capable of making trouble all on his own. He doesn't even need my help.

Halfway through the following morning, he and I were called to Milady's tower. House and I had been on the best of terms since I had returned the beautiful silver key, so it was maybe that alone which prompted it to whisk us straight up to the tower, saving us the wearisome climb.

Or perhaps it was urgency. That prospect made my heart beat faster, and I hastened into Milady's tower-top chamber with some speed.

My curtsey was sloppy. 'Milady,' I said.

Jay, right behind me, made his bow with no prompting from me. 'Good morning, Milady.'

'Vesper,' she said. 'Jay. Thank you for coming so quickly.'

'House gave us a lift,' I said.

'Thank you, House.' The air glittered. 'I am sorry to dispatch you again so soon after your last... adventure. I am aware that you must both be tired. But there is a matter of some urgency requiring immediate attention.'

How intriguing. 'We are at your disposal,' I said.

'Always,' said Jay. Was he still worried about getting fired?

Milady actually hesitated. That is never a good sign. 'Jay, you showed enormous presence of mind in thinking to extract books from Farringale, and I applaud you.'

'Thank you,' he said.

'But on that topic...'

My heart sank with a nameless sense of foreboding — and quickened with an equally nameless feeling of excitement. I exchanged a look with Jay, whose face registered much the same feelings as my own.

'Yes?' said Jay.

'There is something of a problem. Please report to Valerie at once.'

'Yes, Milady.' Jay and I turned as one, already hastening away.

But Milady wasn't quite finished with us. 'Ves?'

'Yes ma'am.'

'Please prepare yourself for some instances of... poor language.'

'From *Val*?' I said, incredulous. I have never known Valerie to use even a mild expletive. But supposing she did, why would Milady think it necessary to warn us?

'You will see what I mean when you reach the library. Go quickly, please.'

We went.

'Gudgeon!' roared a voice as we approached the library door. 'Canker-blossom! Dismal, hedge-born, logger-headed puttock! Churlish, thou art, and full beef-witted! A plague upon thee, and thrice over!'

Needless to say, it was not Val.

As Jay and I burst through the door and arrived, breathless and astonished, in the library foyer, the voice -- a full-throated, sonorous male roar -- took up its insults anew. 'Weedy dewberry!' it cried. 'Idle-headed wagtail!'

Val was seated behind her desk, remonstrating wearily with the voice by way of sentences but half-uttered. 'I meant only that--' she began, but was interrupted with a renewed cry of: 'Hedge-born!'

'Now really, that is *too* much!' said Val sharply.

'Too much for *thee*, lily-liver, and no doubt!' retorted the voice.

This exchange continued, but Jay and I were none the wiser for listening to it, for as far as we could see, the library was empty besides ourselves and Val.

'Er, Val?' I said after a while.

She looked at me with an air of long-suffering irritation, her hands folded tightly around a large, leather-bound book. 'Hello, Ves, Jay. Sent by Milady? Lucky you.' Her words were half drowned out by a renewed tirade from the disembodied voice, which she did a creditable job of ignoring.

Jay gave up. 'Valerie,' he said gravely. '*What the hell is this?*'

Valerie rolled her eyes towards the ceiling, and dropped her ancient, fragile, handsome-looking tome onto her desk, where it landed with a great *thump*.

I had never seen Val so careless with any book, let alone one of great age, and could only stare in astonishment.

But the book did not lie meekly where it had been put, as most are wont to do. *This* book leapt smartly off the desk, took up a position some three inches before Val's face, and began to dance up and down in a fine display of high temper. 'Hedge-pig!' it roared. 'I shall have thy *guts* for such goatish treatment!'

'The book,' said Jay faintly. 'The *book* is talking.'

Val merely nodded once.

'That's... different,' said I.

Val sighed, and put her face in her hands. 'Tell me about it.'

Toil and Trouble

Modern Magick, 2

Charlotte E. English

1

Guess who was landed with the job of looking after the foul-mouthed book?

'Get this horrid thing out of my library!' said Val. It was an order, but she looked at me in a desperate, pleading way which, as her friend, I could not ignore. 'Ves!'

'Something must certainly be done about it,' I agreed, though my mind was blank as to what, exactly, one could do with an unusually lively sixteenth-century tome with all the tender sensibility of a guttersnipe.

'Base, beetle-headed fool!' raged the book, hovering still before poor Valerie's face. 'Thou hast cracked my spine!'

'Beetle-headed?' whispered Jay to me. 'Now it's just making them up.'

'I have not!' protested Val, and truly, I could hardly think of a more vicious insult to direct at our head librarian. She'd probably die before she would handle an old book so carelessly as to damage it. 'But I will, if you don't stop,' she added, and I blinked, shocked.

'*Cracked*,' repeated the book. 'Next thou shalt bend thyself to the creasing of my pages! To the turning of my very corners, and the pinching of them, until, full broken, they have not the means of righting themselves!'

'I suppose "dog-eared" must be a recently coined term,' reflected Jay, watching the book with the dispassionate, arms-folded stance of an intrigued scholar.

'I like his version,' I protested. 'Verbose, elegant, poetic—'

'Windy, flowery and over the top.'

I had long suspected that Jay lacked something in the way of soul. Here was complete proof.

'*Jay!*' thundered Valerie, making both of us jump. Admittedly, she did have to raise her voice considerably in order to be heard over the abominable book, which ranted on and on, unabashed. 'This is your doing, and you will fix it at once!'

'Mine?' gasped Jay. 'How is it my fault?!'

'You brought it here!'

'Together with several other works of great historical interest, all of which are far better-behaved,' I reminded her.

'Yes,' said Valerie, and smiled. 'Thank you for those, Jay.'

'You're welcome.'

'But *get rid of this one!*'

Jay looked not only reluctant to saddle himself with such an object (and who could blame him), but also at a loss as to what to do with it if he did. It was only about his third or fourth week with the Society, after all, and this was a species of magickal heritage that even the veterans amongst us had never seen or heard of before (most assuredly including yours truly). So I hastily stepped forward and, feeling heroic and martyred, swept up the book.

'Thank you, Ves,' said Valerie, instantly mollified.

I only sighed. 'May I ask how it came to start talking? For it was as silent as any a book should be, all the way here from Farringale.'

'I opened it.'

'That's it?'

'That's it. It started shrieking blue murder at once, and I did not even get to read any of it because the vile thing kept slamming itself upon my fingers.'

'A deserved torment, craven wench,' the book informed her.

Valerie cast it a look of intense dislike. 'Sorry to land you with that, Ves,' she said. 'But I can't have it in the library all day. It's making far too much noise.'

She was right, of course. We were only in the library's entrance hall, in fact, where Val's grand desk stood; the library itself was through a handsome archway a few feet to my left, whereupon it stretched away and away for some distance. Nonetheless, I had no doubt that the book's ringing tones could be heard all the way at the bottom of the library, which would be pleasing the Society's scholars to no end.

'I don't suppose you have any suggestions…?' I ventured, feeling almost as much at a loss as Jay.

Valerie massaged her temples. There were deep shadows under her dark eyes, and I wondered how long she'd been grappling with the book before we'd finally arrived. 'I don't know exactly, but there's no doubt this is one of our weirder acquisitions. A curse, or a haunting? You might try Zareen.'

'Oh, yes,' I said. 'This is right up her alley.'

'Good luck.' She gave me a grim smile, which I just about managed to return.

Away went Jay and I.

• • • • • • • • • •

Ordinarily, Jay is much better at finding his way around than me, and I am forced to follow him about like a trusting little lamb while he marches us off to wherever we're going. But not at Home. It's a huge, sprawling old place, and while it was built in the sixteen-hundreds it's had all kinds of additions, alterations and expansions made in the centuries since. Having spent more than a decade wandering its winding passages, I know it extremely well.

Thus I was able to sweep out of the library, chin high, and strut confidently away, with Jay trailing meekly along behind me. Felt good. I waited for Jay's inevitable complaint — on the topic of Zareen, most likely, towards whom he has reportedly developed an instant (and mutual) antipathy — but he was silent.

So was the book.

This surprised me so much that I stopped walking, having travelled only about twenty paces down the tapestried corridor. 'Hello?' I said, tentatively.

'To whom do you speak?' said the book, after a moment's pause.

'Why, to you.'

'Well met, lady.'

'How polite. I had rather expected curses.'

'Thou hast not merited such treatment.'

Jay said, 'Better not open it.'

I had to agree. Cradling the book carefully, I ventured on, and Jay fell in beside me. We had not far to go. The structure at Home is as chaotic in the organisational sense as in the geographical; we are loosely separated into divisions, but there is so much bleed-over between the daily duties, challenges and obstacles faced by our various groups that the structure often falls down. Jay and I, for example, are officially part of Acquisitions, but I'm periodically seconded into Research (happy days, those), and I wouldn't be at all surprised if Jay ends up handed off to Zareen's division more often than he's going to like.

Technically, Zareen is part of Research, albeit in an unusual capacity. But she consults for Development from time to time, and I bump into her in Acquisitions here and there, too. She runs an obscure little division almost single-handedly, clumsily shelved under Research because nobody knows what else to call it. And since it has never been given its own, official name, we've collectively dubbed it the Toil and Trouble division.

In other words: when anything particularly weird comes up, we all call in Zareen.

She's usually holed up not far from the library, in a tiny nook of a room buried deep in the west wing. The door is always shut.

'Would you mind knocking?' I said to Jay once we had arrived. 'I don't want to risk dropping the book.'

'Perish the thought.' Jay shuddered, and knocked smartly upon the door. He then adopted a pose of such studied nonchalance as clearly displayed his discomfort, and I tried my best not to notice.

'Hang on a minute!' yelled Zareen. There came some clattering noises from the other side of the door, and we were left to enjoy the chill of the dim, stone-walled corridor (bare of tapestries, paintings or anything else in this part of the House) for half a minute longer.

Then the door swung open, apparently by itself, revealing Zareen seated at a desk tucked into the corner of the room. The place was a mess, as usual; books and notepads were stacked everywhere, along with a host of such peculiar paraphernalia I'd have no idea where to begin in describing it. Case in point, though: a collection of skulls, apparently human, sat clustered at one end of her desk, except that they were palm-sized, and as usual she had an odd contraption made of woven string, jewel-charms and bones hung upon the wall above her chair. Her curse-catcher, she calls it. I've never been able to figure out whether its purpose is merely decorative, or functional — and if the latter, what its function is supposed to be.

The lady herself looked me over with considerable goodwill, and then Jay with rather less. She had green streaks in her black hair today, very neatly done, and she sported a matching green jewel in her nose ring.

'Peridot?' I enquired.

'It's new.' Zareen grinned and swung around to face me, giving me a full view of the new jewellery.

'Suits you.'

'Doesn't it?' Zareen turned her amused gaze upon Jay, who bore it rigidly. 'I'm still working on Ves. What do you think, nostril or septum?'

'I've told you,' I said hastily. 'I'll think about it when you find me a good unicorn stud, and not before.'

'You can't wear a unicorn in your nose. Pick something smaller.'

'I can't? Then I'm not getting my nose pierced.'

'Navel maybe,' murmured Zareen, but she was watching Jay.

'Do the women of this miserable age commonly engage in bodily mutilation?'

It was the book speaking, of course, but since I had yet to warn Zareen of its capacity to do so, she narrowed her eyes at the only male in the room: Jay.

'That was not me!' he protested. 'Did you see my mouth move?'

'Just the kind of prissy thing you would say,' retorted Zareen, ignoring his question.

I headed off what was clearly an impending fight by laying the book in front of Zareen. I'd been clutching it to my chest until then, with my arms wrapped tightly around it, and since she was used to seeing me carting books everywhere (who wasn't, indeed?) I don't suppose it had occurred to her to take note of it. But the book got her attention at once, as I'd known it would, for on the front of its dark leather cover there was engraved a motif of a complex star, a flame blossoming at each of its twelve points.

'Ooh,' said Zareen, captivated.

'Don't open it yet,' I warned.

She was itching to do so, already reaching for it. 'What?'

I explained.

Zareen was not impressed.

'You've brought me a centuries-old book from *Farringale*,' she said with emphasis. 'A book no one's read since the sixteen-hundreds, containing who knows what esoteric wisdom, and I can't open it?'

'Well, you can,' I allowed. 'Only get some ear plugs first, maybe.'

'And watch your fingers,' put in Jay.

Zareen scowled at him. 'I've handled difficult artefacts before.'

Jay rolled his eyes. 'By all means, try it.'

Zareen did, though to her credit she looked a little wary, and opened it with a hesitancy unusual for her.

'Fool-born haggard!' erupted the book, right on cue. 'Dost thou *dare* to venture upon mine innards? Thou wouldst disembowel me of all my goodness, wouldst thou, and with narry a *by-your-leave!*' The book slammed shut with a crisp *snap* of disapproval.

'Ow,' said Zareen, shaking the pain out of her fingertips.

Jay, wisely, refrained from airing the *I-told-you-so* I could see hovering upon his lips. Instead he said, 'We're calling him Bill.'

'As in Shakespeare?'

'Quite.'

'Slightly less elegantly verbose, I'd say?'

'His full name is Bill the Boor.'

'Churl,' said the book.

'Boor,' said Jay.

'So,' I said brightly. 'Bit of a problem, no? Val would've skinned me alive if I hadn't taken it away at once, and I'm afraid nobody could think who could possibly fix it but you.'

Alone among those who had come into contact with the wretched book, Zareen looked intrigued — even a little bit excited. 'Nice,' she murmured, and turned the book around on her desk, examining all the features of its covers and spine. She ignored its ongoing diatribe with admirable grace.

'Curse or haunting, do you think?' I asked, remembering Val's words.

'Could be either! Really interesting stuff.'

'I can't tell you how glad we are that you think so.' I had no hesitation in speaking for Jay as well as myself, for I could see the relief on his face. Tinged, maybe, with a hint of fascinated disgust.

Well, it takes most people a little while to get used to Zareen.

She was barely listening, already absorbed in the many questions posed by the book. 'Thanks, Ves,' she said vaguely. 'I'll call you when I've figured it out.'

What bliss it was to walk out of that room, and close the door behind us! We walked quickly away, pursued by the muffled and increasingly distant sounds of sixteenth-century cursing.

'She's got a strong stomach,' I offered.

'Madwoman,' he replied, though he didn't sound as negative as I'd expected. Perhaps Zareen had actually won herself a few points with Jay for her willingness to take the thing off our hands.

'Cup of tea?' said I.

'*Yes.*'

2

I n my room at Home, I've got a little stash of Curiosities, minor artefacts, and assorted odds and ends. Some of them are useful, some of them aren't. Probably my favourite of the latter category is a beautiful old scroll, the real kind, made of vellum and with rowan-wood supports. It even has a tooled-leather case. It's paired with a quill pen — owl feather, not goose! Both are enchanted, so that anything I might choose to write upon mine will appear at once upon the matching scrolls of some other member (or members) of the Society. They used to be standard issue, but they stopped handing them out before I joined. I once found a whole, sorry stack of them in Stores, and took pity on this set because... because they're pretty.

What can I say.

The reason for their obsolescence, of course, is the mobile phone. When we all wander about with smartphones surgically attached to our wrists, who needs quills and scrolls anymore? A sad casualty of cruel, inexorable time.

But, I have to admit, a fair one. For when, a few hours later, my own personal scroll-killer buzzed and began to play *Sussudio,* it got my attention at once, and within two minutes I was rattling back down to Research and Zareen's broom-cupboard of a room.

Zareen opened the door right away. 'You're going to like this,' she said, grinning and ushering me inside.

I eyed the book with misgivings. It lay quiescent upon the desk, quiet as a proverbial church mouse, but I didn't trust it. 'I rather doubt that.'

'Oh, don't worry. It's much nicer now.'

'It is? What did you do to it?'

Zareen wouldn't meet my eye. 'Uh, just some minor tweaks. Never mind that. What do you think I found inside?'

'You've read it!'

'Sort of. There isn't much to read, as it turns out. Only a few pages have been used. It looks like a journal, used to record somebody's progress upon some kind of journey. Late Middle English, I'd say, so it's hard to read, and written in such deplorable chicken-scratch I can hardly make it out. So the destination's unclear — or at least, it was at *first*.'

Zareen was bursting with news, and very smug about it too. I didn't want to stop her, but I had to ask: 'Wait, where's Jay?'

'No idea. Anyway, the—'

'Stop right there.' I grabbed my phone and called Jay, ignoring Zareen's eye-rolling disgust. 'Toil and Trouble,' I told Jay when he answered. 'All due haste.'

'Be right there.'

I put my phone away. 'It's Jay's book,' I said. 'And I'm his... mentor, I suppose. Can't leave him out.'

Zareen waited with an exaggerated display of patience.

'What's the problem with you two, anyway?'

'Oh, nothing really,' Zareen replied with a roll of her eyes. 'I think he's a prude and a stick-in-the-mud and he thinks I'm reckless and irresponsible.' She gave me a half-smile. 'Just squabbles, Ves. Don't worry about it.'

Me, worry? I wanted to disclaim this charge at once, until I realised I was wearing my worried face. I hastily smoothed out my features and adopted an air of proper unconcern. 'I feel responsible for him,' I said by way of explanation.

'I don't think you need to be. I'll say this for him: he's far from stupid, and he'll always be okay.'

'Mm.'

Zareen looked at me shrewdly. 'He feels responsible for you, too, I think.'

'Me!'

Zareen grinned. 'Surprised? He *was* given the job of making sure we don't lose you somewhere.'

'Making sure I don't lose myself somewhere, you mean? Fair.'

'No easy task.'

I couldn't argue with this judgement, since it was true. Thankfully for my dignity, Jay showed up just then. He was polite enough to greet Zareen with a nod, and looked at me. 'What's the news?'

'Your moment's arrived,' I said to Zareen. 'We're ready to be impressed!'

Zareen leaned back in her chair, put her booted feet up on her desk and said, 'It's a treasure map.'

'What?' said Jay. 'Bill?'

'Sort of. The book, as I've just said to Ves, contains a somewhat wandering and confused account of somebody's journey in search of something unidentified, to places unspecified. Not at all edifying, and so poorly written I can't even decipher most of it. Only the first few pages have been written on, and one page at the back, which contains a sketch.'

'A map!' I said.

Zareen nodded, grinning. 'It's got an X-marks-the-spot and everything.' She displayed for us a piece of notepaper, upon which she had apparently copied the map in red pen. Her X in the middle was huge and exuberant, marked in bold.

'How do we know it's a treasure map?' said Jay, prosaically.

I sighed. 'Ancient maps with an X marked somewhere upon them are always treasure maps.'

Zareen nodded. 'That, and there's an obscure reference on the third page to a bounty of some kind, if I'm reading it right. There's no description as to what manner of treasure the writer was after, but he obviously expected to discover some grand prize.'

'Any idea as to the identity of the writer?' I asked.

'None.'

'Did you ask Bill?' said Jay.

'I tried. He wouldn't stop insulting me long enough to answer my questions.'

Jay and I both looked in silence at the book. It hadn't spoken a word since I'd entered the room, fully quarter of an hour before. 'I'm curious,' said Jay. 'How did you shut it up?'

Zareen shifted in her seat, and avoided Jay's eye. And mine. 'Er, I haven't. He's just a bit less noisy now.'

I considered pressing the matter — Zareen was obviously skirting around the edges of something — but on reflection I let it pass. Sometimes it's best to circle around the point. So I said: 'What's the likelihood that Bill, or wherever that voice is coming from, is the same person who wrote the journal entries and sketched the map?'

'You mean, is this a haunting? I don't think so. When he wasn't insulting me, he was protesting against the very idea that he'd write such uncouth nonsense, or hare around searching for treasure just because somebody drew a map. Whatever became of the writer, I don't think it's Bill. And I'm not convinced that the book's haunted by anybody else, either, for he's showed no signs of having any kind of history that he can remember, and ghosts can usually talk about little else. You'll want to interrogate him a bit more yourself, see if you can't get more out of him.'

I reached for the book.

'Later,' added Zareen hastily.

I sat back again. 'So it's not a haunting. A curse, then?'

'Could be, but it's the oddest curse I've ever come across if so. Yes, he was keeping idle hands from opening the book and thereby keeping anybody from reading it, but it's a clumsy form of protection. It didn't take much to get around that problem.'

'Oh?'

Zareen indicated a pair of heavy marble paperweights upon her desk. 'It took a few tries, but I peaced it and put weights upon its pages. Bill went off for a nice little nap, and when he woke up it was too late to take up snapping at my fingers again.' She paused and added reflectively, 'He took it rather well, all things considered, which again leads me to think that he isn't there to deter people from reading it. He's just a bad-tempered grouch.'

'But if he's not a ghost or a curse, what is he?'

'A spell,' said Zareen with a shrug. 'Though I grant you, it's a sophisticated enchantment, and more complex than anything I've ever met with before. Quite intimidating. But considering where you got the thing, I shouldn't be surprised.'

I took it from this that Zareen had no more idea what the spell was intended to accomplish than I did. And how intriguing a puzzle. A complicated enchantment which had gifted an (apparently) ordinary book with sentience — and an extraordinarily foul vocabulary? One which had, considering the nature of that vocabulary, been placed upon the book some four or five hundred years ago? And one which, for all its sophistication, Zareen had managed to get around with quite a simple charm?

Very curious indeed.

'If someone was going to go to all that trouble,' said Jay, 'I wonder why they didn't make it more... polite.'

I couldn't help but be tickled by the idea. 'That's a sense of humour I can appreciate.'

Jay grinned. 'It doesn't quite fit with the legends of old Farringale, though, does it? The royal court, a place of learning and high art, blah blah.'

'You'd expect it to express itself in the courtliest language, and with perfect etiquette.'

Zareen looked shifty again. 'Er, yes. You would.'

'So the map,' said Jay, and leaned over the book to get a closer look at it. 'Where does it lead to?'

Zareen pushed her sketch nearer. 'Might want to consult Val. There's only one word on it, and when I did a search I didn't get any hits.'

'*Drogryre,*' read Jay.

'No hits at all?' I repeated, incredulous.

'Not one. So this place is—'

'—even more lost to the mists of time than Farringale,' I finished.

'Or just an extremely well-kept secret,' suggested Jay. He picked up the map and stuck it in his pocket, then made to collect the book, too.

Zareen stopped him. 'Where are you going with those?'

'To find Drogryre. Isn't that what we do next?'

'Let Ves take the book.'

This requirement made as much sense to me as it did to Jay, who looked irritated. But he complied, stepping back to make room for me.

I picked up the book very carefully, still expecting it to hurl abuse at me. But it remained blissfully quiet.

'Don't open it until you get to the library,' Zareen recommended.

'Why not?' I said.

'It's asleep right now.'

'What do you mean by—' I began, but the door was already closing behind us.

'Bring me back something with bones!' yelled Zareen through the door as we walked away.

'There's something fishy about all that,' said Jay.

I had to agree. We made it halfway back to the library before curiosity overcame the both of us. 'I have to open it,' I said.

'Go on,' said Jay.

We stopped in an alcove beneath a big, bright window and I took hold of the front cover. 'Here we go.'

To my relief, the book suffered itself to be opened without trying to bite my fingers, and without snapping itself shut again. Nor did it drown me in a barrage of abuse.

But it did speak.

'Madam,' said the book. 'You must allow me to tell you how ardently I admire and love you.'

I slammed the book shut.

Silence.

Then Jay said, in a strangled voice, 'Is Bill quoting Pride and Prejudice?'

'Dear Jay,' I said faintly. 'I could not be more impressed with your familiarity with the utterances of Mr. Darcy, I assure you.'

'Why is it coming out of *this* book?' said Jay, ignoring my implied question with superb grace.

Gingerly, I opened it up again. And there, on the first unused page, was the whole of Mr. Darcy's ill-fated proposal to Elizabeth Bennet, written out in Zareen's rounded handwriting.

'Val,' I said slowly, 'is going to kill all of us.'

'Probably with a dessert spoon.'

3

All things considered, Jay and I made an executive decision not to take the book straight back to Val. We carried it instead to my favourite study carrell, which happened to be safely situated two large rooms and a corridor away from the library.

It was pleasant to tuck back up in there again. It's a modest place — just a desk (albeit a splendidly well-preserved nineteenth-century example, all mahogany and moth-er-of-pearl), and a chair (ditto), placed in a concealed alcove off one of the reference rooms. I've spent untold hours there with stacks and stacks of books, researching one obscure topic after another. It's undoubtedly *my* study nook.

Jay took to it at once, for I caught him glancing around with an admiring, speculative look.

'Mine,' I told him.

'Sorry.'

I put the book carefully down upon the desk and — checking first to make sure nobody was too near to us — I opened it again.

'Good morning, madam,' said the book. 'Good morning, sir.'

'You can call me Jay,' said Jay.

'That would be an improper mode of address, sir, particularly in view of the fact that we have not yet been introduced.'

I summoned my best manners, and formally introduced Jay to the book. Jay made a decidedly courtly bow, which impressed me no end.

Then he introduced me, and I felt it incumbent upon me to match his exquisite etiquette with a curtsey.

It was an odd business.

The book was kind enough to overlook the irregularities in our behaviour, mostly because, as he said himself: 'I am not fortunate enough to have a large acquaintance here. In fact, I know no one else except for the odd, vulgar woman with the green hair, whose identity remains a mystery.'

Jay stifled his laughter — barely. 'You have no objection to Ves's pink hair?'

'The arrangement of Miss Vesper's hair might be highly irregular, but there is nothing to fault in her manners.'

I was glad he'd said that, for I was quite attached to my hair colour of the day. Rose pink (the dusky, antique shade), and perfectly curled. 'Thank you, Bill,' I said, beaming.

'We can't call him Bill anymore,' said Jay.

'An unnecessarily abbreviated name,' agreed the book.

'We can still call him Bill,' I offered. 'Darcy's first name was Fitzwilliam.'

'Bill Darcy it is.'

The book objected, but I overrode him. 'Matters are not as they were when you were written, Bill,' I unhappily had to inform him. 'You had better get used to our unnecessarily abbreviated modes of address.'

'If you insist, Miss Vesper.'

I gave up.

Secretly, I rather enjoyed being called "Miss Vesper." Jay, however, did not take so enthusiastically to "Mr Patel". 'That is my father,' he said sternly. 'Jay, please.'

The book heaved a resigned sigh, and capitulated.

Having got the formalities out of the way, it was time to do as Zareen had suggested, and launch a clever and subtle interrogation of Bill. I began with: 'Where does your map lead, Bill?'

'To the grave of my mistress.'

'Mistress?' said Jay.

'*Grave*?' said I.

Jay began to laugh. 'So much for treasure.'

'I do not at all understand the modern fixation upon "treasure",' said Bill in disgust. 'It was all that green woman would talk of.'

'That's acquisitions specialists for you,' I said by way of apology. 'The hearts of magpies, all of us.'

'To return to my mistress,' said Bill stonily, '*She* was the greatest sorceress of the age, and my noble creator. In this respect, perhaps, she was a far greater treasure than any mere gold.'

This was interesting. 'Go on. Why did she make you?'

'I was to serve as her grimoire, but of a far cleverer design than any that had yet been created. My task was to absorb not only my mistress's knowledge but anything else that should come in my way, and to repeat it upon command.'

'That *is* clever!'

'I believe I did save my mistress a great deal of time and trouble,' said Bill modestly. 'And won for her no small number of esoteric secrets, besides.'

Jay brightened at the word "secrets". So did I. Occupational hazard. 'We,' I said to Bill, 'are going to get along very well, I think.'

'It is my dearest wish that we should, Miss Vesper.'

'He definitely likes *you*,' muttered Jay.

I awarded the book a tender little pat of approval. 'What about the map?' I asked. 'And your first few pages? They were not written by your mistress, clearly.'

Bill bristled with indignation, his pages curling in a bookish grimace. 'Her death was sudden—'

'How did she die?' interpolated Jay.

'A form of plague.'

'My condolences.'

'Thank you. Her death was sudden, and I was lost for some years among a number of other, lesser volumes from her collection. We were lodged for a time in the library of the great house, until one day we were stolen by a deplorable varmint of the name of John Wester. If you have read those pages, madam, then you will have already experienced his disgraceful mode of expressing himself and I need not elaborate.'

'I haven't, yet, but you did give a rather excellent demonstration of them.'

The book looked a trifle sheepish, and shuffled about upon the desk. 'I did not, at first, trouble myself to speak much to Wester. I was delighted to be removed from the dusty shelf upon which I had so long languished, and entertained some hopes of finding my new master congenial. And I was curious as to his reasons, for he took only two books from the house's collection, both from my mistress's former possessions: a slim treatise upon the most ancient and respectable practices of star-magick, of which my mistress was a devotee. And me. But if I hoped that his second choice, at least, indicated that he understood some part of my value, I was to be disappointed. He had noticed only that my pages were apparently blank, and secured me in order to serve as a receptacle for his own records. My dignity was sunk indeed.

'The matter which absorbed all his curiosity was the search for my mistress's grave. He was under the impression that some article of great value had been buried with her. He was, in other words, a treasure-hunter. He had received some hint of the grave's location, but I understood that, by the time in question — some years after her death — its precise situation was no longer known.'

'What kind of thing was buried with her?' I said, greatly intrigued.

'That I never learned from him. I am not convinced that he knew it himself. He was an opportunist and an adventurer, and not at all averse to taking a chance.'

'Grave-robbers and thieves, plagues and dark sorceresses,' said Jay. 'This is getting good.'

'Zareen will be delighted.'

Bill gave a slight, polite cough. 'I have almost finished.'

'My apologies. Do go on.'

'I did not particularly take to John Wester,' Bill continued, unnecessarily. 'Particularly since the free use he made of my early pages seeped into my consciousness, as was inevitable, and my turn of phrase inevitably adapted itself to his. I made rather free use of his more vulgar vocabulary, and abused him with such spirit every time he dared to approach me that he soon gave up the endeavour. To my great satisfaction, he rid himself of me by selling me to that rare form of travelling merchant who understands when he has met with an object of true worth. I was sold for a mere few shillings, which was a source of some embarrassment to me, but since I afterwards was placed, through a series of subsequent trades, into the grand collections at the Court of the Trolls, I was able to recover my dignity in time.'

'And there you stayed for hundreds of years, until Jay rescued you.' I beamed at Jay, who smiled uncertainly back.

'I am appalled to learn that my sojourn there was of such extended duration,' said Bill. 'I believe I must have slept through most of it.'

'Very likely.' I fell into a reverie of reflection for a little while, pondering Bill's extraordinary tale. Some few questions stood out, at the end of my musings. 'Did they know what you were, at Farringale? Did you speak to them?'

'Scarcely at all, madam. I knew my vocabulary and general speech to be most unsuited to a place of such vaunted learning.'

'A pity, perhaps. All your potential has been wasted.'

'Until now, Miss Vesper. I have some hopes of enjoying a second spring of activity.'

'What became of John Wester, I wonder?' said Jay. 'Did he ever find the grave?'

'And was there anything of interest in it?' said I. 'Good question. Sadly it seems history has forgotten the answers, though perhaps Val might know something.'

Bill gave his polite cough again. 'I wonder if my apologies might be conveyed to the green woman? I have been disgracefully rude both to her and about her, but it strikes me that, without her interference, I would be still condemned to express myself with all the excessive vulgarity of John Wester's cant.'

'Her name is Zareen—' I began.

'—or Miss Dalir, if you prefer,' Jay put in.

'—and I have no doubt she will forgive you, for she enjoyed the mystery you presented very much indeed.'

'She might be disappointed to learn that you aren't a treasure map, though,' Jay cautioned.

'I doubt it,' I disagreed. 'Given the choice, Zareen would always go for a good disinterring over a treasure hunt.'

Jay looked faintly appalled.

'She always was a trifle macabre that way.' I picked up Bill, cradling him in my arms — I was growing rather fond of him by then, I admit — and squared my shoulders. 'No help for it. It's time to see Val. But we've such a fine story to tell that I hope she won't disembowel us *too* badly.'

'Disembowelling is pretty absolute,' Jay said. 'You either lose your entrails or you don't.'

'I'm hoping Bill can be relied upon to present his side of the story with such style as to spare us that fate.'

'I shall be happy to, madam,' said Bill, slightly muffled.

It occurred to me to be grateful even for John Wester's highly questionable behaviour.

If he had not stolen Bill back in the sixteenth century, then the book may never have ended up at Farringale, and he would never have come to us. Even if he had, without Wester's journalising the book would have retained his original turn of phrase, which I imagined to be extremely civilised — in a Chaucerian kind of way. Middle English is not precisely my strong point.

'You're quite wonderful, Bill,' I said with fervour.

'Thank you, madam.'

•••••••••••

'It's an unusual name,' said Valerie some half an hour later, poring over Zareen's sketch of the map and the single word that adorned it. 'I can't even decide how to pronounce it.'

'Medieval,' said Jay, as though this was both explanation and apology enough.

Val apparently agreed, for she merely nodded.

Our initial half-hour in the library *had* been a bit sticky. While Val was relieved to find our Bill so tidily reformed, she was every bit as horrified by the manner of its accomplishment as I had feared.

'*Ten* years in the dungeons!' she hissed, and began searching through her desk drawers for her phone.

'The House has dungeons?' Jay repeated, awed.

'Excellent ones,' I said. 'They're only cellars really, but "dungeon" sounds much more impressive. And there *are* signs with one or two of them that they might have been built to serve as dungeons in the first place. One of them even has something of the oubliette about it, which is fascinating considering—'

'You're babbling, Ves,' said Jay.

I was. 'Sorry,' I babbled. 'Val, don't murder Zareen. She did us a favour.'

'I'm not going to murder her, I'm going to throw her in the oubliette.'

'She'll love that.'

Val looked uncertain, and stopped searching for her phone. 'She will, won't she? I'll have to think of something else.'

'Disembowelment,' suggested Jay helpfully.

Val's face set into steely lines, and her dark eyes glittered. 'With a spoon.'

'What did I tell you?' I said. 'Stop helping, Jay.'

'Sorry.'

'Listen,' I commanded, and put Bill down upon the desk. 'Tell her, Bill.'

'I am in Miss Dalir's debt,' said Bill obligingly. 'Her methods may have been invasive and uncouth, but the results are so much to my taste that I cannot long hold her coarseness against her.'

Overwhelmed by this display of generosity mixed with disdain, and all couched in such elegant terms, Val could only blink at the book in amazement. 'He really *is* reformed,' she said.

'Oh, completely,' said Jay. 'He delivers his insults in such stately style, now.'

'He's a refined, sophisticated book,' I objected, 'and did not enjoy turning the air blue any more than we enjoyed hearing it.'

Val gave me an odd look.

'He admires and loves Ves,' said Jay. 'Ardently.'

'Apparently it's mutual.' Val's eyebrows went up.

I coughed.

So did Bill.

'Anyway,' I said brightly. 'Bill's creator?'

'I'll see what I can come up with,' Val promised.

'The name doesn't ring any bells?'

'Not quite.'

I wasn't sure what "not quite" meant in this context, but it sounded more promising than "none whatsoever." So I scooped up Jay — not Bill, unfortunately, for Val claimed him for research purposes — and whisked him off. 'It's high time we reported to Milady.'

'The gruelling climb,' Jay groaned.

'It's good for your health.'

'Tell that to my knees when I'm ninety-five.'

I pictured Jay at ninety-five, wizened and white-haired and still grumbling about the stairs. I had to laugh.

'Your sympathy is touching,' said Jay. We had by that time arrived at the first of the several flights of stairs — stone-cut, narrow and winding, naturally — that led up to Milady's aerie tower, and I laughed even harder as Jay visibly braced himself.

I did not really suspect him of deliberately hamming it up. Not until I noticed a secret half-smile just vanishing from his face as he marched away from me, moving upwards at a smart pace.

'You're teasing me,' I said with strong disapproval, and made sure to overtake him at once.

It was Jay's turn to laugh.

$$4$$

'**G**ood morning Vesper, Jay,' said Milady as she admitted us to her room. The air sparkled as her disembodied voice spoke.

'Milady.' I took up my usual station in the centre of the sumptuous blue carpet, and made her a curtsey. Jay produced the same courtly bow he'd offered to Bill earlier.

'Very fine form, Jay,' Milady complimented him.

Jay grinned. 'Thank you.'

'He's been practicing,' I said.

'He will make a fine ambassador to the Courts someday.'

That shut me up. Jay! The Society's representative at the magickal royal courts! Since I'd secretly coveted such posts for some years, I could not help feeling a twinge of envy at the idea.

'Not before you, Ves,' said Jay, apparently reading my feelings. It was so kindly said that I instantly forgave him for his earlier teasing.

'Have you ambassadorial ambitions, Ves?' said Milady.

I sighed. 'I'm a little susceptible to the glamour of the post, I can't deny it. But while I think I would suit such a post well, I would probably grow bored after a while.'

'You would, in fact,' said Jay, though whether he was referring to my assertion of being well-suited to such a job, or to my conviction that it would eventually bore me, I could not determine.

'Very well, I shall not rush to reassign you. And we cannot yet spare Jay from Acquisitions, either. What can you tell me about that terrible book?'

We told her everything about the terrible book. I personally chose to gloss over the close relationship I was beginning to enjoy with dear old Bill, but Jay had no such scruples.

Milady seemed more struck with the book's history than its present configuration. 'I am astounded,' said she when we had finished, 'that this sorceress should have faded so completely from all memory or record, considering the extent of her accomplishments. Such a book must qualify as a great artefact. In fact, I have rarely heard of so spectacular an achievement in magick. Valerie had nothing to tell you?'

'I got the impression she had some kind of an idea,' I replied. 'But too shaky an inkling to share, just yet. I've hopes of hearing something more concrete from her before long.'

'I am sure she can be relied upon to unearth something,' Milady agreed. 'As to the book...' She trailed off into silence, and Jay and I waited patiently while she thought the matter over. 'I think it had better be kept a secret, for the present,' she finally decided. 'Such a powerful object would be so highly sought after, were it known to exist — even now, we have nothing in magick to equal it! I fear there could be trouble over it.'

'Absolutely, Milady,' I said. 'We won't spread it about.'

'Should be easier to keep a lid on it, now that Bill's calmed down,' added Jay.

'Yes,' said Milady. 'There I must agree with Bill. Zareen's methods are somewhat to be deplored, but they do appear to have done the trick this time.'

'That's why we have Zareen,' I said. 'She does the questionable stuff, so most of us don't have to.'

'Not that it stops you from trying,' muttered Jay.

'Sometimes, the strangest tasks require the most difficult procedures,' Milady gracefully agreed, letting Jay's comment pass. I knew that Zareen was often given leeway on this kind of thing, more so than the rest of us. I had never resented it, because I knew it was part of her job; Toil and Trouble, indeed. She paid dearly for the privilege of *not* being decapitated for such transgressions as, say, copying famous proposals of marriage into ancient books.

'Do keep me informed,' said Milady. 'In the meantime, Ves, I understand you have some few articles withdrawn from Stores, which might wish to be replaced?'

'Er, yes.' I felt a little shame-faced. I'd gone a bit mad in the store-rooms on the last mission, and gleefully carted off all manner of shiny charms, magickal trinkets and minor artefacts. Most of which I had not even used, and I had indeed forgotten to return some of them.

I do have terrible hoarding tendencies sometimes.

'Jay,' continued Milady serenely. 'Your sister is in the development labs with Orlando. She is feeling overwhelmed, I believe, and would benefit from some family time.'

'Absolutely,' said Jay.

Knowing ourselves to be dismissed, we made our parting obeisances and left the tower, clattering back down the stairs in some relief. I'd half expected Milady to be appalled at the way we'd handled the book, and was pleased to find that we were not in disgrace.

'Your sister's with *Orlando?*' I asked Jay as we wended our way back down. 'How!'

Orlando's the Development Division's star employee, and a typical eccentric. He's an inventor, of sorts; he mixes old magick with new technology in genius-level ways, and he's responsible for some of our best tools (and weapons). He's very secretive. He lives tucked away up in the attics somewhere, and the only people who are regularly allowed to go into his workrooms are his wife, Miranda, and his assistant, Jeremy.

'She's very bright, and very talented,' said Jay with obvious pride. 'They're considering her for Orlando's new assistant.'

'New? What about Jeremy?'

'They think Orlando could do with some more help.'

Perhaps he could, at that. His inventions were so popular with the Society, I could well believe he might have trouble keeping up with the demand. 'You've a very talented family,' I observed.

Jay smiled. 'Indira will be the best of us. She's had a rough time of it lately, though. No sooner did she arrive here than she broke her arm, and now it sounds like she's homesick. I'd better go right away.'

I realised suddenly that I'd seen her already, a week or two before. Our doctor, Rob, had been tending to her. 'How did she break her arm?'

Jay grimaced. 'Fell down some stairs.'

Perhaps that explained a little of Jay's aversion to them. I filed that away. 'Isn't she a bit young to be apprenticing already? Though perhaps Milady was in a hurry to scoop her up.'

'Yes, and yes,' Jay admitted. 'Though she's older than she looks. She's almost eighteen.'

I'd thought she looked fifteen at most. I felt a surge of sympathy for her, remembering the distressed look on her youthful face when I'd seen her in the infirmary. 'That way to Orlando's secret attic hideaway,' I said a few moments later, pointing down a dark passageway that led away from the second set of stairs. 'He won't let you in, but hopefully he'll send Indira out.'

Jay gave me a salute in thanks, and wandered off. I trailed back downstairs alone, feeling oddly forlorn. Perhaps it was because I had to give up the remains of my hoard to the Stores again. I *do* so like my trinkets.

I wondered, on the way back to my room, how Bill was getting along with Val.

Swimmingly, I found. When I'd finished guiltily gathering up my temporary acquisitions and conveying them back to Stores, I trawled back to the library to find Bill holding court from the centre of Val's desk. His courtiers consisted of the entire library staff — students from research and reference, veterans from the archives, everybody. Val herself sat enthroned in her usual spot, but she looked harassed.

'Madam,' I heard Bill say as I approached. 'You do have the most delightfully smooth fingernails.'

He was addressing Anne from Archives, who blushed to match her fire-red dress and stroked Bill lovingly. 'You're so kind to say so.'

A young man I didn't recognise said: 'What about the curse of Thetford in 1453? Real or hoax?'

'Most likely a hoax,' said Bill firmly. 'The story was fabricated by a linen-weaver called Wymond Bowe, who hated his brother's wife with such a passion that he accused her of sorcery, and claimed that she had cursed the townsfolk with a host of unpleasant ailments. The evidence he presented was certainly spurious, but it is fair to note that the good people of Thetford *did* exhibit an unusually broad range of complaints during that year. There were claims in some quarters that the curse was real (or curses, I should say), and that Bowe was in fact the source of the troubles himself.'

'But you don't believe that.'

Bill considered. 'My mistress was acquainted with Bowe in some distant fashion, and did not give the story much credence.'

'This is brilliant,' said the young man, and immediately began typing furiously into his phone. He snapped Bill's picture.

'Val—' I tried to say, but she could not hear me over the clamour of Bill's audience, and I couldn't get near her either.

But Bill detected my presence, for he cried with alacrity: 'Miss Vesper! Surrounded as

I am with extraordinary beauty, still you cast all others into the shade.'

I began to wonder whether our precious book wasn't so much Bill Darcy as Bill Wickham.

I also wondered a bit about Drogryre. Had the book always been so devastatingly charming? (At least up until it came into contact with John Wester).

'Bill,' I said, pushing my way through to the desk with a brutality born of mild desperation. '*Val.* Can we please clear everyone out?'

Val looked relieved to have an excuse. 'All right, back to work!' she shouted. 'There'll be more Bill later.'

Disgruntled, but somewhat mollified by this appended promise, the library's staff drifted away, leaving me alone with Val.

'Milady wants him kept secret,' I hissed.

'It's a bit late for that order.'

'So I see.' I grimaced. 'I ought to have known Bill would cause an instant sensation.'

'He's like a search engine for magickal history, at least up until the sixteenth century. And he's got a vast deal of information that's never come to light before. Of *course* he's a sensation.'

'Not to mention his talent for flattering with sincerity.'

Bill ruffled his pages. 'It may have escaped your attention, madam, but I can hear you.'

I patted Bill's soft leather cover. 'I mean no disparagement, Bill. You're every girl's dream, aren't you?'

Bill appeared pleased with this tribute, and settled down.

'What can we do?' I said, despairing. 'Milady says there'll be trouble if word spreads, and she could well be right. Can you imagine what a book like this would fetch at auction?'

Val began to look worried. 'Spreads where, though? We might receive a few purchase offers, but I can't think who would cause trouble.'

I could think of a few possibilities, but I kept them to myself. It might never happen, and Val had clearly had a trying enough morning already. 'I'm sure it will be fine,' I said. 'Only perhaps we'll keep him under better wraps for a while.'

'We can try,' said Val.

For the rest of the afternoon, I had some of that rare, lovely stuff they call "free time." Jay didn't reappear, and my favourite activity — browsing in Stores — would put me too much in the way of temptation. So instead I spent it on my other favourite activity: browsing in the library.

With Bill. And Val. And half the rest of the Society. My esteemed colleagues kept wandering in all through the afternoon, having *just* happened to remember some vital errand they had to run in the library and which absolutely could not wait another instant... oh, is that the talking book? A quick peek? Bill, do you happen to know the recipe for Gulgorn's Palliative? It's been lost since at least the early fifteens... you do! Let me jot that down! All right, all right, I'm going. Brilliant book you have there.

This went on all day. It was of no use bleating about Milady's orders; our visitors patently did not care, and it was just as obviously too late for us to bother caring either. Oh, nobody would outright flout Milady's wishes, but it was *so* easy to come up with an excuse to stop by for five minutes, and since everyone else was doing it...?

Milady ought to have known, I thought darkly, when at last Val grew tired of this and closed the library. It was late in the evening by that time, and we had to turn people away at the door. I did not ask where Val stashed Bill for the night; I only established that it was somewhere suitably fiendish by way of security, and properly unguessable.

'You're sure nobody will find him?'

'Perfectly,' said Val wearily.

'He's behind a few stout locks, of course?'

'Of course. Will you please go to bed, Ves.'

'I'm going.' And I did, but I was back in half a minute. 'How many stout locks?'

'Several. *Go!*'

I went, but I passed an unsettled night, my head full of paranoid imaginings. See, I have never been involved with such a spectacular find before. The pressure weighed upon me rather more than I cared to admit to anybody. Upon rising the following morning, I strove to erase the signs of a poor night's rest from my face, or at least to draw attention away from them through the use of my sparkliest cosmetics.

I was accordingly a little late reaching the dining area. It's a bit school-cafeteria down there, to be honest, with great cauldrons of food lined up behind a long series of counters, and little clusters of tables spread about the floor. But they have a way of serving all my favourites — a positive feast of berries this morning, and an entire vat of yoghurt, the full-fat kind — so I don't much mind.

Jay was already seated at our usual table near the biggest window. He had Indira with him. Val was also there, and Rob, and Nell. They looked formidably as though they were holding an emergency council, which hardly seemed reasonable at that hour of the morning.

When I reached the table with my bowl of breakfast delights, I saw a newspaper spread out in the centre. They were the colour pages from the front, the headlines, and my heart sank like a stone because there in enormous letters was the announcement: 'Spectacular Find at the Society!'

And Bill's picture.

5

'Morning!' I said brightly, and slumped into the vacant chair at Jay's elbow. 'Disaster?'

'Not quite,' said Jay, and awarded me half a piece of toast slathered in peanut butter. 'Just some, uh, sub-optimal developments.'

To be honest with you, I really don't need feeding up; I'm quite comfortably proportioned as it is. But who can resist peanut butter on toast? I skipped over the question of Jay's inscrutable motives in sharing his food with me — trying not to notice that he was doing the same for Indira — and focused on the article instead. It was light on information and heavy on rumour, but it had the salient facts down: a book featuring a previously unheard of, and extremely powerful, enchantment had come to light, and stood to revolutionise the way magickal libraries operated. They had spared no efforts to promote the story to its widest extent; every page glittered with come-hither-and-read magick.

To my further dismay, there was another picture inside: Jay holding the book.

I jabbed a finger at it. 'Who took that?'

'No idea,' said Rob grimly. 'But it must have been somebody at Home.'

I glowered into my berry-bowl, and comforted myself with a spoonful of yoghurt. It was one thing for the Society's members to be a bit too seduced by the marvels of Bill to resist making a trip to see him; it was quite another to sell the story to the media, complete with photos.

'Does Milady know?' I asked.

'We're preparing a delegation,' said Rob.

Hence the leaden atmosphere at the table. We were all going to get it in the neck.

'Straight to bed, and without any supper,' I said glumly.

'A thousand lines each,' added Val. '*I must not reveal the Society's secrets to the newspapers.*'

Jay said, 'How long before we get the swarms of reporters beating down the doors?'

'No need to worry about that,' said Rob. 'The House is pretty hard to find, if you're not familiar with the route.'

Jay looked sceptical. 'Journalists have a way of getting around problems like that.'

Val set down her mostly-empty coffee cup with a snap. 'One disaster at a time, if you please.'

'Sorry,' said Jay, contrite. 'Milady first, reporters later.'

· · • • · • • · · ·

The first person dragooned into the role of peace envoy was Nell, seeing as she is our media co-ordinator and suchlike. I don't actually know what her official job title is, if she even has one. She manages a lot of our technical requirements — she's spent decades building a huge database of basically everything we know that we know, and her team fixes all the tech bits that go wrong. She's also responsible for our internet presence (such as it is), which means our website and social media. That makes her our PR person, right? She'll be spending half of *her* morning putting together the kind of press release that puts out fires, or so we hope.

The second person volunteered for duty was yours truly.

'You're so good at it, Ves,' said Nell, fidgeting with her glasses. She had a second pair tucked into the coiffed coils of her grey hair; did she know? Apparently I was not the only person feeling wrong-footed by the events of the night.

'What, exactly, am I good at?' I said, trying not to sound quite so frosty as I felt.

'Making things sound good,' said Nell bluntly.

'Charming people,' muttered Jay.

'Persuading Milady to let you off,' said Rob, though since he teamed his comment with a smile of genuine affection I felt less like kicking him than I did the others.

'You talk a good talk, Ves,' Val said, arranging herself upon the side of my enemies without a trace of apology. 'It's one of your talents.'

'Lucky me,' I muttered.

I looked at Indira, in case she wanted to join in with the stone-throwing. But she stared back at me with big, guarded eyes and said nothing at all.

She looked, to my horror, as though she were more frightened of *me* than the rest of us were of Milady-in-anger.

I set that problem aside.

'Fine,' I said, magnificently gracious. 'Your poor, beleaguered Ves will sally forth and take a few bullets while the rest of you... what?'

'Review security,' said Rob.

'Figure out what in the world to do with Bill,' Val put in.

I looked at Jay, who shrugged. 'I'll come with you.'

'What? Voluntarily?'

'Why not?'

I narrowed my eyes. 'You've seen how hard everybody else worked to get out of this.'

'Except you.'

'I've been betrayed by my own troops, sent forth as sacrificial victim—'

'But with backup.'

I smiled, rather touched. 'That's kind. *So* kind I'd even give you that toast back, if I hadn't already eaten it.'

Jay wrinkled his nose. 'Er, no need to go to extraordinary lengths.'

In the event, Milady wasn't even angry. But she was extremely alarmed, which was far worse.

'Tell me everything,' she ordered, when Nell and Jay and I had trailed into her tower-top room and stood lined up on the carpet like a row of naughty children.

We did, though not in any coherent fashion. Milady listened to our fragmented account of the previous day's happenings in a taut silence that I found excessively uncomfortable. When we arrived at the developments of the morning, and held up the newspaper for her perusal, the air practically vibrated with tension.

When at last we stopped talking over each other, interpolating corrections upon each other's narratives and generally confusing everything, Milady went so long without speaking that I began to wonder whether we'd lost her altogether.

At last, she spoke, and though her words emerged in her usual crisp fashion, and with every appearance of total composure, I could hear a note of something else lying behind them; something like fear. 'While I appreciate Rob's confidence in the elusiveness of this house, and his no doubt excellent efforts to assure our security within it, I must disagree with his conclusions. You are quite right, Jay: those with a strong enough motive to find us will surely contrive a way. That goes for reporters, and some other, rather more unsavoury characters as well. It is my conviction that this troublesome book must be taken out of the House at once, and conveyed to a safer spot.'

That caused a little stir. I exchanged a foreboding look with Jay, who looked as worried as I felt.

'Jay, as our Waymaster, you are able to carry the book farther and faster than anybody else. I encourage you to choose a destination entirely at random; that way, it will be harder for others to guess the book's location, and all but impossible for anyone to follow in any timely fashion. Do not linger at any henges. Take Ves with you; she is a woman of significant resources and will be able to resolve any difficulties that arise.

'Nell, it falls to you to make a suitable announcement. By all means, confirm the find; it is too late to hope to deceive anyone on that score. Don't try to play down either its significance or potential. What I want you to do is to mention, as casually as you can, that the book is no longer at Home. I am not at all concerned what excuse you come up with to explain its removal, provided only that it is unexceptionable. The more mundane, the better. I would not have anybody coming *here* expecting to find that book, nor do I wish it to be known that we are expecting exactly such an attempt.'

This barrage of instructions left all three of us a little stunned. I, being Ves the Glib (apparently) recovered my wits first, and said: 'Forgive me, Milady, but why *are* we expecting such an attempt?' I mean, I'd had no trouble grasping Bill's importance to the magickal communities of Britain, but Milady was talking as though serious trouble was not only likely but inevitable.

Her response was swift, crisp and disdainful. 'Ves. Nell. You have been with us long enough to be only too aware that we are not the only organisation in this country with an interest in ancient magickal artefacts. And you are as well aware that they do not all operate upon the same motives.'

'Chancers, rogues and thieves, the lot of them,' I murmured for Jay's benefit.

'Quite,' said Milady. 'Not all of our rival organisations can fairly be described in such terms, of course, but one or two of them can. In particular, you may have heard rumours of a new group calling themselves Ancestria Magicka.'

Jay choked. 'Really?!'

'I've heard of them,' I confirmed, rolling my eyes. 'Treasure hunters, the worst kind. No respect for heritage. Pirates, if you will.'

'Snappy name,' muttered Jay.

'Formed last year, they have swiftly grown in both power and ambition. I have not made it generally known across the Society, but since January of this year there have been three known attempts by members of Ancestria Magicka to infiltrate our House. They were all foiled by the efforts of Rob Foster and his excellent team, and we do not yet know what, precisely, was their goal. Was it espionage? Theft? And more importantly, have there been other attempts that were successful enough to escape detection altogether?

'The news that somebody from among our own ranks has been responsible for giving news and photographs to the press is a matter of some concern to me. It might have been done thoughtlessly, or it might have been the product of something much more reprehensible. The House itself may be able to provide some information upon this point, and I shall investigate that possibility as soon as possible. But in the meantime, I cannot feel that the book is as safe here as I would like. Its presence here is an open invitation to Ancestria Magicka, and to any other group with similar ambitions. Are there any questions?'

Jay said, 'How long do I have to dance about the country with Bill?'

'You'll be notified when it is safe to return, or you may be called upon to hand off the book to somebody else. You will receive information, Jay.'

'Right.'

'Er,' I said. 'When you spoke of my "resolving difficulties", what exactly did you have in mind?'

'I hardly know, Ves, but Jay's picture with the book has been helpfully spread around, hasn't it? I do not know whether his status as Waymaster is broadly known outside of the Society, but it may well be. It is not impossible that somebody may guess, therefore, what we would do with the book, and come for you. That is why I advise staying away from the henges.'

'In that case I'd like Rob with us, really,' I said, though with only faint hope.

'I cannot spare Rob at this time. He is needed here. But consider yourself approved to take whatever you want from Stores. I know that will please you.'

It did, for I was rarely given so complete a carte blanche. *Whatever I want* meant anything at all, up to and including the shiniest, most powerful toys.

'I want a wand,' I said.

'Take the Sunstone.'

· · · · ●·●· · ·

The Sunstone Wand is one of the Society's prizes. It is a beautiful object, made from spangled Norwegian sunstone all fitted up with silver filigree (well, it *was* made in the nineteenth century, and they were not known for their restrained sense of the aesthetic). It is shorter than you might expect. The long, thin, delicate wands of popular imagination are lovely to look at, but hard to carry around without getting them broken. The Sunstone Wand was made to be used, not just admired, so it is only about a foot in length, and sturdy at half an inch thick.

Wands are popular for channelling magickal energies in all manner of useful ways, but a real wand — the kind you spell with a capital W — is a rare and fine thing indeed. *Those* Wands are made from pure crystal, crafted by a master Spellwright, and they tend to be heirlooms.

I presented myself at Stores in a state of such anticipation I was forgetting to breathe.

This time, Ornelle was there.

'Back already?' said she, eyeing me with the kind of suspicion I have in *no* way deserved.

I eyed her right back. Ornelle's one of the few trolls regularly employed by the Society (most of the others are cooks). She's splendidly sized and invariably splendidly dressed, with a penchant for big, dangly jewellery. A fellow magpie, she's been in charge of Stores for years, and she is ferociously protective of the contents.

I usually try to slip by when she's not there.

'Milady sent me for supplies,' I said, and tried (futilely) to make my short self look just a little bit taller.

'All right.' Ornelle slipped on a pair of bejewelled glasses and took up a clipboard. She proceeded to escort me every step of the way, and made notes about everything I took up. Infuriating. I may sometimes be slow about bringing things back but I'm not a *thief.*

She made some difficulty about the Wand.

'You need the Sunstone again?' There was an offensive emphasis on the word *again*.

'Again!' I echoed in outrage. 'I've only had it once before and that was three years ago!'

'And it took you almost six weeks to bring it back.'

'I needed it for a while.'

'And this time?'

'I don't know. I'm being sent out into the wilds of Britain with a protégé and an artefact to protect, not to mention my own hide. It might take some time.'

Ornelle wanted to make trouble, I could see that she did. But for all that she sometimes distrusts me, she knows I wouldn't outright make up an order from Milady. Who would be mad enough to do that? The truth will always out.

She wrote down: "Sunstone Wand to Cordelia Ves" in big, blocky letters and underlined it, with the date written beside.

When I made to leave, she blocked my way. 'Vesper,' she said very seriously.

'Ornelle.'

'If anything untoward happens to that Wand, I'm repossessing everything you've ever been given.'

Everything? 'You mean like my tea cup?' It's enchanted. Gives a different flavour of tea every time.

'Like your tea cup.'

'And the Curiosity that does my hair?'

'Everything.'

I gulped. 'I will defend it with my life.'

I didn't need such an admonition, of course — we would all defend artefacts like the Sunstone Wand with our lives. That's what we're for. But Ornelle required reassurance, and apparently felt pacified.

'Best of luck,' she said as she cleared out of my way.

I wasn't sure whether she was talking to me or the Wand, but I answered anyway. 'Thanks.'

6

Jay was waiting for me down in the Waymastery Station. I don't suppose anybody else calls it that but me, but it's what it is. Unprepossessing, for all its exalted purpose: just a tiny room in the cellar, unpainted and virtually unfurnished. There's an ancient henge under the floor, and that's what Jay uses to whizz us about.

He had a small shoulder bag with him, which he opened when I came in. I took a peek inside, and saw a cloth-wrapped bundle snugly nestled within.

'Bill?' I ventured.

'Bill,' Jay confirmed.

I patted the bag I carried over my own shoulders. 'I've got your stuff.' Change of clothes, life-saving magickal artefacts, the usual. Indira had dutifully packed up his personal things and left them out for me, while Jay was off securing the book. I could well imagine his task was not an easy one; nobody wanted to see Bill go, and he had to try to squirrel him away without anybody noticing besides. Anyone but Val, that is.

'Ready?' I said, watching Jay's face. He looked worried. A heavy frown creased his brow, and he couldn't stand still.

'Absolutely,' he said, fidgeting with the strap of his bag.

'Except?'

The frown deepened. 'I'm worried about Indira.'

'She'll be fine. It's not like there's an army of orcs marching upon the House, or anything.'

'I'm worried about what happens to her if anything happens to me.'

Oh. 'Er, that's a bit doomy,' I tried. 'We're not in mortal danger.'

'Then why the Sunstone?'

'*Bill* is in mortal danger.' I said this in a whisper, hoping that the book was too well wrapped-up to hear me. '*We* aren't.'

'She's shy. It's hard for her to manage without me.'

'Even for a week or two? She needs to stand on her own feet sometime, Jay, or she'll never be independent.'

He scowled at that; I'd irritated him. 'Let's go, anyway.'

'If I may be permitted my opinion,' said Bill, his voice doubly muffled by the cloth wrappings and the bag. 'The little Spellwright is in no danger, either of harm or mortification.'

'How do you know?' said Jay snappishly.

'She and I have had conversation together. I found her to be bright-minded, and more resilient than elder brothers are inclined to imagine.'

The fact that Bill and Indira had been chatting together was news to me, though perhaps not to Jay, for he just gave me a sideways look and then went on with his preparations to leave. 'I hope you're right,' he said to Bill. I have no idea what he does when he's making ready to use the Ways, so I just stand back and try to keep out of his way.

A breeze picked up in the room, and began to build. 'Off we go,' said Jay, and held out a hand to me.

I took it. Since I met Jay, I have had a little practice at travelling the Ways. Enough to know that it is a disorienting experience, and can leave a person feeling unpleasantly shaken up in the middle. It appears to have an even greater impact upon Jay, but he went about his work with an enviable composure, and betrayed no further signs of unease.

I do wish he had warned me before departure, however. Last time, we had waited until the Winds of the Ways had gathered themselves to quite a height before we set off. This time, the breeze had barely doubled in strength. There I was, tranquil enough yet in the expectation of its being a few more minutes before we would be going anywhere—

—and then I was away, tossing about in the wind like a miserable little leaf and clinging fiercely to Jay while the currents rattled my teeth and did awful things to my hair.

When the winds died down, they left us marooned on top of a low hill looking out over an expanse of drab fields. Stone monuments rose around us, which at first glance I took to be your typical ancient megalithic arrangement — except that, at a second look, the stones looked oddly new.

'I forgot to ask where you were taking us,' I said, a little breathless.

'Milton Keynes.' Jay sat cross-legged upon the ground in a pose of studied nonchalance, and looked around with more apparent satisfaction than I was feeling.

'Milton Keynes.' I got to my feet and took a couple of breaths, waiting until my knees steadied.

'Yes.'

'But *why*.'

'Because of all the places you and I might heroically flee with a magickal book, who'd ever think of Milton Keynes?'

Who indeed. 'And what in the name of Milady's garters is this?' I flicked a finger at the nearest lovely, smooth stone.

'A new henge.'

'*A new henge?*'

'It isn't their age that makes them effective, you know.' Jay picked himself up with some care, and squared his shoulders. 'Built last decade. Part of the city plan.'

One of the hazards of my trade: a tendency to start making overly simplified and accordingly fallible suppositions, for example: the older, the better. 'I suppose it's about as reasonable as putting in a train station.'

Jay's lips quirked in a smile. 'If only there were a few more Waymasters to make use of them. Somebody had dewy-eyed ideas about training up a lot more of us.'

'Can't manufacture that kind of talent.'

'Apparently not. You okay?'

'Of course!' If Jay was determined to be Totally Fine then so was I. I looked around at the uninspiring landscape, and hoisted my bag higher upon my shoulder. 'What now?'

'I don't know. Fancy a cup of tea?'

'Last one to the cafe's a rotten egg.' I began to totter down the hill.

'Which cafe?'

'Any!'

But my phone buzzed before I was more than halfway down the hill, and I hastily grabbed it.

'Ves?' said Val. 'Are you all right?'

'Perfectly. Why wouldn't I be?'

'And Jay?'

I looked round to check, if it would make Val happy, and saw Jay wandering down the hill some way behind me, hands in the pockets of his ever-present leather jacket. 'He's fine. Val, what's the matter?'

Val exhaled in a way that filled me with an unreasonable foreboding. How could I be so unsettled by a sigh? 'Milady had me pull up everything we know about Ancestria Magicka, which proved to be embarrassingly little. So then she had me go comb the world for every new scrap of information I could find — in fact she put the entire library staff on it, and—'

'Val, the suspense is killing me.'

'Sorry. Ves, they have a Waymaster.'

I almost dropped the phone. 'What? How's that possible?'

'Imported her from Hungary. She's been on the job only slightly longer than Jay, but she knows her stuff. Graduate from a top magickal university, comes highly recommended, entire bidding war to employ her. Etc. I'm sending pics. Her name's Katalin Pataki.'

'And you think they'll send her after us.'

'Well, wouldn't you? Why did they go to such lengths to get a Waymaster on the staff, if not for occasions like this?'

'They can't possibly know where we are, though, can they? Jay picked a destination at random, like Milady said. What are they going to do, travel to every single henge in the entire British Isles looking for us?'

'Ves, I don't have time to convey everything I've lately learned about this lot, but I'd advise against underestimating them. They may be new, but they've already got Milady worried.'

Curses. 'Thanks, Val.'

'Be careful.'

I checked the pictures and then put my phone away, a variety of thoughts flitting across my mind. Who *were* these people? They had gone pretty far afield in search of a Waymaster, and poured buckets of money into securing one. Why?

And if they had those kinds of resources to throw around after less than a year... who the hell was funding them?

'Jay,' I said when he reached me. 'We may have a problem.'

'Another one?'

I relayed Val's news, but Jay did not react as I'd expected. He thought for a moment, frowning deeply, and then said: 'A bidding war?'

'That's what she said.'

'A *bidding war*?' He looked thunderstruck. 'You know, my parents told me not to take the first offer I received. They *told* me.'

'So why did you?'

'The Society's legend. How could I refuse?'

'Then it's no good regretting that your salary isn't higher. Can we talk about this later?'

'Right.' Jay shook himself and began to march off, heading for who-knew-where, but after a few paces he slowed again. 'Was Bill under guard all night?'

'No idea. Ask Bill.'

Jay began to root furiously through his bag, and at last extracted the book, stripped of its cloth wrapping. 'Bill, have you been left alone at any time in the past twelve hours or so?'

'No, sir!' said Bill brightly. 'I have been very much admired, and without pause, ever since the news of my existence was gratifyingly taken up.'

'By whom?' I said, warily.

'Oh, by everyone! My acquaintance has expanded enormously.'

'Did anyone tamper with you?' said Jay.

'Decidedly not!' said Bill, outraged at the very idea.

But Jay was not satisfied, and neither was I. 'The problem with Orlando,' he said, turning Bill around in his hands, 'is that he's sometimes too clever by half. Those pearl-things you've got, for example; even a non-magicker could use them. A potent spell perfectly encapsulated inside something inoffensive; no particular skill required to use it, and therefore no discernible trace left for a paranoid Waymaster to discern, or even a touchy, overly talkative grimoire of a book...' As he spoke he was inspecting Bill's covers and turning over page after page, ignoring the book's protests that he was a grimoire of enormous ability and no one could conceal a spell between his own pages and hope to escape detection.

'Ah,' said Jay then, and took up something that sparkled when he held it up to the afternoon sunlight. It was round, and about an inch across; pale and translucent, so much so that I wondered Jay had spotted it at all. The kind of thing, in short, that no one would much take note of. If you didn't know better, you might have said it was some kind of sticker, or a patch, or perhaps a bookmark.

'That's a tracker spell,' I gasped. I had seen them before. Orlando's technicians craft a lot of them, and they're wildly popular across the Society. These aren't the type of thing even a non-magicker could use, but they're among the simplest of charms to manipulate, requiring only a trickle of magick.

Jay tossed it to me. It lay in my palm, warm and faintly buzzing.

I dropped it at once.

'We'd better go.' Jay spoke tersely, already packing Bill away into his bag again.

'My most abject apologies!' Bill was babbling as Jay closed the bag upon him. 'I had no notion—'

'Not your fault, Bill,' I said. 'You've been out of the game for four centuries.' I was looking around as I spoke, as though I expected some kind of obvious course of action to occur to me if I moved my neck and blinked enough.

Blank mind. Palpitating heart. Not good.

'It doesn't matter where we go as long as we go *quickly*,' said Jay, and departed at a jog.

But he was too late, for a flicker of movement atop the hill caught my eye. I stopped, squinting against the light. What was it, a bird? Or worse?

'*Ves!*' yelled Jay behind me.

It was not a bird. A woman stood up there, her figure indistinct in the distance, but I could discern enough to be sure. She matched the photos Val had sent: tall, a shade too thin, long dark hair.

She had a man with her, too. He was holding what looked unpromisingly like a Wand.

I turned tail, and ran like a rabbit after Jay.

By the time I reached Jay, I was already scrambling to retrieve my syrinx pipes. Rooting around inside your own underwear is an inelegant business, but I had not the leisure to care just then. *Why* do the damned things have to wriggle around so much in there? It's not like there is much room to manoeuvre; I cannot be said to be incapable of properly filling out a brassiere.

Fortunately, Jay has observed this process before.

'Behind us!' I panted, and then wished I had not, for Jay took one look and sped up into a proper sprint, and soon began to draw away from me.

'*Stop!*' I yelled. 'We can't outrun them, idiot!' They were gaining on us already, not least because Katalin, curse her, had legs about three times as long as mine.

There — I had it. My fingers touched metal, and I drew out my tiny silver pipes, warm from their snug little hiding place. I set them to my lips and played an urgent melody, no easy task while I was still moving.

Jay didn't stop, but he did slow down. 'How long does it usually take Addie to—'

He didn't need to finish the sentence because Adeline, my beauty, was already whistling down from the skies, her silvery-white coat glittering in the sun. Addie, a rare winged unicorn, and my friend of some years.

'I asked her to hurry,' I said and ran forward to meet her. I was up on her back in seconds and ruthlessly hauled Jay up behind me. Catching hold of the silver rope she's kind enough to wear, I gasped, 'Away, Addie! Doesn't matter where, so long as it's fast.'

She leapt, her huge wings flapping, and we were airborne. Jay clung to me with one arm and clutched Bill with the other, while I kept my anxious gaze upon Katalin and her companion.

'Oh, no...' I muttered after a moment.

'What!' yelled Jay.

'That man! He's got a Wand and he's... yes, I really think he's going to—'

A missile like a tiny, crackling lightning bolt shot past my nose. 'He *is*!' I gasped, outraged.

'They're *shooting at us*?' Jay shouted.

I was too busy scrabbling for my Sunstone to reply.

'What was that you were saying about not being in mortal danger?!'

'I acknowledge myself mistaken upon that point.' I had the Wand out by that time, and as Addie gathered herself and put on an extra burst of speed, I mustered my wits, my resolve and my magick and sent an answering shot back. Then several more for good measure; I *was* feeling a trifle irritated.

I had the satisfaction of seeing Katalin's companion drop his Wand and go on the retreat, arms raised.

My next missile hit him in the stomach, and he dropped.

'Hah!' I crowed, arms raised. 'It's victory for the Sunstone Team!'

'Don't celebrate too early,' cautioned Jay, which was not unreasonable of him, but quite unnecessary. Addie was flying like a bolt of lightning herself by that time, and the two Ancestria Magicka agents soon diminished into tiny, indeterminate specks and disappeared from sight.

I glanced down at the city of Milton Keynes spread out below us. 'Miserable spot, but there's probably some good tea down there somewhere.'

Jay shook his head. 'Too close. We'd better fly on a while.'

Addie bore us generally west. We passed over a number of villages, and when the larger sprawl of Buckingham (thank you, phone) came into view we decided to land.

That part is always tricky; where to come down that's sufficiently discreet? It's always inconvenient when local papers start reporting unicorn sightings. But Addie's far cleverer than I and found us a tree-shaded spot a short walk from the outskirts of the town.

I checked her carefully to make sure she hadn't been hit. She was unharmed, but she was also displeased with me.

'Sorry,' I told her, shame-faced. 'I did not expect to come up against a lightning-throwing Wand-wielding sidekick.'

We left her drinking her fill from a charming river, her silvery sides heaving with exertion. There was plenty of grass about for her to snack upon, and better yet, some tasty-looking spring flowers.

I kissed her nose before we wandered off. 'Best unicorn ever.'

Addie flicked her ears at me, and decisively bit through a sunny narcissus flower. The first of many, I had no doubt.

'Eat them all!' I encouraged as we walked off. 'You've earned them!'

'You're a terrible unicorn parent,' was Jay's verdict upon my behaviour. 'She'll be sick if she eats all those flowers.'

'How do you know?'

Jay had no answer to that.

We found a tea-room in Buckingham and partook liberally of its finest beverages (and a cake or two. How could I help it, when they were serving carrot cake *and* Victoria sponge?). The first thing Jay did (after gulping down a liberal quantity of reviving tea) was to take out Bill and comb through his pages more minutely than before. 'Try not to get too chatty, Bill,' he said in an undertone. 'The people here would be more horrified than charmed by a talking book.'

'Non-magickers?' Bill whispered.

'I'm afraid so.'

There were not many people besides us, thankfully: a pair of elderly ladies having afternoon tea at a window table, and a middle-aged man in a suit drinking coffee and reading a newspaper. None of them paid us the smallest attention.

I could still wish Bill's whisper somewhat less penetrating. 'Am I correct in supposing that I was almost absconded with a little while ago?' he demanded.

'Quite incorrect,' I said with dignity. 'We rescued you in the nick of time.'

'I am glad to hear it. I should not like to fall again into the hands of villainy.'

It took me a moment to remember what he meant by *again*: John Wester, of course, with his grave-robbing tendencies.

While Jay was thus employed, I called Val, and informed her in hushed tones of everything that had happened.

'Crap,' she said, succinctly.

'It was, rather. But we're fine.'

'I'll tell Milady. In light of what you've just said, I doubt she will object to sending Rob after you.'

'I wouldn't mind some help,' I admitted.

'Keep me informed of your whereabouts.'

'Will do.' I hung up.

'I don't see any more tracking charms,' Jay said, and handed Bill off to me. 'Want to check as well?'

I did so, enjoying the feel of Bill's exquisite vellum pages under my hands. They don't make books like that anymore. I reached the end without finding anything untoward, either; but that brought me face-to-face with John Wester's clumsily-sketched map and its label: Drogryre.

I handed Bill back to Jay, thinking. 'Why did John Wester want to find that grave?' I mused aloud. 'Specifically? Bill says he's an opportunist, but he must have had some reason to fix upon that particular spot.'

Jay opened his mouth, but blinked and hesitated. 'Er,' he said.

'Right? Why did he think there was something valuable in there with her?'

'Sometimes people were buried with valuable objects?' suggested Jay.

'That might be it, if she was wealthy. Was she, Bill?'

'Not particularly. My erstwhile mistress did achieve some modicum of prosperity by the end of her life, due to her being in increasingly high demand. But she began destitute, and never arrived at anything that might be termed wealth.'

I frowned. 'So why did Wester think her grave was so important?'

'Are you sure it's her grave that's marked here, Bill?' said Jay, tapping the heavily-inked X with one finger.

'Quite certain. He spoke of it endlessly.'

Reminded of the early journal entries, Jay flipped back to the front of the book. But he was soon obliged to abandon his efforts to make it out, and gave it instead to me.

I saw his problem at once. Neither of us had yet had chance to take a close look at those entries; once we had realised how precious Bill was himself, the scribblings of a thief like Wester had ceased to seem important. I now saw that Wester's musings were written in a style of English which predated anything we might consider easily comprehensible; virtually Chaucerian, in fact. And his handwriting was abominable.

'Of course it's Middle English,' I said with a sigh. 'Zareen said as much. I can read it, but not easily, and not here.'

'We shouldn't linger here any longer, either,' said Jay. 'The trackers may be gone but Katalin and Co. saw the direction we were heading in, and we aren't that far from Milton Keynes.'

I agreed to this without much regret, having finished my tea and sustenance some time since. We packed up and left. I considered retrieving Addie and flying onward, but there were a few objections to that idea, not the least of which was that she was already unhappy with me. So we got on a bus, and spent the rest of the day dawdling dully from town to town by way of a series of rattling, pootling old vehicles. It was quite peaceful, considering the events of earlier in the day, and since nobody showed up to try to wrest Bill from us, neither Jay nor I had any real complaints.

We ended up at a bed-and-breakfast in a town called Quainton, dined in true British fashion upon fish and chips, and then fell asleep in front of my TV.

I woke up just before dawn, and was pleased to note that Jay did not appear to be prone to snoring.

I woke again an hour or two later to find he had unsprawled himself from the other side of my bed and gone back to his own, leaving me in full possession of all the space. This pleased me.

The fact that he had taken Bill with him did not please me nearly so much, as it ruined my plans of having a private chat with the book. I wanted to examine him some more on the topic of Drogryre, her life, and especially her death, in case he should be able to shed any more light on the activities of John Wester. That would have to wait.

I wandered down for breakfast, half expecting to find Jay already there; he was usually an early riser, like me. But I was served with cereal, yoghurt, toast and eggs alone, despite the fact that it was well past eight o' clock.

I took my tea upstairs and tapped upon Jay's door.

No answer.

'Jay?' I put my ear to the door, but heard nothing.

I tried the handle, and finding the door unlocked (... not good), I went in.

No Jay. He was not in the bathroom, either.

What *was* still there was all of his belongings — except for Bill. The shoulder-bag stood empty of book; even the cloth wraps were gone. His favourite leather jacket, the dark one so well-loved its cuffs and collar were scuffed, hung over one of the brass bed-posts.

I stood a moment in growing horror, trying to convince myself that there was some plausible, non-terrifying explanation for the dual and unscheduled absence of both Jay and Bill.

There was not, of course.

8

I ran downstairs.

The landlady only confirmed my worst fears: she had seen nothing of Jay all morning, not a peep since yesterday evening. She had not heard anything in the night that might have sounded suspiciously like a break-in by magickal marauders; but then, neither had I. At dawn, Jay had been sleeping comfortably in front of a desultorily flickering television. A couple of hours later, he'd vanished.

I stood in Jay's abandoned room, dithering like a ninny while my mind turned in confused circles. These are the moments in life when one would wish to be a picture of unflappable resolve, brimming with self-confidence and perfectly clear upon the best course of action. My brain would only consent to ask foolish questions. *Where was Jay?* No way to tell. *Why had he gone?* Well, he probably hadn't stepped out for coffee without his jacket, wallet or keys.

Then Rob showed up.

I was informed of his presence when my landlady — a mild retiree with a taste for forties fashions — stood diffidently on the tiny landing outside our rooms and called: 'Dear? There is a gentleman to see you.'

I thought first of Katalin's mysterious sidekick, and marched downstairs with my Wand in my hand, ready to wrest Jay from him by hook or by crook. But of course, the man patiently awaiting me in the hall was Rob. He was looking extra forbidding: with his dark frame swathed in even darker clothes, no wonder my landlady had seemed a bit nervous. He looked like the riot police, or maybe an assassin.

'No!' I yelped when I saw him, and stopped, frozen, two-thirds of the way down the stairs. 'Go away!'

'Morning, Ves,' said Rob, unperturbed. 'Why?'

'Because when I tell you what's happened you'll have to kill me.'

'I might kill *somebody*,' Rob allowed — not at all to the reassurance of my poor landlady, who was, at that moment, creeping past us into the safety of her living-room. 'But never you. What's the matter?'

'I've lost the book.' I sat down heavily upon the stairs and clutched at my hair, whose jaunty pink colour seemed quite inappropriate just then.

Rob didn't move. 'That is unfortunate.'

'*And* I've lost Jay.'

That gave him greater pause. He blinked, uttered, 'Ah,' and fell silent.

'Just make it quick,' I pleaded. 'I probably deserve to suffer, but I haven't the courage.'

Rob came forward and extended a hand. Reluctantly, I allowed myself to be hauled back to my feet. 'Calm, Ves,' he said, more kindly than I felt I deserved. 'It isn't your fault.'

'Of course it is! If I wasn't responsible for keeping them safe then who was?'

'Jay is not helpless.'

'He's never been sent out by himself yet. I'm here because I'm supposed to be competent. Milady said I could be relied upon to handle any "difficulties" that "might happen to arise"! And I haven't! I was *asleep*, and Jay was hauled off like a sack of potatoes!'

'Not necessarily.'

'What do you mean, not necessarily? That is *clearly* the case.'

Rob made no reply, exactly. He only said, 'Jay is clever,' which did not appear to relate to anything. 'Tell me what's happened.'

I brought him up to speed with as much detail as I could manage, finishing with, 'I don't even know how they found us in this wretched—' I broke off as a horrible idea occurred to me. I did not pause to explain; I merely turned and high-tailed it back up the stairs.

Jay's jacket. I all but tore it off the bedpost and rummaged through the pockets. Lots of detritus came out; I have too much respect for Jay's dignity to describe every article of it.

And there. At the bottom of his left pocket, hidden under a crumpled-up handkerchief, was a tiny round sparkling thing: one of Orlando's tracker charms.

'*Crap.*'

Rob had come in behind me. I handed it off to him without another word, and began to pace. How had it failed to occur to me to check Jay's clothes? Or my own! If someone had got close enough to Bill to stick a tracking-charm on him, it wasn't so far-fetched to imagine that the same someone might have done something similar to Jay. According to the news, at least, he was both the discoverer and the keeper of the precious book.

I engaged in a hasty scout of my own attire, courtesy of my lovely spangled Sunstone. It was a rather menial duty for such a magnificent heirloom, but the Wand was remarkably effective at detecting magick. I came up with nothing, or nothing besides the usual: the charmed ring I wear that adjusts the colour of my hair, the spell that keeps ladders from forming in my tights, that kind of thing. No trackers.

'I suppose they only wanted Jay,' I said, stashing the Wand.

'I wonder why.' Rob had gone quiet and tense in that focused way he has, and was examining the contents of Jay's abandoned room like a police detective. He called somebody. 'We have a mole at Home,' he said into it, tersely. 'Someone got a tracker-charm onto Jay, as well as the book, and they're both missing. Vesper's unharmed. Tell Milady.'

I began to feel calmer. Rob has that effect: he's completely unflappable.

So am I, usually, or at least more so. But I'd never lost a priceless artefact and a protégé in one day before.

'Where is the nearest henge?' said Rob next.

I caught his train of thought at once. 'Yes! They'd want to whisk off right away, wouldn't they? The easiest thing would probably be to go back to Milton Keynes.' I could not say this with any great certainty; I am after all legendary for my inability to find my way around.

Rob delicately refrained from saying this, though he did take the precaution of checking my theory on his phone. 'Milton Keynes it is,' he said, and fell to gathering up Jay's things. 'Let's go.'

I whistled up Addie again, and one of her friends, too — a sturdy stallion Rob's ridden before. We made the trip back to Milton Keynes' shiny new henge in record time, but we were still too late. The hilltop was a grey, empty space, an overcast morning and my disappointed hopes combining to render it a desolate scene.

We waited a full hour, just in case we had somehow managed to beat Jay's abductors to the site. But nobody came.

Rob was on his phone for a fair bit of this time, conveying the news to, and receiving advice from, various members of the Society. At length — bored, probably, of watching me hop anxiously about the hilltop like a rabbit on speed — he collected me up and escorted me kindly down the hill again. 'We're going Home,' he said, a shade grimly.

'How?'

'The boring way. By train.'

'What does Milady say?'

'Nothing about the immediate evisceration of one Cordelia Vesper, if that's what you mean.'

I heaved a small, inward sigh of relief. 'And what else?'

'Theories abound as to why Jay's vanished with the book, and—'

'Don't say it like that,' I begged, feeling compelled to interrupt. 'You make it sound like Jay thieved the book and ran.'

'Well, one or two people who dislike Jay are saying more or less that. But nobody who knows him would imagine it possible.'

'Who could dislike Jay?!'

'His unique skills put him in a powerful position, and power will always attract enemies.'

'Haters,' I muttered. I wondered suddenly whether Indira had heard the news. I hoped not, yet; much as I was at fault, I would rather tell her about her brother's disappearance myself. That way, I could make sure she was all right. Wherever he was, Jay would be worrying something awful about her.

'Milady's had Val researching Ancestria Magicka for the past two days,' Rob continued. 'She's now got the entire Research and Library Division on it, and has thrown them a lot of extra resources, to boot. She's confident they will soon come up with something that will help us to help Jay.'

'And Bill.'

'And Bill, though Jay is the Society's priority.'

I hoped this was because he's brilliant rather than because he's the first Waymaster we've had in nearly a decade.

'Also,' Rob added. 'Val said: Tell Ves to stop fussing.'

'Fussing?'

'Running around like a headless chicken.'

'I hope you told her that I am the very picture of cool composure, as always.'

Rob gave me a sideways look. 'Why would I ever tell her anything else?'

I patted his arm. 'I love you.'

'I know.'

· · · · ● · ● · · · ·

When we arrived Home a few hours later, we went straight up to Milady's tower — the quick way. And by that I mean that House itself appeared to have got caught up in the sense of urgency Jay's vanishment had caused and gave us a lift straight up to the top. We went from the entrance hall to Milady's tower-top room in one step.

'Thank you, House,' I murmured. House and I have had a little conversation together before. I would not presume to call us friends, but we've been introduced, and one would never expect to sweep by an acquaintance unacknowledged.

'It's good to see you are well, Ves,' Milady greeted me.

I curtsied. 'I was in no danger, for they did not appear to want me.'

'An interesting point to note, indeed. Thank you for fetching her back so promptly, Rob. What have you both to report?'

'Nothing new,' Rob answered. 'We were not able to catch up with Katalin Pataki or her colleague, nor did we discover any clues as to Jay's whereabouts.'

'Is there any evidence that Pataki is behind the theft and kidnapping?'

'No solid evidence, though considering the encounter Jay and Ves had with those two yesterday, it seems too obvious a conclusion to be discounted.'

'I cannot disagree. Ves, I'd like you to go directly to Valerie, if you please. She may already have useful information to convey, and if not, your research skills will no doubt be wanted.'

'Yes, ma'am.'

'An attempt to recover Jay, and also the book, must be made very soon. I have sent envoys to Ancestria Magicka already in hopes of securing Jay's swift release by diplomatic means, if not the return of the book. But I cannot hold out much hope of its success; they are likely to meet only with a total denial of any involvement whatsoever. Therefore, our methods must be more direct.'

'Please tell me I am to be part of the team,' I said.

'I would not dream of excluding you, Ves. You will be very much needed.'

Phew.

'You also, Rob.'

Double phew. 'Is the identity of our traitor yet known?'

Milady's voice turned cold. 'Not yet.'

'It could be someone from Research.'

'And Valerie therefore has orders to collate all gleaned information discreetly, and to keep her silence on the topic of any planned response. As must the two of you.'

We readily agreed, of course, though I did so with a heavy heart. To have to keep secrets within my own organisation, and from people I have known for years! A painful duty.

I was reassured, though, to find that no suspicion had attached to *me*. If there were those who could doubt Jay's loyalty so far as to accuse him of stealing the book, well, I had my detractors, too. I had not lacked for opportunities to sabotage our little mission, and Jay's disappearance had happened while I was asleep in the very next room. Who was to say I hadn't had a hand in it all? I was comforted to find that Milady was in no way disposed to consider it likely, nor were Rob or Val.

It's good to have friends.

• • • ● • ● • • • •

Val greeted me with a shrewd, narrow-eyed look. She sat behind her huge desk like a queen, as always; straight-backed, imperious, and far too knowing.

'Have you been eating?' she said.

I opened my mouth to protest that nothing — *nothing* — could long divide me and food, but then I realised I had not eaten since breakfast, and the prospect of doing so only induced a feeling of nausea.

So I swept this aside.

'I've been sent to help,' I said brightly. I tried, as I crossed to Val's desk, to walk with the supreme confidence of an unflappable woman, and took some comfort in the smart *rap-rap-rapping* sound my heels made upon the polished wooden floor.

Val was not convinced.

'Sit down before you fall over,' she said, with — was it, really? — a roll of her eyes.

My knees *were* feeling a bit weak, so I meekly obeyed. 'I feel so feeble.'

'Why, because you're worried? Come off it, Ves. You'd be equal to anything, if only it were *you* who'd been swiped. You'd be out of there in no time, pink hair flying, leaving the place a smoking ruin behind you. It's unusual for you to have to fear for someone else.'

It was the feeling of impotence that bothered me; I rarely felt so much at a loss. 'You don't... think they would harm him?' I hazarded.

'Never,' said Val with reassuring confidence. 'He is far too valuable.'

True. Waymasters do not grow on trees. 'What have you found out?'

'Right. Come with me.' Val glided out from behind her desk and sent her chair zipping for the main doors, an act which surprised me for a second. Chatting comfortably with Val at her own, name-plaqued desk was as customary as eating lunch.

But Milady's exhortation had not fallen upon deaf ears. I followed obediently behind Val's hovering chair — I tend to call it a wheelchair but only because it's the common parlance; the chair has no wheels because it flies. Val took me to my own hidden study carrel, and, with an air of mild disgust at the necessity, sealed it up with a slick silencing charm. The air sparkled in a way I found oddly reassuring; no one was going to be listening in on us.

Val tapped her impeccably-manicured fingernails upon the carrel's desk for a moment, apparently deciding where to begin.

9

'They're elusive,' Val finally said. 'Secretive to a fault, and yes, I am well aware of the irony of my calling *them* secretive when we are all employed by a woman whose sole identifiable presence consists of a disembodied voice and an old-fashioned mode of address. Nonetheless. Two days of digging and we don't have much.

'We know that Ancestria Magicka was formed last June, but we only know that because there was a brief press release about it in the Magickal Herald at the end of June. It described the organisation as "formed for the efficient, professional retrieval of artefacts of great cultural value" or something to that effect, and it puts a nice shine on what they do, but it didn't take long for them to develop a reputation for the kind of efficiency that consists more of smash-and-grab thuggery than sleek professionalism.

'We don't know who founded it or how they are funded, except that the Hidden Ministry certainly has no involvement. They are fully independent, which means largely unmonitored. We've found the names of only a few of their operatives, including Katalin Pataki. Her regular partner is George Mercer, who is known to carry a Sardonyx Wand. He was almost certainly the man you and Jay encountered at Milton Keynes.

'They've been recruiting aggressively. Milady revealed we have lost two prospective employees this year to superior offers from Ancestria Magicka. Considering the bidding war over Ms. Pataki, it's clear that they are not at all strapped for cash.'

Unlike us, I thought. We do all right, but that's about it, and we are more heavily reliant upon Ministry funding than Milady would like. *They are* so *interfering,* she had once complained to me, in an unusually forthcoming mood. With no such ties and no shortage of resources, Ancestria Magicka was in an enviable position indeed.

'Their goals remain unclear,' Val continued. 'They are rumoured to have secured at least two Great Treasures this year already, one at auction and one an original find, together with quite the list of lesser artefacts. But what they have done with them is anybody's guess. Sold them? Stashed them? Anything claimed by Ancestria tends to disappear without trace.'

I gripped the desk. '*Not* Jay.'

'This is the first I have heard of their absconding with a person. Crude as their methods are reported to be, they are not known for brutality. I imagine it likely that they have a clear purpose in mind for Jay.'

'Like ransom?'

'Unlikely. They do not need money, and while the Society is known to be in possession of some few Treasures ourselves, there are plenty still out in the world for them to pursue first, with greater ease and lesser risk. And why take only Jay, if all they wanted was a hostage? Why not you? You are a senior acquisitions specialist with quite the reputation outside the Society. They might well imagine your abduction would inspire a comfortable spirit of co-operation in Milady.'

I wondered if it would. Trying to mentally calculate one's own probable value to one's employers is a grisly business, however, so I soon abandoned the project.

I felt a little reassured by Val's logic, but it did not escape me that her recital had not yet included anything that might help us to find Jay. 'Where do they hide out?' I asked.

'Exactly.'

'Exactly?'

'I've spent all day on that very question, and I've had four other people on it, too. So's Nell. Ancestria Magicka has a pretty major internet presence, as it turns out; far more than we do. A slick, lovely website promoting their services in the best possible light, and carefully couched in terms that would not too much alarm any non-magicker who happened upon it. Nell's got a couple of people working on it, but without much progress. The website's registered to a shoe shop in Wolverhampton.'

'A shoe shop?'

'Currently specialises in orthopaedic shoes. Family business, established 1969.'

I put my head in my hands. 'Have you got anything useful at all?'

'Just one thing. Maybe.'

'A maybe thing.'

Val nodded. 'A year ago last February, a strange case came up in the property market: Ashdown Castle in Cheshire was suddenly sold. A fifteenth-century mansion with strong magickal connections ought not to have gone ownerless for very long, but the place was in a state of such near-total ruin that it was essentially valueless. I was surprised to hear of its sale, and even more surprised to learn that — by rumour at least — the sale price ran into the millions. The old place has some attractive heritage, to be sure; it's supposed to have been built by the Beaumonts, one of the most prominent magickal families of medieval England, and as with all such places it's said to be littered with history, old magick and secrets. But to pay several million for a ruin?'

'You think Ancestria Magicka bought it?'

'The idea occurred to me. They'd need a base of operations, and what better site for a group even more obsessed with all things old, obscure and priceless than we are? I thought little of the matter at the time, but I put it in my Mysteries folder and I dug it up this morning.' Val paused, perhaps for effect. 'There's little to be found about its new owners, which immediately made me more suspicious. All I could find was a name, or half a name — Becket. And guess who shares that surname?'

'Wha... oh. The shoe-sellers of Wolverhampton?'

'The same! Before you ask: no, I do not think that family has anything to do with it. They're squarely non-magickal, and characterised by the kind of dull respectability that absolutely precludes the possibility of such interesting shenanigans. I *do* think that our friends at Ancestria are going to extraordinary lengths to maintain secrecy about their doings, though, and they're probably using a few such unremarkable names and addresses as a blind.'

'It's thin,' I said.

'I know. But it's worth investigating.'

I nodded, distracted. Somebody had walked past our hideaway four times in the space of five minutes, back and forth, back and forth. A slim, shortish figure I recognised, moving at speed, her dark hair swinging.

'What's Indira doing?' I said, frowning.

'Looking for something,' murmured Val, and dissolved the protective charm around the carrel with a flick of her fingers.

I set off after Indira. I found her soon enough, for she was coming back my way yet again. She stopped when she saw me and gave me a wide-eyed stare.

'Hello,' I said cordially.

'I was looking for you,' said Indira.

'Here I am. What can I do for you?' I was trying to be as approachable as possible, and hoping I was not coming off as patronising. It was obviously too late to break the news of her brother's disappearance; her manner proclaimed she was already well informed.

Indira has the air of a schoolgirl as well as the appearance of one. She has been impeccably dressed every time I have seen her, but with none of Jay's flair. She wears neat, plain blouses and skirts, her hair always tied up into a perfect, severe ponytail. Her manner is self-contained and withdrawn; I might have called her reserved, if I didn't know she was shy. She looks as though she never knowingly puts a foot wrong, and wouldn't dream of doing so either, which makes the arm-sling an incongruous addition to her wardrobe.

I wondered what kind of person was hiding behind all that conscientious, slightly desperate perfection.

Indira put a phone into my hands. 'Jay's tracking charm is missing.'

I knew it for Jay's phone at once. Not because there was anything distinctive about it, as such; the latest iPhone, plain black case, the same thing at least fifty Society employees probably carried (Indira included). I knew it for Jay's because I had, only the week before, rather wickedly adorned it with a sparkly green butterfly sticker on the top left corner. For some reason, he'd left it there.

There was certainly no sign of a tracking charm anywhere on it. 'Does he always use them?'

Indira managed a tiny smile. 'He's always losing things. He was like that from a child. When he arrived here he got a whole batch of tracker-patches from Development and stuck them on everything he owns. I know, because he gave the leftovers to me.'

'He couldn't have just forgotten to put one on his phone?'

'No chance. The two items Jay loses the most often are his phone and his keys. They're the first things he would put trackers on.'

My hopes leapt for a second, until I remembered that Jay's keys had been in his jacket pocket, which was even now lying forlornly upon the bed in his empty room. 'Perhaps it fell off?' I suggested.

'They don't fall off.'

Indira spoke with certainty, and I had no power of arguing with her. Not being prone to misplacing my stuff, I have rarely had occasion to use them. 'You have some theory, I think?'

Indira hesitated. 'I think... he must have removed it deliberately. And if he did that, he has probably taken it with him.'

My mind raced, and came up blank. 'I don't know how they work. What do you do to locate the charm, if you have lost the object it's guarding?'

'They come in pairs. You keep one somewhere safe, and put its pair on whatever you want to keep track of. Then you can use one to lead you to the other. Jay's got an entire book of them.'

I began to feel the kind of wild, surging hope that tends to end in crashing disappointment, and did my best to contain it. 'Do you know where the book is?'

'No. That's why I came to you.'

'Forgive me, but you must know your brother far better than I.'

Indira's awkwardness manifestly tripled. She looked at her feet. 'I, um... cannot get into his room.'

Uh.

A vision of myself only an hour past drifted through my head. I had casually infiltrated Jay's room — skulked my way inside, in fact, since it *did* feel weird to be in there uninvited, and when Jay was absent. Feeling guiltily like an interloper, I'd placed his jacket and his other bits and pieces onto his bed and immediately fled. It had never occurred to me that he might have sealed off his room to everybody *but* me.

I could imagine well enough why he would keep that space private from a sister who had to be a least a decade his junior, however close they appeared to be. Why he would grant free access to me was a different problem, one I had no answer to whatsoever.

'He speaks highly of you,' said Indira to the floor.

Oh. 'Goodness, we aren't — it isn't like—'

'Oh, I know!' Indira hastily interjected, and with a degree of horror I could only find slightly insulting. 'I would never think *that*! I only meant that he trusts you.'

I let all of this pass; we were wasting time. 'Come on,' I said, and led the way smartly back to the main stairs. I had paid little close attention to all the flotsam and jetsam in Jay's pockets when I had made my frantic search before; I had been looking for a stray tracker-patch like the one Jay had found in the book, and nothing else had appeared relevant at the time. But I vaguely recalled the presence of a little booklet of some kind; I had probably mentally passed it off as a pocket notebook, however unnecessary such an accessory might be to a man with a smartphone. But that booklet, I was now willing to hope, contained all of Jay's paired tracking charms.

10

The next couple of hours got pretty exciting.

Indira and I hurried through the House to Jay's room. All the dorms are on the upper floors, and while there's space set aside for families (Miranda and Orlando, for example, have a suite of rooms they share with their daughter), the singles amongst us are housed in separate wings: one for the ladies, one for the gents.

What can I say. No one will be surprised to hear that Milady can be old-fashioned.

I'd had a bit of trouble finding Jay's room earlier in the day, and I wish I could say that the prior experience rendered it simple for me to find it again. It did not. I dithered and doubted and we wandered back and forth, but eventually found our way through the rabbit-warren of dormitories to the white-painted door which bore Jay's name. I unlocked it with a touch and in we went.

Or, in *I* went. Indira hovered in the doorway, trying not to look at anything. She need not have scrupled. Jay has only been with us for a few weeks, so he has not yet had time to personalise his room very much. It looks more or less as it was issued: a plain, white-painted chamber with a comfyish bed, chest of drawers, wardrobe, window overlooking the grounds. There were no pictures anywhere, few possessions strewn about; little, in short, to incriminate the owner in any fashion that might trouble either his sister or himself.

'He isn't going to mind,' I said to Indira, feeling mildly exasperated.

'If he wanted me in here he would have given me access.'

It was hard to argue with that, so I didn't try. I went straight to the jacket laid upon the bed and began a hasty riffle through its pockets; for all my stout words I would not feel entirely comfortable until I was safely on the right side of Jay's door again.

I found the booklet, withdrew it with hands that only slightly trembled, and flipped it open.

There inside were neat rows of translucent jellyish circles, glinting with magic.

'We've got them,' I told Indira, who sagged with relief. I put the booklet directly into her hands as I withdrew, and locked the door again behind me.

'Now what?' I said.

'I'll take this to Development. They aren't tuned to me, so they'll have to be cracked, and I'm only just learning—'

'Get it to Orlando.'

Indira blanched. '*Orlando*? But he's—'

'Dauntingly important, and eccentric to boot. I know. But he invented these things; nobody knows better than he how they work, and no one will get the job done faster. We have no time to waste.'

Indira looked ready to die of fright, but to her credit she mastered herself, and gave me what was probably meant to be an assured nod. 'Right.'

'I'd go with you,' I said, relenting a bit. 'But in this you have the advantage of me. I'm not allowed anywhere near Orlando's lab.'

She gave a lopsided, scared-looking smile, as though the prospect of her own relative importance to mine alarmed more than appeased her. 'Right,' she said again.

Away she went.

I was a little puzzled by her serene manner of talking about *cracking* Jay's tracking charms, but I was rapidly learning that Indira had a rather complicated sense of honour. Wresting the secrets from her brother's utility spells in order to rescue him from dire peril was one thing; *going into his room without permission* in order to secure the charms in the first place was quite another.

I spared a brief thought to wonder what manner of relationship those two had enjoyed through childhood, and went off to rejoin Val.

• • • • • • • • • •

About half an hour later, Indira was back. At a run.

The library was crowded, though surprisingly quiet for all that; everyone was variously intent upon their stacks of books, aged scrolls, or tab computers. Once in a while somebody went running for Val with some promising note, footnote, or anecdote, most of which were regretfully dismissed. Indira balked a moment at this vision of industrious humanity, but steeled herself far enough to make her way to the desk I had appropriated.

'Ves!' she said — very quietly, as though to be overheard by any of the people around me would be an unthinkable torment. 'Sutton Weaver.'

'What?' I put aside the book I'd been flipping through — a sixteenth-century traveller's journal wherein a woman called Alice Glover, engaged in jaunting through much of northern England, gave accounts of many of the great houses of the area, including some of those in Cheshire. I hadn't yet found any references to Ashdown Castle.

'Sutton Weaver,' repeated Indira. 'One of Jay's tracking charms is there, or about two miles distant. It's in—'

'I warn you,' I said, sitting up. 'If you say "Cheshire" I may kiss you.'

'Cheshire,' whispered Indira, backing quickly away.

I held up my hands. 'I didn't mean it.'

'Oh...' She collected herself. 'Um, Orlando's sent someone to Milady with the news.'

'Right. Let's go see Val.'

Val had Jay's location pinpointed within minutes. 'That,' she said with a scholar's relish, 'is Ashdown Castle.'

I felt elated, and also indignant. Milady's "diplomatic" measures had, as expected, achieved nothing; Ancestria Magicka emphatically denied having had anything to do with the disappearance of either Jay or Bill. They had even been so insulting as to commiserate with us on the loss of two such recent acquisitions (and to refer to Jay as an acquisition made me mad as fire). And they'd stashed him after all!

Val caught the look on my face. 'Remember, none of this is evidence.'

'I know. Just a series of incredible coincidences.'

'Yes.'

'You don't believe there's another explanation any more than I do.'

'Nope.'

I looked at Indira. 'Good job. Thank you.'

She blushed a shade or two darker. 'Um.'

I didn't wait for her to squirrel up some words. I was off to Milady, with the feeling that if she did not authorise an immediate expedition to pick up Jay, well, I was going anyway.

Val made me stop. 'Ves, Ashdown Castle won't be easy to find. It hasn't been marked on any map since the 1530s. It will be behind layers of spells for concealment, confusion, misdirection, everything.'

'I realise.'

'Much like this House.'

'What's your point?'

'How long did it take you to find us, when you first arrived?'

Two days, even with instructions. I did not want to have to say that out loud, not in front of Indira.

Val gave me a meaningful look. 'You'll need help. Don't bomb out of here in such a hurry that you forget that.'

I saluted, with only the mildest irony. She was, after all, quite right. 'Thanks, Val.'

Half an hour later, we were on the road. *We* consisted of me and Rob, travelling in my car (I own a Mini, the Countryman sort. Blue. Yes, it's very beautiful). Ahead of us was a second car conveying Indira, and Melissa from Acquisitions. Indira had Jay's charm-book on hand, its secrets now fully in her control courtesy of Orlando. Melissa is something of an expert in what we shall give the civilised name of *infiltration*. No concealment spells can long stand up to *her*.

Milady was as supportive of our immediate departure as I could wish, though she did ask one or two inconvenient questions.

'What will you do once you locate the castle?'

'Something fiendishly clever and more than a little heroic.'

'Please answer more sensibly, Ves. This is serious.'

'I *know* that. I have no answer to make. I don't know what we'll do when we get there; it's my job, and Rob's, to figure that out. Which is a more petrifying prospect today than it has ever been before.'

'I have no doubt you are both fully equal to the challenge.'

'Thank you. Are you sure it is wise to take Indira?'

'No, but she appears to have the knack of locating her brother.'

'Melissa could do that.'

'Probably, but it would take time to make over that duty to her, and were you not desirous of an instant departure?'

'Yes...'

'What's more, Indira begged hard to be included.'

'Forgive me, ma'am, but you are not always so receptive to pleas.'

'What would you do if I forbade you to go?'

'Go anyway.'

'Mm. Indira has not quite the same level of resolve, but until her brother is retrieved she will not have a moment's peace.'

'Very kind of you, Milady.'

'Besides that, I am interested to see how she does in the field. The question of her future with the Society is not yet fully decided.'

That's Milady for you: kindness wrapped in ruthless practicality, or maybe the other way around.

I suppose it's necessary if you are in command of two hundred people.

I made no further objection, only hoping in private that I would not manage to lose shy, tremulous Indira the same way I'd mislaid her brother. If I did, Jay wouldn't even have to kill me; I'd save him the trouble and immolate myself.

Focus, Ves. Act now, panic later.

We made the trip in under two hours, though it was difficult to know exactly when we had arrived. We drove through Sutton Weaver and out the other side, then performed a rough circle around it through a series of narrow, bumpy little roads. No castle appeared on the horizon to enliven the expense of green, flat fields.

Not a surprise, but not helpful either.

Rob dialled. 'Mel,' he said to his phone. 'Needing a better plan.' He listened for a minute, then shut it off. 'Pull over somewhere,' he said to me. 'We're on foot for the rest.'

I found a spot by the side of the road that seemed safe enough, and pulled my car as far over into the grassy verge as I dared (blessing my choice of a Countryman all the while). Out we got. Neither Mel nor Indira paused at all; they conferred briefly together, then set off into the field, leaving Rob and me to follow them.

If anything, Indira seemed to be leading the way. She had Jay's location to work from, I supposed, which at least gave her a direction to head in. It would be down to Melissa to

—

— well, for example, to wave a magick Wand and make a castle appear. Which she did.

I've oversimplified the process a little, to be sure. She certainly took up her Wand — a sparkling amethyst specimen I have occasionally eyed myself — but she did not flourish it about. She merely tapped it against her lip in a gesture more thoughtful than flamboyant, and *bits* of a castle rippled into view: a section of brown brick wall with a heavy timber door, and a glimpse of a moat.

The vision wavered like water, and vanished again.

'Oh, yes,' said Melissa, as though she had mislaid her keys and happened to come across them again. 'There it is.' She proceeded to do a bit of Wand-waving, but in an odd, graceless way: she poked at the air before her as though sticking pins in something, and then began to jab and slash. With each gesture more of the castle appeared; Melissa was tearing away the illusions which concealed it, like a dressmaker armed with a stout pair of scissors.

At length, the whole building was revealed: a fanciful structure despite the plain brown bricks, all sloping roofs and arched windows, its various wings and annexes piled higgledy-piggledy against one another. It was unusually large, but I spied at least one section which looked as though it had been added sometime after the castle's original construction.

'Jay is this way,' said Indira, and pointed. She indicated a corner of the castle which boasted a splendid fairytale tower, round-walled, with a conical roof and a single long, arched window. Was Jay at the top? I made a mental note to be ready with sleeping beauty jokes, which could not fail to endear me to Jay.

We advanced, veering a little left in the direction of that corner turret.

I found this puzzling. Melissa and Indira seemed intent upon simply walking openly into Ashdown Castle, picking up Jay and Bill and (presumably) walking out again. 'Er,' I said after half a minute. 'Should we not... I don't know, *skulk* or something?'

'I want to attract some attention,' said Melissa.

'Um. Why?'

'Because in about twelve seconds, Rob and I will kick up a ruckus while you and Indira *skulk* into the castle and heroically extract Jay.'

'Couldn't we have talked about this before?'

'I've only just decided it.'

I swallowed my irritation, which flared up all the more at the words *I've decided.* Who appointed Melissa Supreme Leader of our expedition anyway?! But since I could come up with no better plan, it did not behove me to complain.

Instead, I wielded my lovely spangled Sunstone Wand and wove some concealment charms of my own, first around myself and then around Indira. By the time I had finished, anyone glancing only cursorily at the spot I was standing in would see nothing; I'd made of myself a wisp of breeze, and Indira was an errant ray of sunlight.

Not a moment too soon, either, for about two minutes later a palpable shock rippled through the floor and pulsed in the air before us; we had hit the castle's next layer of defence, a magickal field which repelled anyone not authorised to enter. We had exactly the same kind of thing set up at Home.

It is not easy to pass such a structure, but with a pair of Wands at our disposal, Melissa and I were well prepared. My Sunstone buzzed with magick; I tapped the tip of the Wand against Melissa's and the power doubled. We turned them upon the repelling field before us and burned away a fair-sized hole. A warm wind billowed through from the other side.

'Go,' said Melissa tersely.

I went first, glancing back just once to see Rob standing poised a few feet behind me, legs braced, chin lifted: ready for anything.

I didn't like to leave him or Melissa to take the heat for us, but it would not be fair of me to doubt their ability to deal with it. I hopped through the hole we'd made, pulling Indira after me — and almost died of fright to find Katalin Pataki and George Mercer not ten feet away from us.

11

I tensed, trying to keep Indira behind me while I kept a close watch on the two Ancestria Magicka agents. Would they spot us? Melissa's plan of serving as decoy had been put to an unexpectedly early test.

They did not. Something caught Mercer's attention; his eyes shifted briefly in our direction, and a faint frown flitted across his face. But Melissa spoke up just then, and his attention returned to her.

'Hi,' she said. 'So we know that, officially, you had nothing to do with the disappearance of Jay Patel and the book he found at Farringale. But unofficially, we all know that's rubbish. We come to offer a bargain. Keep the book. Return Jay.'

Katalin smiled. 'And if Mr. Patel does not wish to return to the Society?'

Mercer said, at the same time, 'You propose to do what to us, exactly, if we do not agree?'

They needed a lesson or two in negotiation, I thought privately. Typically it would be more productive to pursue only one line of argument at a time; two would confuse the issue and weaken the impact of both. But perhaps they had not been working together long.

Lucky that I had often had cause to test my concealment charms before. I know them to be virtually foolproof. I walked nonchalantly past Pataki and Mercer, drawing Indira with me. She looked far more concerned by the situation than I felt; she crept past them, oh-so-carefully, casting frequent nervous glances in their direction. I tried to reassure her by patting her on the arm, but I do not think my gesture was much heeded.

She relaxed a bit once we were safely past, and had covered a distance of some thirty feet or so. We were rapidly drawing up to the castle by then, and I was engaged in searching for the nearest and most convenient way in.

Indira gave a tiny sigh of relief.

'We were in no danger,' I told her.

'No danger? We were practically standing on their toes!'

'No danger whatsoever.'

Indira frowned. 'What did she mean about Jay's not wanting to return to us?'

'She was trying to manipulate Melissa, that's all. Obviously they would like to keep both Jay and the book, and without our making too much trouble for them over either.'

'I don't think they can care all that much about our making trouble. This seems like an obvious challenge to the Society.'

'Not quite, as they've officially denied it from the beginning. It's a gambit, a throw of the dice to see what happens. It isn't a declaration of war, yet.'

'Yet?'

'That will probably come in time.' We were prowling around the base of the turret by that time, and I'd spied a way in.

Good points: the door was not barred or padlocked and a cautious probe of its magickal defences revealed nothing I did not feel able to handle with the help of my spangled Wand.

Bad points: Historic buildings have a way of being odd, whimsical and downright contrary sometimes, and this one was a prime example. There was a door in the tower, but it was inexplicably situated halfway up the building. There were no stairs leading up to it, nor any sign that there had ever been any.

'Hm,' I said. I wished for a second that I had brought my Chair with me. I, like everyone else, have a flying specimen; Val and I had both gone for tall, wing-backed chairs with comfortably padded seats, high-rising armrests and plush velvet upholstery. Hers is in green, mine's burgundy. With my Chair, we could whizz up to the door in no time; in fact we could go all the way up to the window, and skip the door entirely.

Of course, I would have had to travel the entire distance by Chair, for there's no way I could ever fit it in my Mini. And two hours by Chair in uncertain April weather is nobody's idea of a good time. Not now that there are cars.

So, no Chair. We would have to do it the tiring way.

'How far has your education progressed?' I asked Indira.

'My magickal education? Um, the... the usual?' She looked at me uncertainly.

'More specifically, can you levitate?'

'Oh! Yes.' Indira proved this by instantly levitating herself up to a distance of about two feet from the ground, smiling at me in that hopeful, shy way she has, like a puppy wishing for praise.

'Er,' I said. 'Yes, that's very good.' It was more than good. Levitation is one of the more difficult arts; some otherwise very powerful magickers at the Society cannot manage it at all. Even one such as yours truly, among the finer practitioners of levitation at Home, can do it only with difficulty, and I have never managed to levitate myself more than about ten feet up without serious strain.

Indira levitated in the same way she breathed: effortlessly. And she hovered there, two feet up, with no visible sign that she was tiring at all. She looked like she could sail up ten feet and more still with similar ease, and I suppressed just the faintest, unworthy tinge of jealousy.

She will be the best of us, Jay had said, and I could see what he meant.

I took a deep breath.

'Right,' I said decisively. 'We're going to levitate to the door.' Which, happily, looked to be only eight or nine feet up; I might manage to accomplish the business without embarrassing myself. 'I will take care of its defences and then we'll go in and get Jay. He's still in there?'

Indira nodded. 'Probably in the top— oh, no. Wait a moment.' She frowned and consulted her book of Jay's charms again. 'He's moved a bit, he's— oh! He's coming down.'

The door swung open above our heads, and Jay appeared. 'Hi,' he said, and then dropped down to land beside us with the grace of a panther.

I eyed him with some displeasure. 'Hi? That's it?'

'Hail, fair rescuers,' Jay said, with a smile for me. 'I am full honoured by your braving the dangers of Ashdown in order to retrieve me... oh, wait. You *are* here for me? You aren't just here for the book?'

I waited for him to explode at me over Indira's presence, but he greeted her with a swift peck on the cheek and a brotherly pat of approval, and showed no signs of displeasure.

I felt, once again, that I had not quite got the measure of Jay.

'We're here for both,' I said, and Jay made a show of wiping his brow in relief. 'Do you have the book?'

'No, but I know where it is. Come on.' Jay led the way around the turret and on, presumably leading us to some other entrance. Mindful of threats and bristling with caution, Indira and I followed.

Indira put Jay's charm book into her brother's hand, and he tucked it away with a smile of thanks. 'I knew you'd figure that out,' he told her.

She gave that shy smile. 'How did you know we were here?'

'Because Ves shines like a bloody beacon.'

I blanched. 'Er. I do?'

'Yes, but don't worry. Anyone who didn't know you would just think that a small sun had popped by for a visit.'

'Reassuring.' I wasted a little time trying to decide what Jay meant, exactly; it's never been mentioned before. But probably it had something to do with my being unusually, er, *amplified* by the Sunstone Wand, and anyway, the more important question was: had Pataki and Mercer observed the same thing, and pretended not to notice?

'We might want to be careful, then,' I said. 'They probably know we are here.' I wrestled with the Wand a bit, hopeful of diminishing my beacon-ness by a shade or two.

Jay dampened me with a wave of his hand. I don't know how to describe it other than to say that; I felt quenched, like he had thrown a bucket of water over me. Then I understood what he had meant: I had been positively ablaze with magick, and had not even noticed.

'Were you angry, by chance?' Jay said to me.

'Of course I was angry! They thieved Bill and kidnapped you!'

'They certainly did thieve Bill, which was disgraceful and nothing can exonerate them from that piece of infamy. But they did not kidnap me, precisely.'

'They didn't?'

'They offered me a job.'

I blinked. 'And?'

'And I accepted.'

Indira gasped. I stifled an impulse to kick him somewhere painful.

Jay laughed. 'Only temporarily. What better way to get a look around their HQ than to walk in here as a new recruit? And I wanted a shot at getting Bill back.'

'So they just let you walk in here?'

'Sort of. I've been under close supervision, and they have as yet withheld all privileges.'

I looked around. 'You are remarkably alone for a man under close supervision.'

'Well, when I saw you two on the approach I knew it was time to end the charade. I ditched my supervisor and broke out of the tower.'

Indira clutched at her brother's arm, probably experiencing feelings of knee-weakening relief.

I was experiencing feelings more like incandescent rage.

'You're blazing again, Ves,' said Jay, and I again had to suffer the quenching sensation. It is not especially pleasant.

'I would not blaze if you wouldn't keep making me angry,' I said tightly.

He stopped, and looked at me in genuine surprise. 'How did I do that?'

I controlled myself with an effort. 'You let us imagine you kidnapped.'

'I thought you would realise what I was up to.'

'*How was I supposed to realise that?!*'

'Um.' Jay looked at his sister. 'Right. I see. I'm sorry.'

Indira looked at the floor.

I took a slow breath, and let go of my need to punch him. Not without some regret. 'Another time, could you possibly get word to me about your wily plans?'

'I can try. I didn't have a phone, of course, and nobody would let me borrow one for some reason.'

'*For some reason.* Are you sure they believed your show of willingness to jump ships?'

'I don't see why not.' Jay began walking again. 'They asked me what the Society was paying me, then offered me ten times that.'

'*TEN TIMES?*'

Jay cast me a look of mild irritation. 'Ves, if we are going to engage in any kind of stealth mission here you're going to need to *stop with the blazing.*'

Ten times. For goodness' sake! The Society paid its staff as well as it could afford to, and if Jay's salary was anything like mine (and it would be, considering his Waymasterness) then he was by no means hard done to. Ten times more! Who could afford that?

I felt a faint twinge of nerves. 'Er. You do actually intend to turn that down, right?'

Jay rolled his eyes. 'Obviously.'

'Obviously? Not many people would say no to that kind of money.'

'I think you are doing "people" an injustice, but since I at least am not overburdened with avarice I think we can all stop worrying about that. Ah.' Jay stopped before an apparently featureless patch of brick wall, and stared at it with palpable satisfaction. 'Here we go.' He spoke a word I did not understand, and one of the bricks glowed. He touched his fingers to the shiny brick, and the wall fell away.

'Secret passwords?' I said in disgust. 'Really?'

Jay grinned. 'These people are a bit old-school.' He led the way through the not-wall, while Indira followed and I brought up the rear.

'The irony of hearing the words *old school* uttered with such derision by a member of the Society for Magickal Heritage.'

'Fair. Perhaps I meant staggeringly cliché, but I'm not complaining. My sojourn into espionage has borne fruit.' He stopped talking and stopped walking at the same time, though we had not yet proceeded far into the castle. The door-in-the-wall had brought us, incongruously, into a muddy boot-room wherein many pairs of Wellingtons and assorted hiking boots were littered about. Beyond that was the kind of chilly, bleak hallway to be found in the servants' quarters of any house of at least moderate size that saw use during the Victorian period. Jay stopped us before the typical green baize-covered door, the more or less soundproof kind that muffle all those undesirable noises that emanate from the service parts of the house. Perfectly insufferable to have to listen to the clamour of one's dinner being cooked, isn't it?

Only this one was not quite soundproof, because I could hear something coming from the other side. Someone was singing.

If you intend thus to disdain,
It does the more enrapture me,
And even so, I still remain
A lover in captivity.

The melody was familiar, and so was the voice.

'Why,' I whispered to Jay, 'is Bill singing Greensleeves?'

'Er.' Cautiously, Jay pulled open the door an inch or so. The song immediately swelled in volume, as Bill launched full-throated into the chorus.

Greensleeves was all my joy!
Greensleeves was my delight!
Greensleeves was my heart of gold!

And who but my lady greensleeves!

'Were you wearing green yesterday?' Jay murmured.

'With pink hair? Don't be ridiculous.'

Jay swung the door open. Considering this decision I expected to find the room beyond empty except for Bill, but it was not.

We'd come out in what looked to be a tiny library, though the chamber was barely larger than the boot-room. The walls were crowded with bookcases fitted edge-to-edge, each crammed full of books. Bill lay enthroned in splendour upon a central table, open to display one of John Wester's journal pages.

Seated before him and wearing a long-suffering expression was the kind of cardi-clad middle-aged lady you might expect to see serving dinner at a school cafeteria, or perhaps selling raffle tickets at a Women's Institute fundraising drive. Whatever instant (and doubtless unfair) judgements one might make about such a person, the last thing *I* expected was that she would detect the sounds of Jay's approach almost before it seemed possible, be out of her chair and facing us in about two seconds flat, and hurling hexes at us with the help of a pretty jade Wand.

12

Somehow, the Patels were ready for this. Indira had a very good, very stout shield charm up in no time, which absorbed the first wave of the indignant woman's hexery. Jay meanwhile threw a hex of his own in response, a neat, clever piece of magick which would have knocked her out on the spot if it had hit her. Sadly, she proved to have remarkable reflexes, too, and ducked.

Through all of this ruckus, Bill warbled on.

'Come on, Amelia,' said Jay, throwing another hex. 'You know the book isn't yours.'

She made no reply to this, choosing to focus all her attention on the next wave of dark curses.

Hm.

I plucked a sleep-bead from one of my emergency supplies pockets. No use expecting to get her to swallow it; not with hexes, reflexes and a Wand at her disposal. Instead I threw the bead up, blasted it with a shot of energy from my own spangly Wand, and watched in satisfaction as it sprayed the curse-happy woman in the most potent sleep potion our technicians are capable of brewing.

The woman uttered a word I shall not repeat here, cast me a look of utter hatred, and dropped like a stone.

'I need some of those,' said Jay.

Greensleeves was all my joy! sang Bill.

I went over to him at once and patted his pages. 'Bill.'

Greensleeves was my delight!

'Bill! Stop!'

Bill stopped. 'Miss Vesper?'

'The same. We are about to effect your rescue, and it would be preferable if you were a bit quieter. Early modern love songs might be delightful but they do attract more notice than would be desirable.'

'I cannot begin to express the extent of my gratitude,' said Bill. 'I shall consider myself under an obligation to you for the rest of my natural life.'

How long is a book's natural life? Probably much longer than mine. 'You don't like *Ancestria Magicka*, I take it?'

'If you are referring to these scoundrels who have wrested me from you, then your surmise is correct.'

They did not appear to have mistreated Bill, in fairness to them. He lay atop a particularly plush cushion, his spine perfectly supported. He had an entire table to himself, and they had let him go on singing to his heart's content (though that might have been because he would not oblige them so far as to shut up). He had not been damaged, as far as I could see.

I thought it interesting, and possibly significant, that the woman I had felled had apparently been studying John Wester's journal entries when we had come in. In all the excitement about Bill's unusual composition, we had rather overlooked the contents of his pages; what were they but the ramblings of a robber and a thief? But if *Ancestria Magicka* thought differently, then I wanted to know why. I busied myself snapping pictures of each of Bill's pages that bore writing (except for Zareen's section). These I sent through to Val. I sent a note with them: *Decipher?*

Then I scooped up Bill.

'It is good to be with you again,' said Bill, which was sweet of him.

'Sometime you'll have to tell me who Milady Greensleeves is,' I said.

During my hasty camera-session with Bill, Indira had busied herself with searching the outer garments of the sleeping woman. Jay snatched up the notebook she had left upon the table, and leafed speedily through it. He showed me something interesting: Amelia had made an ink sketch of the map at the back of Bill's pages, with annotations.

'Hang onto that,' I said.

'Mm.' Jay pocketed it. There were two doors in the room: one leading back the way we had come, the other to who-knew-where-else. Retracing our steps was the obvious solution if we wanted to get out, and Jay clearly agreed, for he made for the door at speed. But before he reached it, there came the sounds of heavy footsteps approaching from the other side. 'Uh oh,' said Jay, pivoted, and dashed for the other door at a run.

Indira got there before him. She tugged mightily upon the door but to her chagrin, it did not budge. 'Locked,' she reported.

Well, no surprise there. They had stashed the most valuable book in the world in this tiny library, with only Amelia to look after it; they were hardly going to leave the main door unlocked.

The other door swung open to reveal George Mercer, and Katalin Pataki right behind him.

'See,' said Mercer with grim satisfaction. 'I knew he was full of shit.' He had the air and the accent of a public school boy, and the clothes to match. I wondered which of our most respected establishments had been responsible for turning out such a fine specimen.

Katalin regarded Jay with some disappointment, though she said, in her thick Hungarian accent: 'Is he, though? Let me have the book, Jay.'

'That is Mr. Patel to you,' said Bill.

Jay grinned, and backed up until he was shoulder-to-shoulder with Indira and me. He took Bill from me, probably in order to leave my hands free to wield my Wand.

Katalin, though, interpreted his actions differently. 'Good,' she purred. 'Mr. Patel has more sense than to imagine us as the enemy. Our goals are the same, are they not?'

'As what?' I demanded. 'The Society doesn't steal.'

'We stole nothing. Upon learning that an active Waymaster happened to be the current keeper of a remarkable book, we naturally approached him with an attractive offer of employment. One which he would be a fool to turn down.' Katalin smiled at Jay.

'It is not my book, of course,' said Jay. 'If anyone can claim right of ownership over it, that would be the Troll Court.'

Katalin's smile widened. 'Finders, keepers,' she purred.

My mind travelled back over all the Treasures, Curiosities, rare books and other artefacts I had tracked down and rescued from destruction over my decade with the Society. Finders, keepers? 'Oh, if *only!* I would be filthy rich by now, and retiring to my own island.'

'About that,' said Mercer. 'We're instructed to extend a similarly lucrative offer to

Specialists Cordelia Vesper and Indira Patel.' He waved a document at me, as though that might convince me if his words did not. 'Ancestria Magicka is in need of people with your unique talents.'

Indira looked flabbergasted.

I felt a twinge of curiosity. 'Are you?' I murmured. 'Instructed by whom?'

Mercer's mouth twitched with annoyance. 'You will meet your new employers once you have accepted their generous offer.'

'Like Jay has?'

Mercer looked Jay over expressionlessly. 'Mr. Patel's actions have delivered not only a Waymaster and the book to our Castle but a highly experienced acquisitions specialist and one of the most promising spellwrights the University has ever encountered. Our organisation is very pleased with him.'

All of this was sounding horribly like they had no intention of allowing us to turn down their offer. 'We do have a choice, I suppose?' I said acidly.

'Of course,' said Mercer, and gave me a polite, insincere smile. 'You will find us to be perfectly civilised. Regrettably, however, it will not be in our power to permit you to leave Ashdown with the book in your possession.'

'Think about it, Ves,' said Katalin, and I blinked at her in surprise at her use of my nickname. 'Ten times the salary, ten times the freedom! We are sent all over the world, to the farthest corners of the globe. We have already retrieved ancient Treasures the likes of which you have never seen.'

I admit, I experienced a faint twinge of wistful desire at this picture of well-salaried freedom. But the feeling did not last long. 'All of which you directly repatriated to their home countries, of course?' I said.

Katalin's mouth set into a hard line of disappointment. 'You are wasted on the Society.'

'It may be something of a raggle-taggle organisation,' I admitted, 'without the re-sources to pay island-purchasing salaries, and I cannot deny that I am sometimes chafed by Milady's rules. But the work we do is far more important than you will ever understand.'

Katalin shrugged, and looked at Indira.

I wondered what the poor girl would manage to say under such pressure as that; even small-talking with her new colleagues at the Society's cafeteria often left her tongue-tied.

But I underestimated her. She might only have been able to utter one word, but it was the right word, and spoken with a conviction which must preclude all argument. 'No,' she said.

Katalin sighed. 'I suppose that means you will be leaving us too, Mr. Patel?'

'Correct.'

'The book, then, please.' She held out her hands to receive it.

Jay only gripped it tighter. 'I'm afraid not.'

Katalin and George Mercer exchanged the kind of grim glance that had to mean big trouble for the three of us. Fortunately, we were all at that moment distracted by the terrific sound of crashing glass that might, for example, be indicative of a window breaking.

'Ah,' said Rob, peering in through the ragged hole where there had, only a moment ago, been big, bright panes of glass. I caught a glimpse of Melissa standing just behind him.

Excellent.

'Indira. Chairs,' I said, already making for the nearest one to me. I did not have time to explain, and could only hope that she would grasp my meaning.

See, Rob and I have been out on quite a few missions together before. There was this one time, several years ago now, where he and I got into a pretty difficult situation. There was Rob, there was me, there was a locked room halfway up an unreasonably tall building, and there was a rabid ogre. Enough said? But Rob had put his hand to the glass and pulled one of his fabulously destructive tricks; the entire window turned black-as-night and fell outwards, and when I had witched us up a couple of Chairs we flew serenely away into the sunset.

I never did find out what became of the ogre.

The timing had been slightly tighter before, but then, I had not had the Wand. This time it was the work of a few seconds to persuade my chosen chair — a fairly comfy, tapestry-clad armchair type thing — that it was livelier in nature than it had ever before imagined itself to be, and might rather enjoy taking flight. Indira, to my relief (if not much to my surprise) caught on right away, and made short work of an engraved oak desk chair until it actually began to dance on its four rigid legs.

We witched up three more, during which time Katalin Pataki was unwise enough to make an advance upon Rob and Melissa, while George tried to wrench Bill from Jay. The latter encounter ended with Jay shoving the book through the window into Melissa's hands — a risky manoeuvre, which very nearly resulted in Katalin's swiping it on the spot

— and then (to my exasperation) he abandoned magick altogether in favour of fisticuffs.

I did not linger to watch the two men swing at each other. I pointed my Wand in Katalin's direction. It was unfair, really; she was facing Rob and Melissa, and too engaged in opposing their joint attacks to have any leisure to attend to me. I shot a binding charm at her, nicely amplified by the power of the Sunstone Wand, and she collapsed in a motionless heap. Almost motionless. She was twitching a bit.

I assuaged my slightly guilty conscience by remembering how very unscrupulous most of her organisation's activities had thus far been, and shoved her out of the way of the window. 'Sorry,' I said brightly, ignoring the way her eyes blazed hatred in my general direction. 'But I can't let you have Bill. We've grown fond of each other.'

I bundled Indira out of the window next, desk chair and all. She shot into the sky beyond, clutching the side of her Chair with her one good arm, and almost as rigid with fright as Katalin was with magick. I made a note to send her to the infirmary once we got home; she might be in need of a little therapy.

Melissa went next in my fine tapestry Chair, taking Bill with her. Good.

As one, Rob and I turned to Jay.

He wasn't doing badly, to be fair to him. Not badly at all. His face displayed the evidence of George Mercer's talents at fisticuffs, and he had obviously taken more than one hit judging from the damage. But Mercer was little better off, and I admit to taking some small satisfaction at the mess Jay had made both of his artlessly tumbled curls and his coolly self-possessed demeanour.

Nonetheless, it was high time to cut in. Rob — taking advantage of Mercer's distraction in much the same shameless way I had taken advantage of Katalin's — felled our public school tosser with a solid punch to the jaw, while I shoved a Chair under Jay's legs until he toppled into it. I sent him out the window with a flick of the Wand.

With a startled yelp and what might have been a vicious curse upon my ancestors, he disappeared.

Rob and I followed.

Flying by Chair is quite the experience, and it's really something to do it as part of a small flock. I lounged back at my ease, much better off than poor Indira, for my chosen vehicle had a wide seat and tall arms to keep me from falling out. But it was her first time; she would soon develop a better eye for this kind of thing. And she had got herself out of the library speedily, efficiently and successfully. I was very pleased with her.

Melissa, I noted, had caught up, and steadied Indira with a firm grip on the back of her Chair. She was in no danger of falling off, injured arm notwithstanding; good.

I steered clear of Jay, at least until we made it back to our abandoned cars. He had a fine brooding-glower-of-displeasure going on which I did not wish to tangle with.

He opted to ride with Indira.

I opted to attribute this to a positive cause, like brotherly concern rather than Ves-avoidance.

We made it back to our cars unpursued, piled hastily into them and drove away, Bill in such fine fettle that he began singing again. The strains of *Greensleeves* hung dulcet upon the air, fading into silence as Melissa's car pulled out ahead of us.

We had to leave the Chairs behind, of course, and I do wonder a little what might have become of our escape-pods. I would like to apologise right now to any dog-walker or jogger who might have been puzzled to discover a cluster of library chairs abandoned on the edge of a field, apparently a long way from anywhere. I promise, the explanation is perfectly reasonable.

13

By the time we arrived back at Home, Jay still had not quite forgiven me for bundling him out of Ashdown library like a sack of clothes. He was waiting for me in the hall, cool as a marble statue, with Indira at his elbow and no sign of Melissa.

'Hello,' I said, with a hopeful smile. I cannot absolutely confirm that I did not employ surreptitious use of the puppy eyes, too.

'We need to see Milady right away,' said Jay, unmoved.

'I did not, by my interference, mean any slight upon your very excellent abilities.'

'I was fine.'

I tried not to stare too obviously at the bruises on his face. 'I know!'

Apparently I failed, for the brow came down in annoyance and he involuntarily touched the biggest of the bruises: a great monster of a thing adorning his right cheek. 'No one's ever died of a little bruise.'

'I mean... I'm not a doctor, but that probably isn't true.'

I thought I saw the corner of Jay's mouth twitch, but I was probably mistaken. 'Shall we go?' said he, and gestured for me to precede him up the main stairs.

Desperate times, desperate measures. As I ascended, I burst into a spirited rendition of *Something Happened on the Way to Heaven* (neither the words nor the melody accurate, but one does one's best).

'Is that... are you using Phil Collins against me?' It wasn't his mouth that was twitching this time; there was a definite spasm going on in his left eye.

'Who can resist Phil!'

'One or two people,' muttered Indira, though when I looked at her she tried her best to outdo her brother's statue impression.

'So,' said Jay meaningfully, and pointed in the direction of Milady's tower: up. 'Heaven's that way.'

I sang about paradise, sashaying up the stairs.

'It can't be heaven *and* paradise up there,' said Jay. 'Pick one.'

'I say both.'

'You're just hoping for a promotion.'

'I was recently offered a rather tempting job opportunity, which I very loyally turned down. A raise isn't too much to hope for, is it?'

'Wretch.' I may not have been able to see Jay anymore, having smartly turned my back upon him. I could, however, hear the smile.

Hah.

'Bill!' I called. 'I have no doubt that you and Milady will be delighted with one another.'

'I shall be happy to make the acquaintance of so esteemed a person,' Bill replied 'Her ladyship...?' Bill trailed off into an expectant pause.

'Yes,' said Jay.

'Her ladyship of which family?'

Bill, bless him, was labouring under the impression that Milady had a name. Or that any of us might know what it is.

'Just Milady, Bill,' I called, as Jay floundered for a response.

'Milady is a title, not a name.'

'In this case, it is both.'

Bill was silent, either with indignation or with shock, I couldn't tell which.

'Welcome back, Jay,' said Milady when we reached her tower room. The air sparkled with a special brilliance which usually meant that her ladyship was extra pleased. That of course meant that she had been extra worried, even if she had shown little sign of it before.

'Thank you, Milady,' said Jay with a bow. 'It is good to be back.'

'Indira rocked it,' I announced, making the poor girl blush.

'Did she? I cannot say I am surprised.'

'And Jay was not kidnapped at all, the wretch.'

Silence. There was a quality to the air that suggested Milady's eyebrows might have been raised a little high, had she corporeal presence enough to display it.

Jay rolled his eyes at me. 'May I explain?'

'Pray do.'

He explained. I did not find his reasons any more satisfactory than last time, though to his credit he only made himself out to be *somewhat* stupendously the hero. He accepted Milady's admonishments — rather milder than mine — with reasonable grace.

Then Milady ruined everything by saying: 'That was very clever, Jay. Good work.'

Jay smirked at me. I considered it only fair to respond by sticking out my tongue at him.

Indira watched this exchange with wide, wide eyes.

We followed this by apprising Milady of everything that had happened since our urgent departure for Ashdown Castle, a discussion that proceeded at some length. At long last, Bill made himself known by shuffling his covers in irritation, wafting dust everywhere.

'Where have you been keeping that?' I said to him in astonishment. He'd spent several hours in Val's care, and ought therefore to have emerged spotlessly dust-free.

'I reserve a small supply in case it should prove necessary,' said Bill loftily.

'Displeasure registered.'

'Thank you.'

I made introductions, which was an awkward business considering it was between an unusually loquacious book and an unusually disembodied voice. Bill, to my disgust, turned on the charm so much that I suspected him of snobbery.

Jay passed Amelia's notebook to me. It was open at the page with her ink-drawing of the map. 'There's something odd about them,' he said, interrupting Bill's compliments upon the unusual beauty of Milady's rich, heavenly voice (his words, not mine). It occurred to me to marvel a moment at the transformation: that we (or Zareen) should have succeeded in turning a foul-mouthed wretch of a book into a silver-tongued charmer. Behold, the power of literature.

'In which particular respect?' said Milady.

Jay paused a moment to gather his thoughts. 'Amelia spent a long time with Bill,' he began. 'Studying him, probably, at least at first. But she spent a lot more time talking to him.'

'Impertinent woman,' muttered Bill.

Jay smiled faintly. 'Or trying to, as Bill flatly refused to talk to anyone but me or Ves.

So, they pulled me off supervising the construction of their new henge, and—'

'A new *henge*?' interrupted Milady.

Apparently we had forgotten to tell her about Milton Keynes. 'At the top of a tower,' said Jay. 'Breeze blocks. Ugly in the extreme, but functional enough.'

I almost dropped the notebook. 'They're making a henge out of *concrete*?'

'I'm afraid so.'

'Have they no soul?'

'Not a scrap between them. Anyway, they had me interrogating Bill on Amelia's behalf for more than half the day, and she chose a strange line of enquiry. I expected the kinds of questions our lot were asking — burning historical questions no one has ever found the answer to; details about his life and history; the nature of the enchantments that made him; that sort of thing. But all Amelia wanted to know about was his creator, and where she is buried.'

'I see,' said Milady. 'And what is known about this person that might account for so extraordinary a display of interest?'

'Nowhere near enough. Even Bill's information could not satisfy Amelia, exactly.'

'I was unable to give information about the precise location of my former mistress's grave,' Bill put in. 'On account of not having been chosen to be present at her burial.'

I eyed the map in Amelia's notebook. Her annotations were difficult to read, but they looked like place names, sometimes scrawled with a question mark beside them. The map itself wasn't very helpful, not even the original; it had no distinct features about it, no labels, no directions. It consisted only of a few hastily-inked lines which might have related to virtually anything — roads, hills, rivers...

'It may seem obvious,' I began apologetically, 'but did you ask Amelia why she wanted to know about Bill's former mistress?'

'I did, as nonchalantly as I could. She just looked at me like she couldn't believe I would ask such a stupid question, like the answer should have been perfectly obvious.'

I sighed. 'Any guesses, Bill?'

'I know nothing of my mistress that might explain this unseemly interest in the manner or location of her demise.'

John Wester, whoever he was, had been peculiarly absorbed by the search for Drogryre's grave. Ancestria Magicka, centuries later, were intent upon following in his footsteps — indeed, by Jay's account they were more interested in that question than they were in anything else Bill had to offer. Which, considering the utterly remarkable nature of him, was extraordinary. What did they expect to find in Drogryre's grave that was of greater value than Bill himself?

'Do you know where she died?' I asked him.

'Lavenham. That is the town in which we had taken up residence when she became ill, and quickly died.'

'Of the plague.'

'The sweating sickness.'

My ears pricked up a bit at that, which may sound macabre but many a historian would react the same way. The sweating sickness was a strange form of plague which cropped up out of nowhere in about 1485 and vanished some sixty or so years later, never to be heard of again. More oddly still, it was confined to England for some years, and only belatedly spread into Ireland and Europe. It's still sometimes referred to as the "English Sweat". No theory as to its possible causes can account for all of its recorded symptoms.

And the best part of all, *of all*, is this: the very first symptom of having contracted this plague consisted of an overpowering sense of dread. In other words, one felt one's doom rapidly approaching.

I realise I sound like Zareen, but how fabulously weird is all of that?

Of course, all things considered (especially that last part) it is highly likely that the sweating sickness was of magickal origin. While it is fair to say that the historians of the non-magickal world are a shade more confused about it all than we are, it is also fair to note that none of *us* has ever yet managed to uncover the plague's original author either.

'Bill!' I said. 'What was the cause of the sweating sickness?'

'I have no information on that topic.'

It was worth a try.

So, Drogryre rocked the magickal world back in the fifteenth century, produced a feat of such remarkable power as Bill, but somehow never achieved any prominent position within magickal history in spite of this — perhaps because she died of the sweat soon afterwards.

Or perhaps not.

'I need to talk to Zareen,' I said.

'An excellent notion. Go at once,' said Milady. 'There'll be chocolate in the pot.'

· · ● · ● · ● · · ·

There was, too, though it took a few moments to spot it in the midst of Zareen's clutter. One of Milady's favourite eighteenth-century tea pots, an elegant silver specimen, stood at one corner of the desk, its tall spout steaming in a promising fashion.

Zareen lounged in her chair, booted feet on the desk as usual. She had one smallish ancient-looking book in her hands and about seven more stacked in front of her. When she saw me, she set down her book and adjusted her posture to a more respectable configuration — sweeping the pot onto the floor in the process.

I caught it with a flick of a finger, and carefully floated it back up to the table-top. 'Don't waste the chocolate!' I chided.

'Never,' said Zareen fervently. Milady had thoughtfully provided two cups — two, because Jay and Indira had taken themselves off someplace else. To my regret they had escorted Bill along with them, though no one had seemed very interested in explaining to me where they were going or what they proposed to do with the book.

I tried not to feel hurt.

Zareen and I fell upon the chocolate (not literally). I was feeling strained and tired after such a long, chaotic, stressful day, and guzzled my restorative chocolate more quickly than could ever be called ladylike. I felt better.

This done, I caught Zareen up on recent developments. Her eyes, like mine, brightened at the words "sweating sickness". We are a peculiar bunch, aren't we? 'So Drogryre was part of the first wave of the sweat,' Zareen mused when I had finished. 'One of the very first to die.'

'Seems so.'

'Hmm.'

'Do you suppose that has anything to do with this unseemly eagerness to dig her up again?'

'I don't see how, but you never know.'

I dismissed this with a wave. A careful one, since I was on my second cup of chocolate. 'Questions! What's so special about Drogryre? Why haven't we heard of her, when she seems to have been absurdly powerful and pretty clever besides? How have *they* heard of her, and what's the interest in her place of rest? And who the hell is John Wester? — Oh!'

Wester. Right.' I'd forgotten I had sent the pages over to Val, nor had I checked since for a response. I did that.

There was a string of messages from Val.

Ves, said the first one. *Much as I applaud your initiative, you're an idiot if you think I hadn't taken copies of my own the moment I got your precious book into my sticky little hands.*

Well, that was fair.

Idiosyncratic use of English, said the next one. *Generally classifiable as Late Middle English, but eccentric enough in spelling, grammar etc to suggest Wester wasn't far from being illiterate. Wondering therefore why he purloined Bill at all, and what motive he had for writing any of his adventures down.*

Good questions, those.

About half of his entries are of little use. They ramble about seemingly irrelevant incidents: what he procured for lunch that day, for example, and an insult that was levelled at him by a rude cloth vendor, where (more interestingly) he was trying to buy silk. Silk!

Nothing we know about W suggests he was rich enough for silk garments, or of that kind of social standing either. The man seems to have come into some money and was blowing it in fine style. Surmising that his pursuit of the grave might not have been spontaneous. Somebody paid him. Theft of Bill no coincidence, perhaps. Was he keeping records to satisfy whoever was bankrolling his quest?

He hated Lavenham. Noisy, crowded and without beauty, he says. But he had no thoughts of going elsewhere; too convinced that D's grave must be somewhere nearby. Guessing that his rough map shows some part of the town, though comparing it to contemporary maps of the place has not yet yielded anything. Little indication of where he got the map, though he does say he paid a grave-digger ten shillings for information.

Ten shillings! That was a lot, for the time.

Journal ends abruptly, said Val's final message. *Seemed to think he was near to finding the grave, though did not give further details. Off he went in a spirit of high expectation, and... who knows. Did he find the grave, but for some reason abandon the journal? Did something happen to him? Cannot discover. No reference to a John Wester anywhere that seems relevant.*

As I read this last message, a final one popped up saying simply: *Nor Drogryre either.*

'Zareen,' I said. 'We are in dire need of your macabre mystery-solving skills.'

Zareen smirked. 'What is my quest?'

I thought. There were lists of outstanding questions here, but I couldn't reasonably dump them all on Zareen. What did we most want to know?

'Drogryre,' I decided. 'There is something about her that doesn't add up. Why is there no record of her? We know of many powerful witches and sorcerers from the time; why not her?'

'There must be something, somewhere,' said Zareen, already reaching for her tab. 'Something's put the wind up our friends at Ancestria Magicka, anyway.'

'Exactly. They've found something that we haven't, perhaps because they're looking in different places.'

Zareen frowned, thoughtful. 'I wonder if she was a sorceress,' she mused.

'What?'

'Well. We prize *some* magickal history, but there are parts we would prefer to forget. Or if not to forget, exactly, then we at least refrain from honouring those kinds of practitioners. Think black magick, Ves. Simplistic term, I know, but it's your necromancers, your wicked witches, your demon-summoning gutter-dwellers... those kinds of people.' Zareen maintained this narration without looking at me, her fingers flickering over her screen. 'Real life as we know it is full of shining characters, of great deeds, grand powers and magnificent achievements... course, it's also full of shit, and history is no different. But nobody wants to turn over the rocks and look at the shitty stuff.'

'Except you,' I said.

Zareen's smile flashed. 'Except for me. You need a strong stomach for it, sometimes, but there's some interesting stuff down there. And I happen to think it is important to know the worst of one's past as well as the best. Now, here's something interesting.' She passed her tab to me.

She had found an entry from somebody's blog, dated 2012. *Lavenham's Secret History of Witchcraft*, read the title.

I skimmed through the post (it was long). Written, I had no trouble guessing, by a non-magicker, it nonetheless contained some promising hints: *Did you know that the quaint, quirky town of Lavenham was once the site of some of the most horrific witch trials of the 1600s?*

'They had a coven?' I said, blinking. 'Huh.' I shouldn't have been surprised, really. Lavenham might be a small, nothing-much place now, but back in Drogryre's time it was a bustling merchant town. It wasn't that unlikely for a coven to put down roots there.

Zareen retrieved her tab. 'By the looks of it, more than one, and not just the shiny kind either.'

'You mean they had one of *those* kinds of covens?'

'Ohh, yes. The town's supposed to have declined a long way by the seventeenth, so if they had that much activity still going on even then, I'd be willing to bet it was quite the happenin' scene a century or two earlier.'

Magickers only form covens when they want to do something really difficult, something requiring the pooling of a lot of magickal power. Sometimes people do it for good, noble reasons; lots of covens were formed to battle the Sweat, for example. Lavenham might well have had one or two of those.

But as with all areas of human endeavour, some covens were (or are) formed for slightly less heroic reasons, too. Like, just for instance... 'Raising the dead?' I suggested.

Zareen grinned. 'Oh, I *hope* so.'

14

'U'ndead sorceresses,' I said. 'Lovely.'

'I love you,' said Zareen.

I blinked. 'Thank you. Er, why?'

'It's been an *age* since I last had a good corpse-raising mystery to sink my teeth into.'

I winced a bit inside. The near juxtaposition of *corpse* and *teeth-sinking* was doing unfortunate things to my brain. 'Thank you for those mental images.'

'Always welcome, my darling.'

'You really are pleased with me, aren't you?'

She beamed at me.

'Then you should be pleased with Jay, too. He got the book.'

Her smiled faded. 'So, new questions. I cannot yet say whether Drogryre was involved with any of these covens, or if so, which type. But somebody really wanted to find her grave, and I'd say it's an awfully big coincidence that the area happens to have a history of necromancy as well.'

'Bill said Wester expected to find some kind of treasure.'

'He might have been promised something by way of a reward, if he was successful. Or they might have guaranteed his interest by telling him there were riches to be uncovered.'

'So you don't think there was treasure?'

'From what you've told me, Bill dismissed the idea, and he ought to know. That said...' Zareen sat back again. 'There was sometimes a tradition for magickers being buried with things like their grimoires, their Wands, their familiars (mummified), or any other personal artefacts they possessed some strong connection to. But I think Bill would have known about things like that.'

'Bill *was* her grimoire.'

'Eventually. I doubt she pulled Bill out of her hat the moment she took up magick. He's the kind of accomplishment that crowns a lifetime career, and presumably she had some other, more ordinary grimoire throughout her life up to that point. Even if she did, though, it's unlikely either Wester or Ancestria Magicka had any interest in that. Bill ought to have been enough.'

'So no treasure, no grimoire, probably no artefacts.'

'I'm telling you! It has to be necromancy.'

'Maybe back then, but now? The woman's been nothing but bone for centuries. What could anybody hope to accomplish with the skeleton of a long-dead sorceress? If they want to raise a strong magicker from the dead, how about somebody, er, fresher?'

That gave Zareen pause. 'It is harder with the recently deceased,' she said, though with a little doubt. 'People keep track of corpses nowadays. Nobody dies of plague and gets chucked into mass graves anymore. It's one thing to go dig in a field somewhere for somebody long-forgotten; quite another to crash an active graveyard and walk off with someone's grandmother.'

'Still, though,' I persisted. 'When you raise a magicker from the dead, what's the intent?'

'Enslavement to your will.'

'Right — as an undead being still capable of practicing magick, in some form or another. You want to purloin their abilities for your own use, which is why deceased Waymasters tend to have a round-the-clock guard posted over their graves for about six months straight. If this is the goal, do you think a crumbling old skeleton would be of any interest to anybody?'

Zareen frowned. 'I feel like I know the answer to this, but it's not coming to mind.'

'The answer?'

Zareen lunged for her tab again, and then wandered off to feverishly scan her bookshelves. 'There's something about skeletons,' she muttered. 'I once read about a spate of grave-robbings — fifty years or so ago now — that puzzled everyone at the time for the same reasons you've just come up with. The graves that were targeted were all the resting places of magickers, and all ancient. None of the disinterred were under three hundred years dead. What would anybody want with a crop of crumbling old bones, as you put it? I don't remember now if that mystery was ever solved, *but,* there was another case in the late Victorian era where someone went so far as to advertise. Advertise! Some chap was paying well for the bones of magickers, with a fat bonus offered for a complete skeleton. He was shut down pretty quickly, and no record remains as to what he wanted to do with the bones.' Zareen wandered from shelf to shelf as she spoke, occasionally tapping at her tab. I realised I had entirely lost her attention, and stood up.

'Let me know what you dig up,' I said.

Zareen grinned, not too lost in thought to appreciate my execrable pun. 'Will do.'

My phone buzzed as I stepped out into the corridor. Jay calling.

'Can I borrow Bill?' I said without preamble.

A slight pause. 'By "borrow", do you secretly mean "elope with to the border"?'

'No.'

'Then yes. But quickly, we're leaving for Lavenham any minute.'

'We are? What for?'

'Drogryre's grave.'

'You found something!'

'Not as such. It occurred to Milady that Amelia will notice her notebook missing as soon as she wakes up — which probably happened about an hour and a half ago — and she and her esteemed colleagues will probably speed up the timetable on whatever they are doing accordingly. Ergo, she would like us on the scene.'

'Genius.' Why bother figuring out the site of the grave ourselves, if we could just let them do it and then follow? 'Provided we can find them, of course.'

'I put my tracker on Mercer.'

'You... you did? When?'

'In the middle of that fist-fight you were so eager to break up.'

Ah.

To hide my embarrassment, I hastily told Jay about Zareen's theory. 'Great,' he said. 'She can do that, you and I are going to go do this.'

'Yes, sir.'

He hung up.

It had not occurred to him to mention where he was, or anything useful like that. Nor had it occurred to me to ask. So, I merely checked that I still had my Sunstone Wand within reach, and headed off to the Waypoint in the cellar.

Though I did pop back into Zareen's room first.

'Zar, we're going grave-hunting.'

She was up out of her chair like a shot. 'Don't you dare go without me!'

'Wouldn't dream of it.' I grinned.

She tried to take all seven of her books along, then regretfully bowed to practicality and set four of them back. Then another one.

'Corpse-hunting now, reading later,' I told her.

The last two went back onto the desk with a *thump*. 'There's vital information somewhere in there.'

'They will wait for you. Boots! Phone! Quickly!'

Zareen scurried about in a brief frenzy, and within moments we were both on our way downstairs.

I could have left her to read in peace, of course, and in some ways that would have been ideal; we were in need of information. But I wanted her with us for two reasons.

One: the pall of corpse-thieving, bone-harvesting, undead-raising shenanigans hanging over this business was growing thicker by the hour, and we had no one better to deal with that kind of thing than Zareen.

Two: If we went grave-robbing without her, she would literally never forgive me.

Jay took Zareen's presence with admirable grace, while Zareen took the simpler expedient of virtually ignoring him. That was all right. Better that than sniping at each other. Jay had Bill with him, and I could not contain a coo of delight as the lovely heavy tome was put into my hands. 'You have five minutes,' said Jay. 'Then put him somewhere out of sight.'

'Bill!' I said, as Jay began his preparations for departure. 'Quick! What do you know about raising the dead?'

'I can assure you!' said Bill. 'My mistress was never a friend to that sort of activity!'

'So you don't know anything?'

'Nothing at all!'

Was it my imagination, or did cool, composed Bill sound a little bit shrill?

Hmm.

Zareen said, 'How about bone-harvesting, Bill? Specifically magicker's bones.'

Bill merely said, 'How good it is to see you again, Miss Dalir.'

'Thank you,' said Zareen. 'That's lovely.'

'I am rather lovely,' said Bill.

'Utterly. Now answer the question.'

Bill gave a bookish sigh, and shuffled his pages. 'I am no expert, you understand…'

'We understand completely.'

'…but my mistress did have one or two bone talismans in her possession at the time of her death.'

'Talismans?' said Zareen. 'What were they for?'

'They held unusual protective powers, usually along similar lines to their original owners' abilities.'

'So if I died, someone could use my bones to protect against curses?'

'If you possess a talent for hexes, Miss Dalir, then yes.'

Zareen shrugged this away, unimpressed.

'Superstition?' I asked her in an undertone.

'Sounds like it to me. Codswallop.'

We weren't getting very far with Bill, and Jay's whirling Winds were beginning to whirl in earnest. I raised my voice to be heard over the noise and half-shouted, 'What about a complete skeleton, Bill? What if somebody got hold of every bone in Zareen's body?'

Bill went very quiet.

'Bill!'

'Miss Vesper,' he finally said. 'Miss Dalir. I hold you both in the very highest esteem, and therefore permit me to advise you never to allow yourselves to be caught up in anything of that nature.'

'Why? What does it do?'

'And should you happen to die in untoward circumstances, I hope you will ensure that your loved ones will keep your remains safe from any such interference.'

Zareen's eyes may have lit up at the words *untoward circumstances,* but I felt confused — and slightly alarmed. Bill was serious, very serious. 'Why, Bill?' I tried again.

But Bill would say no more.

'Put the book away, Ves!' Jay ordered, and I obeyed, because to drop Bill somewhere in between here and East Anglia would be more than my job's worth.

And away we went.

I could not decide whether I was more relieved or disgusted by Zareen's manner of handling the journey, for she was untouched by it. We emerged inside a circle of sapling birches in the midst of a tiny copse, and Zareen strolled into the adjacent wheat field not only with perfect composure but actually with a great yawn, as though the whole process was on the duller side of human endeavour.

Jay and I exchanged a look of mutual aggravation, and I am certain we shared a mutual resolve to show no sign of discomfort whatsoever.

Said copse proved to be in between two great, rolling fields, and on the not-too-distant horizon was a town. 'Is that Lavenham?' I asked Jay.

'Well,' he said with a tiny smile. 'I hope so.'

'Are they here yet?'

Jay shook his head.

'Onward!' said Zareen, smiling in the evening sunshine as the spring breezes ruffled her glossy black hair. She took off for Lavenham at an easy, loping run, looking like an advert for washing powder, or possibly for hair care products.

'She doesn't get out of the study much,' I said to Jay by way of apology.

He grunted.

Lavenham, to my delight, was roaring drunk. The buildings looked as though it had been raining brandy for the past two hundred years and they couldn't stop giggling. Crooked, timber-framed, oddly-coloured old things, they wobbled and swayed and leaned against each other for support. Next to this wild display of character, the newer constructs looked drab and featureless. It wasn't difficult to find our way to the oldest parts of the town, where Drogryre's grave must be. We bought chips from a tiny chip shop and hastily devoured them on our way through the narrow streets, eyes everywhere at once, yet with no idea what we were looking for. I suppose we thought something obvious would pop out at us when we walked past it; that we'd know it when we saw it.

Well, it didn't.

'So,' I said after a while, when we had walked past the same perpendicular-gothic church twice over. We had checked the graveyard, just in case there happened to be a stone conveniently engraved with "Here lies Drogryre, sorceress and possible necromancer, 1485." There was not. 'If you were a fifteenth-century grave digger, where would you say is the most obvious place to bury a plague victim?'

'Or several,' said Zareen.

Or several. How were we going to pick Drogryre's individual skeleton out of a whole pile of bones? A problem to deal with... later.

'Church graveyards would fill up pretty quickly,' said Zareen. 'They'd be buried in a plague pit.' She had her phone out as she said this and was furiously typing something.

'Somewhere out beyond the edges of the town,' added Jay. 'I wouldn't bury plague-ridden corpses in my back garden.'

'Good point.' We needed to avoid the old town, then. What was empty land a few hundred years ago had probably been developed with new buildings somewhere in the last century or so, and these were spread out around Lavenham in every direction. Where to go?

'That way,' said Zareen after a minute, and pointed in what seemed to me to be a random direction.

'What?'

'This way.' Zareen set off, waving her phone at us. 'A probable plague pit was discovered in 1963 when the foundations were being dug for a new building.'

'They built a new house over a pitfull of plague victims?' Revolted, I hurried after Zareen.

'No, they built the house somewhere else.'

Jay said: 'Er, how did you find this out?'

A fair question. I had conducted a thorough search for information about the town and its environs, too, and come up with very little on the topic.

'Database,' said Zareen unhelpfully.

'What?'

'I have access to a database for this kind of stuff.'

'Plague pits?!'

'Plague pits, burial sites of unusual significance, haunted houses. Mostly with some link to magick somewhere along the line, but not always.' She turned to flash a brilliant smile in Jay's direction, thoroughly aware of how appalled he was. 'That kind of stuff.'

Jay walked in silence for a moment. 'I don't know whether to be more aghast that such a thing exists, or that you take such obvious delight in it.'

'This is why I brought Zareen,' I told him. 'She's vital to our quest.'

Jay muttered something I could not hear.

We trawled all the way to the other side of the town again, and at length arrived at... a car park.

'Hm.' Zareen frowned. 'I didn't notice anything about it being paved over.'

I stamped a foot on the smooth tarmac. It yielded not one whit.

Jay coughed. It sounded suspiciously like a strangled laugh.

'It is of no consequence,' said Bill suddenly from inside my bag. 'My mistress is not here.'

15

I fumbled the bag open and dragged Bill out. 'What do you mean, she isn't here?'

'She is not here. I detect no trace of her presence.'

'Bill, she's been dead for more than five hundred years. There is nothing left of her to detect.'

'That is not necessarily true. A strong bond was formed between us, and I would know if she was nearby.'

Damn it. 'I take it you haven't sensed any trace of her presence anywhere else?'

'I am afraid not.'

'Not even at the churchyard?'

'No.'

I felt, for one awful moment, like hurling Bill into the nearest of the puddles left by last night's rain. I contained the impulse. It wasn't his fault that we were apparently barking up the wrong tree.

'Any sign of *them*?' I asked Jay.

He shook his head. 'Nowhere near here.'

I began to get a bad feeling. 'Bill. Are you certain your mistress died here?'

'Perfectly.'

'I hate to be insensitive, but truly? You... did you see her die?'

Bill hesitated. 'Well, no.'

Damn it.

'She became very ill indeed, and with such speed that her imminent demise was inevitable. Soon afterwards, she... well, she never came back for me again, and some little time later the contents of her house were removed, including me.'

'Maybe she didn't die.'

'But.' Bill's voice developed a forlorn quality. 'Why then did she never return for me?'

'Good question.'

'Call Val,' said Jay.

My thought, too, but it was not necessary. My phone began to buzz at that moment, and it was Val calling. I put her on speaker.

'Ves!' she said. 'We have all been a bunch of idiots, and I thought you would like to know.'

'You mean our favourite plague-ridden sorceress didn't die in Lavenham?'

'So you figured that out.'

'Only just.'

'How?'

'Well, we're in Lavenham and she isn't.'

Val snorted. 'Zareen's idea interested me, so I went looking in some other, less accessible places—'

'Which ones?' I said quickly. If you catch Val off guard, she will occasionally let something slip.

Not this time. 'Let's just call them the dark depths of forbidden knowledge and leave it at that. Anyway, there is no record whatsoever of any sorceress, witch or other magicker anywhere in Suffolk of the name of Drogryre. Not five hundred years ago, and not ever.'

'Oh.'

'There is, however, quite a lot about a major sorceress called Diota *Greyer*, commonly called Dio.'

This time, it was my own self I felt like hurling into a puddle. Dio Greyer. I had seen for myself that Wester's handwriting was terrible, and Val had told me that his spelling and punctuation were decidedly eccentric. Why had it not occurred to me that we might have interpreted her name wrongly? And for that matter... 'Why didn't we stumble over her before?' I asked Val.

'Because she's not the type of sorceress we like to remember. She was the High Witch of Lavenham's black coven until 1485 when she suddenly disappeared. Serious necromancy,

Ves, the really nasty stuff.'

'Bill's absolutely certain she was very ill.'

'She might well have caught the Sweat, but not everyone died of it. Or it might have been something else, like a hex. This is an era when people lived in daily terror of demons and evil spirits, after all. Remember Wharram Percy? Graves stuffed with decapitated corpses? People believed the dead could come back and attack the living, partly thanks to the activities of people like Dio Greyer. And they were terrified enough of this to mutilate and burn their recently deceased in order to prevent it. She would not have been popular, if her neighbours discovered what she was doing.'

That raised some interesting possibilities. 'Do you think that was why people were looking for her grave? To burn her bones, so she couldn't come back?'

'Maybe. Doesn't explain Ancestria Magicka's interest in her now, though.'

'Harvesting the bones as talismans? Protection against undeath, or the undead?'

'Maybe, but it seems a bit far-fetched. There are plenty of easier ways to accomplish that.'

'What about Wester?'

'Wester. Well. Either he gave up, or he, too, figured out she wasn't in Lavenham and followed her trail somewhere else — leaving Bill behind, for some reason.'

'Where does her trail go, Val?'

'Brace yourself.'

'Braced.'

'Right. There aren't any more recorded references to a Dio Greyer after 1485, so at first I was still inclined to think she'd died that year. But! A few years later, there was a kerfuffle at a town only about fourteen miles from Lavenham when a conspiracy was uncovered. Somebody called Edyth Grey (and coven) was brought in to resurrect a recently-deceased earl and restore him to power instead of his son, who was unpopular. A couple of years after that, an alderman was witnessed to have died suddenly one night when he choked on a bone at dinner — only to reappear the next morning, in poor health but apparently alive. He "lived" for another week, during which time he completed some important business which was very much in the interests of the masters of a local wool guild. There are half a dozen more stories like this one across Suffolk, all within an approximately ten-year period.'

'So Dio Greyer survived the Sweat (or her dose of hexing), fled Lavenham in a hurry

on pain of decapitation and burning, and became a freelance necromancer-for-hire elsewhere.'

'Looks like it.'

'I think I'm going to like her,' said Zareen.

'Undoubtedly. In case you're interested, Edyth (or Edita) Grey died in 1496 at Bury St.
Edmunds.'

'Of?'

'Hanging.'

I felt a chill at those words, and Bill's earlier warning floated back through my mind.
If death-by-hanging did not qualify as *untoward circumstances,* what could? 'You're certain?'

'Yes. Unfortunately, so's Ancestria Magicka. Amelia's notebook mentions "Bury",
which threw me off for a while because there's a town in the Manchester area with that
name. But it's common shorthand for Bury St. Edmunds, too.'

'Val, you are a miracle.'

'I know.'

'Bury St. Edmunds?' said Zareen when I'd hung up. She had an arrested look, and her
mind was obviously somewhere else.

'Does that ring some bells?'

'Maybe.' She disappeared into her phone.

'There's a bus,' said Jay. 'Leaves from the Swan in ten minutes. Half an hour's ride.'

'Where's the Swan?'

'We passed it twice an hour ago, but... no, never mind. This way. We can make it if we
run.'

We ran.

• • • • • • • • • •

'They're here,' said Jay the moment we got off the bus in the centre of Bury St. Edmunds.

'Where exactly?' I asked.

'Look, I don't know what Indira and Orlando did to these things to get so specific a
reading on my position at Ashdown, but I can't replicate it. You've used these things, Ves.'

'Not much, actually. I rarely lose things.'

Jay looked faintly abashed. 'Oh. Well, they work best within a fairly short range. The closer you are to the tracker-bead, the more accurately you'll be able to pinpoint its location.'

'Oh! A warmer-warmer-warmest type thing.'

'Exactly. We aren't close enough to Mercer right now to pin him down to a street or whatever, but he's within probably about ten miles of us.'

'You should ask Indira what they did. It might be useful to know.'

'She probably wouldn't tell me. Keeping secrets is the only way she can one-up me, most of the time.' He stuck his hands into the pockets of his favourite dark leather jacket — now happily restored to him — and looked around. 'So, where did they bury hanged corpses five hundred years ago?'

'Forget it,' said Zareen.

'What?'

'Forget where they buried anybody. She isn't there.' She spoke with a kind of suppressed excitement, and her eyes were shining. 'Who's up for a ghost hunt?'

Jay looked uncertain, as well he might. It was almost eight o' clock, and the sun was sinking into the horizon. 'Explain?' he said.

'What do you two know about haunted houses?'

'Sod all,' said Jay.

'Same,' said I. 'Is there much to know?'

Zareen rolled her eyes. 'All right, my sceptical friends. Most so-called haunted houses aren't haunted at all, I grant you that much, and many that are can boast no more than an occasional flicker of spirit activity. But this is not the whole story. Scattered across our beloved country are a handful of seriously, properly haunted buildings. They could more accurately be termed *possessed,* in fact. This rarely happens by accident, and it's difficult to arrange.'

'We're a bit pressed for time, Zareen,' said Jay.

'I *know.* This is important.'

'Okay, sorry.'

Zareen took a deep breath. 'A spirit is more likely to linger after death if they died suddenly, or at a time when it seemed particularly important to them to be alive for a while longer. If you want to harness such a spirit for something like this, it's customary to bury the body under the floor of a house, or better yet in the walls themselves. Then, through use of a few charms and spells which (I need hardly add) are horribly illegal these days, you can bind the poor soul to the house itself.'

'Why would you want to?' I asked.

'It makes for a kind of bastardised version of *our* House. Doors that open and close by themselves, hopefully when you want them to. Lights which switch on and off as required, temperature regulation, immediate repulsion of anybody you don't want stepping over the threshold. Et cetera. The more powerful the spirit and the better the binding, the more interesting the options.'

It turned my stomach to imagine such a practice in anything like the same context as our beloved House. Magickal slavery of a tormented spirit wasn't something I wanted to connect with my Home, or with Milady. But I put the idea out of my head; something to think about later. 'All right, so... you think this is what's become of Greyer?'

'Her last known place of residence prior to her execution was at the end of Maynewater Lane. About a year after her death, people began to say that the house was haunted. The residents fled, and it was taken instead by one Maud Grey, who lived there in spite of its haunting for twelve years before the house mysteriously disappeared.'

'A *house* disappeared?' said Jay incredulously.

'Well,' Zareen amended. 'It was only a small one. A cottage, really. It reappeared here and there for the next couple of decades before vanishing for good, and eventually a new house was built on the spot. And look.' Zareen held out her phone. On the screen was a picture of an old, hand-inked map of the town in the fifteenth century; she had zoomed in over Maynewater Lane. 'Can we have Bill a sec?'

I saw her point at once. I hauled Bill out of his bag and opened him up to the page with Wester's crude map. The lines obviously correlated with those of the map Zareen had found, and my heart leapt with excitement. 'The X is where her house used to be?'

'Yep!'

'Hey, we've found her. Good job.'

Zareen beamed at me.

'Maud Grey,' Jay mused. 'Family?'

'Probably a sister.'

Jay nodded. 'So we've found her, but on the other hand... er, any idea where the house went to?'

'Well, there are scattered accounts over the next few hundred years of people sighting cottages or even entire mansions which vanish into the mist, or which simply aren't there when they come back. There appear to be three such stories that match up.' She checked her screen. '1572. A timber-framed cottage was spotted by a farmer on Tut Hill, but a day later it was gone. 1678, the sister of the local vicar saw a cottage fade into the mist in much the same spot. And in 1737, a tradesman's wife was held up on the road outside a ramshackle cottage in the same parish. The highwayman went in and the carriage rolled on, but the next day the cottage was gone and the robber was never found.'

'On to Tut Hill!' I said. 'Um, where is it?'

Zareen smiled at me. 'It's close.'

'Quickly,' said Jay. 'Because unless my trackers are talking rubbish, we're likely to be beaten to it.'

16

Tut Hill proved to be a long, long road clambering gently up an incline. It ran from Bury St. Edmunds out to a village called Fornham something, and it was mostly house-free. Only once we got as far as the village did we begin to see low stone walls and a smattering of properties set a little way back from the road.

It would have been nice if we had arrived to find a crumbling old cottage conveniently glowing in the dark, or overflowing with angry spirits, or something of the kind. But the houses there were mere ordinary brick structures, varied in style and age, all looking perfectly innocuous in the low light of late evening. A few had lights shining in the windows.

'What a fine vision of peace,' murmured Zareen approvingly.

I felt somewhat crestfallen. 'Either the cottage is very well camouflaged,' I suggested, 'or it is not here.'

'Could be either,' said Zareen cheerfully. Checking her maps, she pointed back the way we had come. 'I don't think any of the sightings ever came up this far. We've overshot the mark.'

My feet were hurting by then, for we had been trekking a while, and for a moment I felt like applying a heavy object to the general area of Zareen's head. I swallowed these unworthy feelings, and turned about, dragging Bill out of my bag as I did so. 'Bill,' I said gravely, 'we are in dire need of your assistance.'

'How may I be of use, Miss Vesper?'

He sounded sleepy. 'You weren't dozing, were you?'

'No! I have been fully alert since our last conversation! I assure you, I have not missed a single—' He stopped, and if a book could be said to grow *tense*, well, Bill was about as relaxed as a block of concrete just then. 'My mistress!' he said, in a proper hollow gasp, like he was in a highly dramatic stage play.

'See. I was hoping you might say something like that.' I held him out before me as we trudged a ways back down the hill. 'Lead the way, Mister Bill, if you please.'

Bill was off like a shot, dragging me behind him like he was an overexcited terrier and I the mere human appendage on the other end of the lead.

We plunged through a gap in the blackthorn hedge, and into the field beyond. Near enough pitch dark by then, and free of the lights of any nearby houses, there was little to see by; I had to trust to Bill's good sense (did he have any?) and hope he did not lead the three of us into a pit or something. Stumbling over uneven ground, we ventured perhaps a hundred metres into the field — and then stopped.

'She is close,' hissed Bill.

I still saw no house. 'Um, you sure?'

A spectral head flickered into view not two feet from my face, and my heart gave the kind of lurching shudder people sometimes die of. 'What's yer business wit' the Grey house?' it said, teeth clattering. It had hair but no skin, and great hollow eye sockets.

'Social visit,' said Zareen coolly.

There came a sudden rushing noise, as of the displacement of an awful lot of air. It was attended by a distant, high-pitched screaming which grew rapidly closer, and then there was the shadowy bulk of a cottage looming directly before us. It screamed wordless fury in a woman's voice, and Bill flinched in my hands.

'Say no more,' I muttered.

'Hello, Mistress,' said Bill weakly.

The screaming stopped.

The front door opened, and an eerie glow emanated from within.

'Right then,' I said, and stepped forward, Jay at my elbow.

Zareen flung out an arm, halting us both before we'd gone more than a pace or two. '*Please*,' she said witheringly. 'If this doesn't qualify as Toil and Trouble, I'll eat my skulls.'

'Thank you for that mental image.'

'You're welcome.' Zareen sauntered off in the direction of the beckoning door, and Jay and I fell in step behind her.

'Where are they?' I whispered to Jay.

'Gaining on us. We have, maybe, ten minutes.'

'Excellent.'

'Excellent?' It was too dark to see Jay giving me the side-eye, but I could feel it. 'You're hatching plots, aren't you?'

'Jay. *Always.*'

'Right.'

Zareen stopped in front of the door, and gave her Society symbol. We all have the three-crossed-wands part, that's the Society bit. Mine has a winged unicorn superimposed over them. Zareen's turned out to have a skull added on. Not quite human; the eyes were too big, and it had horns.

'Er,' said Jay.

'Don't ask,' I said hastily. 'Never ask.'

'Dio Greyer?' Zareen was saying. 'Maud Grey? We are here from the Society for Magickal Heritage to—'

'—warn you of a dire plot against you,' I interposed. 'Formulated by a vile organisation calling themselves Ancestria Magicka.'

'Er,' said Jay and Zareen as one.

There was a tense silence, and then the door yawned wider. Zareen rolled her eyes at me as she went in.

'You managed to use the words "vile" and "dire" in the same sentence,' muttered Jay as he followed. 'Nice work.'

'There's much to be said for drama.' Jay, sadly, beat me to the door, so I contented myself with bringing up the rear.

The interior was a low-ceilinged, white-washed, scrupulously neat little cottage, with all the leaning door frames, exposed beams and stone floors one would expect of the period. Some things were unusual, though — like the lumpy stonework just inside the door behind which Dio Greyer's bones were presumably interred, considering the way Bill instantly plastered himself to it.

'Bill,' I hissed. 'You're hugging a wall.'

'Communing with my creator,' Bill replied, rather muffled.

Considering the kind of company I was in just then, I refrained from pointing out that

Bill's creator was deservedly hanged for some decidedly questionable behaviour. I suppose it's like continuing to love your parents, even if they turn out to be psychos. The argument usually runs along the lines of "Well, I only have one mother/father/creator/whatever," as if that's reason enough all by itself. Apparently, for Bill, it was.

Then again, I had no actual proof that Bill's endearing gesture was voluntary. I certainly found it impossible to peel him *off* the wall again, when I tried.

Hmm.

'My codex!' said Dio Greyer's voice. 'Thou has't returned!'

'Well…' I demurred, redoubling my efforts to retrieve Bill. 'We had not exactly intended to—'

I stopped, because she was not listening to me. The floor shook, and the walls howled: 'Hear that, wretch! Five hundr'd years to right thy miserable failings!'

Somebody replied, a somebody with the baritone rumble of a large man. But he, I was guessing, was probably as corporeal as Dio Greyer by this time, for those tones came out of thin air, and seemed to emanate from everywhere at once. 'Beef-witted churls!' he snarled. 'Have I not faithfully served thee these five centuries and more? What use these gudgeons?'

'Gudgeons they may be, but they have brought my codex,' purred Dio. 'Which is more than I can say for *thee.*'

'Had thou not made a puppet of me, I would have done all that and more! But thou must be jaunting hither and thither, and ever on! Have me hauling thy stone and bones and plaster about like turnips, because thou didst *require* it, and never a day's rest!' The walls shuddered, and the floor trembled so hard I almost lost my footing. Stones rumbled, plaster flaked, and somewhere at the back of my mind Dio Greyer was screaming again.

'Er,' I intervened. 'Mr. Wester?'

There came a shocked silence. Then: 'How didst thou come by my name?'

'It's in the book,' I said, apologetically. 'Why did you sell it?'

And there I'd made a mistake. '*Sold?*' shrieked Dio Greyer, at such a pitch as to shatter my ears. 'SOLD! Lying wretch! Thieving lily-liver! Didst thou not have courage enough to speak truth to thy mistress!'

'Thou didst slay me anyway,' rejoined Wester. 'I ought to have spoken truth to thee, were it all the vengeance I could win. Yes, I sold thy miserable codex! A foul-mouthed object! I was well rid of it.'

'And if it was foul-mouthed, I know at whose door to lay the fault!'

The argument went on in similar style for some time, and with such heat that the three of us were forgotten. We gathered into a protective knot (for we felt as though an earthquake raged around us, so much did the cottage rumble and sway with the force of Greyer and Wester's fury).

'So,' I said. 'Wester discovered where to find Dio, and got rid of Bill along the way — only she was not quite as dead as she was supposed to be, and he found himself slightly unpopular when he arrived. With Maud, too.'

'Understandably,' said Zareen. 'And the sisters slew him and stuffed him into the walls.'

'Not quite so understandably.'

'It was rather rude.'

'What did he mean about hauling the house around?'

Jay frowned. 'I have an idea about that.' He strode to the nearest wall and hammered upon it, ignoring, with enviable dignity, the rain of plaster-powder that fell upon his head. 'Hey!' he bellowed. 'Shut it!'

To my surprise, this worked. 'Hast thou something to share, little man?' said Dio acidly.

'A question,' Jay answered. 'For John Wester.'

'Speak,' said Wester.

'Were you a Waymaster, in life?'

'I was among the finest!'

'I suppose that explains why you were tapped to find Greyer's grave.'

'And find it, I did. Along with my own.'

'It was, what, 1508?'

'Mayhap.'

I put the pieces together then, too. Maud Grey had lived in the house for twelve years after her sister's death, and then it had vanished. Courtesy of Wester, an enslaved Waymaster. 'But there's no henge...?' I began.

'Didn't always have to be,' said Jay briefly. 'We're crap at it these days, need all the help we can get. Magickal decline, and all that.'

'So you can't haul entire houses around?'

'No.'

'I'm disappointed.'

Jay stuck out his tongue at me.

'What became of Maud?' I said, more loudly. 'Where's your sister, Dio?'

My question went unanswered, because the front door blew open and two people burst into the room. One of them promptly fell over the worn oak chair I had quietly placed directly in the way of the entrance, and went sprawling. That was Mercer.

The other, Katalin, managed to avoid sharing her colleague's fate by virtue of (apparently) greater dexterity, and instead darted around it. She was aiming for me, but she did not get far. It was as though she ran into an invisible wall, or was grabbed by a pair of invisible hands, for she came to an abrupt stop and was left straining uselessly at thin air.

'What are these?' said Dio dispassionately, as though these new visitors did not even qualify as human.

'Ancestria Magicka,' I said with a bright smile. 'Come to dig out your bones, Dio, and take you away to Ashdown Castle. Isn't that right? And John, too! You will have a fine new home, with a great deal more space to rattle around in.'

'And a much, *much* bigger building to haul about,' added Zareen silkily. 'Like turnips.'

'Lots of turnips,' I added.

Katalin stopped striving to get past Dio's obstruction, and instead bent to help George Mercer to his feet. He had cut his lip on something on his way down, and looked fiercely angry. 'You cannot know what an advantage it is to you,' she said. 'Your House, I mean. To achieve something of the same must be a primary goal of my organisation.'

'We do know it,' Zareen replied. 'And the likes of Greyer and Wester are not going to get you anything like the same effect.'

'Setting aside minor issues such as the ethics of the whole thing, or lack thereof,' I amended.

'Right. There is also that.'

'An approximation will suffice, if it must,' said Mercer.

He did not add that a teleporting castle would have its own benefits, of which we could know nothing. For all our dear House's many talents, perambulating about under its own power isn't one of them.

Wester, however, was not quite pleased with the notion. 'A *castle*?!' he bawled. 'Never! I refuse!'

'Why don't we all go and have a look?' said Katalin peaceably. 'You may find that you like Ashdown. And, Mr. Wester, you will not be unaided.'

That was interesting — and horrifying. How many dead Waymasters did they propose to dig up?

... or kill? Their eagerness to recruit Jay suddenly began to look sinister, and I found myself inching nearer to him.

The same idea had occurred to him, too, judging from the appalled look on his face.

Katalin smiled at him, rather kindly. 'Oh, no,' she said. 'Living Waymasters are much more useful.'

'Reassuring,' muttered Jay. 'Thanks.'

Wester may not approve, but to Dio, the idea of Ashdown held some appeal. 'A castle,' she purred. 'I was made to be a grand lady.'

'Weren't we all,' I said, *sotto voce.*

'I have fine manners,' she continued. 'And all the graces.'

'I do not!' bellowed Wester.

'Thou wilt keep *shut* thy mouth, John!' Dio snapped. 'And do as thou art bid!'

Whatever it was that Dio did to give emphasis to her words, it could not be felt by the living save, perhaps, as a waft of freezing wind that raised the goosebumps on my skin. But that it hurt the dead was indubitable, for Wester gave a great, tearing scream, and began to babble helplessly.

'To Ashdown,' purred Dio. 'The castle. And quickly, my John.'

17

A long-dead, tormented and frightened Waymaster proved not to be the best or safest of pilots. We departed Tut Hill with a sickening lurch, and a rumbling shudder which sent everyone in the room crashing to the floor. We came down some interminable time later with an unpromising *crunch*. For a little while I lay inert, my every muscle aching and my poor head spinning dizzily.

Then Jay was at my side. 'Hup,' he said, and mercilessly hauled me to my feet. 'Steady?'

I was, just about. Shaking knees aside.

Zareen was already vertical, and on her way to the door at a bouncing trot. Katalin and Mercer were on the far side of the bare little room, looking (to my secret relief) quite as shaken as I felt. And wary, too. Why? Had they not got what they wanted in bringing the cottage here?

Assuming we had arrived at the right place, of course. Zareen soon confirmed this, for having opened the front door a crack and peeped through, she proceeded to hurl it wide open and stomped out into the darkness beyond. 'Ashdown ahoy!' she called back.

That was when a third voice spoke. 'Ashdown,' it said, low and cracked. 'I remember that name, of my youth.' It was an old woman's voice, the tones worn and faded by the passage of many a long year.

Dio sighed. 'Go back to sleep, Maud.'

'I think I will not,' said Maud.

'Ah!' I cried. 'How nice to make your acquaintance, Maud Grey. Or is it Greyer?'

'Tis Greyer,' she allowed.

'Good. Excellent.' I looked around. 'And where might you be?'

'They buried me in the back bedchamber,' said Maud.

'Buried?' scoffed Wester. 'Walled thee up, like the devil thou art!'

'I am no devil,' said Maud, winter-dry. Then she laughed, wheezing. 'At least, no more than any Greyer.'

'Who is "they"?' I wondered aloud. 'Who walled you up?'

'My grandson,' she said, with chilling indifference. 'And granddaughter.'

Considering that Maud Greyer had herself interred the body of her own, freshly-hanged sister inside the cottage's walls, I decided I did not wish to know any more about the Greyer family.

Bill, though, had no scruples. '*Ves*,' he hissed, still stuck to the wall. 'Have a care! There is nothing but evil in that one.'

'How do you know?'

'My mistress always greatly feared her sister.'

'That is not true!' shouted Dio.

But Maud chuckled. 'It hath the right of it, thy odd creation. Thou wert always easily cowed.'

I felt a chill of foreboding. Dio Greyer, necromancer and High Witch of a powerful coven, found reason to be terrified of *Maud*? That did not bode well.

Whatever Katalin and George Mercer might know about Maud Greyer, it wasn't reassuring them either. They had gone from wary to outright alarmed at the exchange, and I heard Katalin say in a fraught whisper: '*She* was not supposed to be here!'

'Aye,' said Maud. 'They made fine work of me, did they not? Put it about that I had died of the Sweat, and into the wall I went with none the wiser.' She paused, chillingly, and added in a musing tone, 'I wonder what hath become of my descendants?'

I, for one, did not want to know.

'I would like to be rid of these confines,' continued Maud after a moment. 'These rude walls, how they chafe after five hundred years!'

'You must free me, but not her!' Dio said. Her manner was commanding, but I detected a shrill note of fear somewhere behind.

'And me,' added Wester. 'But never *her*.'

'Thou shalt not leave without me.' Maud's words emerged barely above a whisper, but with a ringing power behind them that rooted me to the spot. 'Thou shalt none of you leave without me.'

The door banged shut behind me. I could not even turn to see if Zareen had come back in; my muscles were frozen, and I could not move an inch.

'I suppose you *had* to make her angry?' said Bill venomously.

The walls rattled, and something dark and liquid began to seep through the whitewash and trickle towards the floor. 'Um,' I said, my lips numb. 'Is that... that isn't *blood*, is it?'

'Yep,' said Zareen, and walked past me into the centre of the floor. 'You'd better stop, Maud Greyer,' she said severely. 'I will stand for no more shenanigans.'

I adored Zareen just then. Not only for facing Maud Greyer and her bleeding walls without a blink, but also for using the word *shenanigans* to describe them.

How exactly she was perambulatory when Jay and I and the two Ancestria Magicka operatives remained glued to the floor, well. That was another question.

'Thou art no match for me,' crooned Maud. 'Fair potential thou dost indeed possess, but thou art but an acorn to my mighty oak.' Blood began to drip from the ceiling, too, and to my horror a crack opened in the floor and swiftly widened. Something pale, unwholesome and smoky seeped through from below.

Zareen took all of this in with narrowed eyes, and nodded. 'You might be right,' she allowed. 'Mercer!'

George Mercer's head snapped up. 'No!'

'It's necessary.'

'It's not. Do something else!'

'Like what?'

Judging from the silence, Mercer had no answer to this.

'Stop being a wimp,' Zareen ordered. 'And stop pretending. The sheep routine's getting boring.'

Mercer growled something, but he proceeded to push away from the wall he'd been leaning on, and ambled over to Zareen. This, apparently, came as much to Katalin's surprise as to mine.

'Zar?' I tried. 'What exactly is going on?'

'Don't worry,' she said briefly. 'But grit your teeth.'

'What?'

She'd linked hands with Mercer, and to my stark horror her eyes turned black. I mean,

Zareen's eyes are almost black anyway, but *all the whites filled in with solid black*, too. 'Can't guarantee this won't hurt a bit,' she said.

Then the same thing happened to the eyes of George Mercer, and I shut my stupid mouth.

'Ves?' said Jay uncertainly.

'Just do as she says,' I said tightly.

Maud Greyer had figured her out, too, and she was *not* pleased. 'Betrayer!' she shrieked, losing her cool in fine style. 'How durst thou turn the Arts against me!' The floor washed over with blood, and it was bubbling and boiling; my feet began to burn. The walls shook so hard I expected the ceiling to come down at any moment and bury us all, and I could hardly hear Maud's continued vituperation over the sounds of stones, tiles and beams all rattling against one another.

Zareen raised her voice to shout over the tumult. 'Five hundred years!' she intoned in an oddly ringing voice. 'Ought to have been enough to learn some bloody manners!'

'Spare me!' shrieked Dio. 'Spare John! We will do as thou dost bid us, and never seek to do thee harm!'

'Sorry,' Zareen said flatly. 'Time's up.' Drops of blood leaked from the corners of her eyes, and from Mercer's.

And, I realised, from mine.

A sharp, fierce pulse of pure power shot through the floor and raced up the walls. It manifested itself as a sea of shadow pouring forth from Zareen and Mercer and swallowed everything in its path — me, Jay, the book, all of it. That sea burned like lava and froze like ice, and every cell in my poor abused body screamed with pain.

So did I.

Somewhere in the distance I was aware of Dio and Maud Greyer and John Wester, making a cacophonous orchestra of indignation, fury and pain. But I had other things to consider, for besides the minor inconvenience of searing agony in my every organ, there were a few structural problems developing. The ceiling was raining chunks of plaster into the pools of blood below, and there came the splintering sound of stone cracking into pieces.

'Zareen!' I bawled. 'You'll bring the roof down!'

Too late. The splintering intensified, and a great, groaning tumult heralded the imminent collapse of the cottage. I had time only to grab what little magick I could muster, tears of blood pouring from my eyes, and weave up a shield before the roof shattered into chunks and rained down upon us.

My shield, shaky and feeble, did not last long. Neither did I. I'd thrown it clumsily over Jay, Zareen, Mercer and Katalin as well as myself, and I had the satisfaction of seeing it deflect at least the first wave of falling stone. But it could not bear up under the rest; my glorious, shimmering bubble dissipated into the air, a great slab of something distressingly solid collided with my head, and I passed out.

I woke up bathed in blood.

I cannot say it is the worst thing that has ever happened to me (don't ask), but it may be imagined that I was not best pleased.

The cottage lay in rubble all over the once neatly-swept floor. Moonlight shone upon the pale face of Zareen looming above me, her eyes thankfully restored to their usual colour. 'You alive, Ves?' she was saying.

I took a breath, every second of which hurt like hell. 'I wish I wasn't.'

Her lips twitched. 'Lies.'

'Fine. I hurt, but I am relieved you didn't manage to kill us all with your freaky shit.'

'Nice work with the shield.'

'Thanks.' I sat up. Jay was leaning against the remains of a wall a few feet away, his black hair almost white with dust and a fresh bruise added to his already sumptuous collection. 'Hi,' he croaked.

'You're not dead either.'

'Nope.'

Mercer was prone, apparently still out cold. Katalin sat guard by his side, cross-legged and heedless of the sticky, congealing blood she was sitting in.

All was quiet. The silence was eerie after all the noise of the past hour or so.

'They're gone?' I said to Zareen.

She nodded once.

'Uh huh. And what was that you did, exactly?'

'Forcible exorcism.' Zareen turned away and bent to pick something out of the rubble.

'Did I know you could do that?'

Zareen didn't answer.

'Zar. Are you a necromancer?' I looked sharply at Mercer. 'And him, too?'

Zareen gave me a long, measuring look, and for a second her eyes flickered once more into deep, black pools. 'Toil and trouble, remember?' she said, and her voice was as bone-dry as Maud Greyer's.

'Does that mean yes?'

'It means, don't ask.' Before I could speak again, she handed me her find — a book. *The* book.

'Oh, Bill,' I sighed, stricken. 'I'm so sorry.'

'It would be ungenerous of me to reproach the heroine of the hour,' said Bill.

I didn't think so. It had not occurred to me to include Bill in my shield, and as a consequence he had been sadly crushed. He now sported three dents in his formerly pristine covers, and some of his pages were torn.

'Zareen's the heroine of the hour,' I said. 'Does it hurt?' I tried to smooth his pages as best I could, a useless gesture.

'I do not possess nerves, Miss Vesper.'

I winced, my own agonies not yet forgotten. 'That sounds nice.'

'It has its moments.'

'What is that noise?' said Jay, and hauled himself to his feet.

'What noise—' I began, but then I heard it: a thin, high-pitched whimpering coming from somewhere nearby.

Walking like an old, old man, Jay limped off into what remained of the next room. There were only the two rooms to the cottage, apparently, and the one we were in was by far the largest. Following Jay, I found what had probably once been the back bedchamber where Maud's remains were interred. It was as empty of furniture as the other room, boasting only a dusty (and now broken) chair. The floor was thick with blood, rubble and debris, but in the wan moonlight that filtered through the empty window-frame I discerned a glimpse of something incongruously brightly coloured.

The whimpering gained in volume.

'There's an animal,' said Jay, and ventured towards the window, stepping through the fallen stones with unusual care. He crouched, and began to pull away the wreckage from the corner.

A flash of pale, yellowish fur emerged, and Jay scooped up something tiny enough to fit into one cupped hand.

'Here,' he said, turning, and offered it to me.

I took it with infinite care, for it was a tiny, delicate creature, probably only recently born, and obviously in distress. It resembled a puppy, except its nose was much larger than that of a typical dog, and its forehead bore the tiny nub of a horn. I suspected, moreover, that when cleaned up and viewed in daylight, its fur would prove to be not so much yellowish as bright, sunny gold.

It was hungry, I concluded, for it seemed intent upon devouring my thumb. Fortunately, it had not yet developed much in the way of teeth.

'Ouch,' I said anyway, wincing a bit.

Jay smiled. 'I think you are the properest person to take care of a tiny fluffy thing, don't you?'

I beamed at him. 'Without doubt. But how did it come to be here?' I made to step past him to investigate the spot in the corner, but Jay got in front of me.

'I wouldn't,' he said.

'Why not?'

His face turned grim. 'There were more.'

I didn't miss his use of the past tense, and my heart sank. 'How many?'

'Two more like this one.'

I tried to get past him again, but he caught me and pushed me back. 'They're dead, Ves. No sense in upsetting yourself.'

'Yes, because I'm marshmallow. You, of course, are made from solid rock.'

He just looked at me, his mouth grim and his eyes sad.

'Fine, fine,' I sighed and turned away, cradling the sole survivor of the wreck. 'Zareen's going to cry, you realise.'

'She shouldn't. They were not crushed. I would rather say they starved.'

'Right. We'd better get this one to Miranda as soon as possible.' I would have fed it on the spot if I could, but what did a baby horned puppy eat? I could offer it a whole feast of only slightly congealed blood lightly seasoned with dust, but I doubted that would serve the purpose.

In the next room, Katalin and Mercer were deep in conversation with Zareen. I watched them for a moment, eyes narrowed, for it seemed to me that Zareen and Mercer were not quite strangers. Indeed, Zar's actions of half an hour before had strongly implied that she knew more about George Mercer than we did. 'Old friends?' I said at last, when a lull offered in the conversation.

Zareen just flashed me an enigmatic look.

'I know, I know. Don't ask. We're leaving on a mercy mission,' I said, showing Zareen the puppy. 'Can you deal with all this?'

It wasn't fair to land her with that job, since by "this" I meant the wrecked cottage, the scattered bones of those who had once been interred within its walls, the sea of blood leaking all over the grounds of Ashdown Castle and, of course, the problem of the two Ancestria Magicka operatives who were still hanging around. But Zareen is equal to anything.

'Go!' she commanded. 'Save the tiny, defenceless thing.'

'We'll send help from Home.'

'That would be nice.'

'Where's the nearest henge?' I said, turning back to Jay.

'Assuming you don't want to break into Ashdown itself at this hour, and in this state... too far to walk.'

I nodded. 'Well then. I wonder if our Chairs are still there?'

18

Miranda was not only eager to assume charge of our find; she was electrified.

Jay and I proceeded directly to her domain once we reached Home. She is the head of our Magickal Beasts division, and presides over extensive premises in the east wing. We found her in the veterinary department, tending to the damaged wing of a black bird with an unusually long, blue beak. 'Can it wait just a second?' she said when we went in, without looking up.

'One or two, but not more.' I didn't say that lightly. Our puppy had abandoned its attempts to eat my fingers almost the moment we had stepped out of the ruined cottage, and over the journey home it had seemed to lose all energy. It (or she, I think) now lay inert in my palm, worryingly lifeless.

'Right.' Miranda gently returned her bird to a large cage near the back of the room, and set it carefully atop a padded perch inside. Then she bustled back to us. She'd had a long day of it herself, by her appearance: her white coat was streaked with bird poop, some kind of animal feed and who-knew-what-else, and her blonde hair had mostly fallen out of its usually neat ponytail. She looked tired and shadow-eyed.

I held out the puppy to her. 'Starving to death. Please help.'

Miranda took my puppy, handling her very gently. She said nothing for several seconds, examining the creature with great care. Her eyes grew rather wide. 'Ves,' she whispered at last, her voice emerging as a croak. 'Where did you find this?'

I told her.

'Hnngh,' she said, and swallowed. 'Er.'

'What?'

'This is a...' she began, then stopped. 'I mean, it *can't* be, but it is.'

'Not making sense,' I offered helpfully.

Miranda shook her head, disbelieving. 'It's a dappledok puppy. They're extinct.'

'What?'

'Dead as dodos. The last known sighting of a live one was recorded in a letter in, like, the late seventeen hundreds.'

I stared. 'Oh.'

'So!' she said. 'I'll be off moving heaven and earth to save this one's life, and later we'll talk more about where you got it. Okay?' Without waiting for an answer, she charged off, taking my tiny puppy with her.

I looked at Jay. 'You've a talent for stumbling over long-lost things, it seems.'

His smile flickered. 'We still have to figure out what to do with the last one.'

I gave a long, long sigh at that, and said: 'I'm pretty sure I know exactly what will become of poor Bill.'

Baron Alban arrived bright and early the next morning. *Too* bright and early. I had no idea how he had managed to receive Milady's summons and act upon them so fast, but I supposed he must have a Waymaster at his disposal. If he wasn't one himself.

Having developed a more than passing acquaintance with the Baron by that time, I was prepared for his probable promptness, and so he found me awake, dressed and intent upon the consumption of my second cup of tea. I was only slightly droopy, and gazed at him with bleary-eyed alertness as he wandered into my usual nook in the first floor common room.

'Ves,' he said with his broad, charming smile. 'You look like you fell under a ceiling.'

I gave him my most withering look, and swallowed a great deal more tea. 'You usually manage to be more complimentary.'

'You look gorgeous. Bruises suit you.'

I waved him to a chair, ignoring that. He looked as well turned-out as ever in a dark blue suit and white shirt, his purple tie elaborately knotted. 'Please take care of Bill,' I implored him.

One brow went up. 'Bill?'

'The book. We call him Bill.'

He inclined his head, as though this declaration made perfect sense. 'Bill will have the best care, naturally. I've hopes that our bookbinders can patch him up a bit, and he'll be safe from your friends at Ancestria Magicka.'

I shrugged at that, and set down my empty cup. 'I doubt they will care about him much longer. They've had time enough to study all his workings, and will probably produce replicas soon enough.'

'And will the Society, also?'

'I have reason to believe that Milady cleared Orlando's agenda entirely in favour of the project.'

He nodded, studying my face. 'You're sad about something.'

'I am sorry for the loss of Bill. He's the most charming book I ever met.' My leave-taking from Bill the night before had been a little painful; he had not been delighted to be separated from me either, though his vanity could not but be pleased at the prospect of becoming a prized treasure of the Troll Court. I'd heard unpromising reports of the puppy, too; Miranda could only confirm that she was still breathing, and wouldn't hazard more.

'The most charming troll you've ever met is still waiting to take you out,' said the Baron, and gave me a hopeful smile.

I couldn't help perking up a bit at that. 'How obliging of him.'

'Just say the word.' He got up, and made me a graceful bow. 'I'd love to stay, but I need to get the book back to the Court. I have an escort and everything.'

'Six ruthless bodyguards?' I peeked behind him, as though there might be a team of dreamily muscle-bound trolls waiting by the door.

'Something like that.' He winked, and gave me a tiny salute. 'Call me.'

I promised.

On his way out, he passed Jay and Indira just coming in. I was intrigued to note that none of them seemed a bit surprised to see one another. 'Good timing,' said Alban with a smile, and then he was gone.

I raised my brows at Jay, but he ignored my silent question and flopped into a chair without speaking.

I looked at Indira, who was taking a seat with more care and more grace, keeping her injured arm well away from the table. 'What was that about?' I asked.

Indira looked guiltily at Jay, and said nothing.

Jay smiled at her. 'Well, go on.'

She glanced at me, and looked quickly away again. Carefully, she bent to retrieve a soft cloth bag from the floor by her feet; I hadn't noticed her carrying it when she came in. She placed this on the table before me, and sat back.

I waited for some explanation, but nothing came. 'I'm to open the bag?'

Indira nodded.

Mystified, I peeped inside. A book lay at the bottom. It was of an ancient style (thick leather covers, vellum pages, heavy silver hinges) but it looked pristine and new. Extracting it with care, I discovered that the covers were tinted dark purple, and the front was embossed with a twelve-pointed star. It weighed less than it looked like it should.

'A book!' I said, not at all enlightened.

'Open it,' said Jay.

I obeyed.

'Madam,' said the book. 'You must allow me to tell you how ardently I admire and love you.'

'Perfect,' whispered Jay, and the book gave a rather smug rustle of its pages.

'Bill?' I choked. 'But— but the Baron just took him!'

'Bill the Second,' said Jay. 'Indira's been working on it ever since we left.'

'Well, Orlando has,' said Indira, hastily disclaiming. 'I've just been, um, helping.'

Jay shook his head slightly. 'More than that. You can't deny this is mostly your own work.'

Indira looked like she wanted very much to deny it, but couldn't truthfully do so.

'That's extremely clever of you,' I said, with total sincerity. I couldn't imagine the depth of skill required to produce such a grimoire; my talents definitely don't lie in that direction. I stroked Bill the Second's covers with faint regret (all right, more than faint), and handed him back to Indira.

She did not take him. Instead, she gave me a stricken look. 'Um, don't you want him?'

'Wha... he's for *me*?'

Indira nodded furiously.

'Am I... am I allowed?'

Indira nodded again. 'This is a, um, prototype. Orlando's working on the finished design and, well, this one's spare. Milady said it was all right.'

Jay's eyes narrowed ever so slightly, but he said nothing.

I was only too glad to gather Bill Two back into my arms and give him a tight hug. 'Thank you,' I said, beaming. 'It will be my honour to work with him.'

Indira smiled back, visibly relieved. 'I'm glad you like him,' she said, already getting out of her chair.

'Won't you have some tea?' I offered, but she was in full retreat by then, and only shook her head as she vanished out the door.

I looked at Jay, and waited.

'She made him especially for you,' he said. 'Stayed up most of the night to finish him, too.'

'Um,' I said. 'Why?'

He shrugged. 'Might be that she's savvy enough to cultivate connections amongst those who are popular at Home. Or... maybe she just likes you.'

'Likes me,' I repeated numbly. 'Right.' Indira was always polite, but she still gave me the impression that she was petrified of me.

I decided that the Patels in general were a hard-to-read bunch.

Before Jay could decide upon a reply, there came the sound of tiny claws clicking against the hard floor, and the yellow dappledok puppy came creeping around the door. Her ears were down, her tail drooped and she trudged wearily in my direction as though the distance between us were almost insurmountable.

But she was alive!

'Puppy!' I blurted, overjoyed. 'Come here!'

The moment she came within reach of the table, Jay bent to scoop her up, and handed her to me. I put her in my lap, whereupon she crawled, shivering, inside my cardigan and disappeared.

I tucked the folds of my clothes around her and sat, smiling like an idiot, until Miranda inevitably appeared. 'Ves!' she said, slightly out of breath. 'Don't hate me, but I think I've lost the puppy.'

I merely pulled aside my cardigan, displaying the ball of yellow fur. 'Winnie the Unipup is fine.'

Miranda sagged against the doorframe in relief, though she looked annoyed, too. 'Look, she shouldn't be taken out of care just now at all, but at the *very* least you need to tell me.'

'I didn't take her! She showed up at the door about four minutes ago.'

Miranda blinked. 'She found her way up here?'

'I swear. Jay, back me up.'

'Every word of Ves's is the truth,' he dutifully declared.

Miranda sighed. 'Fine. Bring her back down once an hour for milk, okay?'

I tucked my cardigan back over my unipup once more, and beamed at Miranda. 'Got it, boss.'

The Striding Spire

Modern Magick, 3

Charlotte E. English

1

Let's just say that my first date with Baron Alban did not go quite as I was hoping.

Expectations: me in a *very* good dress. High heels, great up-do, a bit of lipstick (or perhaps a lot). The Baron looking gorgeous as always in one of his many fine suits, escorting me upon one muscular arm to somewhere lovely. Somewhere with music, perhaps, and good cake.

Reality: Somewhat different.

It began with a phone call.

'Morning, Ves,' came the Baron's deep voice when I picked up. 'Do I disturb?'

'Not at all!' said I brightly, and not altogether truthfully. It was, I had blearily noted as I scooped up my phone, all of half past six in the morning; it was Sunday, and I'd had no intention of getting up for at least three hours yet. I was in bed with my duvet around my chin, and the UniPup, all yellow fur and tiny puppy snores, was asleep on my neck. 'What can I do for you?' It wasn't so easy to speak with a weight on my throat. I hoped she would grow out of that habit by the time she grew much bigger.

'We've been talking about going out sometime for a while, and I was wondering — are you busy today?'

'Today?'

'Yes.'

I thought furiously, but only for about two and a half seconds. 'No!' I said with emphasis. I might have been smiling like an idiot, but that I cannot confirm.

'Great!' He sounded happy, too, which I will not deny was good for my ego. 'I'll pick you up in half an hour.'

'*Half an hour?!*'

'Is... that okay?'

I've been on a few dates in my time, and I will be self-aggrandising enough to own that some of those gentlemen were flatteringly eager. But this was something else. 7am on a Sunday morning? Nobody was *that* eager for my company. 'It's fine,' I said, scooping the puppy off my neck. I laid her gently on the pillow next to me — she didn't wake — and stumbled out of bed. 'As long as there is going to be breakfast involved, and soon.'

'That can be arranged. See you soon, Ves.' And he hung up.

Odd.

But with only twenty-eight minutes of the promised half hour left, I had no time to puzzle over it. What did a Cordelia Vesper wear on a shockingly early-morning breakfast date with the handsomest troll alive? *This* Cordelia Vesper had no idea, and she'd have to figure it out pretty fast.

· · · ● · ● · · · ·

I made it down to the hall with exactly thirty-seven seconds to spare. With May dawning dewily outside, the day promised to be warm and fine, so I had chosen one of my favourite dresses — a knee-length confection of red viscose, printed with roses — and thrown a light cardigan over it. My trusty hair-fixing Curiosity had done fine work for me again, turning my long, loose curls to a deep red almost the same hue as my dress.

There the elegance ended, for it had quickly occurred to me that I couldn't leave the puppy alone. I'd thought briefly of taking her back to Miranda, Boss of Beasts, for the morning's activities, and collecting her again when I got back. But I abandoned that idea almost as quickly as it came up, because the puppy was unlikely to consent. It did not matter what Miranda did to keep the puppy under her eye; she would always escape, by means largely unknown, and find her way back to me. If I left her with Miranda, she'd escape again and come looking — but she would find no trace of me. Would she be upset? I could not take that risk, for she had been starving to death when I'd found her and that was only a few days ago. She was frail, and in need of constant care. I wasn't leaving her behind.

The fact that I had entirely lost my heart to the little beast was neither here nor there, of course. But who could help it? She was completely adorable. She had the kind of silky fur that begged to be touched, and it was bright gold. Perky little ears, enormous nose, tiny unicorn horn — what's not to love about all that? She was affectionate, too, and she made me feel needed.

If that makes for a rather pathetic vision of me, I can only apologise.

Anyway, having decided to take her along, I was then obliged to add an inelegantly enormous bag to my attire. It had to be big enough to hold a significant supply of milk for the puppy, for she had to be fed once an hour and I had no idea how long the Baron intended to monopolise my company. She got cold easily, too, even in the balmy weather, so I stashed blankets and fluffies galore to wrap her up in at need. Then I made a nest in the top for the puppy, installed her therein, and tramped down to the hall, already annoyed by the heavy, unwieldy bag by the time I had made it down a mere two of the House's many winding flights of stairs.

C'est la vie.

There was no sign of the Baron, but when I peeped out of the grand front door I saw him at once. Being Baron Alban, he simply cannot do anything in either a conventional way or a low-key way. Why wear a typical suit, however well-cut, when you can appear in a splendid top hat and a nineteenth-century frock coat? Or a nice set of nineteen-thirties tweeds, as was the case today, and he had the car to match. Don't ask me what kind of car it was, for I haven't the first clue, but it had the swanky, exaggerated curves of a proper old-time automobile, and it gleamed in gorgeous British Racing Green. Alban sat at the wheel, wearing tan leather driving gloves and a dark fedora. He grinned as I trotted out into the driveway, and tipped his hat to me.

He then proceeded to get out and hold the passenger door for me, which made me feel quite the lady — at least until the shoulder-bag I had lumbered myself with swung around as I was getting in, knocking me off-balance, and I all but fell into the seat. My poor dignity.

I hastily checked to make sure the puppy was unharmed, and found her to be fast asleep.

Alban returned to the driver's seat, and I took the opportunity to stash the bag safely by my feet, propped securely upright so the puppy would not fall out.

'I know the best place for breakfast,' he informed me as he turned the car, and my stomach was very happy to hear it.

We drove for about twenty minutes, and I began to suspect some kind of shenanigans. Now, I am notorious at Home for being spectacularly poor at finding my way around, and it is partly because I struggle to recognise places I have already been to, if it is nowhere especially familiar to me. So at first I was not troubled by the fact that the roads we were hurtling down rung no bells whatsoever with me; was I likely to remember this particular country road, hedge-lined and flanked by fields, over another almost exactly like it? No.

But after a while, there began to be a change. The hawthorn, blackthorn and hazel hedges ceased to look quite so much like hawthorn, blackthorn or hazel and developed a different appearance altogether. They were taller, for one, and thicker, their leaves a brighter green and oddly curly. Some of them were dotted with star-like flowers of unusual size. The roads that ran in between lost their tarmac-look and became a smooth stone, pale and apparently indestructible, considering the total lack of holes (and believe me, back country roads with no holes in are pretty rare). When a bird flew overhead that in no way resembled an English bird, but more nearly reminded me of a hare with wings, I was certain. 'Just where exactly are we?' I asked.

'The Troll Roads,' answered the Baron serenely.

'And they are?'

'Hidden ways across the world. It's a tradition dating back hundreds of years, though these days the standard of the roads is a bit higher. They had to be upgraded when cars happened.'

I could see there were a few advantages to these Roads, one of them being a total lack of other traffic. This particular one also had the look of a place where it literally never rains. Quite possibly it did not.

'We're going to my home Enclave,' offered the Baron, when I said no more. 'Rhaditton.'

Rhaditton. The word had the old-fashioned air of a top boarding school, and considering that the Baron was attached to the Troll Court, I could well believe it was a salubrious place, and probably exclusive. 'I did not know you lived so close to us at the Society,' I said.

He grinned at me. 'I don't. That is why we're taking the Troll Roads.'

I blinked. 'They're faster?'

'Much.'

'How?'

'Because they're magick.'

Of course.

He laughed, inferring from my silence — rightly enough — that I found this answer inadequate. 'Waymasters,' he said, more helpfully. 'Quite a number of them have worked on the Roads over the years. The routes aren't as good as a Waymaster in person, of course, but they're not a bad alternative.'

'So what do they do, sort of... swoosh you along?'

'Something like that, yes. Waymasters used to be adept at a range of travel arts, once upon a time. One or two of them still are.'

Jay had said something like that, recently — that Waymastery was a diminished art these days, with magick on the decline. Jay, of course, was still quite able to spirit himself and others from henge to henge in a single step, across vast distances, so his "diminished" arts still looked pretty impressive to me.

Ten minutes later, we rolled up outside the vast, gleaming walls of a city. Seriously, it looked like Minas Tirith or something, all white stone and shining in the sun like a slice of heaven on earth. The gates opened as the Baron's car approached, literally like magick, and in we went.

Aaaand I have never been anywhere so glorious in my life. Eerily glorious, because to go with all the polished stone buildings, intricately carved walls, gilding — yes, actual *gilding* — and general air of improbable luxury, there were none of the things one might normally expect to see in a city that's lived in by real people. Litter here and there, for example. Peeling paint, shabby old houses in need of maintenance, an occasional abandoned bicycle or shopping trolley.

I was left wondering how far people like Baron Alban qualified as *real*. Everything about him was improbably fabulous, including his choice of abode.

I tried not to gawk too obviously as we rolled through street after street of this opulence, and in all likelihood failed. At last we drew up outside a low, greyish stone place with an ornate roof and an array of elegant chairs and tables arranged outside. I don't think they were solid gold, but it was hard to tell.

'Ah, of course,' I said as the car drew to a stop. 'This is how you do cafes in Rhaditton.'

'They do fantastic pancakes,' said the Baron.

Pancakes seemed mundane under the circumstances, but I was soon reassured on this point. A few minutes later, I was seated inside the building in what was probably the best seat in the place, with a fine view out of the grand window all the way down the wide boulevard beyond. Baron Alban sat at my elbow; the bag with the puppy in was set on the seat beside me; and I had a plate of pancakes before me that would make any reasonable person cry with happiness.

Point one: they were troll-sized helpings, approximately the size of dinner plates, and there were a lot of them.

Point two: they were smothered in everything. Everything, everything. Ice cream, fruits in improbable colours that I'd never seen before, some kind of sticky sauce that glistened so invitingly it could only be (as the Baron would put it) magick.

I took a spoonful of all this glory, and almost died.

As I was busy winging my way to heaven upon a tide of sweet delight, Baron Alban sat sipping a tall cup of something steamy, his own plate virtually untouched. He was watching me, with a smile that said, *you are inelegantly devoted to food, but I like it.*

I was unmoved. Nothing was getting in between me and those pancakes, not even the desire to appear cool before the fabulousness that was the Baron.

'What's the bag for?' he said after a while.

Having by that time devoured enough to quieten the complaints of my half-starved stomach, I found myself at leisure to answer him. 'I'll tell you later.'

All right, *briefly* to answer him.

He grinned. 'Fair.'

'If you aren't going to eat,' I said, eyeing his plate with disfavour, 'then you can talk. What's the hurry today?'

'The hurry?' he smiled at me, far too innocently for my liking. 'Just wanted to finally get some time with you.'

'At seven in the morning? I do not buy it, Mister.'

'Actually, "my lord Baron" would be more appropriate,' he said, his grin widening.

'Diversion failed, my lord Baron. What are we doing here?'

'Is it so hard to believe I might merely want your company?'

Thinking of the salubrious city and its equally glamorous residents — I'd seen several gorgeous and gorgeously dressed troll ladies wandering those streets, and an example sat not six feet away at another table — I said, 'Yes.'

To my mild regret, the Baron began to look sheepish. I suppose a small part of me *had* hoped he was just desperate for my company.

Such is life.

He picked up his fork and took a bite of pancake, clearly a delaying tactic.

'Spit it out,' I recommended. 'Not the pancake! The problem.'

'I didn't want you to think I'd invited you just to—'

'I know, I know,' I said. I thought it best to interrupt before things could get any more awkward. 'You were positively dying to see me, and it *also* happens that there's something on your mind?'

He smiled at me, with that twinkle in his bright green eyes that makes it impossible to be annoyed with him. 'Exactly.'

'Always nice to kill two birds with one stone.'

'I always thought that expression unnecessarily bloodthirsty.'

'It is. So the problem is what?'

'Right.' He pushed aside his plate, quite flabbergasting me, and folded his arms upon the table-top. 'I heard a rumour,' he began.

2

'Just the one rumour?' I said. 'Remarkable.'

The Baron's irresistible smile flashed. 'Actually, more than one.'

'Let's have the first one, then.'

'Is it true that there's a leak inside the Society?'

That was unexpected. I filled my mouth with ice cream and fruit, stalling for a few moments to think. What should I tell him?

He wasn't wrong. Things had got pretty interesting at work lately. We'd discovered an incredibly rare and indescribably valuable artefact (a book, talkative); faced off against a new, but nonetheless powerful rival organisation with the downright fatuous name of Ancestria Magicka who were determined to steal it; and almost got eaten alive by a haunted house and its trio of unfriendly ghosts. In the middle of all this, we'd found that word of the chatty book (Bill) had somehow leaked out, despite the fact that it had never left Home. That's how we ended up with Ancestria Magicka on our tails.

Furthermore, it wasn't just information that had gone farther than it should. Someone had actively sabotaged us by putting tracker spells on the book itself. It was clear that somebody at the Society was a turncoat, and that was alarming. But how had the Baron found out?

'Who told you that?' I finally said. 'I wasn't aware that Milady was disposed to chat about it.'

'Someone high up in the Society contacted the Troll Court a few days ago with word of a problem,' answered the Baron. 'Probably Milady herself, in fact. She requested aid.'

'Did they send you to nose around?'

He smiled, sheepish again. 'Might have.'

Hmm. It was plausible enough that Milady might seek aid from the Court. I'd become aware of more than one link between Milady, whoever she was behind the vague title, and the Troll Courts of old; if she could no longer be sure of who to trust at Home, it was not so far-fetched that she would consult her allies.

She had not mentioned it to me, though. Did that mean I, too, was suspect? I didn't think so, but I still felt a slight twinge.

I gave the Baron a brief precis of everything that had happened with the book, which he heard without interruption. 'At present we have no idea who it might be,' I said in conclusion. 'Bill caused a sensation at Home, as you might imagine. For a little while, everybody found some excuse to pass through the Library and gawk at the book. Any of them could have passed information to Ancestria, and far too many had at least some opportunity to plant a tracker spell on it. We know that someone's rotten, but we have no leads whatsoever.'

The Baron took a forkful, and chewed meditatively, his eyes faraway. 'There is a reason Milady contacted the Court,' he finally said. 'There are some ancient magicks that are only really practiced by a rare few nowadays, and the Court makes a habit of collecting them up. Sort of the way you do — preservation tactic. If we don't find and nurture those talents, the magicks might fade away altogether.'

'Quite,' I murmured.

'There used to be something called a Truthseeker, or so it was known until about the middle of the nineteenth century, by which time there were so few of them left that the word itself fell out of use. There are no human Truthseekers anymore, but there is one living who can still employ that art, and he's at the Court.'

This sounded promising. 'And Truthseeking consists of what?'

'A Truthseeker is unusually sensitive to...' He took a mouthful of his drink, and shrugged. 'I don't pretend to know how it works, Ves, you'll have to ask him. But where you and I can only guess at whether or not we're being told the truth, a Truthseeker has a much more solid idea. What's more, they can, to some degree, compel a person to speak the truth. Milady means to question the Society about the Bill incident, and she's requested our Truthseeker's presence at those interviews.'

'Fair enough. But what's your role in all this?'

'I'm the advance party. Seeing as I already have a contact at the Society, and a pretty spectacular one at that—' He paused here to waggle his eyebrows at me, which was far more charming than it had any right to be —'I was sent to get the details straight from the source.'

'Well, you've got the details.' I smiled at him, hoping my lips were not as visibly sugar-crusted as I feared. 'I doubt I've told you anything more than Milady already relayed, though.'

'It's good to get a fuller account.' He was being generous, but he was good at doing it unobtrusively, so I overlooked it. 'The other thing...' he said, and hesitated again.

'Oh yes, rumour number two. Let's hear it.'

'You found something...unusual, recently?'

'My dear Baron, we are the Society for Magickal Heritage and I am one of its finest field agents. Our entire job consists of going out into the world and finding highly interesting things whose existence is probably under threat. Could you be more specific?'

That sheepish smile again. 'Of course. Uh, the existence of this particular thing is not so much under threat as... disputed? Extinguished? Impossible?'

'Oh! You mean the puppy.'

He blinked at me. 'It's a puppy?'

'Not in the way you are thinking. Miranda called it a dappledok pup. No relation to the canine species of creature, I'm fairly sure. I may someday get very, very tired of asking you this, but: how did you hear about that?'

'Milady again, but she was cagey about it. Dropped a hint, primarily by asking if we happened to have any experts on extinct magickal beasts mooching around at the Court.'

'Do you?'

'Yes, but she's somewhere in the Caribbean right now, on the trail of some impossibly rare bird whose name I have forgotten.'

'Were you sent to ask me about the pup, too, or is this mere private curiosity?'

'Some of both.' His eyes strayed to the bag I had left leaning innocently against the back of the adjacent chair.

Too sharp for his own good, that Baron.

'All right, all right,' I said, rolling my eyes at him. 'I'll show you.' I lifted the bag's flap, carefully in case the puppy fell out. But she was still tucked securely in the nest I had made out of three pairs of socks, and still asleep. She was so motionless that for a moment my heart stopped, but when I touched her, I could feel the slow rise and fall of her furred side. I tickled her.

She did not move.

'She sleeps like a champion,' I said to the Baron. 'She has had a hard time of it, though. Her siblings starved, and she wasn't far off going the same way when we found her.'

'Let her sleep, then,' said the Baron, staring at her with his eyes as wide as saucers and a dopey grin on his face.

It wasn't just me who found her utterly charming, then. Reassuring.

She was looking particularly cute, all curled up in a tiny ball barely larger than an orange. She has tufts of goldish hair growing around the base of her little unicorn horn, the tips of which swayed with the rhythm of her breathing.

'I imagine she will wake up soon, for it's time for her feed, and she's not one to miss out on breakfast.' Neither am I, of course, though I have nothing like her excuse. Nobody's ever tried to starve *me*. Nonetheless, I felt that it made us kindred spirits.

I noticed Baron Alban eyeing my cleared plate, probably thinking along similar lines. He refrained, however, from comment.

Wise man.

It probably was more than an hour since she had last had her milk, so I opted to tickle her until she woke. She did so at last with a grumpy little snort, and sat up, stretching. I was ready with her bottle, and she soon clamped her jaws around the teat and got to work.

The Baron and I watched with the breathless silence of brand new, doting parents.

'You know what a dappledok pup is, of course?' said the Baron after a while.

'Other than the fact that it's been completely extinct since the eighteenth century?'

'It has indeed. But before that?'

'No. I asked Miranda but she gabbled something largely incoherent — she was wrestling with a clawed, very unhappy creature at the time, in her defence — and I never did make sense of it.' I'd asked Val, too. Her response had been, "I'll get back to you," which meant that she did not know at that precise moment where the books were on that topic, but she would soon find out.

'Spriggans,' said Alban, incomprehensibly.

'I beg your pardon?'

'Fae-folk, native to Cornwall. Fond of shiny stuff. They bred the dappledoks out of a few other fae beasts, the goal being to create a species with a nose for treasure. They were said to be amazing trackers of anything or anyone carrying gold.'

I was quiet, because only the previous day I had gone into my jewellery drawer for my favourite gold ear-studs and found them missing. I'd assumed I had simply put them somewhere they shouldn't be, but suddenly I wondered.

'How did they come to die out?' I asked.

His mouth twisted in a grimace. 'Think it through, Ves. Cute, largely defenceless little creatures that are literally the road to riches? Spriggans can be unwisely boastful, to boot. Word spread, everyone wanted a dappledok, and... the rate of thefts across Britain, the Enclaves, the Dells, everywhere, positively soared. In the end they were banned. It became illegal to breed them. They survived a while after that, of course, through secret breeding-programmes, but eventually they petered out.'

'Spriggans,' I said.

'Spriggans.'

This was not the very best of news, for the fae-folk can be tricky. To say the least. There are more of them still about than non-magickers tend to think; they've just learned to hide better than they used to. But they can still cause a world of trouble for magickers and non-magickers alike, and spriggans... well, they have a reputation for being among the worst for sheer hell-raising mischief.

I've tried to avoid tangling with the fae as much as possible.

'So did I tell you where I found this pup?' I said.

'Pray do.'

Remember when I said we'd almost been swallowed by a haunted house? That's where we found the pup: curled up in a corner with two others, both dead. And this particular house was the kind that moves around, courtesy of its resident ghost of a Waymaster. It dated from the fourteen hundreds, if not even earlier, and it really felt like it.

I told all this to the Baron.

'Triple haunting?' he mused. 'That's unusual.'

'Yes. But. While I did not have much opportunity to chat with the residents, it did not strike me as likely that any of them would have cared much about operating a secret dappledok breeding programme. What would be the point?'

'So you think someone else might have been using the cottage?'

'Presumably with their consent, yes. It's possible. Or someone merely dumped the pups there. Or the pups might even have found their own way in.'

'In other words, you have no idea.'

'None whatsoever.'

The Baron's green, green eyes laughed at me again. 'Excellent,' he said. 'Good talk.'

I grinned back. 'I might be able to find something out,' I offered.

'Do you know, I was hoping you might say that?'

3

Later, happily replete with pancakes and with the Baron's teasing smile echoing in my mind, I wandered through the corridors at Home with my shoulder bag clutched to my chest, whispering soothing words to the pup. She wanted to get out, but Alban's words made me wary. She was more valuable even than I had imagined; not just supposedly extinct, but a potential source of riches. And if we indeed had a mole wandering these same hallways, it suddenly seemed like a very poor idea to show her off.

I was heading for the east wing, and Miranda's quarters in the Magickal Beasts division. I needed to talk to her right away.

Unusually, she was not to be found among any of her creatures. I trawled through room after room, eyed a seemingly endless succession of cages, pens and indoor paddocks, and though a dazzling array of weird and wonderful creatures met my eyes, there was no Miranda.

I found her at last in the east wing common room, apparently meditating over a cup of coffee, and firmly ensconced in a deep, plumply-stuffed arm chair. At least, she did not look up when I walked in, her gaze remaining fixed upon the window. I looked. There was nothing much going on outside, though the view was quite lovely: sunlight glinted on the meadows surrounding the House, and given the time of year the grasses were all frilly and much strewn with new flowers.

Serene and gorgeous as it was, I didn't think it likely that Miranda was quite so mesmerised by it as all that.

'Mir?' I said, when she still did not appear to notice my presence.

Her head turned, and she blinked at me. 'Ves! Sorry, I was miles away.'

'I noticed. Everything all right?'

'Yep,' she said succinctly, and smiled. Never one for long speeches, Miranda.

I offered her the bag, which she took, setting her coffee cup down on a side table. 'Nice puppy nest,' she commented, opening the flap.

'I've been hearing all about dappledoks today, and the news isn't all good,' I told her. 'You probably know what they were once used for?'

Miranda gave me a quizzical look. 'Used for? There was an odd reference in one letter to "treasure-dogs" and something similar in a book I once browsed through, but it was an offhand comment. Their gold fur is probably enough to account for such notions, and perhaps those horns — they're being conflated with legendary creatures. Superstition more than anything.'

'Perhaps not.' I related the Baron's tale, which prompted a frown from Miranda.

'Banned by who?' she said, once I had finished. 'The Troll Court?'

'That was the implication, though if it succeeded in wiping out the dappledoks I conclude it must have been agreed upon, and enforced by, most of the magickal councils of the day.'

'Which would be highly unusual.'

'Wouldn't it? I got to thinking. A spate of thefts would be unwelcome and disruptive, to be sure, but if the response was such a total and inflexible ban, then I wonder what it was that the pups were digging up?'

'Did you ask his Baronship?'

I had, of course, prior to our leaving the improbably wonderful café. But predictably enough, he had merely twinkled at me and fended off my questions with distractions, charm, counter-questions or, when I proved impervious to any of that, the flat statement of: 'Court secrets, Ves. Sorry.'

He ought to have known better than to say that to me.

'Stonewalled me,' I told Miranda.

'Scandal,' she said with a grin. 'Intriguing.'

'So, I am going to do some digging. In the meantime, the pup is a problem. If there is anybody else floating around who knows that the Legend of Dappledok might have some truth to it, I don't want them finding out that we happen to have one. Do we have anybody good enough at illusion to camouflage a living creature?'

'Oh, several. Leave her with me, and I'll get somebody to come up here and sort her out.'

'If she looks like a chihuahua or a dachshund or something, nobody would question that.'

Miranda shook her head. 'Too mundane. This is the Society, and you're Cordelia Vesper — flamboyant to a fault, and notorious for being up to your elbows in magick all the livelong day. We'll make her look like a miniature gorhound or something.'

'Purple,' I said.

Miranda raised her brows.

'This thing?' I said, raising my left hand to show her the Curiosity I always wear: the ring that changes the colour of my hair. 'It works on animals, too.'

'Hah. Purple it is.'

· · • · • · • · · ·

I disliked walking out of there without my pup with me, but it was in a good cause. Anyway, there is no one at the Society who can be better relied upon to take good care of her than Miranda.

I was on my way to Val, next, but my phone buzzed. When I grabbed it, there was no call to answer or message to read: instead, the lock screen displayed an animated image of a handsome, eighteenth-century chocolate pot of wrought silver, glittering steam coiling from its spout.

Or in other words, Milady wanted to see me.

I changed course at once, and headed for the stairs.

Once I had finished laboriously climbing up to the very top of the tallest tower, I discovered that the summons had not been limited to just me. Waymaster Jay was already there, and — more interestingly — Val. Valerie, Queen of the Library, is rarely dragged all the way up to Milady's tower. It might be because it is somewhat harder for her to get up there than the rest of us, seeing as she's confined to her chair (albeit a witched-up, conveniently floating one). But the House has a helpful way of whisking her anywhere she wants to go in the blink of an eye, so it's more likely that Val simply has the kind of autonomy at Home that the rest of us can only dream of.

I was the last to arrive, apparently, for the tower door closed behind me, and the incorporeal voice of Milady began at once to speak.

'Chairs, please, dear,' she said.

It took me a moment to realise that she had not, in fact, addressed any of the three of us by that unusually endearing title, but had been speaking to the House. Chairs promptly appeared for Jay and me: nice, fatly stuffed ones in tapestry upholstery, very comfy indeed.

This worried me. Milady rarely provided chairs. How long did she expect us to be here for?

I took a chair anyway, sinking gratefully into its plush embrace. I may be well used to the long climb to the top of the House, but I don't care how fit you are, it is still tiring.

Jay smiled at me. 'Had fun?'

Word really travels fast at the Society.

'Yes,' I said. 'There were pancakes.'

'An incomparable date.'

Well, sort of. I was still stinging just a bit from the fact that the Baron's purpose had been so very all business, but I did not feel like admitting that to Jay. Call it pride, if you will. So I said, 'Completely,' and let the subject drop, for Milady interposed.

'Good morning,' she said. 'Thank you all for coming. As you are unhappily aware, we have had a... situation at Home, which has not yet been resolved. And since we are on the brink of another, I consider it wise to discuss our options.'

'Another?' I said, startled.

'Relating to your recent find at the cottage, Ves.'

'We do seem to have a talent for making spectacular, but highly inconvenient finds,' murmured Jay.

'You certainly do,' I said. 'First Bill, then the pup. I wait with breathless anticipation to see what you'll stumble over next.'

Jay flashed me a smug smile.

'And whether or not we will survive it.'

The smile disappeared.

Milady cleared her throat. 'First of all, let me assure you that I do not anticipate a repeat of the Bill incident. While clearly special, a dappledok pup is in no way likely to be as fiercely sought-after as a book like that — or its creator. Nor are its unusual talents widely known about, or much believed in nowadays.'

'Really?' I said. 'The pup is basically a gold mine.'

'Not so much,' said Jay. 'It's not fifteen thirty-seven anymore. People don't store their wealth as stacks of gold or jewels anymore. When they do have valuables, they're in safes — or behind stoutly locked doors protected by house alarms. I wouldn't say a dappledok is useless in two thousand seventeen, but the best she could do is facilitate a few petty thefts.'

'Fair enough,' I had to agree. 'But you're talking about the non-magicker world. What about *our* world? We know little about her talents. Is it just gold and silver she can sniff out? Jewels? What jewels? Imagine if she could stick her little nose to the ground and trundle off after, say, a major Wand or something.'

'And that is a fair point, Ves,' said Milady. 'So I am pleased to hear that you have taken steps to have the pup disguised. It is a reasonable precaution, at least until we are able to discover the extent of the pup's talents.'

'What's the nature of the situation, then?' asked Jay.

'As Ves will already be aware, I have sought help with the matter of the... disloyalty we have sadly suffered among our ranks. I would first like to privately assure you all that I do not in the smallest degree doubt your integrity. I will, however, ask that you submit to an interview with the Truthseeker, like the rest of your peers.'

'A Truthseeker?' Jay whistled. 'I didn't know there were any of those left.'

'There are not many. Regarding the other matter, has it occurred to you to wonder in any detail where the pup came from?'

'Somewhat,' I said. 'I do not think the cottage had much to do with it. For the breed to survive for two centuries, there must have been a concerted effort going on somewhere to preserve it. But if it has remained a secret all this time, then it must be somewhere very, very hidden. How those three pups came to be in the cottage I couldn't say, but it certainly wasn't equipped for a breeding programme on that scale, and it showed no signs of having been inhabited by anybody living for a long time. The source must lie elsewhere.'

'They are also delicate,' Val added. 'Difficult to breed, almost as difficult to nurse to adulthood. It would take specialist knowledge, and a great deal of time and money to bring it off.'

'Which suggests,' I said, 'that somebody out there has a clear purpose in mind for them.'

'Might have been using them for something all along,' said Jay.

Good point. Electrifying point. I sat up, my thoughts awhirl.

'Exactly,' said Milady. 'And that is the situation. I need you to find out more about the dappledoks. Find out what they can really do, and discover where this one came from. It is still illegal to breed dappledok pups; Valerie has gone to significant trouble to verify this. That means that there is a group out there, or even a whole organisation, who have devoted considerable effort to an illegal breeding operation and they will not have done this lightly. It must be put a stop to.'

Thorny issue. On the one hand, protecting magickal beasts was a big part of our job; we were supposed to *prevent* them from dying out, not uphold a law that basically compelled them to do so. But I could not fault Milady's thinking. These pups were something else. There must have been a solid reason for their banning in the first place; that reason, whatever it was, might well be as true now as it was centuries ago.

I tried not to dwell on the fact that our having a dappledok on the premises at all was effectively a crime. What would become of the poor little pup? She was an innocent in the business. It was not her fault that her huge, gawky nose was all kinds of magickal.

That would be a problem for later.

$$4$$

'Yes,' added Milady. 'You may wish to begin by consulting your book.'

'Bill Two? By all means. He probably knows something about dappledoks.'

'Ask him about the Spriggan Dells, too,' Milady suggested. 'Not just the ones in Cornwall. Spriggans spread much beyond the borders of that county some time ago, and it may be no accident that this pup turned up in East Anglia.'

Then again, it might. The cottage did, after all, have a habit of moving around a lot.

Val spoke up. 'Something else you can ask Bill, Ves. Quite a lot of major artefacts have gone missing down the ages. Some of them have turned up again, some haven't yet. I would be interested to hear what Bill knows about that, considering he's spent time at the Library of Farringale.' She frowned. 'Or, his predecessor did. Does Bill Two have all the same information?'

'Yes,' said Jay. 'Indira made an exact duplicate.'

Valerie's eyes gleamed in a way I did not quite like. 'Can I borrow that book, Ves?'

'Are you planning to give it back?'

She thought about that. 'Would "someday" do?'

'Not really.'

'Books belong in the Library!' Val protested.

'But this one's mine!'

Valerie folded her arms, and stared implacably at the spot in mid-air where Milady's voice somehow manifested sparkles. 'Can I request a second duplicate for the Library?'

she said.

'Yes,' said Milady.

Valerie brightened at once. 'I'll talk to Indira.'

'Orlando,' corrected Milady. 'Indira is assisting on this project.'

'Nobody talks to Orlando,' said Valerie, rolling her eyes. 'You mean *send a requisition form up to the attic and hope he notices.*'

'He will notice. Valerie, please continue to consult the Library's existing resources, and relay anything you find to Ves and Jay.'

'Of course, Milady.'

'Jay, I imagine a visit to the site where you found the pup may shortly be in order. If you will be so kind as to facilitate the journey?'

'Certainly.'

'The Spriggan Glades are a different matter. They will have to be consulted, but I do not recommend that you do so immediately. They can be prickly, and difficult to deal with. I am endeavouring to secure a guide for you.'

I wondered if this guide might prove to be, in fact, a spriggan. Could be. Fae folk rarely mixed much with the human worlds, trolls somewhat excepted. They kept to themselves, tucked away in their own Dells, Glades, Knowes and whatever else, and did not much set foot outside. But still, it was not unheard of for a fae to enrol at the Hidden University, and the Society had even had a few on their staff at one point or another. I wouldn't be in the least surprised if Milady's guide turned out to be... unusual.

We stayed a while longer, bouncing thoughts around about the pup and its possible origins. Since it was nothing but speculation, Milady called a halt eventually and sent us off. 'Keep me informed,' she said as we trailed out of the tower.

I made her my usual curtsey on the way out. What can I say, Milady inspires a few old-fashioned impulses. 'Yes, ma'am,' I said.

The air sparkled. 'There's chocolate in the pots.'

· · · ● · ● · · ·

Pots, plural. There was one waiting in my room, and two cups: for Jay and for me. Valerie sent me a snapshot of the second one adorning her desk in the Library: it was gold, and it had purple smoke coming out of the spout.

'Huh,' grunted Jay, eyeing our much more mundane-looking silver one with some suspicion.

'Valerie and Milady go way back,' I told him, contentedly pouring hot chocolate into the two cups. The chocolate itself was too amazing to care very much about the vessel.

'And you two don't? How long have you worked here?'

'Only about a decade.'

He blinked. 'Only? How long's Val been here?'

'Since forever, as far as I can tell.'

'Not, like, literally.'

I grinned, enjoying the stupefied look on his face. 'Probably not literally, but who knows? We are all about secrets at the Society.'

Jay shook his head. 'Bill Two,' he prompted me, accepting his cup from me with a smile of anticipation.

'Right.' I found the strength of will to set my cup down after only a single sip of the deliciously rich contents, and retrieved the Book.

I have a safe in my snug little room. I call it a safe more for convenience than because it represents the arrangement with any particular accuracy. It is actually a... well, it is a chamber pot. Don't judge me. What could be more perfect? It is not even an attractive chamber pot, merely the plain white porcelain kind. It even has a crack in it.

See, if you barge into my room looking for valuables, the last place you bother poking your nose into is the ancient, cobweb-wreathed chamber pot lying under the bed, right in the back corner. If you did, all you would see is a dead spider.

Enchantments can be such fun.

Jay made no comment when I fell to my knees and began rooting under the bed, but one eyebrow rose when I emerged with the chamber pot. 'Did Bill Two urgently need to relieve himself?'

'He is a book, Jay. He is above such things.'

Jay's other eyebrow went up. 'Does he *sleep* in a chamber pot?'

I did something fancy with my hands. It was not at all necessary, of course, but it looks impressive. Without it, the process of magick looks sadly underwhelming.

When I had finished waving my hands about, the chamber pot more nearly resembled a rainbow crystal chest with an enormous lock on the front. Into this I inserted a matching crystal key, and the lid sprung open.

Jay put his face in his hands. 'It's rainbow,' he muttered, muffled.

'Of course it is.' I lifted Bill Two out, left the chest on the bed, and returned to my chair — and my cup of chocolate. 'Right. Hi, Bill Two.' I settled the book in my lap, and took a moment to admire it yet again. It is the big, heavy, ancient-looking kind, with purple leather covers and a twelve-pointed star on the front. Devastatingly handsome.

'Might I be so forward as to request an alternative name?' said the book. 'It is lowering to be addressed by my predecessor's appellation.'

'Of course! I ought to have thought of it before now. Did you have any particular name in mind?'

'Well,' said the book, sounding suddenly diffident. 'I have always rather liked the word "gallimaufry."'

The book that knows everything *would* have a spectacular vocabulary, wouldn't it? 'A wonderful name,' I said.

Jay leaned in my direction. 'What does that mean?' he whispered.

'It means an assortment of different kinds of things.'

'Fitting.'

'Entirely. Gallimaufry it shall be!'

The book riffled its pages contentedly.

'Shall you object very much to being addressed as Galli?' I hazarded. 'Gallimaufry is a lengthy word for regular use.'

'Why not Mauf?' said Jay.

I glared at him. 'Let's not confuse the issue—'

'I find Mauf agreeable,' said the book.

'Um. In that case, Mauf it is.'

Jay smiled.

I took a gulp of chocolate. 'Mauf,' I began. 'We are here to consult you on a matter of some importance.'

The book brightened, and I do mean that literally. The twelve-pointed star embossed into the surface gleamed with silver fire, and the dark purple of the leather lightened a few shades. 'I shall be delighted to help!' Mauf declared.

He liked to feel important. I had already noticed that. 'We rely on you,' I added, laying it on a bit.

Mauf preened. 'How may I assist you?'

'There is a situation at the Society regarding the sudden re-emergence of the dappledok species,' I began.

'Which dappledok species?' said Mauf.

I exchanged a startled look with Jay. 'Which?' I repeated. 'What do you mean?'

'Dappledok is a Dell situated near the south coast of Cornwall,' Mauf informed us. 'Once famed for their talent with beasts of all kinds, its residents engaged in a number of selective breeding programmes and produced an array of hitherto unknown creatures with unusual, and highly desirable, abilities.'

'What?' I gulped chocolate, my head spinning. 'There are *more*?'

'I know of at least eight.'

I looked at Jay, eyes wide. He stared back.

'Um,' I said. 'I don't think Miranda knows anything about that.'

'I don't think Milady even knows,' said Jay. 'Or Valerie either.'

'Right. Bill — Mauf — we are referring to a dog-like creature with golden fur and a single horn between its ears.'

'The Nose-for-Gold, that being the literal translation of the original name in the spriggan tongue. Or Goldnose, as they were informally known in English.'

'That sounds about right.'

'Last referenced somewhere in the seventeen hundreds,' said Mauf. 'Believed to have become extinct sometime thereafter.'

'That agrees with what Miranda told me. It's true that they can sniff out valuable objects?'

'It is, but the use of said power was banned by the Troll Court in 1703, the Magickal Councils of the Dells and Dales in 1704, and most of the various fae monarchs by 1706. This did not, of course, deter very many, and so the breeding of the Goldnoses themselves was subsequently forbidden.'

'Even the fae monarchs banned them?' I said, surprised. 'But were they not created by spriggans?'

'The spriggan queen, Parlewin, was the first to declare them outlawed. It is recorded that her favourite brooch, a gaudy object made from gold and rainbow diamonds, vanished under mysterious circumstances in early 1705 and since her primary rival at court was known to be in possession of a trio of Goldnoses, the culprit seemed, to her majesty, obvious enough.'

Jay grinned. 'Perhaps it did not occur to the original breeders that anyone might be audacious enough to use it on *them.*'

'Mauf,' I said. 'Do you know of anyone who defied the ban?'

'It is written that many did, at first, and the penalties for flouting the law had to be significantly increased. This proved effective, and over the next fifty years or so recorded instances of Goldnoses being bred gradually dwindled to nothing.'

'What penalty did they impose?' asked Jay.

'The worst penalty ever suffered for illegal ownership of a Goldnose was Divesting.'

'Um,' I said as my stomach fell through the floor. 'Is... is that still valid?'

'In some communities, yes,' said Mauf.

'Argh,' I said.

See, Divesting is a nice euphemism for the total stripping of all of a person's magickal abilities. Forever. I do not even know how it is done; few do. Only the highest authorities in the land are capable of it, and it is usually handed out only in cases of extreme misuse of magick.

Was I in danger of *that*, for rescuing a puppy?!

'Do not trouble yourself unduly,' said Mauf kindly. 'This law applies in those magickal communities or countries which date back to the early eighteenth century, namely the Troll Court, the faerie courts, the Magickal Councils of the Dells and Dales, the—'

'But *not* the Hidden Ministry?' I interjected, unable to bear the suspense while Mauf rattled through another forty-three or so such organisations.

'Indeed not. The Ministry was founded in 1787, by which time the problem of the Goldnoses had so far receded into the past that it was not thought necessary to carry over that particular law. As such, Ves, you are presently committing no official crime.'

He did not need to add that this would only hold true until somebody thought it worth their while to write up a new law about it. I decided not to think about that because something more immediately pressing occurred to me. 'But I was when I took the pup into Rhaditton!'

'Arguably only. There is no actual prohibition against having a Goldnose pup with you in Troll territory, provided you are neither engaged in using it nor in breeding more.'

Phew. 'Thank you, Mauf,' I said.

Jay patted my shoulder comfortingly, which I took to mean that my brief panic had been showing on my face. Don't get me wrong, I will cheerfully bend any number of rules when I feel it is necessary. But outright flouting inscribed magickal law is another matter, and this is not exactly an emergency situation going on here. No one wants to risk a Divesting without thoroughly good reason.

I'd lost my train of thought by then, and could not immediately think of what next to enquire of Mauf. Luckily Jay still had his wits about him. 'Mauf, can you think of anybody who might have managed to maintain the Goldnose breed since the eighteenth century into the present, and without detection?'

'Until now,' I amended.

Mauf fell silent for a while. Was he thinking? Could a book like him (or more rightly, it) think, in the real sense of the word? Was he riffling through all his archives? I wondered, not for the first time, how so powerful yet peculiar an enchantment worked.

'Not immediately,' said Mauf at last. 'There are no recorded instances of any concerted breeding programmes in operation since 1727, when a group of renegade spriggans were found to have established a miniature state for themselves in an otherwise abandoned Dell. They were all imprisoned, and it is not written that they ever escaped, or that they were ever released.'

I sighed, a little bit disappointed. But I suppose life would be far too easy if Mauf had an easy answer to everything. Wouldn't it? Challenges are good for the character, right?

Right.

5

'Let's think,' said Jay. 'Hidden Ministry aside, the Goldnoses are still banned in virtually every magickal community there is. It is no mean feat, then, to breed them in spite of the law, and to keep it going for so long. It also takes considerable courage to consistently flout a law which carries such severe penalties for disobedience. Somebody really, really wanted those pups.'

'Takes courage, or confidence?' I suggested. 'You might flout that law with impunity if you felt that you had the right people on your side.'

Jay blinked at me. 'You mean somebody high in authority might be behind this?'

'If not behind it, then at least willing to turn a blind eye — and perhaps to shield those responsible from the consequences, should their activities ever come to light.'

Jay nodded thoughtfully. 'Worryingly plausible. Or, it's the responsibility of some group who felt they had power enough in themselves to ignore the general disapprobation.'

'Maybe it's somebody like us, who falls under the jurisdiction of the Hidden Ministry and therefore is not, technically, acting illegally.'

'But if the Ministry only dates from the late seventeen hundreds, and the pups had already passed out of all knowledge by then, who bridged that gap?'

'Fair point. Perhaps the Ministry isn't the only organisation that hasn't enacted such laws. Mauf?'

'All officially recorded and recognised magickal organisations had agreed upon, and enacted such laws, by 1731,' said Mauf.

'Official?' said Jay. 'Are there unofficial ones?'

'It happens on occasion. They do not tend to last long, however.'

Which made sense. Setting up your own unsanctioned magickal state and proposing therefore to consider yourself above all magickal laws was not exactly widely supported behaviour. The usual consequence would be exactly as that enterprising band of spriggans discovered in 1727 — a speedy dispatch to prison, or something worse. It would be like buying your own island, declaring it an independent country, and expecting every other country in the world to nod, smile and pat you tolerantly on the head while you proceed to set up a factory for nuclear bombs on your tiny slice of paradise. This is not how it works.

But it doesn't stop people from occasionally trying.

'I wonder if some rogue magickal state has somehow gone undetected since the early eighteenth century?' I mused aloud.

'It isn't impossible,' said Jay. 'Not *quite.*'

'It is highly unlikely,' I agreed. 'And perhaps we're thinking too big now.'

'A smaller operation would have the greater chance of success,' said Jay. 'The bigger you are, the more noticeable you tend to be.'

'Some smaller operation with an incurable lust for treasure?' I suggested.

'Why else would you brave all dire consequences to keep a Goldnose handy?'

I nodded. 'I think Milady is right. Somebody needs to have a quiet talk with the spriggans.'

• • • • • • • • • •

Valerie needed to have a quiet talk with Mauf, too, and so did Miranda. His casual revelation that the Dappledok Dell had been responsible for at least eight rare and desirable species of beasts required immediate investigation. I left the book at the Library, pausing only to relay enough of our findings to thoroughly electrify our sedate and dignified Boss Librarian. So energised was she, she almost tore the book right out of my hands.

I left them chatting cosily together, or so I hoped. Knowing Val, it would soon turn into an interrogation.

My next plan was to hustle back up to Milady's tower to relay Mauf's findings — and to see if the guide she had mentioned was here yet. I wanted to be on the road already, for little good ever comes of delaying something important. The sooner we talked to the spriggans of Dappledok, the better.

But I was distracted — twice.

I was halfway up the main stairs when I heard Miranda's voice calling me. I turned back. She had just come through the great doors leading into the east wing and was hastening towards me, her blonde hair half out of its ponytail as usual and a besmeared white coat over her jumper and jeans. A little dog trotted at her heels, and in spite of everything it still took me a moment to recognise my pup.

'What do you think?' said Mir, a bit breathlessly, as she came up to me.

I gazed at the pup. Instead of gold, her fur was now chocolate brown dappled liberally with purple, and there was no trace of the little horn that had adorned her forehead. She now had two horns instead, slightly thicker ones, nestled behind each of her pointed ears. Her nose had shrunk, and turned to an unobtrusive black colour.

In other words, she was a gorhound.

'Wow,' I said intelligently. 'That's amazing.'

Miranda nodded. 'They're good, aren't they?' she said, presumably referring to whichever of our illusionists had worked on the pup.

'Amazing,' I said again. So amazing, in fact, that for a brief, wild moment I wondered whether some switcheroo hadn't been performed, and the tiny Goldnose wasn't now languishing in some hidden nook in the east wing while I was fobbed off with a different creature altogether.

I squashed those ideas very quickly. What reason did I have to distrust Mir? None whatsoever. The illusionists really were that good, that was all.

When the gorhound puppy trotted up to me and rubbed herself all over my leg, my doubts vanished altogether. 'Hi, pup,' I said, and bent to pat her.

'Pup?' said Miranda. 'Doesn't she have a name?'

I know I have been referring to her as *my* pup for a while now, but I knew full well that she was no such thing. She was under my care for a little while, that was all, and if she had taken an obvious shine to me, well — what did that matter? No one was going to leave so rare, so valuable and so, er, *illegal* a beast with me for very long.

So I had not had the presumption to name her. It seemed wiser, somehow. If I did not name her, maybe I could refrain from getting too attached to her.

Hah.

'Pup works just fine,' I said, declining to explain all of this to Miranda.

I think she understood anyway, though, for she gave me a smile of unexpected sympathy and said, 'Perhaps it does, at that.'

It occurred to me that Miranda had probably been in the same situation over and over again. How many beasts had she bred and raised herself, or rescued and tenderly restored to health, only to have to relinquish them into someone else's possession? Or back into the wild? She would grow used to it, I supposed — to a degree. Her attachment to animals of all kinds was legendary at Home, after all.

Miranda gave me a salute and dashed off again, leaving the pup trailing around at my heels. We barely managed to climb four stairs between us that time before I heard the double doors of the front hall swing ponderously open, admitting a blaze of sunshine from outside. I say *heard* because they open with a groaning noise indicative of rusted hinges. They don't have rusted hinges, of course; the House is far too well-maintained to permit of that. But no amount of persuasion, oil-based or otherwise, can convince the doors to stop announcing each new visitor with some unpromising noise or another. I've long since concluded that House does it on purpose. If any building could be supposed to have a sense of humour, it would be ours.

Anyway, when the doors groan like that — or squeal, or cackle, choke — it means someone of note has arrived, so I stopped and went back down the stairs yet again.

I might have been planning to go forward to meet whoever it was, but I swiftly revised all ideas of that kind and stayed firmly put. One judges it prudent, you know, with some visitors.

This one was most definitely of that kind. He was so tall, he had to stoop a long way to fit through the enormous doors, and he did not appear to find that an amusing process at all. He made it into the hall with some effort and stood, his short white hair brushing the high ceiling, looking down upon us puny humans with eyes the size of dinner plates.

All right, maybe not dinner plates. Afternoon tea plates, though, for certain. You could easily eat scones off those bright blue eyeballs.

He wore a long robe of blue cloth embroidered in gold, a white coat over the top, and (more puzzlingly, considering the weather) a pair of blue gloves. In other words, he made not the smallest effort to look like he belonged in any part of the modern world — but then, why should he? He was the size of about six humans put together.

'Giant,' I said faintly.

'So I see,' said Jay from behind me, startling me, for I had not noticed his approach. 'Do we often get giants stopping by?'

I had to think for a minute before I could remember the last time. At least five years ago. 'Nope,' I said succinctly.

'Right, then.'

The giant gave a long, windy sigh and said in lugubrious tones, 'Why must the doors always be so small?'

I pondered that. House is perfectly capable of adjusting proportions at need — be it of windows, chairs, or, indeed, doors. That it had not chosen to do so — and, further, that it had chosen to announce the arrival of this giant with so peculiarly unattractive a groaning noise — suggested to me that House did not altogether approve of our visitor.

Interesting.

Jay and I were not the only Society employs standing, frozen with surprise, in the hall. The giant surveyed the lot of us one by one, and when nobody spoke, he said: 'I am here to see Milady.'

There was no conceivable way he was going to fit in Milady's tower.

'Er,' said Jay in an undertone. 'That's going to be interesting.'

But of course, Milady had anticipated this. 'Welcome, Lord Garrogin,' she suddenly said from somewhere disconcertingly close to my head. 'We have been looking forward to your arrival.'

This, too, was unusual, and I could only answer Jay's questioning stare with a shrug. Yes, it was also a long time since Milady had been known to manifest (sort of) anywhere other than her tower. Yes, that probably meant nothing good either.

What can you do.

'Wonder if he's our guide or the Truthseeker?' whispered Jay.

'The latter,' I said instantly, and hoped I was right. Spriggans are not very tall. I collected that our guide was meant to be someone the spriggan courts might feel more comfortable associating with than a couple of humans, and I couldn't imagine their welcoming the arrival of so vast a being as Lord Garrogin in any such spirit.

I was swiftly proved right, for Milady's voice crisply announced: 'Consultations will shortly begin. Cordelia Vesper and Jay Patel to the Audience Chamber, please.'

That's Milady for you. For one thing, "Convention Chamber" is far too modern a term for her. She prefers "Audience Chamber," as though those summoned were to be presented to some manner of monarch. For another, "consultations" sounds so much nicer than "inquisition", doesn't it?

'Why are we first?' whispered Jay to me as we dutifully headed for the Chamber of Gorgeousness.

'Probably because we're supposed to be on our way to Sprigganland already.'

'If our guide's here.'

'He or she probably is, or they're imminently expected. Milady doesn't waste time.'

'As evidenced by the prompt appearance of Lord Garrogin, Giant, from Parts Unknown.'

'Precisely.'

Lord Garrogin was nowhere in evidence when we arrived at the Audience/Convention Chamber. Milady had probably taken him off for an initial briefing, and was overseeing the pouring of hot chocolate down his gargantuan throat at that very moment. The enormous Inquisition Room (as I would now have to think of it) was echoingly empty, though I was heartened to see that refreshments had been provided: the long, crystalline table running down the centre of the marble-floored hall was absolutely smothered in the refined sorts of dishes that come with polished silver covers. I knew they had tasty things inside them because the air was filled with an enticing medley of aromas.

This circumstance puzzled more than pleased Jay, however. 'That seems… excessive,' he said, nodding his chin at the laden table.

'This is Milady, remember.'

'And?'

I pulled out a velvet-cushioned chair at the bottom of the table and sat on it. 'Well,' I said, stretching. 'There are probably two reasons for it. For one, Milady's really very kind-hearted. I suppose she cannot predict how long each interview will take, and she would hate for us to get hungry while we suffer Lord Garrogin's interrogation.'

Jay sat down next to me. 'Hence enough food for about two hundred people. I suppose the dishes keep everything warm?'

'Undoubtedly.'

'All right. And what's the other reason?'

'Milady is almost as devious as she is kind. Well-fed people are comfortable people, and food puts almost everyone at their ease. The comfier you are, the less guarded you are, and that is probably going to make his lordship's job a bit easier.'

'Remind me never to underestimate Milady.'

'Everyone underestimates Milady.'

Jay chewed his lip. 'But doesn't interrogation make for uneasy people anyway?'

'Depends how good Lord Garrogin is.'

The heavy thud of approaching footsteps announced the arrival of our interrogator, and I wondered whether we ought to stand up. I decided not to.

Jay didn't. And if he was going to politely get to his feet then that sort of meant I had to, as well. I stifled a sigh as I hauled my bones out of the chair again, and watched Lord Garrogin's ponderous approach with, despite my sanguine words, a faint flicker of apprehension. He did make an imposing appearance, no doubt about that. And hadn't I just said that Milady was devious? She had told Jay and me that we were not under suspicion, but that, too, might have been a ploy to put us at our ease.

I wondered distantly when I had become so fretful, and banished those thoughts. Time to focus.

'My lord,' I said as Garrogin reached us.

He nodded to us both, and made his slow way to the head of the table. The chair there was no larger than the ones Jay and I had been sitting in, but that did not last. As the giant approached, the chair twitched and swelled to four times its former size, and it wasn't finished at that. Formerly a sleek, armless dining chair of some silver-coloured wood, it thickened and stretched until its silvery frame bore more of a throne-like appearance, complete with tall arm rests. Its blueish cushions became a rich purple just shy of royal in tone, and it even developed some kind of diamond jewel at the top of its arched back.

House had been Spoken To, I guessed. His Lordship was evidently to be pampered, and Milady had insisted. If there was a touch of the satirical about the excesses of that throne, who was I to judge?

Lord Garrogin — was he in fact some kind of minor princeling, out in giant territory? He could be, I supposed, and that would explain the throne — Lord Garrogin sat down, and the majestic chair bore his weight without a whimper. He sat for a moment looking thoughtfully at us.

Jay and I stared back.

6

'Please have a seat,' the giant finally said. 'Covers, please.'

This last made no sense to me whatsoever, but before I could ask for an explanation, two of the silver dishes shivered and spat their covers into the air, where they promptly vanished. The two dishes hastened to set themselves before us, and I noted with approval (but not much surprise) that mine contained three items: a piece of carrot cake, a custard slice, and a cup of chocolate. Three of my very favourite things.

I peeked at Jay's: it had a fat samosa, a plate of chips, and a cup of tea… no, the contents of the little cup were far too dark for tea.

'Since when are you a coffee drinker?' I whispered to him.

He shot me a vaguely guilty look. 'I like tea as well,' he said defensively.

'Traitor.'

He flicked a chip at me.

We had ended up seated within easy talking distance of Lord Garrogin, but not so close that I could see what his dishes were. I was disappointed. Food is a bit of an interest of mine — big surprise, right? — and I was curious about what kinds of things giants might like to eat.

'Cordelia Vesper,' said Garrogin. 'And Jay Patel. I understand you work together?'

'As of a few weeks ago,' I confirmed, picking up the shiny silver fork that came with my plate and tucking into the cake. 'He's our new Waymaster, and I am training him to join the Acquisitions Division.'

'Tell me about Acquisitions,' said Garrogin. He had a deep, soothing voice, and I genuinely did feel calmed by it. The flutter of nerves in my belly dissipated.

'Well, we are the — the public arm of the Society, I suppose,' I said. 'We track down and retrieve artefacts, treasures, trinkets and curiosities, books, beasts, talismans — anything really — that might be under threat, and make sure they get where they need to go. Sometimes that's here, sometimes elsewhere.'

'We fix problems, too,' Jay said. 'It's not just retrieval. On my first assignment with Ves, we went after a pair of stolen alikats and discovered a disease infesting half the dormant Troll Enclaves in the country. Took a bit to resolve that one.'

'And how did you resolve it?' said Garrogin, in the same even tone.

'In the end, we had to go all the way to Farringale,' said Jay, dipping a chip in ketchup.

That prompted a small reaction from our giant interrogator. 'You entered Farringale? What did you do there?'

So we told him that story, and that got us onto the tale of Bill the Book. By the time we had finished telling him about all of that, my cakes and chocolate were gone, and Jay had wiped his plate clean of chips, ketchup and samosas alike.

Garrogin hadn't touched his dishes at all.

'You have had a lively time of it,' he observed.

'It's never a dull job,' I agreed. 'Though to be fair, it's not usually quite *that* exciting.'

Lord Garrogin nodded thoughtfully, and at last — at *last* — he selected some small morsel of something from his plate and consumed it with ponderous slowness. 'What drew you to the Society?' he asked, looking at Jay.

The question came a bit out of the blue, so I could not blame Jay for looking a trifle startled. But he answered quickly. 'It's legendary, for one thing. Everyone here is really committed to the preservation of our magickal heritage, and... well, without Milady and her recruits, we'd have lost a lot of irreplaceable things by now. That's more important to me than anything. And then my parents both worked here, before I was born. They always had great stories to tell. I never really wanted anything else.'

That interested me, for I'd never heard that Jay's mother and father had been employees here. But Garrogin did not seem disposed to follow up that line of enquiry. Instead he said, with probably deceptive blandness, 'Not even for a much higher salary?'

'The Society pays as much as I need,' said Jay.

Garrogin nodded, and turned his sharp blue gaze upon me. 'And why do you stay,

Cordelia?'

'It's Ves,' I said. 'Cordelia makes me feel like a porcelain doll. I stay for all the reasons Jay just said. There is nothing more important I could do with my time and my skills, is there? And I love the variety, the challenge… no two days are ever the same. I once regretted not being assigned to the Library, but much as I love books and research, I'd probably be getting bored by now.'

Lord Garrogin's eyes narrowed the merest fraction, and my stomach tightened. What had I said to prompt that reaction? But the expression faded, and he actually smiled at us both. Not much, but there was a definite curving of his lips. 'Thank you,' he said, in a tone of dismissal. 'It has been an enlightening conversation.'

He did not appear in any way displeased, so I tried not to conclude that this comment boded ill, and got up from my chair. 'It was a pleasure to meet you,' I said politely.

He inclined his head to us both. 'We will meet again.'

Would we? That definitely sounded ominous.

Jay and I exchanged identical looks of mild concern, and beat a hasty retreat.

· · · ● · ● · · ·

The "consultations" went on all day, but there was no news to be had as to how they were progressing. Jay and I wandered listlessly about the common room for a while, and when neither word nor orders arrived, we decided to arrange our own entertainment.

Extra equipment required: one Valerie, one Mauf, one Library of Dreams.

Objective: find out more about the Dappledok Dell, the spriggan courts, and anything else that seemed pertinent.

We arrived at Val's enormous desk to find her getting very cosy with Mauf.

She had the book laid before her on a thick cushion, unopened. Mauf's cover was glinting with light again; I was rapidly learning that this was a sign of interest with him, perhaps even excitement. Val had a notepad beside her and a pen in one hand, and she was furiously writing notes, one finger tapping frenetically upon Mauf's gorgeous leather cover.

She looked up when Jay and I walked in. 'This is amazing,' she said. 'The library has nothing about any of this. *Nothing.*'

'The Dappledok beasts?' I asked, pulling up a chair. Sitting on the audience side of

Valerie's desk always feels odd. Val's chair is handsome, and elevated on a slight pedestal besides, so she's very much looking down on anybody seated on the other side. Valerie herself can be a touch imposing, too — not that she isn't friendly, of course. But she's a tall, majestic sort of woman with perfect posture and incredibly well-groomed hair, and while she's always been a staunch friend to me, some part of her manner can sometimes feel a bit... brisk, shall we say? It feels a bit like taking a meeting with the approachable but mildly awe-inspiring CEO of some vast, important company.

I cannot say that I mind, though. Val is the undisputed queen of the library, a post she has thoroughly earned, and she deserves every scrap of status that comes with it.

Anyway. 'There were eight different species,' Val said to me. 'Each more remarkable than the last, and I don't say that lightly. Irreplaceable. I cannot believe that so many of them were permitted to pass out of existence — nay, not permitted, but forced to!'

Jay politely broke in upon this discourse. 'How many of them have been banned?'

'Four, of the eight,' she said promptly, then paused. 'Right, Mauf?'

'Correct, madam.'

Apparently my book and Valerie were getting along swimmingly, if one of them was already on a first-name basis. Mauf had a bit of formality to get over. I'd give it about... twenty-five years.

Valerie consulted her notes, flipping back a page or two. 'The Goldnoses, as they were colloquially known, though their correct name was — never mind. Too much detail, Val. They were banned because they facilitated the life of crime far more than anybody was comfortable with. Another species had a talent for lifting curses, which you might think would be a good thing, unless they were being used to circumvent the kinds of curses that have been laid down for good reason — you know the kind of thing, Ves.'

I did. That chamberpot, for example. I had cursed it so that it would do a few, er, rather unpleasant things to anybody who contrived to get into it without my permission. We call that a curse, because it's essentially dark magic, but its use for the protection of personal property (among other things) is common, and widely supported.

'A useful creature to have alongside your Goldnose,' I remarked.

'Extremely. A third was forbidden purely because it could never be cured of its tendency to go wild and bite everybody within range, and since its fangs were venomous this was considered undesirable.'

Jay snorted.

'And finally, the fourth. A sweet little thing, as much like a kitten as the Goldnoses are like adorable little puppies. Only it was bred for its milk, which happens to be hallucinogenic in very bad ways.'

'Hallucinogenic?!' I echoed. 'What was that about?'

Valerie shot me a look. 'Why does anybody manufacture drugs, Ves?'

'Fair point.'

'And the other four?' Jay asked.

'Two of them are on the endangered species list, and the other two became so common that nobody remembers — or cares — where they came from anymore. All of them possess, at most, minor and harmless abilities.'

I thought that over. 'Interesting array of beasties.'

'Isn't it?' Val agreed. 'To the credit of Dappledok, the four that were never banned were pretty terrific achievements. But the *other* four? Odd mixture.'

'I wonder what they were after.'

Valerie shrugged. 'Possibly there was no master plan, they were just experimenting. Exercising their powers. That kind of thing.'

'Then again,' said Jay, 'it has been said that spriggans are known for a love of all things gold.'

Valerie pursed her lips. 'In the same way that humans are, probably. Collectively, we're powerfully influenced by material wealth, but that doesn't make all of us robbers and thieves.'

Jay inclined his head, conceding the point.

'So who was responsible for these creatures?' I asked. 'If Dappledok is anything like most Dells, it's fairly sizeable, and a lot of different people live there. Or did, once upon a time. All we've heard so far is that "spriggans" made the Goldnoses, but that's a broad category.'

'It is far too broad, though it is true enough. Mauf?'

The book glittered with enthusiasm. 'The Dappledok Dell had two main neighbourhoods: one inhabited, predominantly, by spriggans, and the other home to a large community of brownies. Scattered about across the rest was quite the array of other beings, including a few humans. I speak of its heyday, which lasted for much of the seventeenth century. It declined somewhat thereafter, and today it is known as a quiet, reclusive Dell rarely open to outsiders.'

'And the spriggans?' I prompted.

'I am getting to that,' said Mauf, calmly but firmly.

I was abashed. 'Sorry.'

Mauf made a throat-clearing noise. Somehow. 'The spriggans of Dappledok were a mixture of multiple tribes, but the most powerful of them were the Redclovers, who founded a school at Dappledok in 1372. The establishment grew to considerable size over the next two centuries, and was held in such high repute that people travelled to Dappledok from all over Britain to attend. They taught a range of magickal techniques and theories but their specialisation, as I am sure you will not be surprised to hear, was all matters relating to the capture, care, breeding and use of magickal beasts. It is that school, and its attendant workshops, which produced all eight of the species I have previously discussed with Valerie.'

The Redclover School. Interesting.

Jay spoke up. 'Where did you learn all this, Bill? I mean, Mauf?'

'I came across it during my time at the Library of Farringale.'

'Did you absorb *all* the knowledge of that place?'

'To my shame, no. It was not possible to properly converse with those books placed too far away from my shelf. I would estimate that I was only able to exchange information with approximately seven thousand books.'

There was a short silence following this extraordinary statement, during which (judging from their faces) Jay and Valerie were thinking much the same thing as I was.

Seven thousand??!

Had they all been lost volumes, full of information we no longer had access to? If so, Valerie was going to be very, very busy for about the next twelve lifetimes.

Anyway. I forcibly dragged my reeling mind back to the point at hand, albeit with some difficulty. 'Redclover,' I said aloud.

'Spriggans,' Jay added helpfully.

'Dappledok beasts. One ancient mystery at a time, right?'

Jay said, 'Right,' but in tones of deep regret with which I could only sympathise.

My phone buzzed.

I grabbed it from my pocket. 'Ves,' I said.

Unbelievably, and unprecedentedly, Milady's voice echoed into my ear. 'Mabyn Redclover has just arrived at the front hall, Ves. I am much engaged with Lord Garrogin at present, and since Mabyn is to be your guide to Dappledok, may I ask you and Jay to meet her?'

I swiftly agreed, and put away my phone. 'A lady's arrived to see Jay and me,' I announced.

'A lady?' asked Jay.

'Her name is Mabyn.'

Jay gave me a quizzical frown.

'Redclover,' I said with a grin.

Jay's eyes widened, and he shot out of his chair. 'Going.'

We went.

'Keep me posted!' called Valerie after us.

I turned around long enough to make a cross-my-heart gesture, and... and I noticed Mauf still lying before Valerie.

I ran back to grab him.

'Ves! I am not finished!'

'Sorry,' I said with total sincerity, but not at all deterred. 'We're going to need him.'

7

J ay had never met a spriggan before.

Neither had I, in fact, but since it was my sacred duty to be the knowledgeable, world-wise one, I had no intention of telling him that. I went forward to meet Mabyn Redclover with a practiced air of confident ease, and bid her warmly welcome to the Society.

Not that there was anything in her appearance to disgust, or even to disconcert. True, her head was a little overlarge for her body, but she was well-dressed and impeccably groomed and I respect that. She was a foot or so shorter than me (so, in other words, *very* short), and appeared to be of advanced age, judging from her wizened skin and white hair. She wore a sixties-style two-piece suit, jacket and skirt perfectly matched, with low heels and gold earrings. She hadn't gone for the beehive hair, slightly to my disappointment; instead, she had a nicely coiffed bob. We arrived in the hall to find her standing in the middle of it, looking around with obvious interest.

She took off her gloves when I went to greet her, and shook my hand warmly. 'Mabyn Redclover,' she introduced herself. 'I'm with the Ministry. Department of Forbidden Magicks.'

My eyebrows rose. Milady had reached rather high, and was it a coincidence that Ms. Redclover was an expert in magickal misdemeanours? I imagined not.

Jay and I introduced ourselves.

'Pleasure,' she said briskly. 'You are the two I was invited to meet, are you? What may

I do for you?'

'Any connection at all to the Redclovers of Dappledok?' asked Jay.

A faint grimace flickered over her lips, and was gone. 'Once. A long time ago.'

I suppose you would distance yourself from family connections like that, in her line of work. But I wondered, then, why she had never changed her name.

Jay nodded. 'Has Milady described our current situation to you?'

'An outline only. A Dappledok beast has been found?'

'One of the questionable ones.' Jay proceeded to fill in the details. I, meanwhile, tried not to look as though I had the creature in question tucked into the bag hanging from my left shoulder, and hoped that the pup would not choose this of all possible moments to stick her head out for some air.

She didn't, but Ms. Redclover's eyes settled upon me with a shrewd expression I could not quite like. 'You have the pup here?' she said.

I sighed, and lifted the flap of my bag. I did so with some trepidation, in case Ms. Redclover, of Forbidden Magicks, should decide to confiscate her — or worse. But she only looked briefly into the bag, noted the dark shape of the pup curled up in the bottom, and withdrew. 'Disguised?'

'Yes.'

'Excellent illusion.'

I smiled, uncertain. Chit-chat? Surely she must feel some disapproval. 'There were three of them in the cottage,' I elaborated. 'Two failed to survive. We believe there must be some manner of secret breeding programme going on somewhere, and we'd like to get to the bottom of it.'

'So would we,' said Mabyn Redclover, with a thin smile. 'Milady has assigned you to assist me, so we will be working together for a time. I trust that will be agreeable?'

I felt a little surprise. Assigned to work with Mabyn? Had she not been sent to serve as our guide? Just who was in charge here?

It was typical of Milady to couch the situation in rather different terms to us, but the melancholy truth was: Ministry employees outranked us, especially the higher ups. And Ms. Redclover had every appearance of being one of those, from her manicured nails to her air of business-like efficiency. She was the kind of person who confidently expects to be obeyed without question, and that spoke volumes.

'Well, actually—' said Jay.

I coughed, interrupting him. 'That will be fine,' I told her. 'We are ready to depart for Dappledok at once, if that is acceptable to you.'

'Quite.' She looked at Jay. 'You are a Waymaster, yes?'

'I am.'

She nodded, and took — I kid you not — a plastic rain-hood out of a pocket of her suit. This she unfolded, and placed carefully over her perfectly coiffed hair, tying the strings under her chin. 'Right away, then,' she said briskly.

Jay looked at me, and I shrugged. I hoped my shrug would convey something along the lines of, *best to do as the nice lady says,* but to Jay it apparently said something more like *I have no idea, it's your problem,* for his mouth tightened, and he walked off with only a brief nod for Ms. Redclover.

She fell in beside me as I wandered after Jay, fussily adjusting the sit of her rain-hood. 'Terse young man, isn't he?' she said in an undertone.

'He's only been with us for a few weeks yet. I think he's still finding his feet.'

'Ahh,' she said wisely. 'I remember those days.'

I was tempted to ask her how long it had been since she'd felt young and uncertain, but wisely restrained the impulse.

'You were lucky to get him,' she added after a moment.

'We were. He's a highly talented Waymaster. One of the best, I understand, though you'd never hear him say it.'

'The Ministry wanted to bid for him, but Milady was too fast. One or two people were mighty displeased about that.'

My mouth twitched, though I managed to suppress the smug smile that threatened to emerge. 'I am sure Milady was duly apologetic.'

'Most apologetic. Not at all sorry, of course, but most apologetic.'

I did smile at that. Plastic hats or no, I began to feel that Ms. Redclover and I might just get along.

· · ● · ● · ● · · ·

Ms. Redclover went through the Winds of the Ways with her hands carefully clamped over her hair. I privately thought it absurd, until she emerged at a windy henge atop a cliff somewhere in (presumably) Cornwall with her hair intact and I... didn't.

As I nonchalantly shook out my tangled curls I reminded myself that perfect hair isn't everything.

'So,' I said to Jay with a brilliant smile. 'Er, whereabouts are we?'

'Cornwall.'

I looked around. We stood high up over the water on rocky ground covered in feathery green grasses. Great boulders lay everywhere, protruding pugnaciously from the earth, and the sun shone gorgeously over a patchwork of meadows stretching away into the distance. 'Edifying.'

He smiled faintly at me, and pointed over my shoulder. 'That's the sea.'

I stared out over the expanse of glittering blue water. 'So that's what the sea looks like.'

'Watery.'

'Very.'

With a tiny sigh, he said, 'We are as far west in England as you can get, and a long way south. We're somewhere along what they now call the Penwith Heritage Coast, which means we are smack in the middle of spriggan country, and the entrance to the Dappledok Dell is not far from here.'

I gave him a tiny salute. 'Thank you, Captain Geography.'

'You are welcome, Captain History.'

I had half expected him to call me Captain Sparkle or something, but I liked his alternative. 'I've never been to Cornwall,' I admitted.

'Never?' He looked incredulous. 'I thought you'd been in Acquisitions for ten years.'

'I have, but somehow I never ended up in Cornwall.'

'Interesting.

Ms. Redclover gave a slight cough. 'The day marches on,' she observed.

It did, at that. It must be well past noon already, and Jay and I were bantering the afternoon away. 'Sorry,' I said hastily. 'Lead on, Jay?'

He led on. We wended our way around the coastline for half an hour or so, and I had cause to be thankful that I had chosen a jeans-and-flat-shoes combination that morning. I wondered if Ms. Redclover might be regretting her shoe choices a bit, but she trudged on with unimpaired composure and seemed unaffected.

I wondered if her unruffled attitude was Ministry-issue, or innate.

After a while, Jay stopped at what must be a specific point in the largely featureless landscape, though I could see no way to tell. We had gone down a sandy incline to a beach littered with stones, and the cliff rose above us, jagged and rocky and just a bit forbidding, if it hadn't been for the balmy, sunny weather. He stood staring at the rock wall. 'Ms. Redclover?' he said after a while.

'Mabyn, please, Mr. Patel.'

He flashed her one of his charming smiles. 'Jay, then.'

She inclined her head.

'I believe we will need your help to get in.'

Mabyn stepped forward, lips pursed. 'Likely, yes. Dappledok closed its doors to outsiders a long time ago, though never entirely. It *has* been a long time, however...' She let the sentence trail off and began to wander up and down the beach, her keen eyes scanning the rock for signs of... something? Jay and I stood, patiently waiting.

'Ah,' she finally said, and stepped forward. Lifting one thin hand, she knocked thrice upon the rock face and said something in a language I had never heard before.

'Ancient Cornish?' guessed Jay.

'Probably,' I whispered back.

Whatever it was she had said, it soon proved effective. A line of sea-green light snaked down the cliff face, and with the horrific groaning sound of grinding rock, a crack appeared, just wide enough for a spriggan — or indeed, a human — to pass through.

Mabyn went in, beckoning over her shoulder to the two of us.

'After you,' said Jay with a half-bow.

'I promise you, even I cannot manage to get lost between here and the cliff.' The distance was all of, what, twelve feet?

Jay grinned at me. 'I'd like to make sure.'

I stuck my tongue out at him, and followed after Mabyn. And into the Dappledok Dell went we, agog with curiosity (or maybe that last part was just me).

Well, let me tell you, my first glimpse of that ancient Dell was... a little bit of a let-down.

Not that it wasn't beautiful. It was, gloriously so. I have probably mentioned the tendency of the magickal Dells to look... well, magick-drenched. Everything practically glows with vitality and beauty, at least with those that are still thriving; the abandoned ones are a different matter. Dappledok wasn't abandoned. It glittered and glowed.

But it was exactly the same landscape as the one we had just left; in fact, it looked identical, save only for the extra blush of vibrancy to the blue-green water, and the sparkle to the sunlight. I don't know what I had been hoping for. Skies full of rainbows? Meadows chock-full of cute puppy-like creatures frolicking in the sunlight?

Ms. Redclover behaved like a native, for all her attempts to distance herself from her ancient familial home. She set off along the beach at a purposeful walk, with the air of a woman walking a long-familiar route. 'Dapplehaven is just around the corner,' she called over her shoulder.

'What is Dapplehaven?' I asked, hastening to catch up with her.

'The largest town in the Dell. The Redclover School is there.'

Straight to the point, hm? I smothered the desire to go for a long, exploratory hike, and dutifully trotted after Ms. Mabyn Redclover.

But we had not gone very far before three most unpromising things happened one after another.

First, it literally went dark. Not completely pitch, but the sun went pale and watery, like someone had turned down a dimmer switch.

Next, the magickal equivalent of a klaxon sounded from somewhere nearby. It sounds less like a car horn and more like an entire flock of griffins all screaming at once.

When a dark speck appeared on the horizon, I knew we were somewhat in trouble.

'This does not seem good,' said Jay, coming to a sudden halt, and warily eyeing the skies.

Ms. Redclover gave a huffy sigh, and fussed with her hair. 'Always so *prone* to overre-action. Some things never do change, do they?'

I was watching that dark speck in silence. It grew rapidly bigger, proving itself to be winged, with a snaky body and four legs. 'Yep,' I said as it drew nearer. 'Dragon.'

It wasn't all that big of a dragon, in fairness, but it was plenty big enough to ruin our collective day. As it swooped down upon us, jaws gaping, with purple fire streaming from between its fangs, Ms. Redclover shook her head with another huffy sigh and said, 'Oh, *Archibald.*'

8

'Who,' croaked Jay, eyes glued to the descending draconic menace, 'is Archibald?'

I wanted to ask much the same thing, but I had been too busy digging for my Wand. I had not yet got around to returning the Sunstone Wand to Stores after our last adventure, for which oversight (ahem) I was now heartily grateful.

Trouble is, I had not expected to encounter so direct a menace two minutes into the Dappledok Dell, and I had left it somewhere in the depths of my shoulder bag. The pup was sleeping on it, and was remarkably resistant to suggestion. 'Er,' I said, beginning to panic, my fingers scrabbling uselessly for any trace of cool gemstone beneath the pup's thick, fluffy fur. '*Duck!*'

We dived for the floor. The dragon swooped, claws extended, and mercifully missed all three of us.

Wait, no. No, it didn't. Jay and I had hit the floor, but Mabyn Redclover had stood her ground like an idiot, arms crossed, tutting the way Matron used to upon finding ten-year-old Ves reading her book by torchlight well after lights out. (I was a well-behaved child most of the time, I swear).

The dragon, unimpressed with this display of disapproval, scooped her up in its long, polished claws and flew away again.

Mabyn's voice drifted back to us along the balmy spring breeze. 'I will get this sorted out! Wait there.'

Jay and I could only watch, helpless, as the dragon dwindled into the distance, taking our guide with it.

'Well,' said Jay.

I hefted my bag. I had found the Wand by then, disturbing the pup in the process, and she was now sitting up, yawning, her ears perked as she looked around. 'Time to explore after all, then,' I said brightly.

Jay gave me his what-are-you-talking-about look. He does something odd and sceptical with his eyebrows. It's hard to describe. 'Don't you think we ought to help Mabyn?'

'Did she sound distressed to you?'

The what-the-hell face became a frown. 'No. Why didn't she sound distressed?'

'My guess is that the dragon's called Archibald. Or he belongs to someone else with that name.'

'Possibly not the first time she's travelled by dragon?' Jay surmised.

'Possibly not. Shall we go?'

'She said, "Wait there."'

'I know. I heard her.'

'We aren't doing that?'

'Did you especially want to?'

'We should.' Jay said this very gravely. 'She is effectively our boss for today.'

I put the Wand away again. 'All right, then.'

Time passed.

Jay, to his credit, did a champion job of pretending not to be stupefied with boredom. He wandered about, hands shoved into the pockets of his dark leather jacket, an expression of bland interest on his face as he inspected the same outcropping of tan-coloured rock about sixteen times over.

I sat cross-legged on a nearby boulder, the pup in my lap, and stared into space.

After about seven minutes of this, he said, nonchalantly, 'Maybe we could explore a little bit.'

'We could.'

'If we don't go too far?'

'Absolutely.'

'Do you want to lead?'

'Nope.'

He set off.

'Jay,' I said.

'What?'

'How about we go in generally the same direction as the dragon?'

He turned around, scowling. 'I did ask you if you wanted to lead.'

I hopped off my boulder, electing to keep the pup in my arms rather than let her run, and beamed at him. 'Just helping out.'

'It's not the worst idea,' he conceded.

My smile widened.

'Fine. You're right, we'll go this way.'

The dragon had flown off inland, more or less in the direction Mabyn Redclover had been going herself. I judged it likely, therefore, that the dragon (Archibald?) had come from Dapplehaven, and had probably returned there with Mabyn. Why we had been left out of this kidnapping party, I had no idea, though I wasn't about to complain. If I am going to fly, I will do it by winged horse, thank you very much. Or chair. Or, I suppose, airplane. Those are the only three options.

My hypothesis seemed sound, for after a half-hour's wending our way across the uneven curves of a stony hillside feathered with bracken and heath, the walls of a little town came into view surmounting the very top of the peak. At least, it appeared to be of limited size at first, but as we drew nearer, it became clear that the settlement extended much farther back than had initially been apparent. The walls were taller than Jay, and built from a reddish-tan stone obviously hewn from the local hills. Those buildings we could see were mostly constructed from the same material, as well as sturdy oak and pine wood. To my eyes, they looked diminutive, being of course the homes of spriggans and other beings built along smaller lines than humans. But they did not lack vision. Neatly constructed from smooth bricks, with sloping, tiled roofs and mullioned windows, they towered over the town walls, most of them built at least four storeys high.

If this was Dapplehaven, it was a prosperous place despite its reclusive habits.

One particularly tall tower rose in the centre, a round-walled construct made from a much paler stone than the rest, and fitted with a variety of peculiar windows, every one of them a different shape. Its top was crowned with a huge nest made out of what looked like lengths of coloured cloth. It made a cheery sight, in spite of its probable purpose.

I pointed it out to Jay. 'Suppose that's Archibald's house?'

'Looks dragon-sized,' he agreed.

Gradually, I became aware of a problem. Walls there were, but it occurred to me that I had caught no glimpse whatsoever of a gate, or a door, or an archway, or even a window, through which Jay and I might enter the town. We walked on, following the curve of the walls around and around, but no sign of an entrance did we find.

At length, Jay stopped. 'We can't walk around the entire town. If there was going to be anything obvious like a gate, it would have been on the side we approached from — facing the entrance.'

'Are you sure? They stopped taking visitors from Cornwall many years ago.'

'And then moved the gate? Did you see anything on the walls that looked like a bricked-up doorway?'

'No,' I conceded.

'It's got to be a hidden entrance, like the door in the cliff face which only Mabyn could find.'

I heaved a sigh. 'Why do Dells always have to make things so difficult.'

'Because they hate you.'

'Thanks.'

'And me, and the entire unmagicked population of Britain especially.'

'Not altogether unreasonable of them,' I murmured, thinking of many instances of persecution, theft, abuse and other such joys the magicker populations of our country had previously endured. Not to mention that the threat of exposure held more perils now than it ever had before. Imagine what would happen if some well-meaning but excitable non-magicker person discovered somewhere like Dappledok Dell — and managed to prove its existence to the rest of the world. Okay, we're past the point where anybody would be likely to come down here with the torches and the pitchforks and burn the residents at the stake. Instead? Hordes of people would come down here with their Canon 70Ds and their camping gear and their Harry Potter t-shirts and the whole thing would become a theme park inside of about a week.

'So, hidden door,' I said to the wall before me. 'Fun.'

'Maybe it's back where we started,' said Jay. 'Near the portal to Cornwall.'

'Could be.'

'It's probably operated by a word, or a phrase. Something in Ancient Cornish, or whatever it was that Mabyn was speaking.'

'One of the spriggan languages, possibly,' I mused.

'One of them?'

'They have many dialects. Just like humans, isn't that odd?'

He grimaced at me. 'All right, sorry. Do you happen to speak any of them?'

'No. Not having expected to end up in spriggan country, I specialised in old English and Court Algatish, which is the official language of Trolldom at the moment. I dabbled a bit in one or two of the goblin and elf tongues, but I never made much progress with those.'

Jay stared at me, bemused. 'You speak Algatish?'

'Not fluently, but not too badly.'

He visibly shook himself. 'Er. So, we aren't going to make much progress with the door if neither of us can speak any of the likely languages.'

'Gosh, whatever shall we do.' I reached out a hand and rapped politely upon the wall.

'Knock?' said Jay incredulously. 'That's the plan?'

'Just wait.'

It took about thirty-five seconds.

'Who goes there?' snapped an irritable female voice, and a face shimmered into view. She was almost as wizened in appearance as Mabyn, though she was much more addicted to jewellery, and she wore bright lipstick.

'I've always wanted to say *who goes there,*' I whispered to Jay. 'I'd say it with a bit more bombast, though.'

'Er,' said Jay. 'We're from the Society for Magickal Heritage, based in Yorkshire. We are here on an urgent matter of business.'

'We had a guide,' I added helpfully. 'Mabyn Redclover. A dragon made off with her.'

The woman's brows snapped down. 'Wait there,' she grunted, and the vision dissolved.

'I was tempted to say "We come in peace,"' Jay remarked.

'You could have. I doubt she would have got the reference.'

'Next time. So is this how it normally works?'

'What?'

'You just... knock?'

I shrugged. 'It works more often than it doesn't. The Dells certainly don't encourage tourism, but it's not like you're in danger of being put to death for setting foot in here. And she must realise we had to have qualified help to get this far.'

The woman herself appeared shortly afterwards. A line of green fire snaked its way up the wall, tracing the shape of an elegant and surprisingly tall archway, and the stonework within apparently vanished. Our grumpy receptionist stood revealed in all the glory of an early Edwardian tea gown in heliotrope silk, a sash tied round her nipped-in waist. Fashions don't always advance much once a Dell closes its doors to the outside world. Then again, some people just like to dress vintage.

'Mabyn Redclover is currently unavailable,' she snapped.

'We guessed that,' I said.

'Is she all right?' Jay put in.

'Perfectly. What do you think Archibald was going to do, eat her? Credentials please.'

We flashed our Society symbols. Mine has the unicorn superimposed over the three crossed wands, but Jay has only the wands so far. He hasn't yet had time to pick a unique identifier.

I might as well add: no, these are not fakeable. It's like the magickal equivalent of that special paper and holographic stuff they use on cash money to make it hard (if not completely impossible) to fake. No one can use my symbol but me. Val and I tried, once, to fake each other's symbols. The results were not pretty. My face hurt for three weeks afterwards.

'Fine. Come in.' The Edwardian spriggan turned her back on us and stalked back through the archway, which promptly began to display signs that the stone blocks were returning.

'Quick.' I grabbed Jay and dragged him through the arch, just as stone rippled back into place with a nasty grinding sound. Nice if we'd got stuck halfway through when that happened.

'Hospitable,' Jay muttered.

'Habit,' I countered. 'I don't think they get groups here very often.'

The town of Dapplehaven had all the hallmarks of an old, old settlement: narrow streets winding every which way, betraying the absolute absence of a town planner; old stone or timber-framed houses with crumbling facades built onto the front in updated styles; an occasional old well, which may or may not be still in use; doors with the door-knobs in the middle, instead of on the left side; uneven stone-cobbled streets; all of that kind of thing. They had updated a bit, though, for they had wrought iron streetlamps in that charming, late-Victorian style (ornate), and a suspiciously twentieth-century-looking wheelbarrow parked in somebody's front garden (not so ornate).

Our new guide escorted us through several winding streets and at last entered a tall, skinny building with an unfortunate unsteady appearance. By which I mean, it was distinctly leaning at the top.

This did not appear to trouble our guide, who took us through a featureless entrance hall and up three flights of stairs. She shoved open a door in the subsequent hallway and ushered us into it.

Mabyn Redclover sat there on a hard oak chair. Her suit was torn in three places, and — alas! — her hair had very much come a-cropper. She was also missing a shoe.

'Your assistants,' said the Edwardian woman.

'Thanks, Doryty,' said Mabyn sourly. 'I am sure you gave them one of your warm welcomes.'

'Naturally. Wait a moment.'

She left us with Mabyn.

'What got into Archibald?' said Jay, sitting down beside her.

That won him a faint smile. 'We go a long way back.'

'Really? He didn't look all that friendly.'

Mabyn looked away. 'I did not leave on quite the best terms. Those who have the care of Archibald these days were not best pleased to see me back.'

'What about Doryty?' I put in.

'Doryty Redclover. A cousin on my mother's side.'

'Good relationship there?'

'Not really.'

Milady's knowledgeable, well-connected guide turned out to be about the least popular person in Dappledok? Great.

I was in for a headache.

9

I suppose we shouldn't have been surprised. Mabyn Redclover had aligned herself with precisely the type of organisation — and the very department thereof — most likely to be opposed and despised by those who remained loyal to the goals of the Redclover school. She had become a person who made a point of getting in the way of projects like the Redclovers', curtailing their options and limiting their prospects for reasons with which they apparently disagreed. If you were not disposed to consider those kinds of laws as justified, Mabyn's choices would tend to look rather like defection to the enemy.

I wondered what kinds of things they were getting up to at the school these days.

'We need to pay a visit to the Redclover School,' I said.

Mabyn gave me an exasperated look. 'It has been forty years since I left. I thought they might have got over their anger by now, but apparently not. They aren't going to let us anywhere near that school.'

'Not you, perhaps,' said Jay. 'I mean no offence, but Ves and I have angered no one.'

'Yet,' I muttered.

Jay ignored that. 'If we request a tour, as representatives of the Society, surely they would agree?'

'Of course they would,' said Mabyn.

'Great.'

Her lips quirked in a sardonic smile. 'Anything remotely objectionable is well hidden, and believe me, you won't find it without help.' She held up a hand as Jay opened his mouth, forestalling his words. 'I cannot help you there. Forty years, remember? I am out of touch with their present arrangements.'

'Not to worry,' I said. 'I have a plan.'

Jay eyed me warily. 'Is it by chance a Mad Ves Plan?'

'A what?'

'Mad Ves Plans make perfect sense to Ves, but less so to anyone else. They are the result of Ves's unique worldview, combined with a splendid disregard for convention or rule and a degree of blithe recklessness.'

'You don't like my plans?'

'They frighten the life out of me,' said Jay. 'It's therefore galling to have to admit that they sometimes work.'

'Usually,' I corrected.

'All right, usually. So what's the plan?'

'I am going to show them the pup.'

'What? Ves, if they are the ones responsible for breeding that puppy, we'll be in big trouble.'

'I don't think they are. Or *if* they are, they may be unaware that one has got away. They'd be quite interested to hear about that, don't you think?'

'Oh? How do you figure that?'

'Because this place is so reclusive. If this is where the pup came from, how did it end up in a medieval ghost-cottage in East Anglia? If the pup came from here at all, then somebody took it out of Dappledok into England, and that is a circumstance that's likely to be frowned upon by the School. I think they would like to know about it, don't you?'

'Like I said,' said Jay with a sigh. 'Blithe recklessness.'

I looked at Mabyn. 'Would you like to be on better terms with your family again?'

'What,' said Mabyn suspiciously, 'did you have in mind?'

'If, say, you heard about this Goldnose matter and came here out of concern for the school, that might win back a little favour.'

'They would only think I was here to make trouble for them.'

'Which,' Jay put in, 'we very possibly are.'

'Let's just see how it goes, shall we? Anyone who's with me, come along.' I left without waiting for a reply. I knew Jay would follow, and it wasn't especially important whether Mabyn did or not.

I thought for a moment that she would not, but then I heard her uneven footsteps following along behind Jay's — the intermittent *clip* of her one remaining heeled shoe on the stone floor. 'You'll never even find the school without me,' she called.

'Is it that well-hidden?'

'It's more that it's spread all over Dapplehaven by now, and beyond. It had thirteen different buildings last I knew, and that was some time ago. What you'll want is the kennels, which used to be on the north-eastern edge of the town.'

'Lead on,' said Jay with a courtly half-bow.

Mabyn led us all the way back down the stairs again. Her cousin Doryty lingered still in the hall. 'And where are you going?' snapped she when she saw Mabyn.

'To the school.' Mabyn spoke firmly. 'We have come on a matter of some urgency, and I think the school will want to hear of it. Please ask whoever is currently serving as its headmistress to meet us at the kennels.' She did not await a response, but swept out of the front door with her chin held high.

Doryty scowled, but made no move to stop either Jay or I as we went past.

'Headmistress?' Jay wondered. 'It couldn't be a headmaster?'

Mabyn did not appear to hear, and marched on up the street oblivious of Jay's question.

So I hauled out our lovely book. 'Mauf. Is the Redclover School at Dapplehaven always led by a headmistress?'

'Typically,' said Mauf. 'Spriggan society tends strongly towards the matriarchal.'

'I knew I liked them,' I said.

· · · ● · ● · · ·

The kennels, happily, had not been moved in the last forty years, though judging from Mabyn's reaction they had been altered. She led us down myriad curly streets, past a great many houses and little shops (I wanted to investigate some of the latter, but Jay would not let me). The streets were mostly empty, but we passed a few citizens of Dapplehaven here and there — spriggans, mostly, dressed in such a riot of different clothing styles that I could detect no clear pattern. A society with no prevailing fashions? Unusual. We attracted some attention ourselves; I could well believe that they did not often see a couple of humans wandering down their wonky boulevards.

Just where Dapplehaven's houses thinned and gave way to rocky heathland, there was a cluster of low-roofed buildings arranged around a central courtyard. The sounds of yapping and baying announced the kennels' presence rather before they came into view; they were obviously still in use.

But Mabyn looked around with a frown, apparently nonplussed.

'Something the matter?' said Jay.

'There used to be a lot... more,' said Mabyn. 'Of everything.'

The school had downsized its kennels in recent years, hm? Perhaps things were not going so well for them.

The kennels also appeared oddly deserted, in spite of the noise. We wandered about for a while, peeping into each of the white-walled buildings in turn. There were plenty of beasts there, including a litter of gorhounds just like the one my pup presently resembled, but there were no people.

The pup swiftly proved a handful. Her face had popped up out of the bag the moment the first forlorn yap had reached our ears, and she had ridden like that, ears pricked up and on high alert, until we got within sight of the kennels. After that, nothing would restrain her. I managed to catch her as she swarmed out of the bag, but she writhed like a wild thing in my arms and it was like trying to hold on to a thrashing eel. She bested me with embarrassing ease and hit the floor with a bounce.

Off she went at a run.

She did not seem disposed to go far, so I was not unduly worried. She came back into view from time to time, tearing past with her tail flying behind her, jaws wreathed in a huge puppy grin as she went from kennel to kennel, greeting every single other creature there.

It was the pup who finally found signs of sentient life, in a manner of speaking. I had not seen any sign of her for a few minutes, and Jay and Mabyn and I had gathered into a knot in the central courtyard, deprived of any particular objective for the moment and awaiting the arrival of the headmistress (supposing she chose to answer the summons). The pup suddenly erupted from a nearby kennel, vaulting over the door in a single leap, and dashed towards us, tongue lolling.

The door she had just jumped over slammed open in her wake, and a spriggan came dashing out after her. I could swear we had looked into that same building only a few minutes before, and seen no one, so how we could have missed him I do not know. He came barrelling in our direction, but not because he had the slightest interest in us; all his attention was fixed upon the pup.

He swiftly proved himself an adept handler of puppish creatures, for he stymied all her attempts at evasion, anticipating her movements with remarkable prescience, and intercepted her as she swung around behind Mabyn. He pounced, and scooped, and emerged victorious, with a wriggling and indignant pup captured in his arms.

I took brief note of his posture. Was he holding the pup in some special way? I couldn't see how, but by one means or another, he was holding her fast where I had completely failed.

'I am so sorry,' I said to him, holding out my arms to receive her. 'Lacking your aptitude with such creatures, I could not persuade her to stay with me. She's a little over excited by all the company, I'm afraid.'

The spriggan looked up, as though noticing my presence for the first time. His gaze travelled from me to Jay and then to Mabyn, but he betrayed no sign of understanding what I had said.

Mabyn stepped in, to my relief. She spoke to him in a string of incomprehensible words, presumably repeating what I had said, for she gestured once or twice at me.

But the spriggan shook his head, so emphatically that the flat cap he wore almost fell off. He said something in response, with a vehemence I interpreted as excitement. He shook the pup slightly as though to say, *look at this!* And I noticed that he was shaking.

Mabyn winced, and turned to Jay and me. 'He asks where you got a Goldnose pup from.'

'He... he can tell she is not a gorhound?'

'He says he would know a Goldnose anywhere, whatever disguise they wore.'

Oh dear. I hoped there were not too many people around who could so easily see through our deception. 'Please tell him that we are here in hopes of discovering an answer to that very question. We do not know where she came from.'

Mabyn relayed this, which seemed to dumbfound the kennel worker. He stood in thought for a moment, a look of total befuddlement on his face. Then, to my mild indignation, he turned around and wandered off in the direction of the kennel he had emerged from.

'Hey, wait a moment,' I said. 'That's our pup.'

'He is fetching her some milk,' said Mabyn. 'He said a moment ago that she's too thin, and he thinks you have not taken good care of her.'

'She's only been with us a few days!' I protested. 'She was starving to death when we found her.'

'That is hardly surprising,' said a new, unpromisingly stern voice from somewhere behind me. 'She needs a special milk, which I do not suppose she has been getting.'

I turned. Behind me stood a woman almost of my own height — a human woman, not a spriggan — and almost of my own age, too, if I judged correctly. She presented an unassuming appearance, with dark hair drawn into a ponytail and discreet make-up. She wore a deep blue trouser suit with a black blouse. On the lapel of her jacket was a tiny silver pin in the shape of a pegasus.

'You must be in charge,' I guessed.

She inclined her head to me. 'My name is Jenifry Redclover. I am the present head-mistress of the school.'

Now that I looked more closely at her, I detected traces of something else in her face that might indicate a mixed ancestry. Slightly overlarge eyes, for one, and an unusually wide mouth. Still, it did not make much sense for her to share a surname with Mabyn, who could scarcely be more different.

'It is something of an honorific,' she explained, with a faint, unamused smile. 'To become the manager of this school is to become a Redclover, if you were not one already.' I supposed my puzzlement must have shown, which was clumsy of me.

I hastily changed the subject. 'A pleasure to meet you, Ms. Redclover. May I ask whether the pup came from these kennels?'

'That is quite impossible. To so blatantly flout all Magickal Accords would result in the school's permanent closure. It could never be worth the risk, however valuable the Goldnose may be.'

At this point, Mabyn decided to reassert herself. 'I hope that is the truth,' she said in a brisk tone. 'It has come to the attention of the Hidden Ministry of England, Ireland, Scotland and Wales that the breed has resurfaced against all prohibitions. No good can come to those responsible, and if the school is involved there is a great deal of trouble brewing.'

'Hello, Mabyn,' said Jenifry flatly. 'How good of you to return.'

10

Mabyn and Jenifry Redclover, the spriggan and the human headmistress, eyed one another with bristling hostility. 'Must you bring threats?' said Jenifry. 'The school has never offered you the smallest harm.'

'I bring warning, not a threat,' said Mabyn, though she looked nonplussed. 'How do you know me? I do not think we have met.'

'Your portrait still hangs in the heritage gallery.'

Mabyn looked pleased. 'I thought they would have taken that down by now.'

Jay coughed. 'You've an official portrait?'

'She is a former headmistress,' said Jenifry. 'That makes her a part of our history, whatever her subsequent choices may have been.'

'I made them for good reason,' said Mabyn.

Jenifry looked unimpressed. 'I am sure you did. At any rate, I must get to the bottom of this.' She straightened her shoulders, and left in the direction of the kennel which had previously swallowed up the man in the flat cap — and our pup.

Mabyn gave a soft sigh. 'I tried to tell Milady I was the wrong person to send.'

'Milady knows what she is doing,' said Jay. 'I am sure she had her reasons.'

I smiled faintly, remembering the early days of my career at the Society, and the unshakeable faith I, too, had enjoyed in Milady. Not that I doubted her now, as such. But however remarkable she may appear, she was as human as the rest of us somewhere behind the disembodied voice. I hoped Jay was right, and that this time she knew what she was doing.

For myself, I pitied Mabyn. Her job required her to take a hard line against the pup, for the Ministry could no more support the widespread return of the Goldnoses to the world than any of its sister organisations did. But she clearly felt some residual loyalty to her former home, and if she was once the headmistress here... she must have been very dedicated.

'I am sure we can contain this issue before it has chance to cause much trouble,' I told her in my most reassuring tone, secretly crossing my fingers in hope that I was to be proved right. 'Only one pup has been found.'

'If it came from here, there are more,' said Mabyn.

I was worried about that possibility, too, though perhaps not for the same reasons. No matter what the laws said, the Goldnoses were innocent of wrongdoing in themselves; it was only in the hands of the wrong person that they had any power to cause harm. Did they not have a right to exist? Was it not our duty to protect and preserve all magickal creatures, as we did with books and artefacts and treasures — even the dangerous ones? A series of laws that had effectively wiped out several entire species did not sit well with me.

This point of view had nothing whatsoever to do with the heart-rending cuteness of the pup, I swear. I was totally detached and objective.

Anyway, I was concerned that more pups were out there somewhere, starving to death as our pup's siblings had done. And they could be anywhere. Anywhere at all. We needed to find the source before any more of them died, and then Jay and I needed to find a way to protect them — with or without Milady's concurrence. I was fairly sure I could successfully argue that case, but Milady sometimes came down hard on the side of the rules. You never could quite tell which way she would go.

Jenifry Redclover shortly returned, the becapped spriggan with her. I was relieved to see our pup trotting along at their heels, though a bit less pleased to see that the beast had lost her disguise, and was restored to all her gold-furred splendour.

She came straight up to me, and begged to be picked up. I, of course, was delighted to comply.

Mabyn, Jenifry and the kennel worker watched this display of affection in unreadable silence.

Jenifry spoke. 'Jory is confident that the pup did not come from this school. He also says that it is not — it cannot be — a descendent of the last such beasts that were known to exist before the laws forbidding their procreation.'

I blinked. 'What? Why not?'

'Because the horn she bears is out of keeping with that theory. The Goldnose was eventually arrived at through the cross-breeding of a few other species, one of which possessed a horn like the one you see adorning the forehead of your pup. But that feature gradually bred out, and was gone by the time the laws were introduced.'

'So...' I did not know what to say first, so many thoughts were churning in my mind.

'*Is* she a Goldnose?' said Jay.

Jory said something emphatic.

'Yes,' translated Jenifry. 'Her capabilities are not in question. But she is a very early example of the breed.'

'How is that possible?' I gasped.

Jenifry shook her head. 'I do not know. Either someone, somewhere, has been attempting to recreate the species by going back to its beginnings, and starting again from scratch, or... or something far stranger is happening. And I suspect the latter, for according to Jory, most of the creatures who were originally cross-bred to arrive at the Goldnose have been extinct for longer than the Goldnose itself.'

I retrieved the book. 'Mauf,' I said crisply. 'Tell us what you know about the Dappledok pups, otherwise known as the Goldnose species. Everything, please, from the beginning.'

Mauf swelled with importance, almost doubling in size. 'The species commonly known as the Goldnose was primarily the work of one person, a spriggan of the name of Melmidoc Redclover. The idea was conceived in the autumn of 1617, and work swiftly began. The goal was to successfully interbreed a variety of beasts whose collective talents included unusual senses for precious materials of one sort or another, heightened tracking abilities, tenacity, and biddableness. It is noted that the project was completed successfully in a surprisingly short space of time — too short, some said, though no particular theory as to how it was done has ever been presented. Within a few years, the earliest hybrids were being successfully trained to sniff out precious metals and jewels from some distance away.'

'What did these look like?' I said. 'In detail?'

'These earliest of the Goldnoses had pelts of varying colours, and the diminutive "unicorn" horn.'

'But this feature faded over time? The horn?'

'It was felt that the horn was unnecessary, for it served no particular purpose, and it was too distinctive a feature. Subsequent generations were bred selectively to eradicate the horn, though in the process the range of colours was lost, and they became predominantly goldish yellow.'

'By when did that happen?' put in Jay.

'The last recorded instance of a horned Goldnose was noted in 1624.'

Seven years? Within a mere seven years of the project's inception, they were already at the stage of making refinements to an otherwise perfect breed? 'That is far too fast,' I said, puzzled. 'Even if the Goldnoses breed unnaturally quickly, surely that is too fast.'

'Many said so,' agreed Mauf. 'In a letter to her sister in 1621 — subsequently published in a volume entitled, "Diverse Correspondence Between Two Sisters" — the Viscountess of Wroxby observed, "Do you Persist in wishing to bring a Goldnose Pup into your household? I am Persuaded you would never know another moment's peace, being forever deprived of your Jewels &c. And you should consider, that though they may be Fashionable, there is some manner of Mystery surrounding their existence about which I cannot be Easy. I wish you would abandon the notion." Which, by the by, she did.'

'Good to know,' murmured Jay.

Mabyn, who had been trying to find opportunity to speak for a few minutes, now cut in. '*Yes,* that is all very interesting, but what of Melmidoc Redclover? I am certain I have heard that name, but I cannot think how.'

'Melmidoc Redclover was thrice invited to take up the headmastery of the school, but declined, for he preferred to devote all of his time to his various projects. His was the mind behind five of the eight breeds for which the school became famous.'

'Perhaps that is how I have heard of him,' said Mabyn, though she frowned, and her tone was doubtful.

'He is primarily remembered for his disappearances, however,' said Mauf blandly.

'What?' I said.

'*What?*' Mabyn and Jenifry said at the same time.

'Disappearances, plural?' put in Jay.

'He disappeared,' persevered Mauf. 'Repeatedly. Four times were recorded, though there may have been more. The first time was in 1599, at the age of sixteen, when he was but a scholar and had not yet distinguished himself by any particular measure. He was absent for three and a half months, and was either unable or unwilling to give any account of his movements upon his return. He vanished again six years later, for almost a year. His third disappearance came at the more advanced age of forty-three, and lasted only three weeks. And he vanished again, for the fourth and (to my knowledge) final time, in 1630, at the age of forty-seven. He was never seen or heard from again.'

A silence fell which could only be termed Flabbergasted. Yes, with a capital F.

'There is clearly more to this than meets the eye,' said Mabyn.

'I have heard the name,' said Jenifry. 'I have seen him, even. Not in the flesh,' she said hastily, as everyone turned to look at her. 'His portrait. There is a gallery devoted to former headmasters of the school, and some few others whose contributions are considered to be of particular significance. Melmidoc Redclover is one of them. The odd thing is...' She hesitated, a deep frown clouding her brow. 'Your unusually talkative book asserts that he disappeared at the age of forty-seven?'

'So it is written,' said Mauf, somewhat huffily.

'He is, in essence, a library all in one,' offered Jay. 'He has absorbed the entire contents of the library at the Society, and quite a lot of... of other libraries, too.' Perhaps he hesitated to name Farringale just then for fear of derailing the conversation altogether; probably wise of him.

Jenifry gave a faint smile. 'I do not doubt you, for he is obviously a marvellous enchantment. The thing is, this portrait is clearly labelled as Melmidoc Redclover, and judging from the clothes he is wearing, and the style of the painting, it dates indeed from the mid seventeenth century. But... but you see, he is depicted as a rather older man. His hair is entirely grey, his face much more lined than that of a man not yet fifty. I took him to be twenty years above that age, at least.'

Stranger and stranger. 'Could the portrait have been made retrospectively?' I suggested. 'As a commemoration, perhaps, of the man he might have been had he not disappeared?'

'It is possible,' Jenifry conceded. 'But...' she paused again, seeming unsure how to phrase her thoughts. 'It is his expression,' she said. 'The portrait lingered in my memory because it is much more — more *real*, than many of the others. It is not a stiff, staged piece. His face is full of character, and life, and humour. I used to like to look at it. It looks like a portrait taken of a model who was very much alive, and in no way resembles a fading memory of a man who had not been seen for at least twenty years.'

'I cannot imagine, though, why a man would be universally set down as vanished for good if he was not, in fact, gone.'

'Has the painting always hung in that gallery?' asked Jay.

Jenifry blinked. 'I do not know. Mabyn?'

Mabyn slowly shook her head. 'I do not particularly recall it from my day, but that does not mean it was not there. I never did take much of an interest in the gallery.'

'Except for your own portrait,' said Jenifry.

Mabyn took this unabashed. 'Except for that one.'

I called Val. She did not answer, so I left a message for her. 'Val, please find everything you can about one Melmidoc Redclover, of the Redclover school in Dapplehaven. Matter of grave urgency.' I chose not to relay the things we had already learned about him, for they were mightily confusing, and I did not want to influence Val's thinking or cloud her findings.

Next, I called Zareen, who picked up after two rings. 'What's up, Ves?' she said briskly.

'So that mass exorcism you pulled,' I said without preamble. 'I don't suppose it can be undone, can it?'

'You mean can I bring three vaporised ghosts back from oblivion? No.'

'Damnit.'

'Why?'

I filled her in. It took a few minutes. When I had finished, she gave a low whistle. When she spoke, I could hear her grin. 'Nice little mystery you have there. So you were wanting to ask them a few questions?'

'I was. The thing is, Zar, that there is a pattern emerging here. This began with a vanishing house, and now we have a vanishing Redclover on our hands to boot. Coincidence?'

'No such thing as,' she said cheerily.

'Yes there is.'

'Fine, but not often. Tell you what, there's one thing I can do.'

'Anything would be good.'

'I've wondered before about all the places that house was going to. I dug up a few instances of its wandering about near (or in) the town of Bury St. Edmunds, but I never looked beyond — and there are gaps of years between most of those reported sightings. I'll see if I can find out where else it might have been parking itself.'

'Especially around the first half of the seventeenth century,' I said. 'Those were the Melmidoc Redclover years.'

'I'll do my best. Don't get your hopes up too high though, Ves. It wasn't a distinctive cottage, and unless other people saw it literally vanish into the mist, I won't be able to track it.'

'Do what you can,' I said. 'Thanks, Zar.'

I hung up, to find that the rest of my companions had gone into a huddle. Jay looked up as I joined them. 'We have a plan,' he told me, with great solemnity. 'Jenifry is to investigate the portrait. Mabyn is going to "raid" the school and scour its records.'

'Raid?' I echoed, intrigued by the emphasis he had laid on the word.

'The school is a little… private, about its records,' said Jenifry, a little shamefaced. 'Even I have been unable to gain access to everything, and that has occasionally made me curious. Jay thought that Mabyn might be able to make better progress, if she makes a show of authority.'

Mabyn looked as though she would very much enjoy making a show of authority.

'Good idea,' I said. 'And when that fails?'

'When?' Jay looked a bit hurt.

'It is a good idea as a diversion,' I said, as gently as I could. 'But if you get pushy with people, they usually push back. At best, they'll make a show of compliance while secretly opposing you every step of the way. While someone is kindly showing Mabyn around the records room, with a suitable show of deference, someone else will be quietly relabelling, or hiding, or outright removing, anything that isn't judged to be suitable for public consumption.'

Jay frowned. 'What do you suggest, then?'

'Mabyn and Jenifry proceed as planned. Meanwhile, you and I will infiltrate the records room and have a poke around. And if we spot anybody trying to hustle any juicy-looking boxes of papers out of the way, we can intercept them.'

'You just like sneaking around,' said Jay.

'I do, actually. I adore sneaking around.' I beamed at him.

I detected traces of annoyance in Jenifry's face, though I could not guess at the reason why. Mabyn, though, was more amiable. 'I think she is right,' said she, and my heart warmed to her on the spot. 'There is one problem, though.'

'Oh?' I said. 'What's that?'

She was not looking at me. Her gaze was fixed somewhere over my head, at the approximate level of the horizon. 'Archibald,' she said.

I turned, and there indeed was the purple-scaled vision of dragonhood winging its way rapidly towards us. 'But don't you two go way back?' I said, turning back to Mabyn.

'Archibald obeys the orders of one person only, that being the Mayor,' said Mabyn. 'He is usually employed to summon miscreants to an impromptu audience.'

'Is that what happened before?'

'Yes.'

'But you weren't taken to the Mayor, were you?'

She blinked at me. 'I was. That's Cousin Doryty.'

'She's the *Mayor*?' said Jay. 'What was she doing answering the door?'

Mabyn shrugged. 'Dapplehaven is a peaceful place, most of the time. Perhaps she was bored.'

'Or perhaps she was more interested in our presence here than she let on,' I suggested.

'Either way,' sighed Mabyn, 'Archie is here to pick up at least one of us, and that means Doryty's changed her mind about letting us wander off.'

We turned as one to watch the approach of the dragon called Archibald. He gained on us with appalling speed and swooped, claws extended. I tried to convince myself that he was going for Mabyn again, but no. Those claws reached out, glittering bright silver in the sun, and the person they grabbed this time was — *inevitably* — me.

11

And, as it turned out, Jay. Archibald wrapped one set of claws around my shrinking middle, and the other around Jay, and took off with both of us in tow. We watched, helpless, as Mabyn and Jenifry Redclover receded beneath us — and Jory the kennel-keeper, too, with our pup still in his arms.

'Inconvenient,' observed Jay, the word emerging as a squeak.

Archibald's grip was a bit tight, at that. I was feeling breathless myself, and I felt like I had an iron band vice-tight around my ribs. 'Archie,' I called. 'You couldn't squeeze a bit less, by any chance? We are fragile creatures, prone to breakage.'

The dragon expelled a whistle of air through his nostrils, and to my surprise, huffed out a clear *No*.

'Oh,' I said.

'You might fall,' the dragon explained.

'That would make for some serious breakage,' I had to agree.

'Fair,' said Jay. 'But don't squeeze too tight. We ought to arrive alive at the Mayor's, no?'

'The Mayor?' said Archibald. 'Why would you want to see her?'

'That... isn't that where we are going?'

'No...' said Archibald, and something about the way he said the word struck me as a bit shifty.

I patted his leg with the hand that wasn't clinging desperately to my shoulder-bag, and

Mauf. 'Where are we going, then?' I asked.

'There is something you should see,' said the dragon.

'Oh?'

A pause. 'I... I heard what you were saying,' said Archibald, and he definitely sounded shame-faced now.

'From *how* far away?' Jay yelped.

'I have very good ears,' said Archibald with dignity.

'And a fair bit of magick, too?' I suggested.

'Well, *anyway,*' said the dragon. 'I used to take Melmidoc places.'

'You knew Melmidoc Redclover?'

'His brother was the longest-running Mayor Dapplehaven has ever had,' said Archibald. 'They were always together, and so... we were always together, too.'

Could a dragon be forlorn? Apparently. 'You miss your friends?' I guessed.

'I do not like Doryty,' said Archibald. 'She is foul-tempered.' His enormous tail thrashed.

'We did not like her very much either,' I said soothingly.

'No one does.'

'Odd, then,' said Jay, 'that she is the Mayor. How did that happen?'

'No one else wanted the job. It is very boring.'

I risked a glance down. Archibald was taking us well away from Dapplehaven, and the ground was rising steeply beneath us. We were, I judged, sailing up the side of a low peak I had briefly glimpsed at some distance from the town. It did not, at least from this angle, look scaleable by any normal means.

'Is this where you used to take Melmidoc?' I asked.

'Melmidoc and Drystan,' said Archibald happily. 'All the time!'

Jay put in, 'Have you taken anybody else there since?'

'Once. The Mayor made me do it. They took away everything that was Melmidoc's, and they made it so I am not allowed to land there.'

'They... how did they do that?' said Jay.

'Oh, there are spikes,' said the dragon cheerfully. 'So I will have to drop you.'

'Onto spikes?!'

'There is a bit that is safe,' said Archibald, with enviable serenity. 'You will not break, because you are smaller than I am.'

'How are we...' I began. I had been going to say, *How are we going to get off the mountain*? For if Archibald could not land there, he could not retrieve us either. But the wind whipped my words away as we began to descend towards a windy, and lamentably cold, hilltop, and since we were, moments later, released from Archibald's claws without warning and flying through the air, there was not much point in finishing the sentence.

It hurt, rather a lot.

'Ouch,' croaked Jay, to my relief, for it proved at least that he was alive.

'Nnngh,' I said, somewhat less coherently. I'd landed on one arm and one hip, both of which smarted painfully, particularly since the ground up there was all highly uncomfy rock. You'd be surprised how little difference a liberal covering of moss and heath make when falling from... any kind of height at all.

I hauled myself, creakily, to my feet. 'Mauf?' I said. 'Still alive?'

'Can I be said to be living?' answered Mauf, in his dry, didactic tone. 'Arguably—'

'Great,' I cut in. 'Let's talk about that later.' I looked around. Archibald had not been exaggerating about the spikes. The ground was covered in them. They were at least a foot long each, they were made of something as hard and bright silver as steel, and they had sharp points. The spot we had landed in was only a few feet across, and an uneven patch in the ground suggested that there might once have been a tree growing there. I wondered whether Archibald had happened to the tree.

'They really didn't want anybody coming up here,' I said.

'But why not?' Jay turned in a circle, surveying the scene. There wasn't much to see. The peak of the hill was not very wide, and it declined steeply on all sides to the ground some way below. We had a fine view over Dappledok Dell, and it made for a glorious vision: rolling dales, vibrant meadows, and the town of Dapplehaven nestled adorably in the middle.

Lovely, but unhelpful. All there seemed to be at the top was a roughly circular space full of spikes.

'Archibald?' I looked up, but he had gone. 'Did he expect this to somehow make sense to us?' I said with a sigh.

Jay looked around again. 'Are we missing something obvious? What's up here?'

'Spikes.'

'All right. Why are there spikes up here?'

'To prevent Archibald from landing.'

'Why?'

'Because he was bringing people like Melmidoc up here, and someone disliked that for... reasons unknown.'

'Those are the obvious answers. What about the less obvious? Maybe these spikes were not aimed at Archibald.'

'How many dragons do you suppose there are in Dappledok? They are not exactly common.'

'It's probably fair to say that most magickal beasts were once a lot more common than they are now,' Jay pointed out. 'But it does not have to be a dragon, does it? I wouldn't think anything could land up here with these in the way.'

I thought about that. 'The ground is quite flat.'

'It is. Unusually flat for the terrain, would you say?'

'I might say that, indeed.'

'And,' said Jay, picking his way through the spikes to the edge of the plateau, 'if some of these bushes and such were to be cleared away, we might discover it to be unusually circular, too.'

'So it's shaped. That suggests that...um.' I hauled Mauf out of the bag again. 'Mauf, do you know anything about this place?'

'No,' said Mauf.

There were, after all, a couple of drawbacks to Mauf the Magick Book. For one thing, he could only know about something if someone had obligingly written it down, and people often did not do that with secrets. For another, there was no getting at what he did know if you didn't come up with the right question.

'Nothing about anything called, say, Dappledok Peak or Mount Dappledok? Something like that?'

'No,' said Mauf again, and then: 'Is that where we are?'

'How about buildings?' said Jay. 'Any lost or unaccounted for—'

'Dapplehaven Tower,' said Mauf.

Jay and I blinked stupidly at each other. 'Um,' I said. 'What?'

'Dapplehaven Tower, occasionally referred to as the Striding Spire. It used to, er, tower over the town of Dapplehaven, if you will excuse the pun, but it was dismantled in 1630.'

'1630! Why was it dismantled?'

'The official reason cited was unstable foundations. There were safety concerns in high winds.'

I jumped up and down a couple of times. 'Would you say there is anything in the world less unstable than solid rock?'

'I would not,' answered Jay.

'Now, why was it called the Striding Spire?' I spoke as calmly as I could, but my heart was racing with excitement in anticipation of Mauf's answer.

'Because it wasn't always observed to stand in the same spot,' said Mauf, confirming all my hopes. 'While it was never described as walking around in any literal sense, it was obviously perambulatory.'

'Melmidoc Redclover disappeared in 1630,' said Jay. 'Do you suppose he walked off with the tower?'

'Or the Striding Spire walked off with him!'

'And for some reason, it never wandered back. So that begs the question: where did the Spire wander off to, and what kept it from returning?'

'Other than the spikes?'

Jay considered them with a raised brow. 'Why would someone want to stop the Spire from striding back?'

'Maybe they disapproved of whatever it was Melmidoc Redclover was doing with it.'

'Melmidoc and Drystan,' corrected Jay. 'Archibald said they were always together, didn't he?'

'And Drystan was a Headmaster.' There was something important to be construed from all of that, but I could not decide what it was. I lifted my chin. 'Archibaaaaald!' I yelled to the sky.

'Dragon likes towers,' observed Jay.

'Seems to.' Archibald reappeared in the sky, winging his way back towards us. 'Archie!' I bellowed. 'Was there a tower here?'

He swooped and grabbed me — but missed Jay. The world lurched and spun crazily as Archibald soared away, banked, turned and dived again towards my hapless partner.

The poor boy stood there, braced for impact, trying manfully not to cringe as the enormous purple dragon bore down on him once again.

A yelp might have escaped him as Archie's claws closed around his chest, but this I cannot confirm.

I, on the other hand, shrieked. There is no other word for it.

'Sometimes it was a tower,' Archibald said as he bore us away from the peak once more. 'I liked that the best, because I could sit at the top. The others were not so comfortable.'

'Others?!' Jay and I said it together, and with emphasis.

'They did not like me to sit on the others,' said the dragon mournfully. 'I was always being sent away. But,' he added in a more considering tone, 'some of them were too small anyway, I did not fit. The tower was the best one.'

'They who?' I said.

'Oh, the people inside.'

I was beginning to feel that Archibald, obliging as he was, lacked something in the way of brain. 'What kind of people were they?' I said, as patiently as I could. 'People like Melmidoc and Drystan?'

'Yes, people like them.'

'Magickal people?'

'People like you,' said Archibald. Then he shook the leg in which he held Jay, not at all to Jay's satisfaction. There was another yelp. 'Some of them were a lot like this one.'

'In what way?' I said, feeling a little desperate. I mean, for *goodness'* sake.

Archie lowered his head to sniff at Jay, his huge nostrils flaring. 'I don't know,' he finally pronounced.

'Waymaster,' Jay yelled despairingly. 'He means Waymasters! Must have been.'

Of course. The Greyers' cottage was perambulatory because it had a dead Waymaster bound into its walls. I hoped that those operating the Striding Spire had not been enslaved ghosts as well, for that promised to cast an entirely different light on the whole Redclover operation. 'Were they... alive?' I asked the dragon.

'Of course they were.' He huffed at my stupidity.

'Jay, when you get amazing enough to haul our entire House around at will, let Milady know! She'll be thrilled.'

The glimpse I caught of Jay's face suggested he felt more nauseated than inspired by the idea. 'That's impossible.'

'It is now, but I suppose it wasn't always.'

'I suddenly feel like a weakling.'

'Utterly feeble,' I agreed. 'Pathetic excuse for a Waymaster.'

'Hey. There are times when you are supposed to *contradict* your friends, Ves.'

'Are there?'

'This was one of those times.'

'Was it?'

I got scowled at. I cannot say it was undeserved.

'By the way, Archie,' I called to the dragon. 'Whereabouts are we going now?'

'Oh. The people you were with are at Doryty's now. Would you not like to go there?'

'That will be fine.'

'I don't have to take you there.'

'No, really. It is a good place to go next.'

'I can take you somewhere else, if you like. Doryty will not like it, but I would not mind.'

'Take us to the Mayor, Archie,' I said firmly. 'Then you will not be in any trouble, and we need to talk to our friends anyway.' I hoped they had put some part of our earlier plan into action, but more likely they were trying to find out what had happened to Jay and me.

'I am always in trouble,' said the dragon gloomily. 'She will not like my taking you to the spikes.'

'She does not have to know about it,' I suggested.

A pause. 'You will not tell her?'

'Never,' I solemnly swore.

'Wouldn't dream of it,' added Jay.

Archibald's long, purple tail swished happily. 'Can I keep you?'

'Uhh. We can't stay all that—'

'Of course you can,' interrupted Jay, with a wink at me. 'You're the best dragon I've ever met.'

Archibald puffed up, much the same way Mauf did when praised. Though perhaps not so literally. 'Would you like to be the Mayor?' he replied. 'It is a boring job, but I would make it interesting! We could fly places, and...' He trailed off, apparently unable to think of anything else fun he and Jay could do when Jay was the Mayor of Dapplehaven.

Jay suppressed a laugh with admirable grace, and said only: 'I'll give it some thought, Archie.'

12

Archie returned us to the tall building inside which we had previously discovered Mabyn languishing alone, and with only one shoe. She was there again, though this time she had halted in the entrance hall. She had the headmistress with her, and the Mayor.

Doryty, Mayor of Dapplehaven, had acquired a socking great amulet from somewhere. It was huge, and very shiny, and it hung around her neck from a heavy gold chain. It looked vaguely like a chain of office, which I suppose is exactly what it was. She had decided to display her authority.

Mabyn was holding our pup in what was essentially a choke hold. The pup, mesmerised by the Mayor's gleaming jewellery, gave a heartrending whimper of protest, and writhed helplessly in that grip; apparently, the bigger the slab of precious materials on display, the greater the poor pup's lust to, er, acquire it.

Headmistress Jenifry stood, arms folded, lips tight with disdain, while the two spriggans bawled at one another.

'The Ministry has every right to demand access to any and all records belonging to any and all magickal establishments!' Mabyn was saying as we went in. At some volume. 'Dappledok Dell may not be precisely under its direct jurisdiction, but—'

'Exactly!' shouted the Mayor. 'Dappledok Dell, and by extension the Redclover School, answers only to those fae courts to which we have historically pledged fealty, and besides those to the Magickal Council of Dells and Dales, to the Commission for Fae

Heritage and History, to—'

'I *know* all that,' hissed Mabyn. 'If you insist upon listing every single one we shall be here all day.'

'The Hidden Ministry would not be on that list!' persevered Mayor Doryty. 'It is an organisation by, and exclusively for, human members of the magickal communities, and Dappledok has always been a strictly spriggan or brownie haven—'

'Oh? And the fact that the current headmistress of your precious school is human is neither here nor there, I suppose?'

'It is irregular,' hissed the Mayor. 'But Ms. Redclover is not entirely without the prerequisite heritage, and—'

'Cousin,' said Jenifry Redclover, from between clenched teeth. 'Our associate from the Hidden Ministry has a point, and you know it. Can you not see, that all this obstinacy only encourages the notion that the school has something to hide?'

'What would it have to hide?' demanded the Mayor. 'We have obeyed every stricture placed upon our work, no matter how it has interfered with the school's mission, and since time immemorial!'

'We?' said Jenifry. 'The school is under *my* mastery, Doryty, not yours. Town business is your affair. School business is mine. We are finished here.' She bestowed a curt nod upon the fuming Mayor of Dapplehaven and turned to the door. 'Oh!' she said, upon seeing Jay and I. 'Excellent. We were most concerned.'

'I can see that,' I said drily.

Mabyn unceremoniously dumped my whimpering pup into my arms, whereupon I was too busy trying to keep hold of her to engage any further in conversation with Jenifry.

Mayor Doryty, meanwhile, was rendered still angrier by the reappearance of Jay and I. 'How did you get back in!' she fumed.

'Oh?' said Jay politely. 'Were we supposed to be thrown out?'

Doryty clenched her fists, as though she would like to express her displeasure by inappropriately physical means. In the end, she merely stalked past Jay into the street, roaring as she went, 'Archi*baaaald!*'

'My "cousin" always opposed my appointment to the headmastery,' observed Jenifry, watching this retreat with a tiny, mirthless smile.

'Who appoints the headmistress, then?' I inquired.

'The school has a board of governors. Doryty is one of them, of course, but she was overruled by the rest.'

'Why does she hate you?'

'Because I'm neither a spriggan, nor a Redclover. It is the only time in the entire history of the school that a headmaster has been drawn from neither stock. It's by her insistence that I ended up having to take the Redclover name.'

'Family matters,' I murmured. 'Always tricky.'

'Time to raid the records,' put in Jay. 'And quickly. We're already late.'

Mabyn paused in dusting pup hair off her suit. 'Where did Archie take you, if he didn't throw you out?'

'Take us to the school, if you will,' said Jay to Mabyn and Jenifry both. 'And we'll fill you in on the way.'

• • • • • • • • • • • •

Which we did, or rather Jay did, because halfway across town I got a call.

'Twas Valerie. 'Ves,' she said crisply. 'Would you like to tell me why you're asking questions about Melmidoc Redclover?'

'Why, is there a problem?'

'Only a total, and virtually impenetrable, block on all information about him. I've tried everywhere. Regular internet has no hits, the magick net has only a vague reference or two behind a big "classified information" wall, we've turned up nothing much in our own library, and when I tried to call in the Baron he came back with no luck either. What does Mauf say?'

'One or two interesting things, which I shall shortly relay, only I didn't want to prejudice whatever you might find— wait. Did you say *virtually* impenetrable?'

'I did, actually.' Val's tone turned smug. 'I haven't been Queen of the Library for so long for nothing, you know.'

'Val! Did you hack something?'

'Sort of, in the magickal sense. Yes. Aided and abetted by your excellent and obliging Baron, so if we're in trouble later, it's all his fault.'

'Did you tell him that?'

'I did. He twinkled at me. How did that date go, anyway?'

'We're wandering off the point here. What did you two reprehensible sneaks manage to dig up?'

'Nothing concrete, but listen. We couldn't get around the classified information barriers, so we decided to find out why everything about him is classified to begin with. That order came down from somewhere way high in the Ministry, Ves, and it was classified under section-something-I-can't-remember of the Magickal Accords of Someday-or-Other pertaining to forbidden uses of magickal arts.'

'We sort of knew that. It's those beasts. He was the mastermind behind the various Dappledok species that were banned.'

'Yes...' Valerie said thoughtfully. 'But, Ves, they don't classify stuff like that. Those kinds of offences, however unusual, would typically fall under more or less mundane misuse of a magickal beast and he'd have a public record of misdemeanour. In fact, he more or less does, though your Baron had to pull some strings to get hold of it as the Ministry's buried it rather deep.'

'He's not *my* Baron, Val — oh, never mind. Spit it out. What else did you find?'

'Does the name *the Striding Spire* mean anything to you?'

'Why, yes. Yes, it does.'

'Right. That's something else your chap Melmidoc was responsible for, and while quite a lot of people were unhappy with him for those thieving little wretches we call the Dappledok Pups — by the way, there were rumours of a thief operating at Home for about six hours, did you know that? Until this morning, when Miranda found a cache of jewels your adorable little friend had hidden away. If the man had a slew of such creations to his name, I'm wondering why they didn't just lynch him and have done with it.'

'*Val.*'

'Sorry. Anyway, somebody was very seriously unhappy with him about that Spire. But even your Baron's contact at the Ministry couldn't find out why. It's that top secret, Ves.'

'Cool.'

'No. Not cool. You are digging your nose into things a lot of important people would like to keep hidden, and by the way there is an *entire ministry* whose purpose is to keep that kind of stuff nicely buried out of sight.'

'Of non-magicker humans, Val! I don't count!'

'You do. I do. There are some things no one is supposed to know.'

'I will bear it in mind.'

'Or in other words, you are wholly unmoved.'

'Of course I am.' We were approaching a handsome brick building with twisty turrets and big, glittery windows by that time, and since its every architectural feature screamed *prestigious school* to this ex-pupil of a prestigious school, I judged that we had arrived at the Redclover educational establishment's main building. 'I have to go,' I said to Valerie. 'But one thing: Mauf told us Melmidoc Redclover had a fine disappearing act going on, which culminated in his total vanishment somewhere in 1630. He also had a brother, Drystan, who was Mayor of Dapplehaven, and they had a tame dragon at their disposal. And that Spire? It, too, had a habit of going walkabout, hence the name, and they took it down the same year Mel disappeared. Can you call Zar? She's digging into that perambulatory cottage business.'

'On it,' said Valerie, and hung up.

I put away my phone, and sidled up to Jay. 'Top, *top* secret stuff,' I told him, brimming with excitement. 'Even Valerie can't find out much about Melmidoc.'

To my disappointment, Jay's reaction was an instant frown. 'Then should we be investigating it at all? We don't need to know more about Melmidoc Redclover, he's been dead for centuries. We're getting diverted from the main point.'

'What was the main point again?'

'Find out where your pup came from, and how it got into the Greyer cottage?'

'Right! Right. But, Jay, everything has to be related. Don't you see that?'

'No.'

'Striding Spire, cottage that goes walkabout. A supposedly extinct Goldnose pup in one, and its original creator in the other. Coincidence? Surely not!'

'Whether it is or not is beside the point. If we've hit a wall with our investigation, we should send what we've found through to the Ministry and let them deal with it.'

'They are dealing with it. They sent us Mabyn, with whose help we now propose to peruse a stash of records entirely unrelated to the Ministry. To quote Doryty the Angry Mayor, the Hidden Ministry has no jurisdiction over the Redclover School, and therefore, the school can do whatever it wants with its records.'

Jay opened his mouth to object again, judging from the lingering frown.

I put my hand over it. 'Jay! Aren't you curious?'

He nodded, still frowning fiercely.

'You realise Milady hires people like us for Acquisitions precisely because we're curious? And tenacious! And difficult to deter!' I optimistically removed my hand.

'Tautology,' said Jay. 'Difficult to deter is the exact definition of tenacious.'

Or in other words, he withdrew his opposition but would in no way be compelled to say so. 'Milady has our back,' I said, beaming at him. 'The Ministry isn't always right, Jay. That's the hard truth about the job we do. We have occasionally ignored Milady's strictures when the need was great enough, and once in a while we have to ignore the Ministry's, too.'

'Why is the need so great this time?'

'Think about it, Jay. What reasonable explanation can you come up with for this pup's existence?' I was still clutching her furry little body to my chest, though she had quietened down now that the Mayor and her shiny jewellery was no longer in sight.

'None whatsoever,' Jay admitted.

'Exactly. Which means something very strange is going on, and will probably continue to go on. We need to find out if there are more of these beasts somewhere, and save them, and get a few specimens for Miranda so she won't kill us. We need to find out how it was possible, apparently, to pluck this one out of, seemingly, nowhere, and plunk it down in a haunted cottage somewhere in Suffolk. And we need to find out why the spriggan responsible for such remarkable, even if questionable, achievements disappeared, and what any of this has got to do with buildings that jaunt about all over the country.'

'Fine, fine,' Jay sighed. 'Colour me convinced.'

I rewarded him with a peck on the cheek and a sunny smile. 'To quote Valerie in all her wisdom: if we're in trouble later, it's all my fault.'

'Valerie said that?'

'Mostly. She's actually blaming the Baron.'

'Good choice.'

We'd paused outside the front door of the school, and so absorbed in conversation had I been that it only then occurred to me that we had been standing there a while. Mabyn of the Ministry and Headmistress Jenifry stood near the door, wearing identical expressions of disquiet, their faces lifted to the air.

'What's the matter?' I asked.

'You can't smell that?' said Jenifry.

I sniffed, and caught a whiff of something acrid. 'Is... is that smoke?'

'It is,' said Jay grimly. 'And it's coming from inside.'

Jenifry hauled uselessly upon the great stained-glass door. 'It's locked. The school's closed by now.'

'Is there a back entrance?' said Jay, already moving.

'This way.' Jenifry led the way at a run, and we followed, all the way around to the back of the great brick pile.

There was a back door, a humble-looking portal of ancient oak with heavy, black iron hinges. It was open, which was nice. And there was a small inferno of flames erupting out of it, which was less so.

13

S o, the main building of the Redclover School was burning down before our eyes. Nice. Worst thing of all? They were not normal, orange-looking flames. They were bright purple, which meant a magickal fire, the kind that leaves nothing to chance.

Jenifry watched for a moment, her face very grim. 'There are measures in place to deal with a fire,' she said. 'But of course, they're all inside the building.'

'Are there likely to be any people in there?' I said, trying not to imagine what it might be like to be one of them just then.

Thankfully, Jenifry shook her head. 'Nothing goes on in here outside of school hours. Jacoby, our caretaker, evicts anyone still lingering by four o'clock, and closes up the building.'

I checked. It was well after half past four.

'Who do we know who might have an aptitude for purple fire?' said Jay, standing at a safe distance with his arms tightly folded.

'A certain purple dragon?' I hazarded.

'Jenifry,' said Jay. 'The records are all in there?'

She nodded. 'Cellar vaults.'

'Was Mabyn right? Does Archibald only answer to the Mayor?'

'He's meant to, and that's normally the case. He might make an exception if he likes you, but Doryty pretends to know nothing about that.'

'So it was probably Doryty who ordered the fire, but it might not have been?'

'Correct.'

Jay looked up into the sky. So did I, and Jenifry, and Mabyn. 'Archibald!' Jay shouted.

No answer came.

'Damn it,' he sighed.

Jenifry was pacing about, staring fretfully at the fire. 'I can make it rain out here for a while, but of what use is that when the fire is in there?'

'How far from that door are the cellar stairs?' I asked her. 'And is there likely to be a locked door in the way?'

'Not far. You'd go down a short corridor and into the rear hall, the stairs are on the left. Yes, there's a locked door, but I have the key. Not that it matters now.'

'It might. Where are these fire-defence measures you mentioned?'

'In every room. There's a bell to the right of every door.'

'Right then.' I shoved the pup — dozing by then — into Jay's arms and set off. Before anybody could stop me, I dived for the purple-flaming door.

This may seem foolhardy of me, but seriously, one of my top talents is shielding magick. All the more so when I happen to have the marvellously amplifying powers of a major Wand at my disposal, which handily, I did. With my Sunstone beauty in my hand, it was the work of a moment to summon an ethereal ward which enclosed me from head to foot, and it was virtually unbreakable.

It was not a perfect solution, though. Main problem: to be that effective, it is also air tight, and that means there is only so long I can stay inside without suffocating.

So I made it quick.

It was my first time wandering about in a blazing inferno, and despite the unusually attractive colour of the flames, I cannot say that I enjoyed it. The corridor Jenifry had described was a tunnel of fire and smoke, and I could see nothing but roaring, hungry flames. It took some nerve to walk through, watching the fire try desperately to claim me, and trusting to my ward to keep them off me. More heat leaked through than I had anticipated, and by the time I reached the rear hall I was shaking violently with fright and sweating profusely.

First: deal with the fire. I soon found one of the bells, positioned just beside the door-frame where Jenifry had said it would be. It was a shimmering crystal creation, exquisitely pretty, and very fae-looking. When I rang it, a clear, tinkling sound pealed through the hall, but I could barely hear it over the near-deafening roar of the fire. Nothing seemed to happen.

I rang it a second time, just in case, and that was all I had time for. If I was going to carry off the second part of my plan, I had to move.

Stairs on the left. There was a door there, which would soon catch alight; flames were licking at the bottom, and all around the frame. Having palmed Jenifry's key ring as I ran past her (ask me another time when and where I learned that skill), I had the means in hand to unlock it. Unfortunately, I had to reach beyond the ward to touch anything, and my hands were shaking so badly that I almost dropped the keyring three times before I found the right key. The *heat*! I could feel my skin burning as I desperately turned the key in the lock, and almost died of relief when it turned and the door swung open.

I all but fell into the blissfully dark, non-flaming stairwell beyond, and hastened down into the cool of the cellar.

It wouldn't be long before the fire spread, so I worked quickly. I made a light, first, by way of several balls of blue fire (yes, the irony was not lost on me) which I sent to float overhead. They illuminated a spacious, open-plan cellar chamber with plain stone walls, many of them lined with bookcases. A long, low chest-of-drawers with at least a hundred drawers in it took up much of the centre of the room, and a couple of study tables occupied the rest.

All of this I dismissed. Nothing sensitive or secret would be kept anywhere so obvious, or so easily accessed. There would be another, hidden chamber somewhere.

I had no time to conduct a search.

'Mauf!' I hauled the book out of my bag, wondering why I hadn't thought to leave him safely with Jay, but blessing my oversight. 'Quick. Help. According to your vast knowledge of secrets, where's a likely place for a secret room in a cellar underneath the Redclover school?'

I was gabbling, but Mauf got me. 'Is there some reason you did not pose this question to the current headmistress?'

'Because I am looking for old, long-buried information which she, apparently, is not privy to. Super secret, Mauf. Think back to the age of Melmidoc.' I stopped. 'Wait. Can you just... absorb whatever it is? In that way that you do, with other books?'

'If you leave me down here for a few weeks, perhaps I could,' admitted Mauf. 'Do we have a few weeks?'

'We have a few minutes.'

'Then you'll have to find it the hard way.'

'And quickly.' I suppressed the urge to panic. *This is an archives repository, Ves. You are comfortable with archives. Archives are your friend, even if they are about to be set aflame.*

Deep breaths. Yes.

'Second cellar,' suggested Mauf. 'Down underneath. Trap door.'

'Do you see a trap door? Because I don't!'

'I do not *see* anything, I am a book.'

I had wondered before whether Mauf was aware of his surroundings in the visual sense, and if so, how. But this was not exactly the perfect time to ask. 'Any other ideas?' I said desperately. I was by that time running from bookcase to bookcase, shoving at all the oldest ones in case they should happen to swing or turn or vaporise, but nothing happened. I had closed the door on the fire, but smoke was pouring down the stairs and beginning to fill the room, and it was getting hard to breathe.

Then I heard the door slam open, and heavy footsteps thudded down the stairs. 'Ves!'

'Jay? You freaking idiot, what are you *doing?*' He had a ward up, but it was shaky, and already falling apart. This had not, apparently, deterred him from plunging into a burning building.

'What am *I* doing? What are *you* doing?!' Jay bellowed back. 'You are completely bloody insane, and we have thirty seconds to get out of here.'

I extended my superior shield to cover both of us, not that it would help us for much longer. 'But I don't have—'

'Forget it! It's not here.'

'*What?*'

'How about we run first, talk later?'

I might have been willing to risk my own hide for another shot at those papers, but not Jay's. I let him bundle me back up the stairs, Mauf clutched in my left hand and the Sunstone Wand in my right. We almost got lost in the hall, for it was solid smoke by then and we could hardly see. The noise of crackling flames was monstrous, and even my ward began to falter; heat blazed through and began to burn.

But Jay and his sense of direction got us out somehow. We emerged, coughing, into the blissful sunshine of late afternoon, and fresh, clear air had never felt so exquisite. We ran a long way from the door before we stopped, gasping and choking. I was shaking violently. So was Jay.

'Idiot,' I finally told him, when I had recovered breath enough. 'You could have been killed.'

'So could you!'

'I was about to come back!'

'That's a total lie. You were on the opposite side of the cellar to the door, fumbling with a bloody bookcase. You had that foolhardy scholarly zeal going on, didn't you?'

'If you are referring to my academic fervour,' I said imperiously, 'take my advice, and don't ever tell Val you gave it so dismissive a name.'

'Valerie's dedication could never be called into question, but even she would not be fool enough to get herself burned to a crisp in the pursuit of a piece of paper!'

'Are you calling me a fool?' I demanded.

'Yes!'

I found that I had no immediate response to so emphatic a declaration, for he... had a point. 'It was an important piece of paper,' I said in my defence.

'Nothing is that important. And, as I was trying to tell you, what we are looking for probably wasn't in there anyway.'

'Then why has somebody burned the bloody building?' I said, about ready to burst with frustration.

'Maybe they were poorly informed. If it was Doryty the Mayor, well, I am not sure anyone would accuse her of being quite the brightest spark. I'm beginning to think they give that job to the village idiot just to keep them quiet.' Jay suddenly swept me up in a hug, the kind that makes your bones creak. My response was little better than a surprised squeak, and he had squished out all the air I might have used to speak, so I just hung there.

'Your hair is burned,' said Jay in my ear, and let me go.

'*What.*' I checked. He was right. 'Damn it.'

'A fair sacrifice to make for a book?' said Jay, straight-faced.

'Always. Speaking of which...' I put the Wand away and turned my attention to Mauf. 'You okay in there, Maufie?'

'That would be Mauf*ry*,' said Mauf.

'I know how the word goes, I was just — never mind. Glad to see you're unscathed.' I put him away, ignoring his protests. 'So, then,' I said to Jay. 'Where are these super-secret papers, if not in there? Oh, hang on.' I went over to Jenifry, who was pacing about, arms wrapped around her waist, her face turned to the beautiful burning building. 'Those bells,' I said. 'I hit them a few times, but... it doesn't look like they are working.'

She stared at me. 'Then someone has deactivated them.'

'Yes,' I said pleasantly. 'I wonder who it could possibly have been?'

Jenifry's cool composure was unimpaired. 'What do you mean?'

I meant that, as headmistress, Jenifry had the knowledge, the means and the access to everything she would need in order to pull off this little manoeuvre. She knew what the fire defences were, where they were, how they worked, and how to disrupt them. She knew when the building closed, and therefore, when it was safe to set a fire intended only to destroy documents. And she had notably failed to make any efforts whatsoever to bring in help, ostensibly relying on the fire defences to render that unnecessary.

I had slightly mistrusted her apparent helpfulness before, for I had expected some reticence; some challenge to our authority, some attempt to defend the rights of the school. I was now disposed to see it as highly suspicious, but there was not time to have that conversation with her just then. 'You know what I mean,' I told her. 'Luckily, no one died. Why don't you deal with this, and we'll go deal with the other thing somewhere else?'

She began to say something, but I turned my back on her and re-joined Jay.

'I think she has us beaten when it comes to diversions,' I commented.

'Hands down, no contest.' He grimaced. 'Good to know that the old diversion trick works so well.'

'So. Where do you suppose the papers really are?'

'Yes. If the headmistress of this school is willing to destroy her own buildings to keep us away from those papers, don't you think we ought—'

'No.'

That won me a flat stare. 'Is that it? No?'

'We've had this conversation.'

He sighed. 'Fine. Mabyn?'

I had almost forgotten Mabyn, for she had hung back in silence ever since we had emerged from the school building, and had excelled so well at being unobtrusive that I had looked straight past her. But now she stepped forward, visibly gathering resolve, and nodded to me. 'Courageous,' she said.

'Thank you.'

Jay rolled his eyes, but mercifully held his peace.

'When I was headmistress,' began Mabyn, and paused to hand the pup back into my arms. I was welcomed with a lick to my chin, which was nice, though the pup immediately sneezed, which was less so. 'There was…' She stopped, and sighed, and said in a stony voice: 'The reason I am so despised in Dapplehaven is as follows. The post of headmistress of the Redclover School is the highest possible post of authority in this town. The Mayor is barely more than a figurehead, or a distraction. As headmistress, you possess the fullest powers and authority, and access to absolutely everything. You are also bound to lifetime secrecy. In abandoning my post, deserting the town and, as they see it, joining the opposition, I broke a great many sacred promises. And now, perhaps I must break more.' She took a deep breath, and cast an eye over the retreating figure of Jenifry "Redclover" — who had, apparently, decided at last to do something about the fire. 'The head teacher's quarters are deceptive. The house — Jenifry's house at present, I suppose — looks to be naught but a cottage, but it is much more than that. Anything troublesome, sensitive, especially powerful or dangerous is likely to be kept there.'

'How do we get in?' I said promptly.

'Only the present incumbent of the post can get in.'

'A previous one could not?'

Mabyn's lips flattened into a thin line. 'I doubt it.'

'Can we try?'

Poor Mabyn gave me the helpless look of a woman who is trapped, and knows it. 'We can try,' she conceded. 'But what about Jenifry? She will be on the watch for exactly such an attempt.'

And she would, too, knowing that her fiery diversion was no longer holding us.

Happily, an answer presented itself at that very moment. 'Hello,' came a hopeful voice from some way over our heads. 'Did you need anything burning? I have some fire left. It's purple.'

Archibald descended from above. He did indeed have some fire left; it wreathed his gigantic, scaled body in a crackling shroud, pouring white smoke. We all backed hastily away.

'Archie,' I greeted him warmly. 'Did Jenifry make you burn things?'

'Oh, no!' he said, shocked. 'She would never make me do anything.'

'No?' I said, surprised and dismayed, for that made mincemeat of our neat and tidy theory.

'She's my friend.'

Jay's eyes narrowed. 'Did she ask you to burn things.'

'Yes,' said the dragon, his wings drooping. 'And she promised me a treat afterwards, but there has not been anything.'

I sighed inwardly. Did the portrait of Melmidoc really exist, or had Jenifry fabricated that little mystery in hope of distracting us?

'Would you say *we* are your friends?' I said.

'Yes. Especially that one.' Archie pointed the tip of his fiery tail at Jay, who took an involuntary step back. 'Are you the Mayor yet?'

Jay blinked. 'Ah, no. But we could pretend, if you like?'

Archie gave a wide dragon smile, flashing pearly fangs. 'I like games.'

'I thought you might.'

So, we set fire to Dapplehaven.

<h1 style="text-align:center">14</h1>

All right, we didn't set fire to all of it. Not even very much of it. But enough to keep Headmistress Jenifry very busy indeed, and the Mayor, too. It caused a great deal of frustration, I believe. Jenifry knew what we were up to, and we knew that she knew, but she was in charge here. She could hardly leave her precious town to burn, and its people with it, while she protected her own home. That kind of thing never does a person's public reputation any good, now does it?

We'd chosen empty buildings in disparate parts of the town. Being conscientious, heritage-preserving citizens of the world, we had also selected buildings of little value, material or otherwise, and preferably those with easy access to a body of water besides. And considering Jenifry's professed talent for calling down rain, little real damage would be done, all told. That said, I privately resolved to leave out those details when I made my report to Milady. Why bother her with trifles?

Archibald performed his part with gusto. By the time we had finished, his cloak of purple flame had diminished significantly, and we were no longer in danger of being fried alive if we got too close to him.

Which was convenient, because it was time and past for us to hightail it out of there, and over to Jenifry's cottage. Or whatever it really was.

Archibald was happy to oblige.

'Wait!' I cried, as he reached one vast foot towards me, his claws still crackling with flame. 'You still have too much fire, Archie. We will burn.'

'Oh.' He regarded his foot in pensive silence for a moment, and I felt a twinge of apprehension. What unpromising mental processes might I have sparked in that dim brain of his?

We were in a meadow on the edge of Dapplehaven at the time. A half-ruined barn of ragged oak planks was situated a ways to our left, purple flames licking up the empty frame of its doorway. If there had ever been a farmhouse that went with it, that building was long gone.

Archibald turned his head, coughed, and belched a gout of weak lavender fire all over the grass.

The grass promptly caught alight.

'There,' said the dragon, inspecting his polished claws with greater satisfaction.

The fire roared up towards my feet. 'Er, time to go!'

Oof. Archibald swept me up, then Jay. Mabyn he caught in one back foot, almost as an afterthought as he rose into the skies. I heard her distant squawk of protest, and silently sympathised.

Archibald's getaway was not quite so speedy as I had hoped, for he paused, circling the air, to admire his handiwork. The ground below was rather more ablaze than I had bargained for.

'Note to ourselves,' said Jay, eyeing our retaliatory diversion with dismay. 'Be careful when playing with dragons.'

'I would not hurt you,' said Archibald, in an injured tone.

Jay patted his leg comfortingly. 'I know you would not.'

Archibald smiled, and puffed a jaunty little ball of fire into the air.

'At least, not deliberately,' Jay amended, as Archie's fireball missed his head by inches.

Mercifully, Archibald flew on after that.

The house of the headmistress proved to be a humble-looking place, though it was amply provided with a large garden ringing the cottage all around. Timber-framed, white-washed and crooked, with a neatly thatched roof, it was spriggan-sized, which must cause Jenifry no end of inconvenience.

It was not, of course, unattended. Archibald landed in the middle of the stone-cobbled street outside of it, but he had trouble squashing his huge bulk even into the widest part of the thoroughfare, and a sweep of his wings upset a cart full of fruit an outraged spriggan was trying to hawk on the corner.

'Jay,' I said, when my adorable and well-meaning partner began picking up spilled produce. 'Focus. Urgent task at hand.'

He smiled sheepishly, handed off the fruit he had collected to the stall holder (who cursed him roundly for his efforts, and tried to box his ears), and re-joined me. Mabyn was already halfway up the street, striding towards Jenifry's cottage with her Minister demeanour firmly in place. Brisk of step, chin high, she swept towards the two guards stationed outside of the front door, looking formidable indeed.

Jay and I hastened to catch up, leaving Archibald to reason with the stallholder.

'I request access,' Mabyn was saying when we reached the house. 'As a former head-mistress of Redclover School, and on behalf of the Hidden Ministry, who has reason to suspect—'

'Nobody goes in,' said one of the guards, a relatively beefy-looking spriggan with a domed, shinily bald head and a fine purple uniform. 'Ms. Redclover's orders.'

'*I* am Ms. Redclover,' said Mabyn impatiently.

I was beginning to think that half the citizens of Dapplehaven were called Redclover, and perhaps they really were, for the guards looked most unimpressed.

'We were told that somebody might make an attempt,' said the second guard, a near perfect match for the first, save that he had a full head of dark hair scrupulously coiffed. He looked us over, his leathery face cold. 'If you persist, we are instructed to arrest you at once.'

'You cannot arrest me!' spluttered Mabyn. 'As a representative of the Hidden Ministry, I am immune to all—'

'Ms. Redclover said to make special effort to repel any Ministry folk,' interrupted Guard the First. 'You are immune to nothing, and I suggest you leave at once.'

Mabyn was slow on the uptake and continued to argue. Jay and I exchanged a thoughtful look.

'Usual trick, then?' said Jay.

'I'm thinking so.' I rooted in my heavy and ever-present bag — I will have the right shoulder of a wrestler, at this rate — for my usual supplies, though it took me a moment to find them around the soft, sleeping bulk of Pup and the angled, leather-clad shape of Mauf. I really ought to organise my things a bit better.

But I found them. Two of Orlando's best sleep-pearls, each about an inch across, and encased in a jellyish coating. I gave one to Jay.

I'd retrieved my Wand, too. I threw my pearl up in the air, zapped it with a wave of the Wand, and it burst in a shower of pearly rain all over the nearest guard.

Jay threw his, and I zapped that too.

'Hey—' said Guard the First, as he fell sideways into the road.

Guard the Second followed suit, without uttering so much as a syllable.

They lay there, charmingly inert, and snoring repulsively.

'That shouldn't keep working so well,' Jay said, stepping over the nearest guard.

'Maybe I need a new signature trick,' I agreed. 'You know, the last time I tried to re-order a batch, I got an interrogation from Enchantments? They thought I might be putting them to some manner of misuse.' I reached the door, and tried it. Locked. 'Any keys on those gents?'

'What kind of misuse?' said Jay, bending down to pat the guards' pockets. He shook his head.

'They asked the usual kinds of questions. Was I experiencing any excess pressure at work, that I had been unwilling to report? Was I feeling any strain? When had I last taken time off?'

Jay shook his head at me: no keys. 'People use them to self-medicate?' he said incredulously.

I shook my head back at him, but in my case it indicated despair. 'You are so very new, aren't you?'

Mabyn gave a vast, noisy yawn, and toppled slowly into the street.

'Oops,' I said, regarding her recumbent and deeply asleep form with a twinge of guilt. 'I hoped she wouldn't get caught in it.'

'She could probably use a nap,' said Jay. 'Seems stressed.'

Jay and I quickly moved all three of our victims, the intended and the unintended, to the edge of the street, out of the way of any passing dangers.

'Time for the big guns,' I said, and dived back into my bag. I had a lot of bits and pieces in there, rattling around in the bottom. Not quite as many as usual, since Ornelle, Keeper of Stores, had lately made me hand back virtually everything I'd had on loan (joy-killer extraordinaire). But Orlando's people keep me well-supplied with consumables, and I had a really juicy one in there.

Somewhere.

'Ah!' I crowed, and from the depths of the Receptacle of Everything I produced a stick of bubble gum.

Jay looked at me. He had That Face again. 'Gum? Really?'

'It looks like gum.' I unwrapped it, softened it in my fingers for a moment, then stuck it to the front door of Jenifry's house. 'But you really do not want to eat it.'

I waited.

It began to crackle after a moment, and then it melted into a trickling slime which dripped slowly down the door, taking the wood with it. All of it. Fine old oak planks dissolved into slush and dribbled away, leaving the doorframe nicely empty.

'Don't ever let me eat one of those by mistake,' Jay said as he followed me inside.

'You won't. They taste like poo, and I mean that more or less literally. Safety measure.'

Jay made a gagging noise.

Jenifry had not left it to her guards and her locked door alone to keep us out, of course, but I was ready for that. I flicked the Sunstone Wand as we walked in, surrounding us both in one of my best wards. When the magickal alarm flared, sending waves of searing purple light flooding the interior of the cottage, the surge of power bounced harmlessly off our shared shield, making my ears ring but causing no lasting harm.

'What is it with purple around here?' I muttered.

'You love purple.'

'Exactly. It's *my* signature colour.'

'At least it proposes to be pretty while it fries us to a crisp,' said Jay. 'That has to count for something.'

'My room defences have rainbow fire,' I said proudly.

'Really?'

'No. But not for lack of trying.'

'Is it purple?'

'... Yes. Yes, it is.'

The cottage, as Mabyn had warned us, appeared to be just that: a modest abode, with only a few rooms, and everything in them of the most mundane. Jenifry had a small living room equipped with a worn green velvet sofa and matching chairs, and an array of suitable books. Her kitchen was charmingly old-fashioned, and she had a bedroom at the back.

That was it.

It took Jay and I less than five minutes to explore all this, and we met back in the little hallway, wearing, I imagine, identical expressions of frustration.

'No signs of any secret doorways, I suppose?' I said.

'Nothing so promising. You didn't run into any hidden staircases or trapdoors?'

'Nope.'

It occurred to me to wish that we had asked Mabyn for more detail, though in fairness I imagine every inhabitant of the cottage has their own ways of concealing the secret spaces. Would Mabyn's information have been of any use?

It might at least have been a place to start. Now we had nothing, and Mabyn lay outside in the street, asleep. She would remain so for at least an hour.

My bag rustled, and the pup poked up its head, sniffing the air. I patted her. 'Sweet pup, I wish you could help, but I do not suppose there is anything around here that might interest—' I stopped, because she was writhing like a mad thing to be let down, and succeeded in falling out of the bag altogether before I could catch her. She landed with a snort, but she was up again in seconds, her enormous nose drawing in great gulps of air.

That nose adhered itself to the floor, and off she went, tail high and wagging with excitement.

She went into the kitchen.

'Right, then,' said Jay, and we followed.

But when we reached the kitchen, the pup was not there.

I went back out into the hallway, in case she had sneaked past us somehow, but she was not there, either.

'Huh,' I said.

Jay joined me, and stood regarding the doorway thoughtfully. 'She didn't go straight through, did she?'

'She was circling a bit, but she was following a scent of some kind, so that would account for it.'

'It might.' Jay approached the door again. Rather than walking in a straight line into the kitchen, he did as the pup had done: circled his way over the threshold in an arc, turning a full circle before he went through.

He still ended up in the kitchen, but that had given me an idea.

'I think she went the other way about,' I told him, and stepped forward to try it. 'And with these kinds of things, it is nearly always widdershins that—'

'—does the job,' I finished, after a pause, for my own anti-clockwise circle had landed me in another room, but it was not the kitchen, and there was no Jay.

There was, however, the pup.

15

'**G**ood job, puppy,' I whispered, awed.

For this room was larger than the rest of the cottage put together, and it was packed full. It looked like it might once have been a barn, or something of the like, for it consisted of a large open space with a high ceiling supported by thick, crooked beams, and the windows were near the top of the walls. Shelves, chests of drawers and bookcases were everywhere in evidence, to the pup's delight, for many of them bore objects of obvious value: jewellery, Wands, trinkets and Curiosities, even one or two genuine Treasures as far as I could tell. There were a great many books as well, and — to my relief — a section which was clearly designated for the storage of papers.

I made straight for that, and by the time Jay found his way through the sneaky enchantment on Jenifry's kitchen door, I was up to my eyeballs in crumbling old documents. Figuratively speaking.

'Soooo,' said Jay with a low whistle, walking up behind me. 'Do you suppose all this is legally held?'

'Probably not, considering how eager they've been to hide it. Help me with this, Jay?' I had found a set of four bookcases fitted edge-to-edge and back-to-back, and their shelves were stuffed with old books, proper scrolls with ribbon bindings, notebooks, journals, and everything of that sort. There was so much of it, and we did not have much time before Jenifry would appear — or send someone else to intercept us.

Jay took a look at the job that lay before us, and blanched. 'Try Mauf,' he suggested.

'He says he needs time to absorb this much information.'

'We don't need him to absorb it all, but he may be able to identify what we need.'

So I extracted Mauf. 'Dearest book, if you can contrive to find out whether any of these books and such were written by, or predominantly about, the brothers Melmidoc and Drystan Redclover, our gratitude would know no bounds.'

'I cannot do much with gratitude,' remarked Mauf. 'Do you have something more concrete?'

'What did you have in mind?'

'I want a proper ribbon bookmark. Silk, not polyester. And a sleeping bag.'

'A sleeping— never mind. I will get you anything you like, as long as you're quick.'

'Bookcase to your left,' instructed Mauf. 'Second shelf from the top, third book from the end. Melmidoc's journal of his discoveries, covering the years 1618 to 1630. Bookcase behind that, bottom shelf, a small notebook with crumbling pages — *how* embarrassing — entitled "A Mayor's Recollections of Service," written by Drystan Redclover.'

We hurriedly collected both.

I took the liberty of kissing Mauf's front cover soundly. 'Best book ever.'

The book gave what sounded like a cough, if the rustling of dry pages could ever be termed such. 'That spire you were asking me about. Is that also of interest?'

'Yes!'

'Scroll, bottom shelf. The one with the sumptuous tassels. "An Account of the Deliberations of the Dappledok Council Regarding the Matter of the Spire." I advise you to take all three in that pile.'

I gave him another kiss. 'I love you,' I said as I stuffed him back in the bag.

His response was too muffled to be understood.

I put the books and scrolls in on top of him, trusting that he would enjoy the company sufficiently to forgive me the indignity.

'Time to go,' I told Jay.

He cast a brief, agonised look at the contents of that building, and I could hardly blame him, for I, too, desperately wanted to explore. But he did not argue, perhaps because there came a kerfuffle from the doorway at just that moment, and a voice called belligerently: 'You are trespassing upon private property, and are hereby arrested on the orders of the Mayor!'

Interestingly, whoever it was did not burst straight in, as might be expected. 'I think they are afraid of us,' I remarked.

'Maybe it was the pile of unconscious bodies outside the front door that did it,' mused Jay.

'Could be that. Can you levitate?'

'Badly.' He looked up at the distant windows, and sighed. 'You're thinking of those, aren't you?'

'I am afraid so.' I looked around in irritation, for while there was no shortage of storage spaces, and even a desk against the far wall, there was not a single chair in sight. So much for flying.

'Come on in!' I trilled. 'We give ourselves up!'

On which note, I grasped Jay's hand and shot up into the air, dragging him with me.

I cannot say it was our most successful effort ever. We made it about four feet before we began to wobble, and promptly sank halfway back down again.

Our assailants found their courage and came striding through the door, looking warily about. They were guards like the two we had felled, wearing the same uniforms, though these were equipped with proper Wands: a Jade, and by the looks of it an Opal.

These they levelled at us. 'Stop where you are,' commanded one.

Well, we tried. Hovering for long in mid-air is a talent neither of us possesses, however, so we drifted inexorably back floorwards again. 'Sorry,' I giggled.

The pup trotted over to me, grinning a canine grin, her tail wagging exuberantly. She had an amethyst Wand in her mouth, which she presented to me with great pride.

'Oh, thank you!' I said, accepting it with alacrity. I gave her a luxurious pat, for what a clever, good pup she was!

A guard took it off me moments later.

'That was a gift,' I said indignantly.

'It is stolen property. What else have you taken?'

I rolled my eyes, and sighed. 'Fine, fine.' I unpacked the bag again, offloading all our acquisitions into the wrinkled palms of the belligerent guard.

'Any more?' he prompted when I had finished. 'You will submit to a search.'

Jay did so quiescently enough, but I was not feeling so docile, for if they found Mauf, were they going to believe that the book belonged to me, and not to Jenifry? So as they searched Jay, I cast about for an alternative solution. Sadly, I couldn't get at my brilliant sleep pearls without attracting notice, and I was not perfectly certain that I had any left, anyway.

'I suppose it doesn't have to be a chair,' I said, and kicked over the nearest bookcase. It took a couple of attempts, for it was heavy oak, but it toppled with a nice *bang*, and all its books fell off onto the floor. I felt a pang of guilt over that, for many of them were old and fragile. But needs must.

The other guard had more of his wits about him than I was hoping. He flicked his Opal Wand at me, and succeeded in paralysing my every muscle. I fought, but to no avail; I could barely breathe.

Then the pup sank her teeth into his ankle, making him screech in a fashion I found most satisfying. She followed that up with an athletic jump, closed her slightly bloody jaws around his Wand, and cheerfully pinched it from him.

The paralysis eased.

'Right,' I said. 'We're going.' I bent to scoop up the pup, Wand and all, and at the same time persuaded the nice, empty bookcase that it was feeling energetic. Jay took care of the guard who had hold of him with a solid punch to the face, and jumped onto the bookcase with me.

Up we went.

'The books!' Jay cried.

'Never mind. Mauf's got it.'

'I hope so.'

'Me too. Hup.' I didn't bother opening the nearest window, for the guards were still down there, and one of them still wielded a Wand. So I smashed it, and sent Jay through first.

'Woah,' he gasped as he clambered out. 'Careful, Ves.'

'It's not that far up.' I accepted his help, however, letting him pull me through the window and out onto the roof.

I was immediately obliged to retract my statement, for the ground yawned a long way below; plenty far enough for a mere Ves to go fatally squish, should she fall.

I hung onto Jay. 'Unexpected,' I remarked.

'Any idea where we are?' Jay asked, and that was a fair question, for I had not quite grasped that the view was wholly unfamiliar, and also notably lacking in a town. We were up somewhere high, a clifftop perhaps, and a green valley lay below us, with a pearly lagoon cutting into one side of it. In Dapplehaven we emphatically were not.

My phone rang.

Jay took the squirming pup off me, at some peril to his life, and promptly sat down on the roof. Said roof was also incongruous, by the by, for it was not a barn roof. It was instead rounded, with a peak in the middle, and covered in slate pieces. Also, the window we had climbed through was gone.

I dug out my phone. 'Val,' I said, perhaps a bit shakily. 'This is a bad time.'

'Is your life in imminent danger?' said she crisply.

I tested my footing. Reasonably sound. I followed Jay's example and sat on my haunches, and felt a bit better. 'Probably not.'

'Probably?'

'I mean, we're stuck on a roof with no way to get down, but we probably won't die just yet.'

'Great. Because this is important.'

Another voice cut in: Zareen's. 'Ves, this is *way* important. That cottage? The Greyer place?'

'I remember it,' I said drily.

'Right, listen. I've tracked it everywhere I can, and I admit that it is hard to do, because of its sheer mundanity — nondescript to say the least, right? — but still. Vanishing buildings tend to attract notice, but this one has only done so patchily. In the, what, five hundred years since it began to go walkabout, there have been only a handful of recorded sightings of any vanishing building of its general description. It might have been quietly camouflaged in some unremarkable spot for a lot of that time, sure, but — get this, Ves — I did find one or two other recorded sightings of just such a cottage.'

'And?' I said, not following at all.

'They date from *before* 1508.'

My thoughts spun. '1508, wasn't that the year that Maud Greyer—'

'Killed John Wester and stuffed him into the walls. Yes.'

'But if Waymaster Wester was the one moving the cottage about, how could it have been moving around before that year? Are you sure it was the same place?'

'It's impossible to be entirely sure, but how many late medieval timber-framed dwellings do you know of that had a habit of wandering about?'

'There could have been more. Waymasters were more common, once.'

'They were. And it could be a different building that was spotted mid-vanishment near

Colchester in 1432, or that was seen to appear out of nowhere near Ipswich in 1398. But Ves, there's more.'

My hands were getting cold, way up high as we were, for the wind was chilly and it was growing late in the day. I gripped the phone tighter, hugged my bag closer to myself, and said as patiently as I could: 'Go on.'

Val came back on. 'I've been looking into that Spire. Did you manage to find the papers you were after?'

'Yes, but haven't had chance to look at them yet.'

'Right. No tower-like building has ever been sighted moving around Britain the way the Greyer's cottage did, and I think a place like that would attract some notice, wouldn't you? So I went looking for any such reports from Dells or Enclaves or other magickal communities, and bingo. There are a few such cases. Did you get any description of the Spire, by chance?'

'No. My source was a dragon of little brain, who is weak on things like details.'

'There was a tower that used to appear in the heart of the Meyvale Dell, a predominantly sylph community, in the fifteen hundreds. It was said to be all white, but it shone blue at twilight. What does that sound like to you?'

'Starstone, but that wasn't developed into a building material until the early 1600s, so it can't be.'

'Another such tower was spotted twice on the edges of the Barraby Troll Enclave, early 1500s. And there are more such examples, Ves, going back another three centuries.'

My head spun. 'It can't have been starstone.'

'Ves. Get off that roof and go through those papers. I need you to find out whether the tower your Dappledok folk called the Striding Spire was built out of starstone, which would have been brand new and exciting at the time.'

'But—' I stopped, confused. 'But Val, it can't have been starstone.'

'Just find out, Ves. Stop overthinking it.'

I wanted to remonstrate with her some more, but she hung up on me.

Damnit.

I looked at Jay, but before I had chance to relay what Valerie and Zareen had said, he simply gave me a meaningful look and pointed down over the edge of the roof.

I inched my way thither, and peeped.

Below us stretched a tall, slender tower made from blocks of bright white stone tinged faintly with blue — a blue that would flare to brilliance when the sun went down.

I called Val back. 'Val? I think we've found the Spire.'

16

'Y ou've found the *Spire*?' echoed Val in disbelief. 'The actual building itself?'

'The actual one.'

'Where is it?'

'I don't know, but we are sitting on it.'

'...that's the roof you're stuck on?'

'Right.'

'And you don't know where you are?'

I told her about the cottage, and the secret barn, and the window we had climbed out of. 'I cannot tell if we are in Dappledok Dell anymore,' I concluded. 'I see a valley below with a lagoon in it, the latter having weird iridescent water, and I don't remember that from the Dell. I've a glimpse of sea, more normal colour. And that's it. No houses, no settlements, no sign of habitation whatsoever.'

'Can you get down?'

'No. Not without calling Adeline, and for one thing I am not sure she could make it to wherever we are. For another, I don't fancy trying to get on her back while she's hovering in mid-air about fifty feet off the ground.'

There was silence for a moment. 'Hang on, Ves,' said Val, and hung up.

I looked at Jay.

'Does this kind of thing happen often?' he asked. He had his knees drawn up to his chest and his jacket wrapped around them. We were both getting cold.

'Predicaments of this exact type, no, but in a more general sense... constantly.'

He nodded thoughtfully. 'There is a window,' he said after a moment. 'I explored a bit while you were talking. It's on the other side, about eight feet down.'

'Open?'

'No. But big enough to climb through.'

That did not really augur much. Setting aside the problem of how to reach the window without falling to our deaths, what would happen if we did? Would it prove to be another window like the ones in the barn, and we'd climb through it only to end up somewhere else? I did not want to lose track of this Spire just yet.

On the other hand, we could not just sit on the roof forever, either.

'Levitate?' I said, without much hope. Our joint performance at that art had not covered either of us in glory earlier on.

Jay looked as dubious as I felt. 'I think we'd die.'

'Chances of it are high.'

'If I die without saying goodbye to Indira, she'll kill me.'

'A fate worse than mere ordinary death by falling off a building, no doubt.'

'Much worse.' He looked around, perhaps hoping someone might have left a convenient chair on the roof somewhere. Or a bookcase, we were not picky.

'Did you come across any loose slates while you were daringly risking a plummet to the ground?' I asked him.

He gave me a flat stare. 'You are not witching up a roof tile.'

'I know it's dangerous, but—'

'Dangerous? Have you seen the size of these things?' He selected one to demonstrate with, thus answering my question as to whether or not he had found any loose ones. 'You could barely fit both feet on it,' he said, holding the dark, aged slate up to show me. 'It is windy up here, there is nothing to hold onto, and you would die.'

'There is a building to hold onto!'

'Yes. An extremely tall building, and we are at the top!'

'I just want to use it as a levitation aid. We can inch our way down, stone by stone—'

'How are you still alive?' Jay had folded his arms. It's always a bad sign when he does that.

'Because my ideas are not as crazy as you think, and I have had a lot of practice at slightly foolhardy escapades.'

'Slightly?'

I held out my hands for the slate. 'What if I promise faithfully not to expire?'

He did not hand over the slate, so I set about finding another one.

This prompted a sigh from Jay. 'Ves, I am genuinely worried about this.'

I flashed him a quick smile. 'Me too. But it is going to take Val a while to figure out where we are, if she can at all. In the meantime, we are without food or shelter, and we can hardly sleep up here without falling off. There is only so long we can safely remain aloft, and that means we have to take a risk or two to sort ourselves out.'

With obvious reluctance, Jay passed me his roof tile. 'I am going to thank our lucky stars that your talent for enchanting flying objects is vastly superior to your talent for levitation.'

'Practice, Jay, not luck. Like I said, I've got into trouble before.'

'Do you practice levitation, too?'

'Constantly.'

He grinned at me, though it was a strained expression.

I took up my Sunstone Wand, and set about witching up the slate. The process was much the same, even if the object was rather different, and before long the slate was bobbing buoyantly at my feet.

My pride made it imperative to hide the frisson of panic that shot through me at the prospect of stepping onto it, so I composed my face into a fair impression of serenity, and managed the business as confidently as I could.

Jay sat not far away, hands out, poised to catch me if I somehow managed to fall in his general direction. His face was creased with worry. 'That won't hold your weight,' he said.

'I have reinforced it a bit.' It still felt precarious, though, and Jay had been right about the wind: it buffeted me about atop the too-lightweight tile, and whenever I tried to release my grip on the roof and straighten up, I was almost blown backwards.

So I did it the graceless, undignified way, inching down the roof like a backwards crab, both hands clinging tightly to the tiles within reach. The part where I had to go over the edge was too horrible to recount in any detail. Suffice it to say that the ground yawned far, far below, I absolutely did *not* look down (much), and a great gust of wind caught me halfway through my descent and slammed me against the wall of the tower, almost breaking my fragile levitation aid.

But, I reached the window. Reassuringly big, it was neatly rectangular, and filled in with many small, diamond-shaped panes of glass. It was closed, and locked, and also handsome and old; I did not want to have to employ Rob's trick, and break the whole thing.

So I finagled it. An unlocking charm, amplified by my precious Wand, did the trick; a latch clicked, and to my infinite relief, the central section of the window creaked open.

I shoved it the rest of the way, and all but fell into the room beyond. I received a faceful of dust, first of all, for the floor was thick with it — everything was thick with it. Choking, I drew a fold of my gauzy scarf over my mouth, and held a brief exploration party.

I was not back in the barn, to my relief, nor did I seem to have been transported anywhere else. The room was round-walled, and appeared to be of the right dimensions to fit the tower. Someone had made a comfortable home here, once: a matched pair of elegant, upholstered arm chairs of early seventeenth-century style stood near a stone hearth, with a low table in between. Better yet, an array of bookcases ringed the walls, all stuffed with dust-covered books. I badly wanted to peruse those, of course, but first things first: would one of those chairs fit out of the window...?

It would not, so I chose a stout oak stool which stood near the hearth and enchanted that instead. Within an agreeably short space of time, Jay stood in the tower-top room with me, and without having to brave the same death-defying stunt as I had. The pup, too, was relieved to get her paws on solid ground again, and hopped out of the bag to perform an exploratory circuit of the room, nose to the floor.

Jay still looked shaken, so I gave him a swift hug — and then moved right on to the books.

'Melmidoc's place?' Jay surmised.

'And Drystan both, I'd think, judging from the... chairs...' I lost track of my train of thought somewhere in there, for those books. Those *books!* For a girl with the soul of a librarian, they were like twelve Christmases all in one. Even a cursory inspection soon revealed that they comprised a genuine trove of Treasures, spanning every age from the seventeenth century backwards. My hands shook slightly as I snapped a picture for Val. She would probably faint.

'Ves.' Jay came over, with a book in his hands. He had wiped most of the dust off it, and opened it to the title page. 'What do you make of this?'

It was a genuine illuminated manuscript. That first page was painstakingly inscribed in cramped, but exquisitely neat calligraphic print, the kind that used to take monks an entire day to complete. The text was framed with images inked in gloriously vivid colours, depicting a variety of beasts that were indubitably magickal in nature, though I recognised almost none of them. Were they all extinct?

'I had a leaf through,' said Jay, and took a deep breath. 'Do you see what that says?' And he pointed to a word, prominently placed on the first page, in scrolling handwriting.

Dramary.

I couldn't breathe.

'Dramary?' I squeaked. 'Is this Dramary's Bestiary?'

Jay just nodded. There weren't words.

See, Dramary's Bestiary is the kind of book people like Miranda cry themselves to sleep over. There are a scant few surviving references to it as one of the most complete examples of its type, an exhaustive dictionary of every species of magickal beast known to exist during the years it was written, most of which are no longer with us now. Those years were somewhere between 1097 and 1108, by the by, as near as we can judge. The last known copy of the book burned when Lord Torrant's library caught fire in 1907, taking the rest of the house with it. All we have left is a few sketch copies made by Torrant's secretary in 1904.

'Miranda will die,' I predicted. 'Of pure, unadulterated joy.'

'So will Val,' said Jay. 'But, Ves, it... it can't be Dramary's Bestiary, surely?'

'Why not? It looks like it.' I turned a few pages. I had seen the Torrant sketches before, and while I would need to see them again to make certain that they were a match for this book, I was fairly convinced. The style of the illustrations was very similar.

'Does nothing strike you as odd about this book?' said Jay.

'Besides its existence at all? Not really.'

'It's too new. Look at it.' Jay showed me its binding, which was, to be fair, unusually sound for a thousand year old book. The colours, too, were scarcely faded, and the ink still quite dark. It looked aged, but in a way that suggested it had been sitting on a shelf for a few centuries, not a millennium.

I exchanged a long, considering look with Jay, and some of Val's words floated back through my mind.

Earlier on, faced with the problem of risking a potentially fatal descent from the roof of the Striding Spire, or dying of exposure on top of it, I had not fully focused on everything that Val had said. But I did then.

There was the problem of the starstone, and the starstone Spire's apparent sightings well before that ought to have been possible.

There was the fact that the Spire itself had been spotted at various intervals down a number of centuries, though everything we had learned about it suggested it had only been built in the early seventeenth century.

There was Zareen's report about the Greyer cottage and its similar patterns of movement — and the fact that it had, to all appearances, been nowhere at all for considerable periods of time.

And then that book.

'My bag,' I said. 'I need Mauf.'

Jay pointed silently to the window, beneath which he had deposited my ever-present shoulder bag. I hauled Mauf out of it and said breathlessly: 'Mauf, those books and such you were canoodling with earlier. Did you get chance to, er, find out what they know?'

'I did not have full opportunity to absorb every word, Miss Vesper, but I believe I acquired the majority.'

'Magnificent you. Tell me one thing: is there anything in there to confirm when the building known as the Striding Spire was built?'

'There was not.'

My heart sank with disappointment.

'There was, however, reference to a building called the Starstone Spire, which was built in 1611.'

My heart almost stopped with excitement. 'Mauf! Who built it?'

'Its construction was ordered by Drystan Redclover, Mayor of Dappledok Dell, though it is noted that his brother Melmidoc was as active a participant in the process as the Mayor.'

'Jay,' I said, and my voice shook. 'In your Waymaster training, did you ever hear tell of a time when Waymasters could — could cross large expanses of time as well as distance?'

'Never.' Jay was clutching the Bestiary like it was his new born first child, and I noticed his hands were shaking too. 'Ves, if that was ever true, it would be the kind of discovery that... hell, it would set the world on fire.'

17

'**O**h, it would,' I agreed. 'And that would give, for example, the Hidden Ministry strong reason to keep it secret, wouldn't you say?'

'No wonder Val had a hard time digging anything up.'

The pup jumped up onto one of the chairs and lay down in a cloud of dust. I could almost swear that she winked at me. 'The Greyer cottage. John Wester was a more powerful Waymaster even than we thought, Jay, for that cottage — it must have taken a jaunt back a few centuries, and quite recently.'

Jay eyed the sleepy pup with an air of dejection. 'And Zareen nuked it.'

'She is going to be gutted.'

'But the Spire?' Jay looked around at the room we were in, as though its décor might yield some manner of clue. 'It seems dead to me.'

'Long abandoned,' I agreed. 'Can you, I don't know, sense the presence of another Waymaster somehow?'

'How would I do that?'

I shrugged. 'Mauf, is there anything in those papers about how the Starstone Spire worked?'

'Or what it did?' put in Jay.

'Little that is likely to be of interest to you,' answered the book. 'Its recorded purpose was merely residential. It was a private project of the Redclover brothers, and its tendency to perambulate was only noted much later. And without the full approval of the Dappledok Councils.'

'There's no mention of its time-wandering capabilities?' I asked.

'None, but there are notes regarding its habit of disappearing without trace fairly often. I believe the writer assumed the Spire had simply gone to another Dell, or to somewhere in Britain. They may not have been aware of the possibility of an alternative.'

That was interesting. It implied that those brothers had developed the Spire's more remarkable capabilities themselves, privately, and without sharing it with the school or the town. Then again, why should they? Had we not already agreed that such powers would attract all kinds of attention, some of it very wrong indeed?

But what had happened to them?

The light dimmed momentarily, as though a cloud had crossed in front of the setting sun — or something moving much faster than that. I looked out of the window.

A trio of winged horses was on the approach. With the sun behind them, they were in silhouette, and I could not see who was riding them. 'I really hope this is Rob,' I said to Jay. 'Because I am starving.'

It wasn't Rob, but it was Zareen, and Miranda, and to my particular surprise, Baron Alban. It was the Baron who contrived to bring his steed up outside the window, and grinned in at us. 'Need a ride?'

'That, and dinner.'

He doffed his hat — a grey trilby, today — to me. 'Yours to command, my lady.'

We opted not to climb out of the window again, not when there were perfectly good stairs to be used. I took the pup under one arm, only to be immediately relieved of her by Miranda at the bottom, who gathered her up with a mother's tenderness and cooed something incomprehensible at her.

I realised, guiltily, that I had missed her last couple of feeds. I hoped Miranda would forgive me, considering the circumstances.

'You haven't been feeding her, have you?' said Miranda, fixing me with a gimlet eye.

So much for that. 'Yes!' I yelped. 'Except for the last few hours, but there was that whole stuck-on-the-roof thing, and we were distracted by...'

With a tut, Miranda walked off, already rummaging in her bag for a milk bottle.

'Dramary's Bestiary and time travel,' I finished.

The Baron grabbed me in a hug, the squeezy kind. '*Yes*, you little vixen! Is it true?'

'Er,' I choked. 'Cannot yet confirm, but all signs point to yes.'

Zareen punched the air. '*I knew it.*'

'Oh? Since when?'

'Since all that digging Val and I did. It didn't add up, unless you factor in possible time leaps.'

'Mauf's got some records stashed which we can go through for more detail,' I told her, tapping the Baron's head until he set me on my feet again. 'And there's a lot of books in there.'

Zareen nodded. 'Milady's sending an incursion, soon as I confirm we've got you.'

'How did you find us, anyway?'

'Iridescent water. That was a good tip. Val found a reference to a mermaid cove, and there's some old legend that says the waters turned pearly with the tears of some dumb princess or something. I daresay there's another explanation. You are in Nautilus Cove, in case you're interested, and it's sort of tucked into the Norfolk coast. Hi, Jay.'

Jay, engaged in stuffing Dramary's Bestiary (with great care) into my shoulder bag, merely nodded her way.

Zareen eyed the book hungrily. 'Is that really Dramary's Bestiary?'

'Seems to be,' said Jay.

Her fingers twitched. 'Damn it. I'm going to have to wait in line behind Mir, aren't I?'

'And Val, I should say.'

'And me,' said the Baron.

Zareen scowled at them both. 'I mean, I saved everybody's hide a fortnight ago with my amazing powers of exorcism, but sure. You can make me wait behind the Baron.'

'And destroyed the only building more or less known to be capable of time leaps,' said Jay, with a crooked smile.

'I did, didn't I?' groaned Zareen, and put her face in her hands.

Baron Alban gave the rump of his silver horse a friendly pat. 'Shall we go?'

I wanted to stay and read every word of every book in that library, of course, but I also really needed a plateful of crumpets and a bucket of tea. So I said, 'Tally ho,' and hopped up onto the Baron's horse. He mounted behind me, wound an arm around my waist, and nudged the beautiful creature into motion.

'Hold on tight,' he said in my ear.

Weary, cold and worn out with excitement, I had energy only to respond with a single syllable, and not even a meaningful one. 'Mm,' I said, at my most intelligent.

He chuckled. 'Hang in there, Ves. We'll get you fed shortly.'

· · • · • · • · · · ·

'It is unfortunate,' said Milady the following day, 'that your findings were not more concrete. However, I have a few points of interest to share.'

Jay and I had returned Home to a fine feast of a dinner, and to my relief we had been permitted to spend the remainder of the evening recovering from our escapades, uninterrupted by any summons from Milady. She had even give us sufficient time, upon the following morning, to sleep in.

I felt loved.

At eleven sharp the next morning the summons had come, and by then I was more than ready to report, for I was dying of curiosity upon one or two points. House had provided chairs for us in Milady's tower, which was nice. I had bagsied the purple one and sat straight-backed therein, stubbornly resisting the temptation to sprawl out comfortably. It was that kind of chair. Jay had a plush red number to my right. Milady, as ever, was a sparkle in the air, and there was nobody else present.

It had not taken all that long to make our report, since much of its contents had already found its way to Milady via Valerie and Zareen. The bit about the Starstone Spire prompted a silence from Milady which I wanted to call enthralled, but which might rather have been grim.

'Firstly,' continued Milady, 'I have received an enquiry from the Hidden Ministry as to your doings and findings in Dappledok Dell. Naturally I returned a comprehensive answer, and have subsequently received a strict order of secrecy. No part of your discoveries, or any theories as to their possible meanings, are to be shared outside of this Society. Indeed, I have been strongly encouraged to refrain from mentioning it to anybody within the Society either, though they did not quite have the temerity to order my silence there as well.'

Interesting.

Jay gave a whistle. 'Sounds like we might be on to something.'

'I fear so, Jay.'

'Permission to keep digging?' I said hopefully.

'I am sorry, Ves, but no. Not at this time. And I hope this will not be one of those occasions when you take it upon yourself to skirt around my decision.'

I tried my best to look innocent, which was probably about as successful as all the other times. 'Would I?'

'Please refrain. You have too much common sense to imagine that it would be in any way wise. The Ministry is correct to fear the consequences of a general discovery of any of the Redclover brothers' more remarkable achievements.'

'But — but only imagine! Today, we are reduced to grubbing about in the dirt salvaging what little can be retrieved of a much-decayed heritage, and that's less and less every year. But if we could go back, nothing like Dramary's Bestiary need ever be lost again. No species will ever be extinct beyond revival, no great Treasures — the kinds that save lives, even! — will ever be destroyed or lost. We could do so much more good!'

'Yes, but for every advantage you could name, there is the less desirable alternative. Some Treasures are better lost, there is not room in this world for every magickal beast to survive, and while the Bestiary is a delight, it is still only a book. Time is cruel, Ves, but some of its more brutal effects are sadly necessary, however much we may wish it otherwise.'

I was too busy choking internally over the words "only a book" to reply. I was disappointed, too. Milady's arguments made sense overall, but the fact that they were coming from her made rather less. She could be a lot more rules-oriented than me, sure, but she was also extremely dedicated to the Society, and its goals. How could she flatly turn down such an opportunity?

'What if the wrong people got hold of a functional Striding Spire, or Greyers' Cottage?' said Jay, who obviously had more of his wits intact. 'What if Ancestria Magicka—' He came to an abrupt halt, his eyes wide.

'Precisely,' said Milady.

Oh.

Oh, dear.

I had wondered before what was the real purpose behind Ancestria Magicka. On the face of it, they were doing the same kinds of things as we were, albeit with different motives. Tracking down lost artefacts and retrieving them, restoring them, saving them — whatever you wanted to call it. Their ultimate intentions might be more materialistic than altruistic, but it was essentially the same gig. We weren't the only two such organisations in Britain, either, not to mention the rest of the world.

But someone had gone to enormous trouble and expense to found Ancestria Magicka, very recently. Emphasis on the expense. They had been kitted out with the very best of everything and everyone — and why? I wasn't exaggerating when I said there was less and less left of our magickal heritage to salvage. Could they hope to find enough valuable Treasures to justify the extraordinary amounts of money they were shelling out? Either they were confident that they could, somehow, or they were being backed by somebody with oodles of money to burn, and no particular concern how much of it they lost.

If the former… how were they so confident they could do better than we could? The Society was founded eons ago, it had many years of experience behind it, and while it wasn't nearly so well-funded as Ancestria Magicka, it still managed to attract many top professionals in our shared field. We did well.

And we still didn't get hold of anywhere near enough valuables to cover our costs, even had we been disposed to sell them, which wasn't at all the point.

What if we were not the first people in modern history to rediscover the Redclover brothers and their Striding Spire? Or what if somebody had stumbled over the Greyer Cottage, or a similar example?

That would be a pretty strong motive for somebody moneyed and ambitious to go all-in at this game. And Ancestria Magicka had sent some of their best agents out in pursuit of the Greyer Cottage, with the apparent goal of coercing its resident spirits into working for their organisation instead. We had assumed that all they wanted was to set up their headquarters, Ashdown Castle, as an equivalent to our own, dear House — with extra perambulatory capabilities as a bonus. But what if they had known more than we did? What if they had actually been after John Wester because he was the only surviving (more or less) Waymaster who could leap through time, as well as space?

Hang on, though. What if John Wester wasn't the only one left? What if there were more?

'Um,' I said, and swallowed something like bile. 'What else do they know that we do not?'

'Too much,' said Milady grimly. 'And I am sorry to add that Lord Garrogin's hunt for a double agent has ended in failure. According to his conclusions, no one at Home was responsible for feeding information about the book to Ancestria Magicka, or for secreting a tracking enchantment between its pages. This means either that someone anticipated his involvement, and has contrived a way to lie successfully even to a Truthseeker, or that there is some other explanation, the details of which I cannot begin to guess.'

'That's a problem,' I said weakly.

'Zareen, I am afraid to say, came under particularly close scrutiny, considering her apparent prior acquaintance with George Mercer.'

'It cannot have been Zar,' I said quickly.

'I believe it to be most unlikely myself,' said Milady. 'The worst I am inclined to believe is that she may, in an unguarded moment, have let something slip about the book. But that she would go to the lengths of compromising its security, I am much more in doubt. However.'

I did not like the way Milady said *however*. Her voice had gone all cold.

'If she indeed has connections with a member of an opposing organisation, whose motives and possible information we have increasing reason to fear, then those connections must be put to use for the benefit of the Society. I do not believe either of you will much like the next assignment I have in mind for you, but you must accept my apologies.'

I now understood what Mabyn had meant when she had described Milady as *apologetic, but not at all sorry*. 'Anything you require of us shall of course be carried out, Milady,' I said as stoutly as I could.

'I know, Ves,' she replied. 'I need you to find out the nature of Zareen's acquaintance with Mercer, and how close they are. I also need you to ascertain the extent of Zareen's loyalty to the Society.'

'I don't need to do that last part,' I said. 'I know her to be entirely loyal.'

'Would you stake your life on it, my Ves?'

'Without hesitation.' Zareen has been a member of the Society for almost as long as I have, and she has always had my back. I have always had hers. I could not doubt her, any more than I could doubt my left arm or my right leg.

Jay shifted in his seat, but thankfully said nothing.

Milady was silent for a time.

'Zareen has told me that she met Mercer at school,' Milady finally said. 'And that there is little contact between them now. I hope the latter is not quite true, for we *must* learn what the group calling themselves Ancestria Magicka know, and with minimal further loss of time. If, as we fear, they are ahead of us in the matter of the Spire, or other, equivalent resources, they must be interfered with before they have chance to do anything too damaging with this dangerous knowledge. Your assignment, then, is as follows.'

Milady can be the queen of dramatic pauses, when she wants to. Jay and I waited. I, at least, might have been holding my breath.

'I require you to go renegade,' said Milady in a dispassionate tone. 'To my infinite regret, my two best Acquisitions Specialists and I have been unable to agree regarding your recent findings, and the three of us have parted ways. Zareen shall join you. Your goal is to found a more forward-thinking establishment, without me and my hidebound, restrictive notions. You will leave this House tomorrow morning with everything you can carry, and no more. Temporary accommodation will be provided for you. Your contact will be Rob, who, poor man, cannot at all decide whether he would like to remain with the Society or join in with your exciting new adventure. Others may secretly offer you what aid they may. I imagine my recent decisions may prove sadly unpopular with all manner of my employees.'

I, too dumbfounded to speak, could only nod. Jay said nothing either.

Milady's middle name had better be "Devious", or I shall be sorely disappointed.

'This news shall of course reach Ancestria Magicka by way of Zareen and George Mercer,' continued Milady. 'I shall be most interested to know what their response to it will prove to be.'

I found my voice. 'To be clear, Milady. Are we to actually pursue any of these fictional goals during our sojourn away from Home?'

'That I leave in your capable hands, Ves. Yours too, Jay. I am sure you will know just how to proceed.'

In other words, Milady could not officially tell us to investigate the Spire, or the Greyer Cottage, any further. If it were known that she had done so, the future of the entire Society could be at risk — being, as we are, dependent upon the Ministry's goodwill, not to mention funding.

But she could no more ignore this development than we could. The alternative, then? Put us in a position where we could do it without, apparently, her official sanction, and she could deny all knowledge of it later.

That put us in an interesting predicament, for if the Hidden Ministry found out what we were up to, it would be more difficult for Milady, no longer our employer, to shield us from the consequences.

On the other hand, for a little while we had more or less total freedom to do as we chose. Dangerous or not, that was going to be a hell of a lot of fun.

Jay, though, was struggling. 'Is... um, does this amount to official permission to...?'

'No,' said Milady.

'It amounts to unofficial permission,' said I.

The sparkle in the air brightened for a moment, which I had always taken to be Milady's way of laughing at us. Nicely, of course. 'Listen to Ves,' she told Jay. 'Do as she thinks best. She will not lead you too far astray.'

'Or at least, not much farther than is justifiable,' I amended. And considering that we had just been given an unofficial order to kick over pretty much all the traces, quite a lot was going to be justifiable.

'Dismissed, then,' said Milady. 'There's chocolate in the pot, and you may take the pot with you when you leave.'

I heaved a small, inward sigh of relief. To brave the dangers of the Ministry, Ancestria Magicka, the Spire and clear and consistent misdemeanour all at once was one thing. To do it without a drop of Milady's finest hot chocolate was quite another.

'Stop by Zareen's on your way down,' added Milady. 'You will find her reasonably well-informed already.'

• • • • • • • • • •

'This is not what I had in mind when I joined the Society,' said Jay a short while later.

We were huddled up in Zareen's tiny cubbyhole of a room, what we colloquially call the Toil and Trouble division. We were sharing the chocolate three ways, Zareen in her big chair with her feet on the desk, Jay and I perching on the edges of the latter.

'You thought it would be straightforward, did you?' said Zareen, without much sympathy.

'It was when my parents worked here,' he said, rather defensively.

'Division?' said Zareen.

'Enchantments, and Beasts.'

Zareen waved a hand dismissively. 'Tame stuff. Welcome to Acquisitions and Research. Much more fun.'

'Much more confusing,' said Jay.

I felt some sympathy for him, I really did. He was the type to prefer to play by the rules. It made him feel better. What was he supposed to do with a job where the rules changed by the day, and where you could be officially (unofficially) ordered to ignore them all? He wasn't going to find it easy.

'We'll make a maverick of you yet,' I said to him, with a reassuring pat to his shoulder.

'Great,' he muttered.

'So let's get this straight,' said Zareen, finishing her chocolate with an appreciative slurp and setting her empty cup upon the desk. 'We're to sort of found our own Society splinter group, independent of Milady's authority or influence, with some degree of help from supposed rogue agents within the Society. I'm to make George believe we've gone rebel, in case Ancestria wants to take another shot at recruiting us, and if they do, we're to find out what they know about the Spire — and anything else we can dig up, too. Oh, and if we can manage to find out how the Spire worked, and whether there are any more functional examples left in the world, then we get bonus points.'

'That's pretty much it,' I said. 'Oh — if we can find another Dappledok pup, too, Miranda will love us forever. She wants a breeding pair.'

'The Ministry might have let us keep the current one, but they'll never go for our having a breeding pair.'

'Milady will talk them round. Or ignore them.'

Jay snorted.

Zareen silently checked about twelve things off on her fingers. 'Right. Easy,' she said, with a roll of her eyes, and reached for her phone.

'So how do you know George Mercer?' I put in, as she waited for whoever it was to pick up.

'Met him at the School of Weird.'

'The what?'

'The Seminary for the Stranger Arts. Already an adorable euphemism. They mean the Dark and Dire Arts of course, but nobody quite went for that title for some reason. The students call it the School of Weird. Oh,' she said then into her phone. 'Hi, darling. We need to talk. Usual place? Great. Tonight, eight o'clock.' She hung up.

'George?' I guessed.

She nodded.

So much for little real contact between them. But then, Milady had probably known that. Zar didn't hobnob with George Mercer in the same way that she and Jay and I were in no way sallying forth to disobey all the Ministry's sternest orders with Milady's semi-official sanction.

'Excellent,' I said to Zareen. 'Can we come?'

'No.'

'Please?'

A pause, and a glare from Zareen. 'Oh, fine,' she said, capitulating with a sigh. 'I never could resist the Ves puppy eyes for long.'

I grinned smugly. 'I know.'

Also By Charlotte E. English

Modern Magick

The Road to Farringale

Toil and Trouble

The Striding Spire

The Fifth Britain

Royalty and Ruin

Music and Misadventure

The Wonders of Vale

The Heart of Hyndorin

Alchemy and Argent

The Magick of Merlin

Dancing and Disaster

The Fate of Farringale

House of Werth

Wyrde and Wayward
Wyrde and Wicked
Wyrde and Wild
Wyrde and Wondrous